THE TRUTH WIL

Wilde Fae

A KINGDOM OF MONSTERS

USA TODAY AND INTERNATIONAL BESTSELLING AUTHOR

KATE KING

This book is a work of fiction. All characters, names, places, and incidents, either are the product of the author's imagination or are used fictitiously. Any resemblance to real persons, living or dead, events, or locales, is purely coincidental.

First Cover edition October, 2024

Cover design and typography: Flowers and Forensics

Formatting and Edge Design (Printed edges edition): Painted Wings Publishing Services

Unique Character Art: @damianintheden, Rin Mitchell

Published by Wicked Good Romance

For the readers who have been with me from the beginning. I hope you're ready to finally get some answers.

CONTENT WARNING

Wilde Fae

A KINGDOM OF MONSTERS

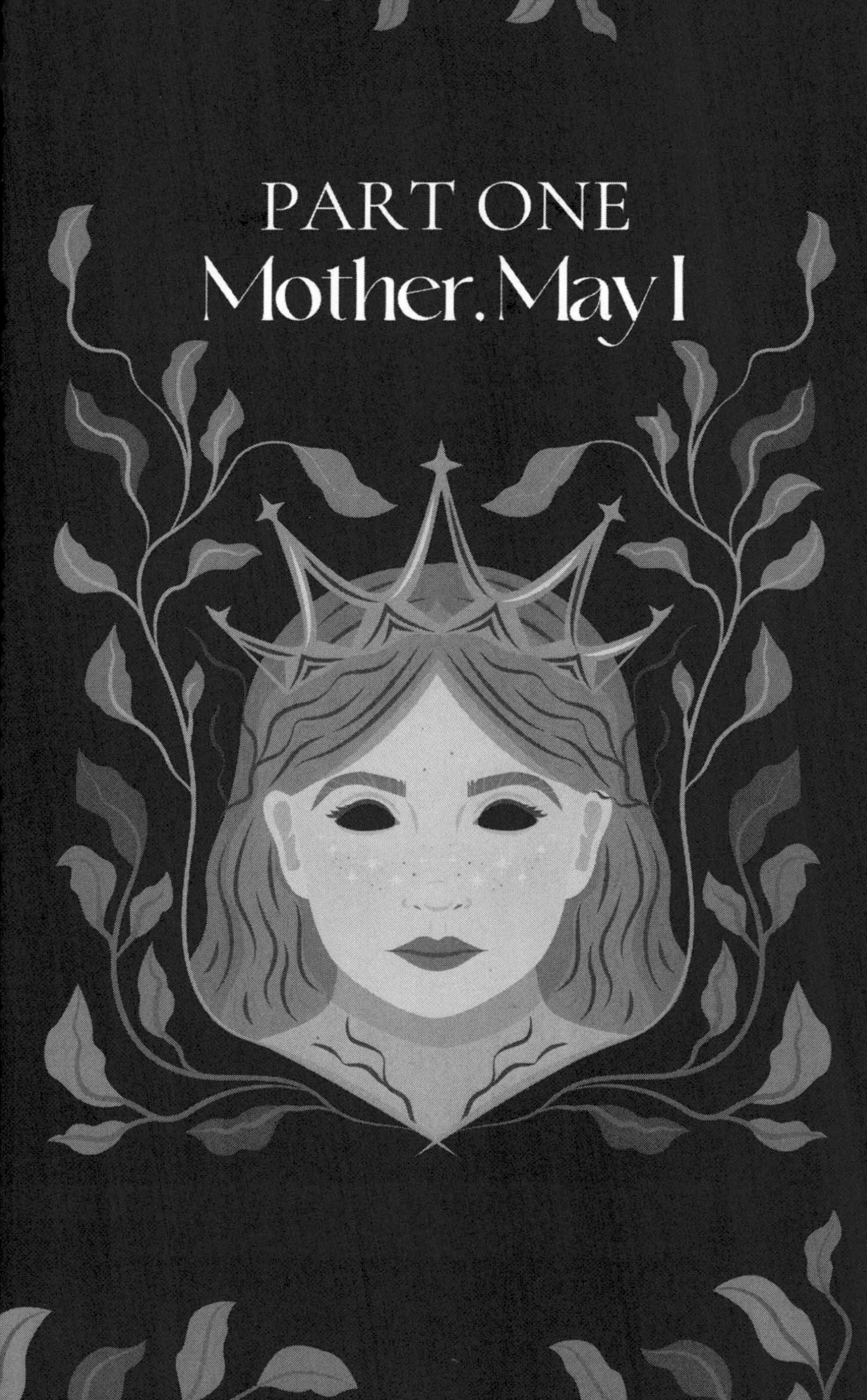
PART ONE
Mother. May I

1
LONNIE

THE OBSIDIAN PALACE, EVERLAST CITY - TWO MONTHS SINCE ESCAPING FROM UNDERNEATH

I jerked awake, sitting up in bed with an audible gasp.

My heart pounded double time, and I felt the gooseflesh rising on my arms as I stared into the pitch black of the darkened room.

It was only a dream—a nightmare really, yet my body didn't seem to know that. Terror still clung to me, even as the details of whatever my mind had conjured seemed to slip away faster than I could hold on to them.

In my dream, I'd been standing in a throne room. Outside the window the sunflowers swayed in the field, shadowed by the purple mountain rising over them. There was someone laughing…

Hmmm.

It didn't sound like a nightmare, but the details were twisted. Fuzzy. Leaving only a sense of wrongness behind.

I sighed, and tried to stand up, only to find my legs trapped beneath the blankets. This was nothing new. In fact, I nearly always woke to find myself held tightly, tangled with either Bael or Scion—often both.

I shifted my head and saw Scion peacefully asleep next to me. His chest rose and fell rhythmically, and his strong, lean legs were tangled with mine, his arm draped casually over my waist. With a slight smile, I turned over, expecting to see Bael lying on my other side. My forehead wrinkled as I noticed the space on the right side of the bed was empty. Strange.

Now more awake than ever, I carefully extracted myself from Scion's strong embrace, my body aching as I rolled off the bed and onto the cold, wooden floor. The moonlight shone through the window, illuminating my bare feet as I tiptoed to the adjoining bathing room.

I closed the door and leaned against it for a moment, breathing heavily. My body still seemed to shake with residual tremors from my dream. I shook my head, blinking quickly to banish the rest of the haze on my mind. Whatever I'd dreamed, it didn't matter. I'd been plagued by overly vivid dreams for some time now. Some seemed almost like visions, but this didn't seem to be one of those. Merely my mind, creating images out of all the fear I'd felt in the last year…nothing more.

A drink of water was sure to help.

I pushed off the door, and walked blindly across the dark room toward the sink. With a wave of my hand, I lit the lamps along the walls of the circular room, making the reflections of flickering orange flames dance across the walls.

I leaned both hands on the edges of the marble sink basin, and stared up through my lashes at myself in the oversized gold-framed mirror. The face staring back at me seemed almost unfamiliar, like that of a stranger. I had the same pale skin, the same freckles, the same wide brown eyes…but something seemed different, and I couldn't put a finger on what that might be.

I shook my head to clear it, and leaned over the sink and twisted the faucet handle, feeling the cool water run over my fingers. I greedily took a gulp of water before splashing it on my flushed cheeks. Standing straight again, I gave my reflection a final mutinous glance before extinguishing the lights and returning to the dark bedchamber.

Now feeling more awake, my attention returned to the bed. Scion's slow and steady breaths filled the silence, but there was no sign of Bael.

I squinted at the window. Outside, the dark silhouettes of towering trees were just barely visible. In the distance, a faint blue glow signaled the approach of dawn. It was unusually early for my mate to have gotten out of bed, but he was nowhere to be found. Snatching a long silk dressing gown from a nearby chair, I shrugged it on and crept out into the hall to search for him.

The castle was still asleep, and the corridors were dark and quiet as I moved silently down the hall. I felt like a wraith, haunting the empty castle, my long sink robe fanning out behind me like a trail of mist. That feeling wasn't helped by the occasional crumbling stone or smashed door, now common in the once pristine palace.

It had been nearly two months since my mates and I returned from Underneath. To them, that was a mere blink of an eye in their immortal lives, but for me, it felt like an eternity. We were once again residing in the obsidian palace, but almost nothing felt the same as the last time we'd been here.

For one thing, the smoothly running court was now in near disarray. Since the battle with the rebellion, the castle had been undergoing a never-ending restoration. The east tower where I'd once slept in Scion's old room was nearly back to normal, and the entrance hall looked as splendid as it ever had. Still, not every sign of the battle had been erased and the effects of the battle still lingered in the daily running of the court. Many of the former guards and servants had either been killed or escaped. Those who remained split their loyalty between the Everlasts and the rebellion, and struggled to keep up with daily tasks while the damaged castle was stuck in a state of constant repair.

For another, the royal family was fractured. Gwydion and Thalia remained in Overcast with Raewyn, Oberon and Elfwyn. It had been confirmed that Lysander was killed during the battle, and no one had seen or heard from Aine since we'd left her in Inbetwixt. The only members of the Everlast family remaining in the capital were Bael, Scion, Scion's mother Mairead—and oddly enough, Ambrose.

Since we'd returned from Underneath, Ambrose had thrown himself entirely into restoring the castle, to the point that I rarely saw him outside of the occasional meal, or passing in the hallways.

I'd thought—or perhaps feared—that once we returned to the mainland Ambrose would disappear again. Instead, we were all living in a state of uneasy tension. The animosity between Ambrose and the rest of his family—particularly between him and Scion—had not lessened. If not for the fact that they maintained the common goal of ending the curse on their family, I was sure it would have come to blows.

Clearly sensing this, Ambrose had distanced himself as much as possible from Bael and Scion, and me by extension. So, while two months ago I'd thought we were something like friends, now I felt like barely more than strangers.

I reached the end of the hall and turned the corner toward the grand staircase, only to jump back in surprise as a large shape loomed toward me out of the darkness. I shrieked, raising a hand already filled with dancing blue flames.

"Careful, love." Ambrose held his hands up, as if in surrender. "The last thing we need is another burnt corridor to clean up."

I let out a relieved breath and lowered my hand. "What are you doing here?" I demanded.

Ambrose raised his eyebrow at me, perhaps taken aback by my accusatory tone. I couldn't find it in myself to feel guilty for snapping at him. It felt as if my very thoughts had summoned him, and I was filled with frustration and something like embarrassment at the very idea.

"I could ask you the same question," Ambrose said, a teasing note in his voice. "Why are you up?"

"Nightmare," I said briskly. "And I was looking for Bael."

Ambrose tilted his head at me, almost concerned. "Is he missing?"

"I doubt it," I replied, already edging away toward the stairs. "I mean, he's missing in the sense that I don't know where he went, but I'm sure he's just downstairs somewhere."

Ambrose quickly turned to fall in step beside me as I continued toward the grand staircase. "I'll help you look."

I stiffened. A large part of me didn't want that. Any time spent alone with Ambrose sent my mind reeling. Still, another part of me missed talking to him. I looked up at him, meaning to ask if he could so easily abandon whatever he'd been doing. Instead, however, I found myself caught in his penetrating gaze.

Like all Fae, Ambrose was almost supernaturally handsome. I'd noticed that from the very moment we first met—it would have been impossible not to. He looked a lot like Scion, except that his eyes were dark and his hair was an almost luminescent silver. He wore it in a long intricate braid on one side, and shaved close to the scalp on the other revealing the dark tattoos that climbed up his neck and over the side of his head. His pointed ears were adorned with a collection of gold hoops, as well as a single bone, which stabbed through the top of his right ear like a tiny dagger.

Ambrose blinked at me, his mouth tilting up in an arrogant smirk. I looked down and flushed, suddenly realizing I'd been staring at him for several beats too long.

I cleared my throat, and looked down as we descended the stairs into the entrance hall. "I haven't seen much of you these last weeks."

His smirk died. "No. I've been doing my best to stay out of the way."

"Out of Scion's way, you mean?"

He grimaced. "Exactly. There's no need to provoke him more than I already am with my mere presence."

We crossed the large entrance hall and walked through the door into yet another winding corridor. I pressed my lips together in a flat, considering line. "I don't think–"

"Stop," he interrupted with a laugh. "Whatever you're about to say will only scald your throat. We both know full well that my brother would like nothing more than to stab me in my sleep."

I let out a breath. "True. He hasn't, though. That's something."

"He hasn't only because he thinks you'll all need my help to break the curse. The moment we're finally free of it, I'm sure my days will be numbered."

I frowned at him. He seemed oddly casual–cheerful even–about the idea of his own death at the hands of his brother. Unfortunately, I was quite sure he was correct: Scion was practically foaming at the mouth to get rid of Ambrose, especially since he'd captured me and taken me on his ship to Underneath. Nothing, not even Ambrose helping to free him and Bael from the dungeon would convince Scion that his brother was anything but a monster.

"It could be far worse," I said weakly, trying to ease the discomfort of the situation. "I think Bael likes you, at least,"

"Not really," Ambrose said, still a bit too cheerful. "Except for you, and perhaps Scion, Bael likes everyone and no one exactly the same. Which is to say that he's a friend to anyone who is useful to him, but would slit his own mother's throat without thought if she betrayed him."

"Yeah, well, you can hardly blame him for that. If I had Raewyn for a mother I'd consider slitting her throat at least twice a day."

Ambrose laughed, but I didn't join in.

I'd spoken without thinking, and the mention of mothers always put me in a foul temper. Hoping to ward off my own depression, I changed the subject. "Have you seen anything useful to do with the curse?"

It was Ambrose's turn to look morose. "Not recently. I've been struggling to see anything clearly since we left Underneath."

"Really?" I looked up at him again, surprised. "That's unusual, is it not?"

He shrugged. "Yes and no. Like any other skill, all magic requires regular practice. Admittedly it's been many years since I had to consciously work at improving, but there are new… factors that have changed things for me."

"Factors like what?"

"Nothing you need to worry about now," he said airily. "But don't be surprised if I join you in your practice sessions."

I smiled weakly. There certainly were enough opportunities for him to join me if he wanted to. For the last two months, I'd spent nearly every day practicing my magic.

It was still difficult given that I had no idea what the Source of my power was, or how much there was to pull from, but steadily I'd been getting better. I could conjure flames now at will, and had much better control over setting entire rooms on fire when upset. Best of all, I hadn't summoned any afflicted to me in weeks. Bael theorized–and so far he seemed to be correct–that the better control I had on my power, the less likely it was to call Wilde creatures to me. Why that was, we had no idea, but I was grateful not to have to contend with the vicious monsters of Aftermath on a daily basis.

"Where are you leading us?" Ambrose asked conversationally.

I looked up and realized I hadn't been paying any attention to where we were going. It took me a moment to recognize the corridor, and realize we were still a floor above where I'd intended. I set off again, this time in the right direction toward the servants' stairs. "I'm going to check Bael's old room." I explained. "If he's not himself at the moment, that would be the first place he'd go."

"Ah," Ambrose nodded. "I'd better leave you here, then."

"There's no need to be afraid." I rolled my eyes. "Bael wouldn't hurt you in front of me, even in his other form."

"I don't know about that. I wouldn't want to test the lion's patience. Especially if he thinks I'm encroaching on his territory."

"What, like his room?" I asked flippantly. "I think he's probably over that, given that he has an entire kingdom to call his territory."

Ambrose stopped, turning to face me in the dimly lit corridor, and reached out to push a lock of my hair behind my ear. "Not what I meant, love."

He didn't lower his hand, holding it there tangled in my hair. My breath caught and my heartbeat picked up, pounding loudly enough that we could both hear it clearly in the quiet corridor. I looked up slowly, half dreading the moment when our eyes would meet.

Abruptly, Ambrose pulled back and stepped away, brushing his hands on his jacket as if wiping away dust. He cleared his throat. "Right. Well, I'll just go then."

I merely swayed on the spot feeling a bit drunk. "Okay."

WITHOUT ANOTHER WORD, HE TURNED ON HIS HEEL LEAVING ME alone in the dark hallway.

Barely a few minutes later, I found myself in front of Bael's door. Though he wasn't using the room regularly anymore, the door and the surrounding walls had been repaired. All the soot and debris from the fire had been cleaned up, and there were no more blood stains on the stone floor. Still, I could practically see the bodies that had once lain in the doorway as I knocked and pushed the door open without waiting for a response.

I stepped inside, and immediately knew Bael was there.

"Hello," I crooned, in the same voice I might use to speak to a house cat.

Bael raised his enormous lion head to look at me, and blinked once in greeting. He'd once told me that he couldn't exactly understand my words while in this form, but he knew who I was. Not all that long ago, even that much control over his lion form would have seemed impossible. For many years, he'd been trapped in a constant cycle of bloodlust, but since defeating his father to take the crown of Underneath Bael had been rapidly gaining more and more awareness

Now, his huge yellow eyes tracked me as I closed the door behind me and strode across the room toward the cage. It wasn't locked, I noticed, so I had no difficulty swinging the door open and stepping inside.

Bael growled at me, in what I assumed was a low warning.

I rolled my eyes. "Oh, shut up."

I closed the bars of the cage behind me and then sat on the floor beside the enormous lion, curling into his side and resting my head against his powerfully muscled shoulder. He yawned in response, and put his head back down on his paws, closing his eyes in surrender.

Bael purred, sending rumble through my entire body. I sighed in contentment, and closed my own eyes thinking vaguely I might be able to steal a few more hours of sleep before rising for the day.

As my breathing grew steady and I drifted off again, my thoughts turned back to Ambrose. I wondered suddenly where he'd been going so early when we ran into each other, and then if perhaps he hadn't been going anywhere at all–perhaps he'd simply wanted to see me.

I wasn't sure if I wanted that to be true or not.

Especially, given that I had not one but two mates already.

What was wrong with me, that I couldn't seem to stay away from the Everlast males?

2
LONNIE

THE OBSIDIAN PALACE, EVERLAST CITY

Only a few hours later, the sun was high in the sky and I found myself out on the castle lawn practicing magic.

Several days ago, we'd set up targets—as if for archery practice, and now I furrowed my brows in concentration as I attempted to direct balls of fire toward them. Thus far, I'd managed to burn a large patch of brown grass in the manicured lawn, but the targets stood untouched.

I spread my feet wider apart and relaxed my shoulders, then took a deep breath and conjured another flaming sphere in the palm of my hand. In a single movement, I tossed the ball in the direction of the target. I held my breath for half a second before the flames spun wildly off course. They flickered and died midair, but not before managing to catch a nearby rose bush on fire. I screamed in frustration.

"Careful screaming like that, Rebel." Scion extinguished the bush with a lazy flick of his wrist. "What few servants we have left will think you're being tortured and abandon us before lunch."

"You're not funny."

"I wasn't trying to be." Scion replied from where he lounged on the grass watching me. "I really am concerned about how many servants you've terrified into hiding."

"Fuck off," I grumbled. "Just because you've had no difficulty mastering flames, doesn't mean we can all be so gifted."

Scion shrugged and gave me a rare grin, which lit up his entire face, and set his silver eyes dancing.

Indeed, he'd taken all of one afternoon to learn to swap easily between his own inherent magic talent of shadows and illusions, and the power he'd borrowed from me by way of our mating bond. Now, Scion could make flames in one hand and shadowy ropes in the other, all while barely breaking a sweat. Meanwhile, I was just happy to have stopped lighting buildings on fire by mistake.

It was infuriating.

"Don't be jealous, Rebel," he said with a slightly arrogant smirk. "I've been practicing magic since birth. It's a skill like any other, you'll get used to it. And honestly, I do think that last attempt was better."

"That's not saying much," I grumbled.

"On the contrary," another voice chimed in. "What you've accomplished in these last weeks has been nothing short of remarkable."

I glanced over my shoulder and offered a weak smile. "Thank you, Idris."

Scion scowled, and he didn't have to say anything for me to know precisely what he was thinking. *This motherfucker gets thanks and I get complaining? How is that fair?*

That thought cheered me slightly. "Don't be jealous, my lord," I teased. "Manners are like any skill, you'll get used to them eventually."

My mate scowled, but beside him Idris grinned.

Idris—whom we'd rescued from the prison in Underneath a few months ago—was completely unrecognizable from when we'd first met him. Then, his hair and beard were so long they brushed the floor. He'd been dressed in rags, and while it was clear he wasn't exactly starving under all that filth, he'd dragged around an aura of illness and depression.

Now, that prisoner was gone, replaced by an average looking Fae male. If I passed him in the ballroom at the Obsidian palace, or on the street in Inbetwixt, I wouldn't look twice.

Idris was tall and muscular, with a square face and chin-length black hair. To a human, he would probably appear young—thirty at most. For the Fae, however, the slightly ashen tone to his dark hair and depth of his eyes would imply he was middle aged.

That implication would be incorrect.

Though he didn't look it, Idris was likely the oldest faerie alive. He claimed he'd been imprisoned beneath the castle of Underneath for seven thousand years, which seemed unbelievable but was, nevertheless, possible.

Like all magical beings, Fae were immortal. That term, however, was not entirely correct. To be truly immortal meant that you could not be killed by any means. Nearly all creatures could be killed, provided you knew how to do it properly. The average age of the Fae population was somewhere in the realm of 300. I'd met beings as old as ten centuries, but very few older than that. Most Fae who lived to such an age chose to pass on at some point, returning to the Source when they felt their life was complete. Perhaps Idris had never felt that urge, given that his life was put on hold the moment he'd been imprisoned.

Regardless of what we knew–or didn't know–about the former prisoner, Idris had thus far been a helpful and pleasant guest. Ambrose seemed to trust that he wasn't a danger to us, and that was enough for me. At the very least, he'd been allowed to roam free since we'd arrived in the capital–a privilege that couldn't be taken for granted when it hadn't been extended to all those who returned from Underneath with us.

I glowered, that thought instantly darkening my mood.

Seeming to sense my unease, Scion stood up and strolled over to me. He said nothing, but leaned his cheek against the top of my head for a moment in a silent gesture of affection.

On rare occasions—usually when he thought we were about to die—my prince would share outrageous declarations of love. But on a daily basis, Scion was as incapable of speaking his feelings aloud as he was of lying to my face. Despite my teasing, I wasn't all that bothered by it. I didn't enjoy discussing my feelings either, and anyway, Bael was poetic enough to last all of us an immortal lifetime.

As if reading my thoughts, Scion pulled back suddenly. "Where's Bael?"

I shrugged. "Sleeping, I believe."

Scion frowned. "Again?"

"Not so much again, as 'still.' He changed back into himself early this morning, but still seemed too tired to leave his room."

"That's…unusual." Scion frowned, which sent a spark of anxiety skittering through me.

Since our return from Underneath, I couldn't help but notice that Bael seemed more tired than I had ever seen him before. At first,

I'd thought it was fatigue from the battle with his father, but now I wasn't so sure.

"Why?" I asked quickly. "Do you think he's ill?"

"Probably not..." Scion wouldn't meet my eyes. "It's not as if he could contract a common plague."

I narrowed my eyes, my anxiety rising. The Fae could not lie, and therefore found many creative ways to spin the truth to avoid being forthright. I'd been around the Everlasts–and Scion especially–long enough to know that "probably" and "perhaps" were as good as an omission of wrongdoing.

"I wouldn't concern yourself, Lonnie," Idris said casually.

Scion and I both turned to look at the other Fae male, who stood several paces back from us, with his hands in his pockets. Scion frowned. "Why?"

Idris raised a brow. "Your cousin just gained a powerful amount of new magic. That's taxing on the body, but he'll recover eventually."

Scion looked mollified, nodding as if that made sense, but I was still confused.

"What new magic?" I asked, feeling uncomfortable at being out of the loop.

A momentary expression of annoyance flickered across Scion's too-handsome face, as if he was trying to suppress an eye roll. If this conversation had taken place three months ago, he would have definitely ridiculed my lack of comprehension. But now, it seemed like Scion was making an effort to be more patient and understanding for my sake.

"Bael's never been able to transform at will before," Scion said.

"What changed?"

Scion shrugged. "I'm not sure. I would say it was due to the mating. Mating always results in increased power for both partners. But since you haven't completed your bond, I can't say for sure if that's the reason."

"Maybe it's because he's now the king of Underneath," Idris theorized.

"Maybe," Scion agreed. "Whatever the case, Bael's power has increased, possibly beyond mine."

"Does that bother you?"

He let out a bark of harsh laughter. "No."

Even as I heard the honesty in his answer, I glanced at him, searching for any hint of jealousy or resentment on his face. There was none. "I would have thought you'd envy anyone with stronger magic."

"No, not at all. I—" Scion broke off abruptly, leaving his sentence hanging in mid-air. He let go of me, and turned sharply to look over his shoulder. "By the fucking Source!"

I turned and followed Scion's gaze, already knowing whom I was likely to see. Sure enough, my gaze immediately landed on Ambrose striding toward us.

"Why doesn't he stay in his half of the castle?"

"Which half is that?" I asked blandly.

"Whichever half I am not in," Scion growled.

"He can hear you, you know."

"I hope so," Scion raised his voice to a near yell. "Then maybe the prick would turn around and leave us the fuck alone."

I watched as Ambrose laughed and shook his head, not changing course as he carved a wide path toward us across the lawn. His expression was amused, but otherwise he looked every inch the fierce rebel leader, with his bright white hair falling wildly around his shoulders and his shirt open at the neck to display a hint of his tattoos.

Pointedly ignoring Scion, Ambrose nodded a greeting to Idris, then stopped in front of me and grinned. "Hello, Love. How is practice."

"Er, good…fine…I mean. It's great." I flushed, even as my throat began to burn. He'd flustered me enough to lie by mistake, and I looked down hiding both my face and my watering eyes.

I felt Scion's sharp gaze on me, probably wondering what the hell was wrong with me. It was a good question, really.

Last night had been far less awkward, but perhaps that was because it had been the middle of the night. No one had been around to witness my awkwardness.

Indeed, there was really no need for me to feel so uneasy around Ambrose. On the ship, we were relaxed around each other, almost like friends. But now, I couldn't help but feel on edge.

Perhaps it was because I knew how my mates felt about him, and their mistrust was rubbing off on me. Or perhaps it was due to that night we'd spent together in Underneath. Just because we hadn't slept together, didn't make what I'd done any less embarrassing to think about. Then, there was the strange moment between us last night. It had been so fleeting, I was half sure I'd imagined it.

Or, at least I was, until I glanced up and accidentally met Ambrose's dark eyes. Instantly, I felt scrutinized. Watched. Like I was standing naked on the lawn.

I flushed, and pushed all thoughts of that night out of my mind before everyone could sense my reaction. Fortunately, Scion was clearly too incensed by his brother's presence to examine my strange behavior.

"What do you want?" Scion barked.

Ambrose finally condescended to look at Scion, his posture relaxed and his expression neutral. They were exactly the same height, but somehow Ambrose managed to look down his nose in the way that only an older sibling could. "Calm down, brother. You'll give yourself an aneurysm."

Scion spluttered furiously, but didn't manage to reply before a massive raven swooped low over our heads, drawing everyone's attention. The bird let out a loud caw, and landed on Scion's shoulder, its feathers rustling against my hair as it settled comfortably on its new perch.

"Hello, Quill." I smiled and extended my hand, gently running my fingers along the soft feathers of the bird's neck. Quill chittered in response, as if bidding me good afternoon.

Ambrose made a noise of disgust, and his carefully neutral expression cracked. He glared angrily from Quill to Scion. "Can't you make that thing stay inside?"

Scion sneered. "Are you telling me the mighty Dullahan is afraid of a bird?"

"That's not a bird," Ambrose grumbled. "It's an omen of disaster."

I scratched Quill beneath the beak, and he cocked his head at me, cooing innocently. "I really don't understand why you're all so afraid of a harmless pet."

"Exactly," Scion replied triumphantly, sneering at an affronted Ambrose. "But if you're so bothered, feel free to walk away. I guarantee, we'll take no offense."

Ambrose scowled, first at the raven and then at his brother. Scion scowled back, and I had to bite back a laugh. Their expressions were identical, down to the last dimple.

Aside from their coloring which was entirely opposite, I would have readily believed that Scion and Ambrose were twins. In actuality, Ambrose was nearly two centuries older.

For over a hundred years, Ambrose had been the crown prince of the Everlast dynasty, until he abandoned the family to join the rebellion against the monarchy. With his brother gone, Scion had become the heir-apparent, and the two of them had been on opposing sides of a brewing civil war since before I was even born.

For that reason, among many, Scion hated his brother with an unholy passion. I had loathed him as well, until Ambrose took me captive and we were forced to spend two weeks getting acquainted.

Ambrose possessed the incredible gift of foresight. He was the most powerful seer born in generations, and therefore he'd been burdened since childhood with the knowledge of his family's eventual downfall. It haunted him, until finally, he made the conscious decision to stop passively observing, and instead actively work towards shaping a better future for his family and the entire nation.

Unfortunately, that had meant sacrificing his title, his reputation, and his relationship with his brother. Ambrose had explained all this to me, because I was the only person—aside from himself—whose future he couldn't directly see or influence. Now, I was perhaps the only person on the continent who didn't think he was a monster.

"Was there something you wanted?" I asked Ambrose, hoping to defuse the tension between the brothers.

Ambrose shook his head as if to clear it, and refocused on me. His jet black eyes bore into mine. "I came to tell you that your mother is ready."

I faltered for a moment, startled by his complete attention. "You're not serious."

Ambrose grimaced. "I am. As I expected, hunger was a powerful motivator."

I wrinkled my nose in distaste. "Yes," I muttered grimly. "I know all too well that starving in a cell has a way of making one reevaluate their priorities."

Beside me, Scion stiffened uncomfortably, running one large hand through his hair. Behind us, Idris cleared his throat.

I turned to look at him, having forgotten for a moment that he was here. I gave him an apologetic smile. "I'm sorry. I'm sure you don't want to hear us discussing dungeons."

He shook his head. "Don't worry over it. In my time, we used far harsher methods of persuasion. Your dungeons are very tame compared with what I'd do."

I frowned, a shiver running through me. Part of me wanted to ask what he would do if it were up to him, but a larger part didn't want to know. I supposed it didn't matter. I was technically in charge here, and imprisoning my mother in the very dungeon where I'd nearly died was about the worst thing I could possibly think of.

"Do you want me to go with you to speak with her, Rebel?" Scion asked.

"If anyone should go with her, it's me," Ambrose said pointedly. "I actually know Rhiannon."

"And look how well that's turned out," Scion said acidly. "Did you also order her to kill my mate?"

"Alright, stop," I interrupted before Ambrose could respond. "I'm going alone."

"I'm not sure that's a good idea, love." Ambrose furrowed his brow in concern. "Your mother is clearly harboring some resentment toward you."

I snorted a humorless laugh. "Resentment" was an understatement.

"Having either of you there will only make things worse," I said. "Anyway, it's not as if she can hurt me in her present condition. I'm just going to ask her some questions."

Neither Scion nor Ambrose looked happy, but they didn't argue. We all knew that my mother might hate me enough to kill me, but she hated the Fae more. She'd been perfectly willing to die in Underneath rather than be stuck on a ship with dozens of Fae, and had spent the last three days starving rather than answering a few questions. Unless we wanted her to starve herself to death before providing any answers, I'd have to speak to her alone.

"Take Quill with you," Scion said abruptly.

As if he understood his master's words, the raven jumped into the air and made a circle around our small group before coming to rest on my shoulder.

"Oooph," I grunted, when the bird's weight landed on me. "I'm not sure that's a good idea."

"For once, I agree," Ambrose said begrudgingly. "You should take the bird with you."

"Wasn't it you who was just complaining that he's here at all?"

Ambrose shrugged. "Perhaps the mere presence of such evil will make your mother think twice if she planned to hurt you again."

I couldn't quite tell if Ambrose was joking, but I supposed it wasn't that much of a hardship to take Quill with me. I rolled my eyes and shifted so the raven's weight was more evenly dispersed on my shoulder. "I find it ironic that the only time you two can agree is to gang up on me. Maybe you should set your own example. Isn't there something you can do other than arguing?"

The brothers glanced at each other, then back at me, seeming wary.

"I've been looking through Grandmother's study," Ambrose said slowly.

"Fine. Then do that together." I replied almost too quickly, jumping on the chance like a starving man on a crust of bread.

"Why?" Scion practically growled.

I shrugged, unable to think of a good enough reason why they should have to spend time together. In truth, I wasn't even sure why I cared so much that they put aside their animosity once and for all, but I did. At the very least, it would make my life easier if my mate and my–I shook my head–*his* brother got along.

"I'll bring Quill with me as long as you two promise to try and get along while I'm gone," I promised.

Ambrose seemed unbothered. "Fine."

"And agree not to kill each other," I added.

Pointedly, no one said anything.

3
LONNIE

THE OBSIDIAN PALACE, EVERLAST CITY

Since my earliest recollection, my mother taught me the art of deception. Lie to protect others. Lie to protect myself. Lie to confirm my humanity. Somehow, in all that time it never occurred to me that Mother was lying too.

For the past seven years, I believed my mother was dead until Ambrose revealed to me that not only was she alive, but he also knew her whereabouts. She'd gone to the Unseelie kingdom of Underneath, at least partly, on his orders. However, he hadn't expected her to be living comfortably in Bael's father's castle. No matter how hard I tried, I couldn't think of a single reason why she would have been there. Or—more importantly—why she wouldn't be happy to see me.

If she could lie about that, then what else was she hiding? Perhaps our entire relationship was false. *Maybe she'd never really loved me*

Barely twenty minutes later, I made my way down to the palace dungeons.

The smell hit me first.

It was worse than I remembered, and yet I knew it would only grow stronger when I opened the door. A mixture of sweat and shit and misery. Like rotting bodies and stagnant water.

I stopped at the top of the long stairs and leaned against the wall, my head spinning. This was the other reason I'd wanted to go alone. No one needed to see my reaction to returning to this place–least of all Scion, who had been the one to imprison me here to begin with. I knew he felt haunted by the guilt of that, and I didn't want to make it worse–not when he'd changed so much since then and we were finally in something of a good place.

I held my breath and forced myself to put one foot in front of the other, descending the stairs. Quill let out a mournful cry on my shoulder and dug his talons into my flesh. I glanced up at him, and without knowing how I knew, I was sure he hated being this far from fresh air. "Wait for me on the stairs," I told the raven.

He made a chattering sound that felt suspiciously like *"Thank you,"* and leapt off my shoulder.

At the bottom of the long stairs was a curved wooden door. Once a guard had been stationed here, but now it seemed that the diminished staff saw no reason to waste someone standing outside a closed door all day. I was grateful at least that no one saw me struggling to contain the panic that threatened to overwhelm me.

My hand shaking, I reached for the cool metal knob and pulled the door open. As I'd expected, the smell was 100X worse. The stench of death and despair overwhelmed me, and I struggled to remain standing as I let the door swing closed behind me.

As if I were a puppet on strings, and someone else was guiding my movements, I made my way down the long row of cells. The echo of screams and rattling bars rang in my ears.

"I'm sorry," I whispered to each prisoner as I passed. "I'm sorry. I'm sorry."

I was familiar with how it felt to be kept behind bars, and I felt a large dose of guilt and pity at every single face. I had no idea what these creatures had done to be kept here–many had likely been here for many years since before I was born, but I couldn't help but wonder if that was a mistake. Had they really deserved to be imprisoned, or were they like Idris? Who had been trapped for so long he no longer remembered how or why he'd been placed there.

Tears pricked at my eyes as I ventured deeper into the prison.

Before I'd seen the prison in Underneath, I never would have realized how the cells were organized. Now I understood that more dangerous captives were held in the back where the magic was strongest. Strangely, my mother's cell was at the very back of the long line of cages, only one over from where I'd been held last year.

I stopped in front of her cell and peered inside, guilt overwhelming me.

I hadn't wanted to put her here–I'd argued heavily against it, but had ultimately been outvoted. Even Bael, who usually took my side in everything, thought my mother was potentially too dangerous to roam freely. At least, until she was willing to explain what she'd been doing for the last seven years and how she'd ended up in Underneath.

I still wasn't sure we'd made the right choice. My mother might have tried to kill me, but she was still my mother…at least, I hoped she was.

Mother sat on the cold ground, leaning against the unyielding iron bars of her cell. Her knees were pulled up to her chest and her head bowed down in defeat. She was still dressed in the long, flowing crimson gown she wore in Underneath, but she had discarded the veil that once hid her face. Her once lustrous red hair now sported streaks of gray and hung over her face like a mop.

I let go of the breath I'd been holding. "Mother?"

My mother turned her head, her hair falling to the side, and looked up at me. There was no feeling behind her expression—hardly even any recognition. It was as if I were a stranger. "What do you want?"

I swallowed the lump that immediately rose to my throat, and pushed down the hurt that threatened to consume me. Instead, I reached for one of the lessons my mother had once spent hours hammering into me: Hide your feelings, and don't draw attention to yourself.

I forced my face into a benign, calm expression, and held out the plate of dried fruit and cheese I'd brought for her. "Are you hungry?"

Her eyes narrowed, and I could practically see her wrestling with herself. Finally, a stubborn arrogance took over her features. "Not for your filthy Fae food."

I sighed. Either she'd changed her mind upon seeing me, or Ambrose had a warped opinion of how "ready" Mother was to speak with me. This was going to be unpleasant.

"Suit yourself," I said as lightly as I could manage. "I have nowhere else to be. I can wait. But I imagine you'll change your mind before long. In my experience, one stops caring where the food comes from after several months in prison."

She looked sideways at me again, her eyes narrowing. "How would you know?"

I smiled grimly. "Because I spent a year in the palace dungeon."

She blanched, and for a moment the mother I remembered showed through her angry expression. "A year? How did you survive?"

Another pang of guilt hit me. Humans didn't typically survive this dungeon. I'd promised myself that if my mother didn't give in and answer our questions soon I'd take her out of here. Maybe she knew she was running out of time.

"It seems we both have questions for each other," I said. "I know you must be hungry, no matter what you say. Take the food, and let us talk."

After a moment of consideration, she nodded once. "Fine. Sit."

A tiny spark of triumph lit in my chest. Carefully, I set the tray of food down on the floor, close enough that she could reach it through the bars. Then, I walked back down the hall and retrieved the bench where the guards usually sat. I returned, placed the bench against the wall facing my mother's cell, and sat.

Mother reached a thin wrist through the bars of her cell and selected a husk of bread, all the while watching me carefully. I couldn't help but wonder what she saw–if it was as strange for her as it was for me to see each other after all this time.

Except for a brief glimpse in Underneath and when we were disembarking the ship, I'd hardly seen my mother in almost a decade. The last time we'd sat face to face I'd been barely more than a child. Now, as I assessed her, she looked smaller and shorter than I remembered. Standing, she was probably no more than an inch taller than I. Her face was pale and similar to my own, but more angular. She had lines around her eyes that I did not remember being there before, and her freckles had almost entirely faded.

I sucked in a deep breath. I'd carefully weighed how to begin this conversation, and had decided that the best way was to lay out my expectations beforehand. "I need to ask you some questions. I'm sure you also have questions for me. I will answer whatever you like, in exchange for your honesty."

As I expected, my mother sneered at me. "So you're offering a bargain?"

"Yes," I said flatly. "If you care to see it that way."

"And if I say no?"

I sighed heavily. "I would prefer not to have to threaten you."

She laughed bitterly. "What could you possibly threaten me with that's worse than this?"

I closed my eyes, unable to ignore how familiar her words sounded. I'd said much the same thing when Bael came to offer me a way out of my own cell. "I don't care to argue with you," I said, my eyes still closed. "I know it would be pointless, anyway. I'd love nothing better than for this to be a happy reunion, but until I can determine if you're trustworthy my m—men will never let you go free."

Internally, I winced. I'd intended to say "my mates" and stopped at the last second. Even so, my mother visibly recoiled at my words.

"Those aren't men," she sneered. "They're monsters. I can't believe it—my own daughter willingly becoming a whore for the Fae royals."

I winced. "You have it wrong."

"I don't think so," she snapped. "I saw you with the Everlast prince."

I started to ask which prince she meant, then stopped. It didn't matter. Growing up, my mother hated Fae more than anything else in the world, and it seemed that she hadn't changed.

"Forget about them," I said through gritted teeth. "Let's talk about how you ended up here. You hate the Fae, so how did you find yourself in the court of Underneath?"

She glared at me, her breath heaving with anger, before she sucked in a long calming breath. Before my eyes, she schooled her features into the same flat expression I'd just used on her. "It's a long story."

A shiver of discomfort trailed up my spine. "I told you, I have plenty of time," I replied hastily. "After all these years, I feel like I deserve to hear the whole story."

My mother let out a deep sigh and adjusted her uncomfortable position on the hard, cold floor of her cell. She ran her fingers through her tangled hair before finally starting to speak. "I was brought to this land thirty-two years ago when I was only six years old..."

4
LONNIE

THE DUNGEONS, OBSIDIAN PALACE, EVERLAST CITY

"All these years later, I still remember flashes of my old life," Mother said. "I was often lonely, but well cared for. My family was wealthy, and I didn't see my parents often. I was raised by our housekeeper. She was called Orla, and she was from Ireland—"

"She was from where?" I interrupted.

"A nearby country," she said dismissively "Orla believed in fairies, and she told me stories about them. She warned me not to venture too far into the woods, because the fairies stole pretty children."

I swallowed thickly. I could see where this was going.

I'd known from an early age that my mother was a changeling—a human child stolen from another realm to serve the Fae. She'd spoken about it when telling Rosey and I why we should never trust fairies, however she'd never gone into so much detail.

"One day I was playing in the woods behind my house and I saw them," Mother continued.

"The Fae?" I asked.

She shook her head. “A group of Underfae, though I didn’t know then what they were. They were barely larger than my doll, and dancing in a ring of toadstools. Being only a child, I played with them. Then, only a few days later, I was taken from my bed just as Orla promised.”

“How?” I asked, leaning forward with interest. “Why?”

Mother shook her head, as if she wished to shake the memories from her mind. “Not all humans born outside of Elsewhere can see the Fae. I was told later that all changelings were taken because they had the sight.”

Even here in Elsewhere, not all humans were able to see the tiny creatures that guarded plants and rivers. I’d always been able to see them, but never once had my mother indicated that she could as well.

“I didn’t know you could see the Underfae.” I was unable to keep a slight hint of accusation out of my voice.

“I wish more than anything that I could not,” she spat. “Filthy, evil creatures.”

I ran a weary hand through my hair. If I let her linger too long on this topic, she’d devolve into a bitter rant about the evils of all magic. For a moment, she’d seemed willing to share more than I’d ever learned before. I had to get her back on topic.

“So you were taken from the human realm and brought to Nightshade?” I prompted.

My mother blinked at me, as if she’d forgotten her train of thought. “Yes. I spent ten years in Nightshade serving the court and learning to worship the Source. The court of Nightshade was just as evil and depraved as the capital. Every inch of the city was filled with zealous priests and fanatics, all united in worship of the Source.

"Living there was an absolute nightmare and I swore that one day I would find a way back to my family."

A sick feeling churned in my stomach. "What happened?"

"When I turned 16 I was assigned to be the wife of one of the priests who served at the Source. There was no point in trying to escape after that."

I gazed at her, eyes wide with shock. This was the first time she had ever brought up this topic in our entire relationship. To my knowledge, my mother had never been married; in fact, she always avoided any questions about who my father could be. My mind raced with anticipation, a sudden realization dawning on me.

"How long were you married?" I asked, forcing my tone to remain even.

"Six months," she spat bitterly, her face twisting with the ghost of old pain. "For those six months I was no longer required to work in the kitchens or clean the temples, but I also wasn't allowed outside. Each day I felt more and more like a prisoner, and every evening I dreaded the moment when my husband would return home. If I tried to leave he would have killed me, and often I thought I might simply let him."

I glanced at the floor, simultaneously horrified and morbidly curious. "Why did it only last six months?"

"Because one day I decided I couldn't stand it any longer," she replied bitterly. "I knew one of us had to die, and I didn't much care if it was me or the monster who called himself my husband. So, one night, I waited for him to go to sleep, and stabbed him through the eye with my hairpin."

"And that worked?" I blurted out incredulously.

Mother nodded. "In Nightshade, many things were made from Source-forged steel. My only regret is that he was killed instantly, and never even knew what had happened."

I gaped at her, a whirl of tangled thoughts coursing through my mind. It was little wonder why Mother hated the Fae, when she'd known nothing but cruelty from them.

I couldn't help but notice the similarity between her story, and how I'd first killed one of the Fae, and with that thought, the nervous anticipation that had been building in my stomach collapsed. If she'd killed this nameless Fae priest, he wasn't my father. I wasn't sure if I was relieved or disappointed.

A part of me was angry that I'd never known any of this before…but then, I supposed it made sense. Even if Mother had wanted to talk about her past–and she clearly didn't–I'd been barely more than a child when she was taken away. Hardly old enough to know the truth of what had happened to her.

"So you escaped?" I pushed, wishing to keep her talking. I needed to hear all there was to know, or I might never have the opportunity again–no matter how uncomfortable these stories made me.

"Yes," Mother said. "I ran and made it as far as the Waywoods. I intended to reach the eastern shore and try to find someone who knew how to return to my homeland, but it was barely two weeks before I learned that I hadn't fully escaped my husband after all."

"What do you mean?"

She gave me a pointed look. "I was pregnant."

The anxious bubble in my stomach re-inflated.

My heart pounded quicker and I wrung my hands in my skirt,

the full realization of what she was saying washing over me. "So that would mean that Rosey and I are—"

"Half Fae," she finished for me bitterly. "It's the curse I've borne for twenty-two years. My daughters are monsters."

I stared at her in shocked silence, my heart pounding too loudly in my ears. "Why did you never tell me?"

My mother readjusted her position, pushing her back flatter against the bars of her cage. She assessed me with cold eyes. "If I had, would it have changed anything?"

"Maybe," I snapped. "It might have changed how I felt."

"No," she replied. "If anything, it would have given you a reason to indulge in your unnaturalness. I wanted to raise you both to be human, not let you turn into one of *them*."

A prickle of heat traveled up my spine like angry flames licking at my skin. I sucked in a startled breath.

I straightened, sucking in a deep breath and pushing every shred of feeling to the furthest corners of my mind. Only a few more questions, I told myself grimly. I just need to know the truth once and for all.

"If you always hated us, why did you raise us?" I asked, my voice an eerie calm resonance. "Why not kill us at birth?"

My mother jerked. "I didn't always hate you. I tried to help you not become evil, despite who your father was. I thought I could teach you to suppress your evil side. I could never have killed my own babies, in fact, I destroyed my own life to save you."

"What do you mean?"

"You were born sickly and dying," she replied, her tone flat as if she'd resigned herself to finishing this story no matter what.

"Your sister was born healthy, but I knew the moment I saw you that you wouldn't survive."

I narrowed my eyes at her. "But you were wrong."

She shook her head. "No. I wasn't wrong. You were dying, and there wasn't anything I could do to save you. It would have taken magic."

"But—wait."

My mother wasn't even looking at me now. She spoke into the cell, as if she was divesting herself of years of secrets, unloading them like a weight hanging over her. Her confession was no longer about me, but about her own need for closure.

"As much as I hated it, I'd spent ten years in Nightshade," she continued. "I'd been taught to worship the Source, and I knew the stories of its power. I knew where to take you, so I climbed the mountain, still bleeding, with two infants in my arms. I begged queen Aisling to save my child, and she answered. She offered me a bargain."

"You bargained with gods?"

She nodded. "Aisling agreed to save you, and in exchange I would have to find and save her child. I had no idea who her child was, or how to find them, but I agreed."

"Why?" I spluttered, my mind reeling.

She looked at me blankly. "At the time, it seemed like the obvious choice. My baby was dying, I would have agreed to anything."

I swallowed, willing the lump rising in my throat to disappear. I couldn't cry. I couldn't give in to any anger or sorrow. Not yet. "So obviously, Aisling helped?" I asked, struggling harder than ever to keep my tone even.

"The queen poured her power into you, and the force of it caused the Source to erupt. I watched from the top of the mountain as the city of Nightshade was consumed in fire and molten stone."

"So you're saying it's because of me that the entire city was destroyed."

She shrugged. "I suppose so."

"You don't seem bothered by it. You destroyed an entire city."

"An evil city," she insisted. "At that moment I didn't care, but soon I realized I'd made a mistake."

I almost sagged in relief. She might have done something terrible, but at least she felt some remorse for it— "You couldn't have known, I—"

"As a child you immediately showed signs of magic," she continued, talking over me. "I know I'd made a mistake in saving your life."

A stone dropped into my stomach. I opened my mouth, but no words came out. Another spark of heat crawled over my skin, this time traveling down my arms and lingering in the tips of my fingers.

"I'd been weak," Mother said. "And it cursed you with that foul magic even more than you already were. I tried to teach you to suppress it."

My mind felt numb with shock. I could barely even process what she was saying, much less the hatred in her gaze. "What about the promise you made to Aisling?" I asked, dazedly.

She made an angry noise in the back of her throat. "I had no idea where to look."

"So you joined the rebellion," I finished for her, understanding dawning.

Ambrose had told me how he met my mother during the rebellion. They were comrades, and even after Ambrose became the leader of the rebels, my mother remained under his command.

It was unbelievable to me that Mother would ever work with Fae, but now it made sense. If she was forced to seek them out for information on Aisling's child, she would certainly prefer to associate with those who sought to tear down the Fae monarchy rather than supporting it.

"That's right," Mother confirmed. "King Gancanagh was in the North at that time."

"Trying to take over the rebellion?" I asked, remembering the rest of what Ambrose had explained to me. "Gancanagh first tried to take over the kingdom of Elsewhere, and when he was unsuccessful he returned to Underneath and challenged the former king for that throne."

"Correct," Mother sneered. "I suppose your princes told you that?"

I flattened my lips. They were kings now, not princes, but it didn't seem worth correcting her. "Yes. Did you know that Gancanagh is Bael's father?"

She scowled. "I hardly cared to learn more than passing gossip about the royal family. The Everlasts do not matter to me, nor do they have anything to do with this story."

I bit the inside of my cheek to keep from speaking the retort I longed to throw at her. The Everlasts had everything to do with this story. Their family history was as twisted up in this as mine was.

"Gancanagh told me that he knew where the heir was."

"The heir?" I asked, confused.

Mother narrowed her eyes, seeming annoyed that I didn't understand. "Aisling's child. Her heir."

It was my turn to be annoyed. For someone so filled with hate, my mother certainly knew a lot about Fae history and religion. She spoke of Aisling with no awe or confusion about who she was. I supposed she had learned of the ancient queen while living in the theocratic territory of Nightshade.

"Well, where was the heir?" I asked.

My mother smiled bitterly. "For many years he refused to tell me, holding the information over my head as long as I was willing to work with the rebellion. I assumed he was somewhere in the North, as Gancanagh was equally interested in stamping out the last person who could challenge rule over Elsewhere as I was in finding and freeing him. I kept in contact with him while we lived in the valley near the Source, and all the while tried to keep your magic hidden. Unfortunately, that became impossible."

"What do you mean?"

She looked at me with something akin to disgust. "No matter what I did, that horrible power would leak out. Everywhere you went, you would summon Wilde creatures to you. At first, it was just the Underfae, but then it became worse. As you grew older, any creature with magic would become fixated on you and follow you around like a moth to a flame. You would play in the forest, and come home riding some monster claiming it was tame."

"I don't remember that," I interrupted.

"You were very small. No more than five, and already your power was more than I could handle. I knew by the time you reached adulthood, there would be no chance of hiding it unless

I forced you to stop. I invented rules to prevent you from encountering magic, but you broke them. I tried beating you for it, rewarding you when you surpassed it, but nothing worked. You weren't afraid of me."

"So you taught me to fear the Fae instead."

She nodded. "It wasn't difficult. I paid some members of the rebellion to attack you, so you'd fear both them and the forest."

Unconsciously, my hand flew to my ear. I remembered the attack she spoke of, and she was right—after that, I'd known that the Fae were evil. They were dangerous, and I could never disobey my mother's rules again.

"Why would you bring us to the capital? If you were so worried I'd use magic, why take me to a court full of it?"

She grimaced. "You'd stopped using your powers intentionally, but there were still the occasional incidents. You'd have an argument with your sister, and the afflicted would swarm our home. I knew it was only a matter of time until you realized you had caused the attacks, and it was no random coincidence. Gancanagh visited me once again, and offered to take you from me."

I gasped. "Why?"

She grimaced. "I assume to bring you to Underneath where your powers might help him in his quest to hold on to his throne."

"Why not let him?" I asked bitterly. "If you hated me so much."

"I didn't hate you," she said verdantly. "I hated the magic, but I still foolishly believed I could stamp it out of you with time. At least I might be able to lessen it, after all, your sister was half Fae as well and never showed a shred of that horrible power."

"Yes, she did."

A dark sense of contentment washed over me. I longed to confront my mother with this information, knowing it would undoubtedly infuriate her. It was a small way to get back at her for the pain she had caused me. "Rosey was a seer, she dreamed of the future almost every night."

My mother stopped, her words cut off by her surprise. After a moment, she swallowed, and fixed me with a contemptuously glare. "Liar."

I laughed. "I wish I was lying. You certainly taught me how to do it well. Was that really for protection, or were you just assuring yourself that as long as I could lie I was still mostly human?"

She flinched, and didn't have to answer. I knew I'd hit the nail on the head. How would she react if she knew I struggled with untruths more with every passing day?

"Let me guess," I said wearily. "You were called on by the rebellion seven years ago?"

She nodded. "I was still bound to seek out the heir, and the longer I spent in the capital avoiding my purpose the more restless I felt. I jumped at the opportunity to return to Aftermath to seek him out, with or without Gancanagh's help. I spent years there, searching, and finally realized there was no heir to be found. I contacted the rebellion again, and got myself sent to Underneath to confront Gancanagh after all these years. He owed me the information."

I couldn't help but marvel at how many bargains my mother had managed to strike with Fae royals of all sorts. Was it from experience then, that she'd always forbid me from bargains?

"And did Gancanagh help you find the heir?" I asked, dully. I barely cared about the answer anymore, my mind was too tired, spinning with all the new information.

"He did, in a manner of speaking," she said bitterly. "I couldn't simply ask him. Gancanagh is—was—the worst of his kind. He would never answer a straight question, and would do everything in his power to keep me indebted to him. Unfortunately for him, he laid his own trap quite nicely. His queens were never allowed to be seen or heard, making it all too easy to move in and out of the court as long as I was veiled."

I wondered fleetingly what had happened to the original queen, then decided I didn't want to know. Whether my mother had killed her, or they'd colluded together, I didn't desire to know anything more about Mother's double-life.

"Did you know I'd be at court?" I asked.

"No." Her tone had taken on a hint of discomfort. "Imagine my surprise when I saw you there at dinner. I'd disguised myself as the queen that night, only so I could find a moment to speak with the Dullahan. I had no idea I'd find my own daughter whoring herself out to Fae nobles."

I pinched the bridge of my nose. I didn't even care about the putrid smell of the dungeon anymore. It hardly affected me as I sucked in deep breaths, forcing myself to remain calm and detached. No matter what she said about me it didn't matter. The truth was the most–the only–important thing.

"And did you find him?" I asked, dully. "The heir, I mean. Did Gancanagh help you?"

"I did," she said grimly. "In a manner of speaking. But that hardly matters to me anymore."

"Why is that?" I asked, feeling detached. Like one part of me was asking questions, while the rest was floating outside my body watching the whole thing.

"Because it wasn't worth it," she hissed. "Didn't I always tell you not to bargain with fairies? There is no winning. I made that deal to save your mortal life, but once I'd agreed that was lost anyway. I should have known there was no hope for your humanity," Mother sneered. "Your sister always did a better job of behaving normally than you did. Where is she, anyway? Is she with you, or did she escape this unnatural hell?"

I jerked, her question dragging me back from the edge of madness. I blinked at my mother, a sickly feeling climbing up my throat. "Do you not know?"

"Know what?" she demanded.

I closed my eyes, and swallowed the thick lump in my throat. "Rosey is dead. She died over a year ago."

For a moment my mother stared at me, and I saw the raw, unendurable pain in her eyes. In a way, I was glad of it. Somewhere deep down, my mother cared. Part of her was still the person I remembered, even if she was almost unrecognizable to me right now. But then she blinked, and her eyes went flat and angry once more. "Good," she snapped. "At least she never had to see what you've become."

My mother's words hung in the air, and my mind struggled to comprehend their meaning. My ears were buzzing with a high-pitched sound, and my heart raced so loudly I could feel it pulsing in my head. I gazed at my mother, blinking rapidly as if trying to clear my vision and understand what was happening.

My hands were burning.

Anger and heat coursed through my body in equal measure, the licking flames scorching me from the inside out. For a long moment, I lost track of where I was—who I was. I became nothing but flame, burning, raging, unapologetic and uncontrollable. I was born of death and flames, and maybe that was all I was ever meant for.

Distantly, I heard a scream.

I blinked and black dots filled the edges of my vision. I didn't remember getting to my feet, but I found myself standing before the cell. A haze of smoke filled the room, and struggled to focus on my mother in front of me.

She had managed to get to her feet as well, and now stood eye level with me, only the bars of her cell separating us. Her fingers clenched white around the bars, and her face was twisted with equal terror and contempt.

For the briefest moment, a stray thought flickered at the back of my mind. An evil thought.

I could leave her here.

I could burn this entire castle down, and her with it.

I was the Source; the great equalizer; and like death, I would take no prisoners.

5
AMBROSE
THE OBSIDIAN PALACE, EVERLAST CITY

"You must be fucking joking," Scion snapped. "You're expecting us to look through every book? There must be five thousand volumes in here."

"At least ten thousand, actually," I said blandly. "And yes. We'll have to go through all of them."

Scion gave me a withering look. "What is the point of this, exactly?"

"Aside from appeasing *your* mate? This is Grandmother's study. All these books contain her notes on her visions going back hundreds of years. If there's anywhere in the castle that contains information about the curse, it's here. I would think that might interest you, given that you're currently the most likely to kill us all."

Scion glowered. "I don't know about the *most* likely."

He glanced across the room and I followed his gaze to where Bael was lying on his back on the carpet, one arm behind his head, staring up at the vaulted ceiling. In a way, I was quite glad to see him—both human and awake. Bael had spent many weeks either sleeping, or roaming the lower floors of the castle in his lion form. This was a vast improvement on both.

As if feeling our eyes on him, Bael turned his head to look at us. His yellow eyes flashed, the pupils dilating into slits for half a second before returning to normal. "Did you two say something?" he asked, his tone distant.

Scion shook his head, and turned to the nearest bookcase pulling a volume out at random and flipping to the very center of the book.

It was the first time the three of us had been alone together since…actually, I wasn't sure we'd ever been alone all together. Certainly, it was the first time Scion and I had willingly been in the same room since before I'd left the family, and I supposed I couldn't be surprised there was so much animosity.

Half an hour had passed since Lonnie left to talk to her mother, and I was already feeling the absence of her calming presence. With her around, Scion had avoided direct confrontation with me. Maybe she was changing him–she'd certainly changed me. But now that she was gone, my brother's anger towards me seemed to intensify.

We were standing in the middle of Grandmother Celia's study. The familiar round room stood at the very top of the southern tower—fortunately not one of the towers that had been damaged in the battle several months ago.

It was a perfectly round room with a deep burgundy carpet and floor to ceiling bookshelves on every wall. In the center of the room was an oak desk. On the desk were an enormous statue of a bronze raven, and several stacks of loose parchment.

Many years ago I'd spent entire days here, training to use my talent under the care of Grandmother Celia—the only other omniscient seer in our family. Now, the room felt hollow and empty without her presence.

Scion looked up from his book and grimaced. "This is all ramblings about politics in Nevermore. It's nothing to do with us."

"Pick another book then," I snapped.

"Aren't you supposed to know everything?" my brother said snidely. "Why don't you tell us what book to look in?"

I sighed, pinching the bride of my nose. "I wish I could."

"But—"

"Drop it, Sci," Bael said lazily. "Yelling won't help anything."

"Listen," Scion snapped, rounding on Bael. "If we're all forced to work together I just think it's strange that he—" he glared at me again "—isn't helping. What is the fucking point of being a seer if it doesn't work when it would actually be useful?"

I pressed my lips together to prevent myself from saying something I'd regret and turned my back on Scion. Ironically, I agreed with him, but there wasn't a single fucking thing I could do about it.

On the surface, Scion might be angry about my lack of helpfulness—something that bothered me as well—but deep down, I knew this argument was about far more than my visions. Scion had harbored resentment towards me for most of his life, and he had every right to, but just because I understood him didn't mean I enjoyed the fallout.

It had been foolish to agree to work together to go through Grandmother's office, even if it pleased Lonnie to see us getting along.

"You're being juvenile," I barked.

"And you're being an ass," Scion snapped back.

For some reason I couldn't explain, I felt a smile tugging at my lips. Maybe because this was the longest conversation I'd had with my brother in years, argument or not. Maybe because the argument itself felt so pedantic, like a real fight between siblings. I supposed, I wouldn't really know.

I turned my back so Scion wouldn't see my face as I wrestled with the insane grin that threatened to overtake my forced indifference. Bael caught my eye and smirked.

My cousin was practically a stranger to me. By the time I left the court of Elsewhere, he'd been barely three years old. Still, I could already tell we'd get along well. Bael appeared completely unfazed by everything, except when it came to Lonnie's well-being. On that point, we were in complete agreement. Besides, he seemed to take as much pleasure in antagonizing Scion as I did.

My thoughts were interrupted by a knock on the door. For a second, I thought it was Lonnie, coming back from speaking to her mother. But no, she wouldn't knock. I took a step toward the door, and reached out a hand to open it.

"Who's out there?" Scion asked darkly.

I paused, my hand outstretched, and glanced back at him. "How should I know?"

My brother raised an eyebrow, sneering. "Aren't you supposed to know everything?"

I ground my teeth. Not that Scion could know it, but I hadn't been able to see much of anything since we'd left Underneath. It was clear to me what the problem was: Like almost all seers, I couldn't see any visions of my own future. I couldn't see Lonnie either, for entirely different reasons, and what little I could see of my brother's future was always hazy. Scion was prone to second-guessing everything. That quality allowed him to seal his mating bond with Lonnie without risking death, but it also made it nearly impossible to get a clear vision of his future. Of the people within the castle who mattered, only Bael made a good subject for prophecy. Unfortunately, he'd spent the better part of the last several weeks sleeping. All that combined to build a brick wall in my mind. I couldn't see through it, and if I tried to peer around it I could find no edge to the wall.

I could only conclude that I'd be spending the foreseeable future with Lonnie and Scion, at the very least. A large part of me was glad of that, but it still left me nearly powerless.

The person on the other side of the door knocked again, and I jumped. I'd nearly forgotten about them. Hastily, I swung the door open, and found myself nearly nose to nose with Idris. I took a step back. "Hello."

"I could hear you all shouting down the hall," the other male said by way of greeting. "Thought you might like some help."

I furrowed my brow in slight annoyance, but stepped aside to let him into the room. "We're fine," I said flatly. "You really don't—"

I broke off as Idris shouldered past me and into the room. The hair on the back of my neck stood up.

There was nothing specifically wrong with Idris, per se. I'd spoken to him when he first boarded my ship after Underneath, and I knew he was being truthful when he said he didn't remember exactly how he'd ended up in the palace dungeons. He also had no ill will toward any of us, and didn't intend to harm Lonnie–always my first priority. Still, there was something…odd about the man. Something that I didn't think had anything to do with his being from another millennia.

"What are you looking for?" Idris asked conversationally.

Scion looked up from his book and glared at the male. "Why the fuck does it matter to you?"

I stifled a grin. For once, I wholeheartedly agreed with my brother, though I might have said so more tactfully.

To his credit, Idris took Scion's mood in stride. "It doesn't," he replied easily. "But there's not much else for me to do, is there? You all freed me, I may as well try to be useful."

Bael sat up, cocking his head appraisingly at Idris. "You said you were born seven thousand years ago?"

Idris nodded with a weak smile. "Something like that."

"Well, that would have been the time of Aisling, wouldn't it?"

I went stiff waiting for Idris to reply.

Of course, this wasn't the first time it had occurred to me that seven thousand years was almost exactly the time since the curse on our family was originally enacted. Yet, I didn't exactly believe that Idris was really so old. I believed he thought he was, but then, years–even months–of confinement could easily drive a male insane. It was far more believable that he had lost track of time than that he was truly as old as the legendary queen Aisling.

Before Idris could even open his mouth to reply, the shrill call of a raven pierced the air. We all instinctively turned to face the doorway as, in a flurry of black feathers and sharp talons, Scion's pet raven burst into the room. It swooped low over our heads, landing on his master's shoulder with another urgent screech.

My stomach sank.

I didn't have to understand the bird to know something was wrong. It had been watching Lonnie, and if the bird was here… where was she?

* * *

I ran down the stairs toward the dungeon. Bael had taken the lead and sprinted several paces ahead of me, while Scion took up the rear, seeming to be trying to get more information out of his bird. Whether he could actually talk to the thing, I had no idea, but for once I hoped so.

"We shouldn't have let her go alone," I grumbled to no one in particular. "Rhiannon is more dangerous than she looks, and she's already tried to kill Lonnie once."

"Why do you care?" Scion barked. "She's not your concern."

I opened my mouth to retort, and closed it again.

In a way, he was right. For now, Lonnie really wasn't my concern. And unless I was honest with her, she never would be.

Still, I couldn't keep myself from rushing downstairs with the others to make sure she was safe. I consoled myself with the knowledge that Idris was running along with us, and he certainly had no claim to Lonnie, nor a reason to care aside from general curiosity.

We burst through a round wooden door at the bottom of the stairs and into the hallway which housed the entrance to the dungeons. I turned my head, frantically searching for some sort of danger, only to come crashing to a halt.

Lonnie herself sprinted toward us, running away from the dungeons as if there was some terrible monster chasing her.

Mingled relief and confusion hit me at once, followed by anger. She was alive, yes, but she was crying.

She reached Bael first, and threw herself into his arms, burying her face in his shoulder. He patted her head, while looking over her shoulder at me, confusion across his face.

'What happened?' he mouthed.

I shook my head. I'd never been more frustrated by my inability to see Lonnie's future. My blood pounded in my ears and my adrenaline surged. I wanted to destroy whatever had upset her, or better yet, to have stopped her from encountering whatever it was in the first place.

"Did your mother do something?" Bael demanded, seeming as frustrated as I felt at not knowing how to help her.

She shook her head and sucked in a great rattling breath. "No. Not really–"

"Then what–"

"I did," she sobbed. "I could have killed her!

"Did you kill her?" I asked sharply.

"No," she wailed. "But I wanted to. She's my mother, I can't believe–" she broke off with a shuddering gasp. "She…she upset me, and I nearly destroyed everything."

"What the fuck did she say to you?" Scion demanded angrily.

Lonnie shook her head, her words turning practically incoherent. She buried her face in Bael's shoulder, and I couldn't make out what she was saying, picking up only disconnected phrases, "Aisling" "Rosey" and "Heir" coming out the clearest.

We all glanced at each other over Lonnie's head. Scion looked quite like he wouldn't have minded if Lonnie killed her mother, but Bael looked troubled.

I felt somewhere in the middle.

Unlike Bael and Scion, I'd never had to learn to control destructive combative magic. I had no idea what it was like to get angry and have the ability to level a village in one wave of the hand. I did, however, know far more about killing than any of the others combined. Every decision I'd ever made resulted in someone's death. Sometimes in thousands of deaths, and it never really got easier.

"Take her upstairs," I told Bael. "I'll go check on Rhiannon."

Bael nodded, and scooped Lonnie into his arms. He carried her down the hallway with little effort, looking far more awake than I'd seen him in recent memory.

"If you're going down there, I want to go," Scion demanded.

I glanced at him, and merely nodded. The grand irony of the situation hit me–Lonnie had wanted us to do something together without arguing. Apparently, that was impossible for the time being, yet we agreed on one thing. The most important person in the world was her.

6

LONNIE

THE OBSIDIAN PALACE, EVERLAST CITY

"What are you thinking, little monster?" Bael asked urgently.

I blinked up at him dazedly, feeling slightly disconnected from myself. As if I were in my body, and not. Intellectually, I suspected I had to be in shock, but in practice… "I don't know."

"Talk to me." Bael growled, seeming unable to keep the anger from bubbling up to the surface. "What the hell did she say to you?"

I sighed. "A lot. I know I need to explain it, but I'm so exhausted…"

"Alright," Bael said quickly, changing tactics as quickly as the wind. "Then how about a bath?"

"Do I look that bad?" I asked, with little conviction, as he carried me toward the sweeping stone stairs.

"You're covered in soot," he replied diplomatically. "If I didn't know you were under all those black spots, I'd think you contracted the plague."

"I can't," I replied flatly.

"Can't what?"

"Contract the plague."

We reached the top of the landing, and Bael marched down the hallway, his expression a cross between concern and determination. His tone was light, almost humoring. "And why is that?"

"The Fae don't get sick."

Bael came to an abrupt halt, his posture going rigid. I looked up, startled, and saw that we were mere steps away from a familiar door. It seemed that Ambrose's rebels had been busy repairing the castle, and had managed to reattach the door to Scion's tower bedroom. Whether Bael realized the room had been repaired, or was just returning there out of habit, I wasn't sure, but I was glad to be back on familiar ground.

"What did you say?" Bael asked sharply.

I sighed, and shook my head to clear it of some of the cobwebs. "Let 's go inside. I have a lot to tell you."

* * *

My bath had nearly turned cold by the time I finished relaying Bael with all that my mother had revealed. He sat beside the tub, his back leaning against the wall, watching me. It was a familiar position, reminding me all too clearly of one of the first conversations we'd ever shared. This time, though, I did the majority of the talking, and Bael sat in rapt attention.

"I knew you weren't human," he said finally. "Magical blood always wins out, and believe me little monster, you've been practically leaking magic from your pores since the day I met you."

"You did," I conceded. "You weren't entirely correct, though. I'm still half human."

"That's irrelevant," Bael said immediately, waving my words away.

I frowned. "I think it's extremely relevant."

"Why?" he cocked his head to the side, looking wary. "Do you dislike the idea of being Fae?"

I bit my lip and trailed my fingers over the surface of the lukewarm water, thinking. "I don't know," I said finally. "I suppose not, but I still feel human."

"How would you know what that feels like?" he asked, pragmatically. "If you feel the same as you always have, and you've always been Fae—"

"Half," I corrected.

"Whatever. If you've always felt the same, how would you know that's your human side you're recognizing."

"I don't know," I shrugged. "The only thing I know for sure right now is that if I'd learned this a year ago, I would have been horrified."

He laughed humorlessly. "I think that might be an understatement."

I winced, thinking of how angry and hateful my mother had been when we spoke. I wanted to think she hadn't always been like that, but a large part of me knew that she had. She'd been blindly hateful her entire life, and had taught me to be the same.

"It's confusing," I mused, trying to find words to describe all the complicated feelings swirling inside my head. "I think my mother was right to hate those who treated her the way they did, and to fear the court. We both know humans weren't treated all that well here."

"True," he reasoned. "Fairies like my Uncle Penvalle did horrific things to anyone weaker than them, but that sort of thing isn't universal. I've personally never cut out a servant's tongue, or whatever other horrible things you've accused me of."

I glanced at him. "You've killed humans, though."

He cocked his head at me. "Yes, and so have you. You've also killed Fae, and Unseelie, and quite a few monsters, all the while believing you were entirely human."

I nodded, but my response got stuck somewhere between my throat and my mouth, and I couldn't think of a single thing to say. Fortunately, Bael carried on, saving me the necessity of holding the conversation.

"I think you should stop focusing on which parts of you are human or Fae, and start thinking about what you might be able to do now that you know what your full potential is. You have Source magic, which is far beyond anything Scion, or I, or any other faerie can do."

"Yes, but what does that mean?" I practically whined. "I don't understand anything about how to control it, and so far, it's done nothing for me except nearly kill me time and time again."

"We can find a way to help you control it," Bael said confidently. "Now that we know what your powers are, I'm sure there's someone who knows what to do. Hell, we have journals in the library going back all the way to the time of Aisling. We'll find something."

"I suppose," I muttered, peevishly.

Bael looked at me sideways, and raised an eyebrow. "What's wrong, little monster? You've just discovered that you have more magic than probably anyone else alive, and you don't seem the least bit excited."

I sighed, and pulled my knees up to my chest, wrapping my arms around them. I leaned my head forward against my knee, so I could only just see Bael through the sheet of my wet hair. "It's stupid," I muttered, "But I can't stop thinking about what my mother said about how I always attracted power."

"What do you mean?"

"She said, from the time I was small, that nothing with magic could stay away from me. And that makes sense, I remember how Underfae always followed me, how I could never manage to blend in with the other servants. My entire life, everyone was afraid to be around me because invariably we'd attract the attention of faeries."

"So?" Bael asked, clear confusion in his voice.

"So, don't you think it's suspicious that I should end up here? Your family has controlled Elsewhere for thousands of years because you have the strongest magic ever recorded. I'm only half magical, and somehow I'm the mate to not only one, but th—I mean two of the most powerful royals alive?"

"What are you saying?" Bael asked, slowly.

"What if it's not even real?" I burst out, lifting my head back up to look at him. "What if you wouldn't even be here, except that I'm...compelling you, or something. If all magic is made from the Source, and I'm literally the Source, maybe you're just like the afflicted, or the Underfae. You can't help but try to be near me."

I sucked in a deep breath, having said all that without stopping. I blinked, and suddenly Bael was directly in front of me. He stood so fast, I saw nothing but a gold blue, and then he was standing beside the tub, reaching down, and pulling me to my feet. A cascade of water fell down around me, drenching Bael's clothing.

"Listen, to me." His intense yellow gaze bore into me. "I love you and it has nothing to do with your magic."

"You can't know that," I argued.

"Yes, I can," he said fiercely. "Because if somehow my presence was hurting you, I wouldn't hesitate to walk away. You're not compelling me to do anything, little monster. I want you, always, whether you're the fucking queen of the Fae, or just some fragile servant with a smart mouth."

The corner of my mouth tipped up. "What if I'm neither?"

"That's fine. Go anywhere and be anything you want, as long as I can go with you." He grinned wickedly. "And as long as you promise to keep that smart mouth."

I grinned, and stood up on my toes to kiss his lips. He responded enthusiastically, and I wound my arms around his neck, pulling him closer to me.

I suddenly became very aware that while he was completely clothed, I was naked and dripping wet. I pressed my body flush against his, soaking the front of his tunic and causing the fabric to stick to his muscled chest. In an instant, I felt him harden against me.

With a growl, Bael lifted me off my feet and carried me out of the tub. He didn't bother to walk all the way to the bed in the next room, and merely pressed my back up against the wall. I wrapped my legs around him and held myself up, as I helped pull his soaking wet shirt over his head. Bael growled low in his throat, then leaned forward, fastening his lips around my right breast. His too sharp teeth bit into my nipple, sending a spark of combined pain and pleasure rocketing through me. My pulse pounded low in my core, and I tipped my head back against the wall, whimpering in pleasure.

Abruptly, Bael stopped moving.

I blinked in confusion, pulling back far enough to look at him. "What's wrong?"

He grimaced, his eyes squeezing shut for a moment before he schooled his features back into a smile. "Sorry, little monster. Headache."

"Oh," I frowned, half in disappointment, half in concern. "Are you alright?"

"I'm fine. It'll pass in a minute. Recently I've been getting them a lot, but they never last long."

My eyes narrowed. "That sounds like it could be something serious. What if–"

In answer, Bael pressed a firm kiss to the curve of my neck, making me forget my words mid-sentence. He licked over my skin, sending tingles skittering all over my body. At the same time, he ran one hand up my bare thigh to cup my core.

I made one more half-hearted attempt to question him about the headache. "Are you sure you didn't want to lie down?"

"Actually, yes." Bael smirked. "That sounds perfect."

He carried me across the bathing room and out into the adjoining bedroom. I laughed when I glimpsed his determined expression in the vanity mirror, and caught on to what he was thinking.

Bael dropped me unceremoniously on the bed and I landed on my back in a tangled pile of soft silk sheets. He stood beside the bed, looming over me, his catlike eyes tracking over every inch of my body.

I smiled, and reached out a hand. "Aren't you going to join me?"

Anticipation gripped me as he knelt on the floor, wrapping his long fingers around my calves and pulling me all the way to the edge of the mattress. My breath caught in my throat as his lips pressed against the sensitive skin on the inside of my thigh, sending shivers through my body.

I moaned, my hips rising off the bed of their own accord at the very first touch of his tongue. He pushed my legs wider apart and licked me slowly, dragging his tongue up my center, causing waves of pleasure to wash over me.

I moaned again, and twisted my hips, desperate for more friction. In answer, he splayed his fingers over my stomach, pushing me back down and holding me against the bed all the while administering slow, tortuous pleasure.

With each slow, deliberate swipe, he teased and tantalized me, building up the intensity. With a slow and deliberate motion, he pressed his lips against my throbbing clit, drawing out every keening sound from my lips.

I reached down gripping his shoulders, pulling his face up and toward to look at me. "Fuck me now. I want to come with you inside me."

A low, rumbling growl escaped from the depths of Bael's throat as I tugged him to his feet. With a swift motion, he undid his belt with one hand and leaned forward, his hands pressing down on either side of my head as he loomed over me. His powerful presence filled the room, casting a shadow that seemed to engulf me in its darkness.

I stretched my body, arching my back as far as it could go, meeting his intense golden stare. Without hesitation, he thrust inside me with such force that a deep gasp escaped my lips. "Like this. You want me to fill you when you come?"

Every nerve in my body tingled with pleasure as he filled me completely and the intensity of our connection ignited like fire between us. "Yes," I demanded. "More."

He slammed into me again and withdrew slowly, seeming to enjoy my whine of protest.

His body collided with mine once more, the force causing my back to arch and a whimper to escape my lips. He withdrew slowly, savoring the moment as if it were the ultimate pleasure.

"Faster," I insisted, rolling my hips to increase the friction between us.

Bael's hands tightened around mine, his grip firm and commanding as he held them above my head. His lips grazed across my breast, sending shivers down my spine.

His hand left my wrists and found its way to my hair, tugging back my head so our eyes could meet in an intense gaze that sent electricity through my veins.

Hot. Destructive. All consuming.

Our eyes locked as he pounded into me, hard and frenzied, and my entire body coiled tighter and tighter like I might snap at any moment.

My mouth fell open in a silent scream, my legs instinctively wrapping tightly around him as I trembled from within. He plunged into me again with a force that left me breathless, all the while muttering curses in a language I didn't understand.

My body gave out, surrendering to the intense pleasure that coursed through me. I collapsed onto the bed, my limbs splayed out and trembling from the aftershocks of my orgasm. Beside me, Bael rolled onto his back. His chest rose and fell rapidly as he tried to catch his breath. Our eyes met, and for a moment we simply gazed at each other in silence, basking in the aftermath.

"It's getting harder and harder not to claim you," he said, still looking at me with an intensity that made my stomach feel as if it had turned inside out.

I opened my mouth to reply and closed it again, merely nodding. I was afraid to voice the truth: that I also felt the pressure to complete the bond, and sooner or later we'd have to confront it.

7
LONNIE

THE OBSIDIAN PALACE, EVERLAST CITY

Several hours later, Bael and I lay in bed in comfortable silence.

I shifted slightly, rolling onto my side. Without saying a word, Bael lifted his arm so I could more comfortably rest my head on his shoulder. I smiled. How could there have ever been a time when I was afraid of him?

Of course, Bael had changed since we'd first met, but not in any way that made him less objectively terrifying. He was still a bit loose with his morals, and there was still something slightly unnerving behind his eyes. Like the lion was peering back at me —his Unseelie side trying to force its way out to play. If anything, now that Bael had embraced his Unseelie power instead of suppressing it, there were more reasons to be afraid of him now than there ever were.

But, in that same time, I'd changed as well.

I wasn't sure when it had happened. It might have been when I'd killed King Penvalle, or else when I spent those long months in the dungeon plotting my revenge on the Everlasts. It might also have been when I'd first drank Bael's blood, or when I let myself consciously use magic for the first time. Perhaps it was all those moments, and all the ones in between.

But at some point, I'd ceased to recognize the former version of myself. I'd moved further and further away from my mother's teachings, until now, we had far less in common than I did with the male lying beside me.

"What are you thinking about, little monster?" Bael asked. "You have a strange look on your face."

Rather than tell him exactly what I'd been thinking—which would have been far too embarrassing to voice, even to my mate —I answered a question with a question. How very Fae I was becoming. "Do you think we can trust that what my mother told me is true?"

He sat up slightly, leaning on his elbow facing me. "What do you mean?"

"It just seems very naïve to think she wouldn't lie. After all, she's the one who taught me that deception was our greatest weapon against the Fae."

Bael pursed his lips, thinking. "It's a very intricate story. Even if she wanted to deceive you, I doubt she could have invented something so detailed right there on the spot. I'm inclined to think she was mostly honest. To the extent that she's aware, that is."

"What do you mean by 'to the extent she's aware?'"

"Not all falsehoods are lies, little monster. Sometimes people are simply wrong."

"I suppose."

I pressed my lips together, still feeling uneasy. I believed Mother had been truthful about her life in Nightshade, and even about my birth. As unreliable as it sounded, I also believed the story about Aisling. After all, where else would my magic have come from?

"I'm confused about the heir," I said finally. "And what Aisling wanted my mother to do once she found them. Doesn't it seem strange that there would be no further instructions? No message Aisling wanted to give her child? No specific mission?"

Bael frowned, looking troubled. "Maybe your mother simply forgot to explain that part. You could go ask her."

My frown deepened and I huffed out a long breath. Of course I could go back down to the dungeon, but at what cost?

Allowing myself to be berated again was not high on my list of priorities. Furthermore, I had absolutely no idea what we were going to do with her. We couldn't leave my mother in the dungeon forever, but neither did it seem smart to let her roam free.

"You don't have to get all the answers tonight," Bael said, seeming to understand the direction my thoughts had taken. "There's always tomorrow. Or next week, even. Your mother withstood two months in the dungeon with barely any food or water just to avoid talking to you. She can wait another week for us to decide what to do next."

"Isn't that cruel?"

He smiled grimly. "I don't care much if it is or not. She hurt you, and if Rhiannon were not your mother, I would have killed her for it. I'd have torn out her heart before we ever left Underneath."

I said nothing. His violent fantasies probably should have disturbed me, but I'd long ago accepted that they probably never would. I'd seen Bael literally eat the body of a man who attacked me, and then bathe in his blood. If I still loved him after that, there was likely nothing that could scare me away.

I scooted closer and laid my cheek back on his shoulder, soaking in the near-feverish warmth of his skin and closed my eyes.

"You know what I'd like to understand?" Bael asked, after several long moments. "What does she mean by 'heir?'"

I opened one eye. "What do you mean?"

"Technically we're all heirs of Aisling. My entire family are descendants of the first royals, albeit distant ones. And then there's you. Through your magic, you're probably more connected to her than anyone has ever been."

"It sounded to me like she meant her child, not a distant descendant."

"But that's just it," Bael argued, sitting up straight to look at me. "Aisling lived thousands of years ago, and…" He broke off, leaving his sentence hanging in mid-air. "Oh, fuck."

"What is it?" I asked, sitting up.

In a split second, Bael had jumped to his feet. He moved so quickly I barely saw the blur as he collected his clothing from the floor, and tossed a shirt at me. "Get dressed."

"Why? You just said we could wait a week before speaking to my mother again."

He tugged his trousers on, and ran his fingers through his tangled curls, looking at me with incredulous wonder. "It's not her I want to talk to. If Aisling had a child, they would be nearly seven thousand years old, and as it happens we have a guest downstairs claiming to be exactly that."

My mouth fell open. "You don't think…"

"I don't know, little monster." Bael grinned. "Let's go find out."

* * *

Bael and I dashed down the hallway.

Or rather, I dashed, and he walked briskly beside me, clearly torn between a desire to stay together and frustration that I couldn't go any faster.

"We should prepare for the possibility that Idris has no idea what we're talking about." I panted as we ran. "Or, maybe he is the heir, but he's plotting to overthrow us at this very moment."

"Both are possible," Bael agreed grimly. "But I'm willing to risk it. If Idris really is an heir to Aisling then he could know how to break our curse. That's worth a gamble, no matter the cost."

I nodded in silent agreement as we turned a corner at the end of the long hall. Suddenly, the sound of arguing filled the hall, the angry raised voices echoing off the stone.

Bael stopped walking, and glanced over his shoulder. "By the fucking Source. Now what?"

I didn't bother to stifle my groan.

The voices were clearly recognizable as Scion and Ambrose, and while I couldn't hear what they were saying, the tone and volume was enough to give me an idea.

"Come on." I turned on the spot to go back the way we'd come. "We should go see what's wrong."

"We know what's wrong, little monster. They hate each other just as much today as they did yesterday and every day before that. There's no reason to waste our time playing referees when we could be finding out how to break the curse within the hour."

I bit my lip, feeling conflicted. "You're right, but I'm still going to intervene. I'll hate myself if one of them kills the other before we even reach the guest wing."

Bael rolled his eyes, but turned around and begrudgingly followed me back in the direction of all the yelling.

"If we're taking bets on who comes out alive, my money is on Scion," Bael muttered darkly. "Ambrose is a better physical fighter, but Sci has magic on his side, and he's far angrier."

I frowned. "You've thought about this?"

"Just a bit." Bael gave me a slightly guilty grin. "Like, if for whatever reason I had to fight Ambrose I think it would be a toss-up who'd win."

"Why is that?" I asked, internally kicking myself for feeding into this.

"Ambrose is really old, and he's been fighting far longer than I've been alive. Give me another hundred years or so, and I'll win every time."

"In one hundred years he'll have more experience too."

"Sure, but magic is like wine, and not just because it tastes delicious–" he winked at me "--power gets stronger as you get older, which is an advantage for someone like me. But for seers, more power isn't necessarily a good thing."

"It's not?"

"The more power a seer has, the more they lose touch with the present. They get kind of…strange and distant. Like they're here with you, but really somewhere else."

I scowled. I'd never seen Ambrose do anything like that. He was always alert, always wary of everything and everyone around him. I couldn't imagine what it might look like if he looked at me without his usual intensity.

"I don't know why we're discussing this," I snapped as the distant shouting grew louder. "I don't want any of you to fight."

"Don't worry little monster. Soon it won't matter who will kill whom."

"Why?" I asked, narrowing my eyes at him.

"Well…" He shrugged, almost sheepishly. "I assume Ambrose won't want to stay here much longer now that the question of king has been settled. You're the queen and we're your mates, so unless he was somehow able to kill all three of us, which is doubtful, he'd never have a clear claim to the throne."

"I don't think he wants to hurt any of us," I said flatly.

Bael cocked his head at me in question. "Then what has he been doing for the last several decades?"

"I—" I broke off, unsure what to say.

The time I'd spent on the ship had felt like a lifetime for me, but Bael and Scion hadn't been there with us. Until recently, the only time's they'd seen Ambrose, he'd been attacking them. He'd destroyed their castle and his rebels killed all their guards. The fact that he'd helped rescue them wouldn't fix all the bad blood between them. It was hard to argue that all Ambrose wanted was to rejoin his family after he'd spent years trying to destabilize them. He'd been the leader of the rebellion for longer than I'd been alive, yet somehow I was positive that none of us were in any danger from him or his rebel army.

"He never hurt me while we were on the ship," I said defensively. "And he helped me rescue both of you, and let us use his ship to return from Underneath."

"And that's why he's still breathing," Bael said flippantly. "But you can't honestly think he's going to stay and…what? Go back to being a prince?"

"He's still here now," I argued.

"Sure, because we have to break the curse, but once that's done, and we start rebuilding the court, there's no place for him here anymore. Not after he gave up his title to go raise an army against us. The best thing for everyone would be for him to disappear."

A tiny spark of fear shot through me, but I tamped it down, forcing a neutral expression onto my face. "You're right. I suppose I've just gotten used to all this chaos, I keep forgetting what normal would feel like. If there ever really is a normal."

As if to illustrate my point, at that moment Scion and Ambrose rounded the corner on the opposite end of the hall, walking straight toward us. They were clearly still locked in their argument, both gesturing wildly as they yelled back and forth. They hadn't seen us yet, and we stopped walking, waiting for them to notice our presence.

Bael put a hand on my lower back, and bent to press a kiss to the side of my jaw. "Don't worry, little monster. If Idris knows how to break the curse, hopefully things will be better than normal again soon."

He'd clearly meant that as comforting, but instead I bit my lip, feeling slightly uneasy.

He was very attached to the idea that Idris could know how to help, but I wasn't so sure that was wise. Tonight had only emphasized to me that we didn't know nearly enough about the male we were allowing to live here, and we'd have to put a stop to that, no matter if he turned out to have anything to do with Aisling.

Finally, Ambrose looked up and spotted us standing in the middle of the corridor, clearly waiting for them. He nudged Scion to get his attention, who seemed to think he was being attacked, and immediately raised a fist to–presumably–send Ambrose careening into the opposite wall.

"Hey!" I shouted. "Stop it!"

To his credit, Scion did stop. He froze with his arm still raised, and turned his head to look at me. "Lonnie," he blurted out. "What are you doing there?"

"What the hell are you two doing?" I snapped back. "We could hear you all the way in the guest wing. You sound like spoiled children."

Both Ambrose and Scion turned to look at me. Their expressions were nervous—something I wasn't used to seeing from either of them. When the silence stretched on a beat too long, a feeling of unease began to wash over me.

"What's wrong?" I asked, in a completely different tone.

Again, the awkward silence was almost palpable. Finally, Scion broke, stepping forward. "It's your mother, rebel."

A lump formed in my throat, and I already knew what he was going to say before I even spoke. "What about her?"

"She's gone, love," Ambrose said gravely.

"Gone where?" I demanded, uncomprehending.

"Dead."

8
LONNIE

THE OBSIDIAN PALACE, EVERLAST CITY

There was a strange buzzing in the back of my head I recognized immediately as shock. Dead? How could my mother be dead? I'd just seen her. Just talked to her.

Just wrestled with whether to kill her myself.

Suddenly, a horrible realization hit me and my hand flew to my mouth. "So, I…"

"No," Ambrose said quickly. "I don't think so. She wasn't burned, and you don't have the power to simply end someone's life by willing it so."

He looked conflicted like he wasn't entirely sure if that was true. Like he was wondering if I did in fact have that power, and we simply didn't know it.

"What happened to her?" Bael asked, all the excitement of minutes before lost from his voice.

"I don't know," Ambrose said, sounding more bitter than I would have expected from him. "We went down to talk to her after…well, after you two went upstairs, and she was just gone."

"But she was fine," I cried, disbelieving. "I'd just left her, and I didn't—" I broke off, my voice cracking.

A strange numbness washed over me, enveloping my body and mind in a thick fog. I felt worn out, as if I had been running for miles without rest. And yet, at the same time, I felt disconnected from myself, almost as if I was watching everything unfold from a distance. My emotions were dull and distant, elusive and unattainable. It was like being trapped in a dream, unable to fully grasp reality.

At that moment, a heavy realization washed over me. It was a deep knowing, a certainty that settled in my bones and made them ache. I knew with absolute clarity that I could never have followed through with killing my own mother. No matter how hurt or angry or betrayed I may have felt, the thought of taking her life was inconceivable to me. Her words and actions may have wounded me deeply, but they could never justify such a heinous act. My conscience would not allow it.

So then, the question became: Who did? Who killed her?

"What were you arguing about?" I asked suddenly, glancing up at Scion and then to Ambrose.

"Nothing important, Rebel," Scion ran his hand through his hair. "Just what might have happened to her."

I nodded dully. I'd thought as much.

Unlike other deaths I'd experienced, this felt unreal. I almost didn't believe it, and likely wouldn't until I saw her body for myself. Was it a sudden act of violence that occurred between the time I left her and when Ambrose and Scion found her, or did she simply pass away. With the truth now revealed, perhaps her life's mission was complete.

Without warning, my legs wobbled underneath me, threatening to give out at any moment. In a flash, Bael was there, his strong arms wrapped around my trembling body, steadying me. His deep voice rumbled with reassurance, "You're going to be fine, little monster."

A bleak part of me wanted to agree that yes, I probably would be fine. I'd endured much worse than this before, and probably would again.

Even to my own ears, however, that sounded callus.

I didn't have to say anything as once again, Bael picked me up and carried me the last few paces down the hall toward our room. For the moment, all thoughts of Aisling and Idris were forgotten, and any questions I had about what more secrets my mother might have kept disappeared.

The silence between us was heavy as we entered the room.

Bael carried me across the floor and placed me down gently on the bed. I instinctively curled into a tight ball atop the blankets. A second later, I felt the mattress dip as he lay down beside me.

A moment later, Scion followed. I didn't open my eyes, but I knew it was him from the scent of pine and amber, and the stilted way in which his footsteps crossed the room. Stiffly, like after all this time he still half-expected me to not want him there.

As he sat down on my other side, I moved ever so slightly closer and his posture seemed to relax. He gently placed his large hand on top of my head and began to run his fingers through my messy hair.

Despite my shock and the beginnings of grief, a part of me felt almost calm. Yet…

Practically against my will, my eyes cracked open. I squinted toward the door where Ambrose still hovered on the threshold, reminding me uncontrollably of Scion back at the inn in the forest. On that occasion, it had been Bael who convinced his cousin to join us, but I was quite sure that neither Bael nor Scion would be so generous this time. Which left it up to me to ask for what I wanted. The only question being: what did I want?

My gaze found Ambrose's dark eyes and he gave a tiny jerk of his head, as if to say *"I'll leave you to it."* Then, he stepped back, beginning to pull the door shut behind him.

I sucked in a deep breath, my entire body tingling with anticipation. "Wait! Aren't you staying?"

Beside me, I felt Scion stiffen and hold his breath. His fingers ceased their combing through my hair, and I knew he was watching me. Meanwhile, Ambrose stopped with one foot out the door, and glanced over his shoulder at me. "I'm not sure that's a good idea, lov–Lonnie," he replied, seeming to stumble over my name. "You've just had a shock, and I don't want to make things harder for you."

By "harder" I was sure he meant that he didn't want to keep fighting with Scion in front of me, but I pretended not to understand. "Then don't make them harder. I'm asking you to stay."

Ambrose didn't reply. Instead, he stared at me for a long moment. Then his eyes flicked toward Scion, before he took a tentative step into the room.

Ambrose crossed the room at a torturously slow pace, and walked around the side of the bed nearest Bael, keeping as much distance between himself and Scion as possible. I expected him to join us on the bed, but he didn't. Instead, he reached for the chair beside my vanity table, and spun it around taking a seat beside the window.

It wasn't exactly what I'd wanted, but it was better than if he'd left. I felt…calmer…with all of them here.

I sighed, and lay back down as Scion resumed his stroking of my hair.

"What do you want from us, little monster," Bael asked roughly.

I glanced at him, and a thousand ideas shot through my mind at once. Did I want to rage, or to forget, or talk? I didn't know, and yet I felt comfort in the fact that whatever I said, I was sure I'd face no judgment or resistance from any of them.

My throat ached from holding back tears and my eyes burned with exhaustion. I couldn't bear the thought of facing this alone, so I pleaded with them to stay, to wrap their arms around me and offer comfort in their warm embrace. "Please," I whispered through trembling lips. "Just hold me."

9
LONNIE
THE OBSIDIAN PALACE, EVERLAST CITY

In the days that followed my mother's death everything seemed to pause.

For the entirety of that first night, all three of the Everlasts stayed with me, but by morning Ambrose had disappeared. I thought he might return at nightfall, if only to ask how I was feeling, but he did not. I had half a mind to go find him and ask why he was avoiding me, but I couldn't find the energy.

For that matter, I couldn't find the energy to do much of anything.

All my training came to an abrupt halt and there were no more discussions of Aisling or her heir, or even conversations about the curse. I knew that the men hadn't fully stopped their research and plotting, but no one asked me to participate.

I spent the better part of the next five days in my room playing over every single moment of my final conversation with my mother until I wasn't sure what was a true memory and what was my own conjecture. My depression wasn't nearly as bad as it had been after my sister died, or even all those years ago when I'd first lost my mother. Still, I couldn't completely banish the gloom that settled over me like a funeral shroud, nor the constant questions and feelings of guilt.

It wasn't until the sixth day of my self-imposed confinement that things changed.

It was close to noon, but I lay alone in bed. Bael and Scion had both slept beside me the previous night, but they'd left early in the morning without explaining where they were going. I was fairly certain Bael was spending the majority of his time helping Ambrose search for information about the curse, while Scion seemed to have resumed his former role as master of the castle. Admittedly, however, I hadn't asked for details.

Outside my window, thunder rumbled, the sudden sound making me jump. I glanced across the room at the open window, and was equally startled to find the sky an ominous shade of gray. I hadn't even noticed the light changing in the room as the storm rolled in, and now I jumped to my feet dashing across the room to close the window before the rain soaked the curtains.

I reached up, struggling to close the heavy window when an enormous blue-black shape landed on the stone sill in front of me. I jumped back in alarm, letting out a small shriek. "Quill!"

The raven ruffled his large wings, his feathers glinting with rain. He cocked his head at me, and let out his usual squawk of greeting. *"You look terrible,"* he seemed to say.

I scowled. "Well at least I'm dry."

The bird chittered, seeming to laugh at me. I humphed and waved him into the room so I could finish closing the window just as a flash of lightning lit up the dull gray sky.

Quill hopped off the window ledge and swooped across the room, landing on the foot of the bed instead. He looked at me again, narrowing his beady coal-black eyes. *"When was the last time you left this room?"*

I rolled my eyes, and didn't reply. It seemed stupid to argue with the bird–or rather with my own subconscious. I could take a hint.

Thinking I might at least walk down to the kitchens for a spot of lunch, I strode across the room and yanked open the doors of the mahogany wardrobe. My fingers ran over the rows of neatly hung dresses until I found a midnight blue one that caught my eye. After quickly slipping into it, I braided my long hair into a hasty crown.

Quill leapt off the bed, and I braced myself as he fluttered down on my shoulder. I glanced up at him. "I hope you're not expecting an adventure. I'm not sure I can manage more than a trip to the kitchens today."

He blinked his glassy eyes at me, and for once I have no notion of what he might have been trying to say.

I made my way to the door and threw it open, stepping out into the hallway. Unfortunately, that was where my motivation died.

I wasn't hungry, and otherwise I had nothing to do. I couldn't very well go back to practicing magic when the courtyard was soon to be flooded, and undoubtedly if Bael or Scion were available to keep me company they already would have been here.

My thoughts drifted to Ambrose for a moment, but I quickly dismissed the idea. He was likely busy as well, and more importantly, I didn't think my fragile mood could handle it if he dismissed me.

Frowning, I wandered aimlessly down the hall in the same direction Bael and I had run on the night– *wait.*

I stopped in the middle of the hall, shocked by my realization.

I'd completely forgotten about Idris, and about the theory that Bael and I had begun to craft before everything came crashing down around me, but there was still ample time to speak with him. I assumed Bael had not already done so, or he would have told me. And was this not the perfect opportunity? If Idris was hiding anything about his identity, surely he'd be more willing to talk to me alone.

A renewed sense of purpose coursing through me, I sped up, marching down the hall.

* * *

It didn't take me long to find the mysterious former prisoner.

I descended the stairs into the enormous entrance hall and immediately spotted him, standing just under the stone overhang that sheltered the open doorway, looking outside at the rain. I smiled with genuine excitement. It was a lucky thing to find him here so easily, when this castle was large enough to spend hours getting lost in.

As if he sensed my presence–or perhaps he just heard the tap of my shoes against the stone stairs–Idris turned to look at me.

He offered me a pleasant smile, and I was once again startled by how healthy he looked for someone who had allegedly been imprisoned for thousands of years. Immortal or not, it seemed impossible that he should look so…alive.

Idris's chin-length hair was pushed back from his face, and he was wearing a red embroidered silk jacket and a pair of matching trousers. I guessed he might have borrowed them from Bael, who was both the most likely to lend anyone his clothing, and the closest match to Idris in both height and weight–Scion being several inches taller, and Ambrose far too muscular across the chest and shoulders. As I approached, he raised a hand to wave at me. "Lonnie," he greeted me jovially. "It's good to see you up."

"Thank you," I muttered, flushing slightly.

"If you're looking for your mates, I'm afraid I can't help. I haven't seen any of them all morning."

I waved him off. "I wasn't. I was actually hoping to ask you something."

"Of course, would you like to join me?" He smiled pleasantly and gestured for me to come stand beside him.

I faltered, distracted for a moment. "Join you in what exactly? What are you doing?"

His smile widened. "I enjoy watching the rain. It's been many years since I've seen it."

"Oh, of course. I should have realized." I moved to stand beside him on the threshold and also turned to look at the rain now firmly pelting the front lawn and cobblestone road that led from the castle down to the city. "How are you enjoying the capital?"

Idris smiled again. "I haven't ventured far into the city itself, but the castle is comfortable. Though, I suppose anything is better than where you found me."

I cleared my throat, a slight wave of discomfort washing over me. "That was actually what I wanted to discuss."

He held up a hand to stop me, frowning apologetically. "If you've come to ask more about what I recall from prior to my imprisonment, I'm sorry to tell you that nothing has jogged my memory."

"No, it's not that," I said quickly. "Not precisely at any rate. My mother seemed to think–"

He cocked his head at me, his smile still firmly fixed in place yet for some reason a small shiver traveled down my spine. I wrapped my arms around myself, trying to ward off the damp wind.

"Your mother is the one who tried to kill you in the dungeons, correct?"

"Well yes. She was a flawed person, but–"

"Then why would you take stock in anything she said? She was human, was she not? Doesn't it seem more likely that she lied?"

I narrowed my eyes in annoyance. He hadn't even let me finish my question before he was denying the credibility of my mother's story. Did that mean he had more information than he wanted to share, or was this simply the Fae's tendency to write off humans as untrustworthy?

Seeming to sense my frustration, Idris changed tact. His smile returned, and he put an almost fatherly hand on my shoulder. "I apologize. I should be more sensitive to your recent loss."

"I just wish I knew who killed her?"

He seemed taken aback. "You think someone else killed her? Someone other than yourself, of course."

I scowled openly this time. "I didn't kill her, and yes, I do. Either that or she did it herself, because there's no chance that she dropped dead of natural causes in the few minutes between when I left her and when Scion and Ambrose found her body."

He looked troubled–perhaps sympathetic, but it was hard to tell as I did not know him well. "Is it always so dreary here?" he asked abruptly, changing the subject so fast it gave me whiplash.

I frowned. "I thought you said you enjoyed the rain?"

"No, you misunderstand," he waved me off. "I mean dreary within the castle. All any of you seem to do is stay locked up in that old study, or train as if you're at war."

I opened my mouth to tell him we were at war, then closed it again shaking my head. I supposed we really weren't—not any more, at any rate. It had been Ambrose and his rebellion who had for so long necessitated a strong army presence in the capital, but now that there was an uneasy truce between him and the rest of the family there was little need to prepare for another attack. Furthermore, the realm of Underneath, which had maintained a constant threat for many years, was no longer a concern now that Bael had won the throne.

One could argue that Aftermath still posed a threat, with its Wilde magic and afflicted monsters, but that wasn't a war so to speak.

I supposed Idris was right—we were constantly vigilant for a threat that had no physical form.

"It's complicated," I said vaguely. "And I do not think we are behaving as if there's a war coming. I'm merely training to use my magic better."

"But what for?" he asked, seeming genuinely curious.

"For…I don't know, what do you mean?"

"You have exclusively combative magic, do you not? What is the point of your abilities if not to fight?"

I had no answer for that.

Again, he was correct, but I was not the only one whom that applied to. Neither Bael nor Scion had the sort of magic that could do much else besides killing, yet they'd trained since birth to master their powers. Was I not doing the same?

"I suppose I'm not exactly sure what you're getting at," I said finally.

"I'm merely noting that I've never encountered a royal court that engaged in such little revelry."

"How many royal courts have you encountered?" I asked, raising an eyebrow.

He waved me off. "It was a figure of speech. I only meant, do you not host parties? Throw balls?"

"Er…well I don't, no."

"Why not?"

Again, I found myself at a loss. I was tempted to say that it was not my responsibility, but that wasn't exactly true. I was the queen, after all, and finally I could understand what Idris was getting at. Before the hunts, and especially during the reign of Queen Celia, the Everlasts did throw revels on a weekly basis.

"Are you suggesting I should have a ball? Here? Now?" I said incredulously, waving a hand around the room as if to point out the still damaged castle.

He smiled. "I assume you never had a true coronation feast. Isn't that something to celebrate? Or perhaps your recent marriage."

I pressed my lips together, thinking. "I suppose…"

Idris smiled widely at me in an indulgent way, like a favorite grandparent might smile at a child. "I'm merely suggesting you think about it. Not everything in life needs to be so catastrophic."

With that, he turned on his heel and walked away, leaving me utterly perplexed and no closer to answers than I had been before.

10
SCION

THE OBSIDIAN PALACE, EVERLAST CITY

I slammed my book shut with a snap, and hurled it at the wall. It smacked against the stone with a resounding slap, and slid uselessly to the ground.

Across the room, Ambrose jolted in his seat, eyes wide and eyebrows raised in surprise. "What the fuck was that for?"

"This is pointless," I grumbled. "I'm fucking done."

Ambrose pressed his lips together in a tight line, evidently struggling to hold back whatever retort he'd thought of. "Fine, just go then. You're distracting me, anyway."

I glared mutinously at him.

We were once again sitting in our grandmother's old study, where we'd been pouring over her journals every day this week. The entire process was mind numbing boredom, punctuated only by frustration every time Ambrose opened his mouth and reminded me he was there.

I got to my feet, pacing the study to work off some of the energy that had been building inside me for days. I wished I could blame my mood entirely on Ambrose, but it wasn't only him that was the problem.

We were no closer to figuring out the curse than we'd ever been, and I was starting to feel like it might never be broken. Meanwhile, this castle was starting to feel more like a prison than a privilege, and I'd actually started to miss my time in the army. It had been horrible, but at least I had something to do and there were always people around.

Now, the court was practically empty, what with everyone still hiding in Overcast until things could return to normal. Lonnie was spending all her time training, or most recently, grieving her mother. Bael was constantly disappearing or sleeping, which left me with no one for company aside from the one person whom I'd hoped never to see again.

"Stop pacing," Ambrose barked. "You're distracting me."

I glared at him. "I'm not one of your sycophantic minions."

He looked up. "What does that have to do with anything?"

My lip curled. "I'm merely suggesting that you not try to order me around. You're still breathing because I allow it, and I'll withdraw that privilege if you keep testing me."

His jaw worked, and for half a second his eyes flashed with rage. I could practically see him struggling to hold on to the detached diplomacy he'd been employing since we got off the ship.

"Fine," Ambrose said through gritted teeth. "Understood."

My eye twitched. A large part of me had hoped he'd retaliate, just to give me something to do. If he'd attacked me I would have known exactly what to do with him, but this new more careful version of Ambrose was unnerving.

"If you have something to say, say it," I demanded.

"And let you goad me into a fight? I'd rather not. I'm too busy to kick your ass at the moment."

I scoffed. "I'd like to see you try. I'd melt your brain before you ever drew your sword."

With what looked like an enormous effort, he sucked in a slow breath and lowered his book. He looked up, finally meeting my gaze head on. "I think you'd do better not to underestimate swords," he said in a tone of forced calm. "That scar on your face is healing nicely, by the way. How fortunate you are that Lonnie isn't so superficial as to be disgusted by it. Not all women could be so charitable."

I saw red, rage coursing through me so suddenly that I hardly noticed when shadows began to leak from my fingertips.

I was done with this—done with letting him stay here as if he hadn't tried to destroy the damn room we stood in less than three months ago. I was done with civility, and with tolerating his encroachment on my position. I wasn't even sure I wanted to be the fucking king anymore, but I'd die before I let Ambrose have the role by default.

I took an aggressive step forward. My power lay in illusion, but the illusion of pain wasn't all that different from physical pain. If I wanted to, I could break him right now. I could feed him so much pain that his mind would snap, his body believing it had died and trapping him in an immortal state of agony.

Rashly, I let go of the hold I always kept on my power and let just the smallest tendril of pain reach out and scratch his mind. I held my breath.

There was a long pause where I waited for him to crumple in his chair as so many others had, but as the seconds ticked by nothing happened. I blinked in surprise.

The illusion of pain had never failed before. The shock of it was enough to jerk me back into rational thought, and I took a step backward breathing heavily.

What the fuck was going on?

"If you're going to stand there thinking so hard you may as well keep researching," Ambrose said, his tone maddeningly calm. "We have hundreds more books to go through."

"I told you," I barked, my anger still riding me. "This is pointless. If Grandmother knew something she would have told us."

"Not necessarily." He gave me a condescending glance. "If I saw that you were about to drink poison and die, but then warned you that would happen, you'd likely not drink the poison at all rendering the vision moot. Often the act of staying silent is part of ensuring the future goes in the correct direction."

"Is that what you're doing, now?" I asked bitterly. "Staying silent and letting us all drink the proverbial poison?"

He looked up, and his expression was inscrutable. "If it was I wouldn't tell you, would I?"

"I know you're up to something."

"Always," he agreed, blandly.

I faltered, taken aback by his admission. "I know you're downplaying your visions. You seem to have forgotten that I lived with Grandmother Celia, too. I know what seers are like."

Ambrose frowned, but he couldn't pretend not to know what I meant.

Seers—good ones, at least—were always slightly disconnected from reality. Grandmother Celia had been so enmeshed in the future, that as she grew older she was hardly ever aware of the present. Speaking to her directly was challenging, and even when she was lucid she was always cryptic and often condescending. As if, because you could never know what she knew, you must know nothing at all.

Ambrose had never been exactly like Grandmother—at least not during the handful of conversations I'd had with him since he left to become the Dullahan. The smug prick was certainly just as condescending, yet, for some reason he wasn't displaying any of the usual…fog…that always shrouded his kind. What if he was plotting something? Or worse, attempting to sabotage us…

"I'm not hiding anything like you're suggesting," Ambrose insisted, almost as if he'd read my mind.

"Then you're doing something. You're too *present*."

Ambrose turned toward the window, showing me his back. He stiffened, and ran a hand through his hair. "I haven't had a clear vision in days."

I sneered. "Bullshit. If I didn't know better I'd call you a liar."

"But you do, so don't waste your breath."

"Grandmother Celia always—" I began again.

"Celia and I are not the same," he interrupted.

I faltered, doubt and confusion settling over me. He couldn't be lying—at least not without giving some outward sign of pain, but how could it be possible that he hadn't had any recent visions? "What's wrong with you, then?"

"It's not me—" He abruptly broke off, not finishing his sentence as he whirled to face the door.

The door flung open and Lonnie marched into the room looking harassed. She slammed the door behind her with enough force to rattle the window panes, and stood with her arms crossed glaring at no one in particular.

I blinked in surprise. Indeed, I wasn't sure I'd ever been less pleased to see her—not when I'd just been about to hear whatever Ambrose had been hiding.

Then, I noticed her dark expression and my entire focus shifted. "What's wrong Rebel?"

"I fucking hate fairies," she sighed loudly, before crumpling into a nearby armchair.

I raised an eyebrow. "That's inconvenient."

She looked up, and seemed to realize what she said. Her eyes widened. "I didn't mean like that. I just meant it will never not be frustrating to try and have a direct conversation. Why can you all never answer a damn question with a real answer?"

"Depends on the question, love," Ambrose replied, looking infinitely more cheerful than he had only moments before.

Lonnie laughed hollowly, then looked around the room seeming to take it in for the first time. "Sorry, am I interrupting something?"

"Not really," I told her. "We haven't found a single fucking mention of the curse in any one of these journals."

"How many have you checked?" she asked.

I gestured to the growing pile of books on the desk. The pile had started out modestly, but now was nearly two dozen volumes high, and covered the entire surface of the large desk completely obscuring the statue of the bronze raven. Ambrose had begun stacking more finished books beside his chair, so that soon there would be more volumes off the shelves than on them.

Lonnie groaned, and closed her eyes slumping back in her chair. "I've not had any luck either."

"I didn't know you were trying to help," Ambrose said. "You don't have to, you have more than enough to deal with at the moment."

I glared at him. It wasn't his responsibility to worry about what Lonnie was or wasn't doing. I shifted, turning my back on Ambrose, blocking him from our conversation. I peered down at Lonnie, trying to discern meaning from her annoyed expression. "How are you feeling?"

She bit her lip. "Alright, I suppose."

"Are you certain? You'd be well within your right to stay in bed far longer. Your mother just passed."

"I'm fine," she said stubbornly. Then, perhaps correctly reading my skeptical expression, she added: "No, really, I am. I'm sick of lying around, I want to do something useful. And anyway. I've realized that nothing has really changed. I believed my mother was dead for years. I already grieved for her years ago, and in a lot of ways I feel the same."

"This is different, though."

"Yes, different in that now my last memories of her are unpleasant ones," she said darkly. "She tried to kill me, and then made it all too clear that she wished I was never born."

I growled low in my throat, unable to keep my anger at how she'd been treated from bubbling up to the surface. Oddly, I was sure I heard Ambrose do the same. I glanced over my shoulder at him, narrowing my eyes.

Ambrose cleared his throat, coughing. "I only wish we'd had a chance to ask your mother more questions."

"I know," Lonnie bemoaned. "Which is why I've just tried to speak to Idris."

She quickly explained her unproductive conversation with the mysterious prisoner in blow by blow detail.

"I'm not sure I understand what you were trying to accomplish," I admitted when she'd finished.

"My mother said Aisling asked her to find her heir, and that she'd managed to do it while in Underneath," she explained. "It seems too much of a coincidence that we should meet someone who claims to be as old as Aisling."

Ambrose shook his head. "I don't think Idris has anything to do with this. For all you know, your mother meant *us*. Our entire family are descendants of Aisling."

"Yeah, Bael said something similar. Lonnie frowned, and glanced around the room as if expecting Bael to emerge from behind a bookcase. "Where is he, by the way? I thought he'd be with you."

"Sleeping in his old room," I answered flatly. "Again."

Lonnie's brow furrowed in evident concern, and I could hardly blame her. Bael had been growing increasingly absent over the last few months, but this week had been unusually bad. Lonnie likely didn't realize it, since she'd been locked in her room, but Bael had been spending nearly every hour of the day sleeping in his cage. He'd get up in the evening and drag himself upstairs where he'd climb into bed with Lonnie, pretending to go to sleep as normal.

I'd asked him about it, but he'd laughed me off, refusing to give any clear answer. I'd already decided that if he didn't pull himself together by the end of the week I'd call in a healer and have him assessed.

"Well, I'm going to try and talk to Idris again at the soonest opportunity," Lonnie mused, clearly still following her own train of thought. "There's something…strange about him that I can't put my finger on."

Ambrose shook his head. "I talked to Idris almost the moment he set foot on my ship. He has no interest in harming us. He doesn't even know who he was before prison."

"Doesn't that seem strange, though?" Lonnie burst out, obviously frustrated. "I'm sure he's said something about his past to me before, but I can't recall when."

"I meditated on his future for days," Ambrose argued. "If he were up to something I'd know."

Lonnie glowered. "Maybe he's blocking you somehow. You told me your visions weren't coming as easily."

I straightened, turning to glare pointedly at Ambrose. "What the fuck does that mean?"

He sighed in exasperation, looking annoyed–likely that Lonnie had revealed this shred of information in front of me. "No one is blocking me…at least, not intentionally. All I'm focused on right now is this:" He gestured vaguely in the air as if to indicate the present moment. "There's nothing worth seeing except the future as it relates to the curse."

That made absolutely no fucking sense.

If he was focused on the curse then why couldn't he tell us how to break it? I narrowed my eyes at him, watching intently. There was something I was missing here–something important–and I didn't like feeling in the dark.

"Here, look at this!" Ambrose said, as if desperate to change the subject. "I finally found a mention of the curse. Or, at least of the crown."

"When?" I barked. "Why didn't you say anything?"

"It's a bit hard to get a word in when you're constantly yelling." He reached for the book he'd been reading, and flipped open to a dog-eared page in the middle, before holding it up for us to see.

I stared nonplussed for a long moment before looking up. "I don't see anything."

Ambrose sighed and pointed to the middle of the page. I leaned closer and noticed that between some other random scribblings was a small drawing of a crown with three jewels set into the points.

Frowning, I pulled back, more annoyed than ever. "That's not the same crown. That one has jewels, the obsidian crown is plain."

"I know," Ambrose snapped. "But look at this."

He pointed again at what I'd first taken to be a random scribble. I leaned closer and squinted. In fact, it was a tiny note drawn beneath the crown in Grandmother Celia's familiar loopy scrawl.

The uniter of the realms

"Aisling was called the Uniter," Ambrose said, seemingly for Lonnie's benefit. "Because she was the reason that Elsewhere became a single country rather than four independent kingdoms. I'm sure this is relevant."

Lonnie looked unconvinced. "If you say so, but if that's all there is I don't see how we're going to decipher it. I was really hoping Queen Celia might have written an entire book of instructions on how to break the curse, not just some vague mentions of Aisling here or there."

"I know," Ambrose agreed. "She still may have. There are more books to check."

Lonnie sighed and stood up again, moving toward the door. "Let's hope, because I'm starting to feel like we're fighting that many headed sea monster again. Every time we answer one question, two more appear in its place."

I laughed darkly.

I knew exactly what she meant. The more I thought about the curse, the bleaker everything felt. No one had been able to break it for thousands of years. Maybe it couldn't be done. Maybe we were simply meant to die miserable.

"I'm going to check on Bael." Lonnie's gaze flicked to Ambrose for half a second before returning to me. "Did you want to come with me?"

I ran a frustrated hand through my hair. "I'll join you shortly. We're not done here."

Lonnie glanced from me to Ambrose and nodded looking almost hopeful. For some reason, she clearly wanted us to get along and for the life of me I couldn't understand why.

Lonnie stood on her toes to kiss me lightly on the corner of my mouth, turned on her heel and marched toward the door, her crimson braid coming more unraveled with every step until half her hair was fanning out behind her like a cloak. At the last moment, she seemed to remember she didn't have to waste time running down corridors anymore if she didn't choose to. The air around her shimmered, and she walked straight into nothingness disappearing from sight in the blink of an eye.

I closed my eyes and tilted my head back, groaning. I could feel the exact point where her lips had touched me burn, and it was a steady reminder that I could be spending my time with her, and instead I was trapped in here day after day with my traitorous brother. Life was cruel.

I turned back to Ambrose, intending to pick up my interrogation precisely where we'd left off. Instead, I came to an abrupt halt, staring. I opened my mouth, then quickly closed it again. I was suddenly at a loss for words.

By the fucking Source.

Ambrose wasn't paying any attention to me–in fact, he seemed to have forgotten I was there. He stood with his arms slack at his sides, the book he'd been so emphatically brandishing a moment before hanging limply from his hand. He was staring at the spot where Lonnie had disappeared with a hauntingly familiar expression on his face.

"By the Source, I'm so fucking stupid." I blurted out. "You want her."

Ambrose jerked, and spun toward me. "What?"

"It's so fucking obvious now, I can't believe I didn't see it before. You're looking at her like–" *Like how I'd watched her for months.*

The evidence was clear enough on his face. It was a longing shadowed by torment, and all too familiar.

Ambrose snorted and raised an eyebrow. "I'm looking at her like what? Are you a mind reader now?"

I shook my head, confused but absolutely sure I was right. "You're fixated on her."

He rolled his eyes. "I'll admit she's tempting. If she wanted to climb into my bed I certainly wouldn't say no, but unfortunately she seems satisfied enough already. I suppose there's no accounting for poor taste."

That was bullshit, and I saw right through it immediately.

"Is this why you suddenly care so much about the curse, then?" I demanded. "For Lonnie?"

"It couldn't just be that *I* don't want to die? You're paranoid, Sci."

I barked a harsh laugh. Yes, I was paranoid, which was why I noticed immediately that he hadn't actually denied my accusation.

This was it, then–the thing that I'd been sure I was missing. My brother was enraptured with my mate. Suddenly, so many things became clear: Why he'd kept Lonnie as a guest on his ship rather than a prisoner and agreed to help her rescue us from Underneath. Why he was still here playing librarian rather than raiding army outposts in Aftermath, or whatever the fuck he usually did with his time. Why he kept trying to force peace between him and I.

Now that I saw it, I couldn't believe I'd never noticed before, and I had no idea how to feel about it.

"Fine," I said, as if agreeing with him. "You don't care about her at all. Just say that, and I'll drop it."

He stared at me, and I could practically see the calculation taking place behind his eyes. He knew I'd trapped him. He couldn't lie outright, but if he refused to answer the question I'd get my answer anyway.

"What do you want from me?" he demanded finally. "I'm quite sure you can't hate me any more than you already do, so what do you have to gain from pushing this?"

I looked Ambrose up and down, assessing him as if I'd never seen him before. And maybe, in a way, I hadn't.

I sunk into the armchair that Lonnie had just vacated, and put my elbows on my knees. I waited for the familiar pang of jealousy and even of rage that always accompanied any thoughts of another male even looking at Lonnie. But as I'd half expected that it wouldn't, the feeling never came.

Ambrose watched me warily, as if expecting me to try and attack him again. Strangely, the idea hadn't even occurred to me. I'd been teetering on the edge of violence for days, but now rather than wanting to attack him, I simply wanted to know what was going on.

Was Lonnie aware of his feelings? Was that why, despite everything, she seemed to want him around us? Ambrose had kidnapped her, had her shot with a crossbow, and nearly killed her on countless occasions. I couldn't see what possible redeeming quality she saw in him.

Granted, I also often wondered what she saw in me. I'd treated her just as horribly as Ambrose had–worse, in some respects.

Part of me was starting to worry that she simply liked broken people. She seemed to seek out the worst possible monsters and aimed to rehabilitate us through sheer force of will. If that was the case, my brother would undoubtedly become her next project.

"Say something," Ambrose demanded.

"I can't. I'm thinking."

"Well what are you fucking thinking?" he barked, finally dropping the false serenity he'd been holding on to for weeks.

I shook my head, dazedly, unable to find the words to describe the ideas flitting through my mind. Instead, I decided to test my theory.

I let go of my hold on my power once more, and let a tendril of shadow drift across the room toward my brother. Ambrose eyed it warily, but didn't move. I let the shadow curl around his wrist, squeezing tightly before falling away. Then, for good measure, I tried zapping him with pain. He didn't even twitch.

I let go of the breath I'd been holding. It wasn't all my magic he was immune to then, just the violent aspects–just like Lonnie.

I sighed in resignation. "How long have you known she was your mate?"

He eyed me, somewhere between apprehensive and defiant. "What makes you think that?"

"I can't hurt you." I laughed bitterly. "I can't hurt Bael either even if I wanted to, because it would hurt Lonnie and the bond won't let me. That would have been fucking helpful to know all these years. I could have saved myself the effort of trying."

My brother closed his eyes and sat back down in the chair across from me. I held my breath and waited, half hoping he'd laugh and deny it, or suggest that it was only Lonnie's Source powers that was affecting him the same way it affected every other creature born from magic. That it wasn't the same for him as it was for me.

But I should have known better than to hope.

"I don't remember when I first had the suspicion," he said, slightly defeated. "A few years ago, perhaps."

I narrowed my eyes. "How is that possible when you can't see her future?"

He looked up, startled. "I never said I couldn't see her future."

"I'm not a fucking idiot," I muttered. Admittedly it had taken me far longer than I would have liked to work it out, but now that I had it seemed entirely too obvious. "Lonnie must be immune to you too, which would make it difficult to see much of anything while living in such close proximity."

Ambrose scowled. "I never said you were an idiot. And you're right, but it's not so black and white. For years, I could always see mundane glimpses of her in other people's futures. Nothing of consequence, but I liked seeing flashes of her."

"I used to meditate on her sister's future just to catch a glimpse of Lonnie. It was addictive. Her reactions were always interesting, and she was beautiful–far too beautiful for me to not realize that was part of the appeal. Except, then I noticed that her sister held no interest for me. They were completely identical, but I could always tell the difference. It occurred to me that there might be a reason for that. I guessed she might be…something. If not my mate, then it could be part of her power."

"It could be," I said, almost hopefully. "She draws everyone to her without even realizing it. I noticed long before I ever knew what her magic was. One time, I took her to a brothel in Inbetwixt–"

Ambrose looked up. "You *what*? Why?"

"Looking for you, actually. It doesn't matter. The point is, I nearly lost my mind trying to keep anyone from touching her. She didn't even realize she was doing it, but her presence alone drove people wild."

He nodded. "I know. You should have seen how the crew watched her on the ship."

"I did," I laughed. "I nearly killed at least three of your men."

He laughed, and I found myself smiling back for the briefest moment before the smile slid off my face. For the first time, possibly ever, we were having a real conversation.

I cleared my throat, sitting up straighter. "So, you're sure that's not all this is? She's not affecting you the same way she affects everyone."

His smile slid away, and he shook his head. "No. Maybe once I thought that, but not anymore. I knew for sure when I felt her in the cell beside me in the dungeons. It was—"

"Like being bewitched," I finished almost bitterly.

"Yes."

I sighed, nodding. I'd already known what he'd say, but my thoughts were still in disarray.

In an ideal world, his admission that we shared a mate would have made me forget the last several decades and forgive him on the spot, but this was far from such a utopia. The kindest thing I could say about my brother was that I didn't much care if he lived or died. I couldn't imagine what it would be like to see him every day, or have to pretend to get along for Lonnie's sake.

"Does she know?" I asked.

"I don't think so." He smiled weakly. "She's very good at living in denial, even when the obvious is staring her right in the face."

Truer words had never been spoken–not that I could claim to be any better.

"Well, when are you going to tell her?" I demanded.

"I don't know. I may never tell her, or at least wait until after this is all over."

I frowned, not liking the uncertainty of that answer. More importantly, I didn't think he was being honest with himself. He'd tell her eventually, or she'd find out. I was living proof that it was only possible to live in denial for so long before everything came to a head.

I stood up, and Ambrose looked startled. He stood as well.

"You're not going to tell her yourself?" he stated. Half a question, half a demand.

I shook my head. "No, but you should."

A ghost of a smile flickered across his face. "Are you being magnanimous? That's not like you."

"No," I said acidly. "I'm being selfish, actually. Even if she doesn't recognize it now, eventually she'll realize she's your mate. When that happens, she'll think we hid it from her because we can't get along. She'll think she has to choose."

"Afraid she won't choose you?" he asked–it wasn't a malicious question, just an honest one.

"No. I don't think she'll be able to choose at all and I don't want to find out what would happen if we ask her to."

He nodded and said nothing as I took a step in the direction of the door. I needed to go for a walk and clear my head. Maybe I'd go down to the village and pick a fight with some noblemen, just to work off some of my energy.

"There's one thing I still don't understand," I stopped abruptly in the doorway. "You told me to marry her."

He looked confused. "And? What about it?"

"Why would you do that if you already knew she was your mate? You practically forced us together."

He shrugged again. "Why did you spend so long denying your own mate bond?"

"Because Bael had claimed her first," I replied automatically. "He's like my brother."

Ambrose looked down, refusing to meet my gaze any longer. If I didn't know better I'd think he looked slightly disappointed. "Well, there you go," he said hollowly. "You actually are my brother, even if you don't want to be."

I drew back, startled. I didn't know what to say to that, and retreated quickly from the room. I would definitely be heading down to the village. I really needed to hit something.

11

LONNIE

THE OBSIDIAN PALACE, EVERLAST CITY

I sat at the head of the long breakfast table in the royal dining room shoveling food into my mouth with almost indecent haste.

For the first time in recent memory, nearly all the seats at the dining table were filled.

Scion sat across from me at the other head of the table, holding a large leather-bound book in one hand, and his fork limply in the other. His posture matched that of Ambrose, who sat to my left, also reading. To my right, Bael was cutting up his sausages, seeming more awake and alert than he usually was as of late, and beside Bael, Idris was watching me with evident curiosity.

I glanced up over my breakfast and met Idris's gaze. "Was there something you wanted?"

He smiled, seeming slightly amused. "I was simply wondering if you have somewhere to be this morning. You're eating rather quickly."

"Not exactly," I mumbled through a mouthful of toast. "I just want to begin training on time."

"On time for whom?" Bael asked, his yellow eyes flashing with amusement. "You're training yourself. No one cares when you begin."

"I care," I replied mulishly, washing down my toast with a sip of strong herbal tea. "I think I'm finally close to mastering that trick with the fireballs. Yesterday I nearly managed to hit the target."

"That's amazing, little monster."

"Thank you." I smiled. "Next I'm going to try and make ropes."

It had been several days since I'd resumed training and things had returned to something resembling normal. Or at least, normal for us.

Scion and Ambrose were getting along better, and I could only assume it was due to the time they'd been putting into research. They'd found several more mentions of the crown as well as drawings like the one Ambrose had shown me the other day. At this point, even I had to admit that he was right–Celia clearly had been on to something, though what that thing was I couldn't say.

Despite my initial desire to speak to Idris again, so far I hadn't been able to find a good moment. I was watching him more carefully, but as far as I could tell he wasn't up to anything nefarious. He'd taken to strolling the corridors and the grounds of the castle, or sitting in the garden for hours on end. He didn't go anywhere or meet with anyone. If anything, he seemed bored.

I startled as Ambrose put his book down on the table with a smack. I looked over at him, finding him already watching me with interest.

"You're planning to make ropes next?" he asked. "You mean like Sci?"

I raised my eyebrows at the casual use of Scion's family nickname, but no one else seemed to notice it. I nodded, and heaped some scrambled eggs onto my last piece of toast.

"Will you use flames or shadows?" Bael asked.

"Er, I'd planned to use flames, but I suppose I could try both."

"I can't wait for you to try turning something to dust," Bael said slightly wistfully. "I've never met someone else who could do what I do."

"Let's not get ahead of ourselves," Scion grumbled, not looking up from his book. "The last thing we need is for her to destroy the castle…again."

I glowered at him, but he looked up from his book and grinned, assuring me that he was joking.

"You all are fascinating," Idris said lightly.

I jumped and looked over at him surprised, having almost forgotten we had an audience. "How so?'

"Well, it's just as I was saying the other day. You all are so focused on fighting and whatever it is you're searching for in the library. One would think you were all preparing for a battle."

"Who's to say we're not?" Scion snapped, his eyes narrowing.

"But against whom?" Idris chuckled. "I've never known royals to be so active. Don't you all typically spend your time enjoying yourselves?"

"How would you know?" I said quickly. "Do you remember any royals from before you were imprisoned?"

He looked at me sharply. "I was imprisoned in a castle, dear. I simply meant that Gancanagh's court never did much else besides go hunting and hold banquets."

I furrowed my brow. How he could know that when he'd been trapped in a cell was more than a little suspicious, but I didn't know exactly what to say to challenge him. Perhaps it was better to play along and wait to see if he slipped up again.

"Are you suggesting that we should be throwing parties rather than running the country?" Scion asked, acidly.

"Are you running the country?" Idris asked innocently. "I was under the impression that you left most of the governing to your regional figureheads."

Scion looked sour. He didn't take well to criticism, especially when it came to the well-being of Elsewhere.

In fairness, Idris wasn't precisely wrong.

The cities mostly ran themselves with the oversight of the Governing families. On occasion the lords and ladies of each court would reach out to the capital, usually for money or soldiers, but otherwise we had very little to do with them. As Scion had once explained to me, royalty focused on larger scale problems, such as the ongoing situation in Aftermath and the shifting powers on the continent.

"What do you suggest we do differently," Scion asked. His tone was perfectly pleasant but I could tell from the steely gray glint in his usually silver eyes that our guest was on thin ice.

"I wouldn't presume to know precisely," Idris replied, still smiling. "If it were up to me, however, I might dedicate some time to improving the lives of the people?"

"How so?" Scion snapped, a sickly sweet edge to his tone that made the hair on the back of my neck stand up.

"I understand you have humans and high Fae living together in your city?"

"We do," I answered.

Idris reached for his tea, taking a slow sip. "Then perhaps you should focus on them."

I grimaced. I supposed that wasn't a bad suggestion. Not at all, actually. "I have been wanting to do something to improve Cheapside," I mused.

Idris beamed. "That's an excellent idea. Of course, the humans are an inconvenience but one that is easily remedied."

I stopped eating abruptly and let my fork fall back onto my plate. "Remedied?"

"Well, of course. If you are looking to improve your city I'm sure there's somewhere else the Slúagh could be sent that might make everyone a little more comfortable."

My throat went dry and my pulse sped up, pounding in my temple. I sat up straighter, glaring at Idris. "Somewhere else? Where would you suggest the humans go? Bearing in mind that quite literally every single one of those people is here because either they or their ancestors were stolen from their homes and brought here against their will."

Beside me, Bael reached under the table and gripped my knee. At first, I thought he was trying to tell me to calm down, but then I caught sight of his expression. It was full of cold rage, the likes of which I hadn't seen from him since perhaps the day he killed the guard who'd tormented me in the dungeon.

"Oh, you misunderstand," Idris said jovially. "I didn't mean sending the Slúagh anywhere unpleasant. No, I simply meant that perhaps everyone would be happier with more clear separation. Them included."

"You've certainly thought a lot about it in a very short period of time," I said coldly. "If we were to implement something like that, which settlement would you send me to?"

Idris's benign smile returned at once. "As I said, I wouldn't presume to think I know everything. You wear the crown, after all."

I wrinkled my nose in distaste, and stood up from the table. "I do," I snapped. "And I killed the last king to get it. So, if you'll excuse me I'll be outside training to kill the next prick who thinks he can run this country better than we can."

* * *

A full hour later, I was still angry about breakfast.

I shouldn't have yelled at Idris–not least because I'd essentially proved his point, painting myself as just as rash and violent as I'd ever accused the Everlast family of being. I couldn't even explain to myself exactly what it was that bothered me about Idris. He was clearly prejudiced against humans, but unfortunately that was hardly unusual. In fact, he'd been more polite than most high Fae typically were when discussing the Slúagh.

Maybe it was that the entire conversation brought me back to another time, when I'd had absolutely no agency in my own life and was far too afraid to speak up in my own or anyone else's defense.

Maybe it was that Idris had made me feel helpless. Like nothing we were doing mattered.

I felt like I'd betrayed the version of me who had stolen golden candle sticks to hand out to starving villagers. I'd been in the castle for months now, but we weren't doing anything to help anyone but ourselves. Perhaps we should take a greater hand in governing the cities and improving the lives of the people, but as I'd come to realize over these last months, it was much harder than it appeared from the outside. I could give candlesticks to every citizen of elsewhere and it still wouldn't matter. Real change–real progress–was never so simple.

Letting my anger fuel me, I stood with my legs wide and my shoulders back, facing the same red and white painted targets as last week. The targets remained untouched except by the recent rain and wind, however the patches of dead burnt grass surrounding them were growing gradually closer. It was a nice warm morning, yet the rain from the last several days still clung to the grass. At least that might make it harder for me to light the lawn on fire.

I rolled my shoulders and took a deep breath, before allowing the warmth from within me to travel down my arm to my hand. Instantly, a warm ball of glittering, dancing flames appeared, just barely tickling my flesh as I eyed the center of the target.

"Well done," someone said behind me. "You've really gotten the hang of that."

I whirled around, startled, and had let the fire fly from my hand before my brain was able to register that I recognized the voice.

I gasped, as I beheld Ambrose sauntering toward me across the lawn. He jumped out of the way of the fire, just barely avoiding it. Instead, one of the damp thorny bushes dotting the lawn began to smoke.

"I'm sorry," I said a bit peevishly. "You startled me."

"My fault," Ambrose said, "I should know better than to sneak up on a pretty girl holding a weapon."

I flushed in spite of myself. "Why should it matter if I'm pretty or not?"

"Because the most dangerous things are often the most tempting."

The heat in my cheeks burned hotter and I glanced down, having no idea what to say to that. He really shouldn't have been flirting with me at all, but I couldn't bring myself to tell him to stop. Indeed, my thoughts immediately drifted to our last night in Underneath, and I had to yank my mind back with brutal force.

"What are you doing out here?" I asked tonelessly. "Don't you have more research to do?"

He ran a hand over the shaved side of his head and down the back of his neck. "You left so abruptly, I wanted to make sure you were alright. That meal was..." he looked at a loss for words.

I found the words for him. "That meal was far better than many I've experienced in the palace. Idris is tame compared with your aunt Raewyn, or–" I broke off.

"Or any of us, at one point or another." Ambrose looked uncomfortable. "Believe me, I know, but people can learn and change their minds. You've certainly done more to change the perception of humans than likely anyone else in the history of Elsewhere."

"Right," I said bitterly. "But that's only because I'm not truly human. If I were, I would have died ten times over long before I ever had the chance to influence anyone."

He said nothing, which I took to mean he grasped my point. Somehow, that helped. It wasn't a pleasant topic for any one of us, but at least Ambrose wasn't trying to gloss over my past experiences just because now things had changed.

Making a valiant effort to change the subject, Ambrose nodded toward the target. "Are you going to try again?"

"Yes." I turned away from him, meanwhile conjuring another ball in my hand.

Feeling his eyes on my back, I threw the fire toward the target with as much force as I could manage. For a few seconds it sailed straight at the target. Then, at the last moment the flaming orb spun wildly out of control, arching sideways and very nearly hurtling back in our direction before it plowed into the damp grass. I groaned. "By the fucking Source. I give up!"

Ambrose made a humming sound like he was thinking. "Do you always miss the targets?"

I scowled over my shoulder. "Yes. The grass could tell you that much."

"That's odd. You're throwing hard enough, but it seems like an accuracy issue."

"Yes, I'm bad at throwing," I said acidly. "I don't need you to tell me that."

Ambrose still looked contemplative. "You're not, actually—bad at throwing, that is."

"No, I am. I'm so bad in fact that I've managed to nearly hit almost everyone who's ever come out here to watch me. It's pathetic."

Ambrose's eyes lit up. "Yet you had no trouble throwing the fire directly at me when I startled you. If I hadn't moved it would have hit me straight in the chest, and I was further away than your targets."

I frowned, looking from the targets to the smoking bush behind me that had taken the brunt of my attack. To my surprise, he was right.

"Perhaps I need to be under direct threat?" I theorized. Gods, I hoped that wasn't the answer because the last thing I wanted was to wait until the middle of a real fight to know for sure if I could hit anything.

"Perhaps," Ambrose said in a tone that told me he didn't believe that was the case. He stepped around me and sauntered purposefully toward the target, before standing directly in front of it. "Now try again."

"No!" I said automatically. "What if I hit you?"

He smirked at me. "You won't. Trust me."

Inexplicably, I felt the heat crawling up the back of my neck once again, and I looked down. "Fine, but don't say I didn't warn you if you end up with both halves of your head bald."

He merely nodded for me to begin, and I quickly conjured another fireball and threw it at him. It wasn't my best throw, not my strongest, but still the flames hurtled toward Ambrose's too handsome face and I felt my stomach dip with fear. "Look out!"

At the last possible second, he stepped back, disappearing into the shadows just as the fire sailed through where he would have been standing and smashed into the straw circular target. I gaped, my shock turning to excitement as the flames engulfed the straw, sending great plumes of smoke up into the air. I shrieked, nearly jumping off my feet in excitement.

Ambrose reappeared beside me, just in time for me to spin directly into his chest. He put out his arms to steady me, trapping me in a loose hold.

"Congratulations." He grinned down at me, practically blinding me with his dazzling smile.

I tipped my head nearly all the way back to meet his jet-black gaze. "How did you know that would work?"

"Just a theory," he said, brushing off my admiration as if it was nothing. "I think your abilities are like the Source itself. The fire is merely a conduit, but you could probably learn to conjure other things with time and practice."

"I have no idea what that means," I said, still grinning widely, basking in my success after so many months of having no idea how to control any aspect of my mysterious power.

"The Source is both a magnet and a power Source to all creatures with magic," he explained. "We're all drawn to its power, while at the same time the magic wants to spread out and sustain all of us. No matter how accurately you throw, the magic will seek the best magical vessel in its immediate path. The targets are innate, but the grass and trees are still alive, making them better vessels for power."

"Except if you're standing in the way," I finished, for him.

"Exactly. It's only a theory, though. I could be wrong. Maybe you just harbor a secret desire to light me on fire."

"I don't know about that. If I did, I'm not sure I'd bother to keep it a secret."

"I'll watch my back, then," he replied, still grinning.

It was only at that moment that it dawned on me how very close we were still standing. Ambrose's arms were loose around my waist, somewhere between a hug and an attempt to hold me upright. If I titled my head up just a tiny bit further, I was close enough to run my tongue over the underside of his sharp jaw.

"So, is that the only reason why you came down here?" I asked, my voice suddenly sounding a bit raspy as my throat had gone dry. "To see if I was alright? Or was it to share your theory?"

I held my breath. I wasn't sure what I wanted or expected him to say. That he'd sought me out again because he too couldn't stop thinking about our week on the ship together, or what might have happened if we hadn't stopped that night in Underneath? No, that would be ridiculous and entirely out of character.

And yet…

Ambrose cleared his own throat and stepped back, dropping his arms back to his sides. "No," he said, almost begrudgingly. "I actually wanted to run an idea by you. I thought of it earlier, when Idris was going on about how to rule."

I scowled. "Don't remind me. Did you notice how he seemed to know what was going on in the court of Underneath? I can say from experience that if you're stuck in a dungeon you have no sense of what's happening above you."

Ambrose frowned. "Perhaps he was just guessing?"

"Perhaps, but why aren't you even questioning him?"

Ambrose's brow furrowed. "What do you mean?"

I crossed my arms over my chest. "I mean, where's the male who was suspicious of every tiny detail while we were in Underneath? Where's the army general? You cannot tell me that you survived so long marshaling a rebellion without being just the smallest bit paranoid."

"I survived so long because I always know if someone is about to betray me," he said pointedly. "I told you, I spoke with him that first night on the ship and he made it very clear that he has no intention of hurting us."

I scowled. "Something seems off."

Ambrose looked a bit exasperated, like he was only humoring me. "Perhaps you're right, but that's not what I came to talk to you about."

"Then what is?"

"It occurred to me that you never had a coronation."

I raised an eyebrow. "It hadn't occurred to me that I needed one. Anyway, I don't think the people of Elsewhere would be all that excited to see me, I'm still the human usurper who stole their kingdom, remember?"

"You're not human," he corrected. "And I actually don't think you realize how popular you are among the citizens, especially in the capital. They love you and would be loyal if you asked them to in a way they have never been for us. They see you as a sign of hope, and that things are changing for the better."

My cheeks felt hot once more and I found myself staring at my shoes. "So, you just want to raise morale in the capital?"

"No," Ambrose sighed. "If that was all it was I'd suggest we have a parade of some sort, but I think a coronation might serve a greater purpose."

"Such as?"

He glanced over his shoulder toward the castle for a moment, as if checking that we were well and truly alone before continuing. "I can't stop thinking about how you already have the crown."

I furrowed my brow. "So?"

"So, that should have broken the curse," he said, his tone low and insistent. "Now with what your mother revealed about your connection to Aisling I'm more sure than ever that I was right, and you're the worthy one that the prophecy spoke of."

"I'm not sure about that…" I shifted uncomfortably.

"I am," he replied. "It's the only thing that makes sense."

"What about Scion?" I asked, almost desperately. "You told me while we were on the ship that you spent years trying to mold him into the next ruler from afar."

"I know, but I think that's part of it. I nearly succeeded, don't you see? Everything I did to set up Scion to be the king led him to mating with you and becoming the king consort. I hadn't even planned to use Bael for anything, but I still managed to lead him to becoming the king of Underneath, which is a powerful ally in its own right and support you'll need in the future. The way I see it, the curse should have already broken."

"Maybe it's because I never finished the hunts," I thought aloud. "I never defended the crown."

"That doesn't make sense either," Ambrose insisted. "The hunts were invented after the curse was already cast as a means to find a worthy person. The number and order of events had nothing to do with Aisling, and there's nothing in the history books that implies you have to actually finish them. Only that you must kill the previous monarch, which you did."

"So, what?" I raised my eyebrows. "You think having an official coronation will wake up the gods and remind them they forgot to lift their generations long curse."

I meant it to sound absurd–because it was, but Ambrose only nodded. "Maybe."

I scoffed. "That seems crazy."

"Maybe so, but I don't know what else to do. We've read nearly every book in Celia's library, and there's nothing. No mentions of the curse, not even of Aisling. All I've found was more drawings of that crown with three jewels."

"What jewels?" I asked, distracted.

He ran both hands through his hair, his frustration clearly close to boiling over. "From what I can tell, they're probably just symbolic, likely representing the three territories that came together with Nightshade to form Elsewhere, which is Inbetwixt, Overcast and Nevermore."

"What makes you think that?"

"I recognize one of them–or, at least I think I do. It's the diamond of Nevermore, which has been a prized possession of the province for centuries. The only thing that bothers me is the obsidian crown doesn't have jewels, and it never did."

"How do you know?" I asked, curiously.

"Because it's been in our family since the beginning of the dynasty, and we have numerous records of it. There are paintings of past rulers wearing it, and descriptions in old ballads. There are no jewels."

I had nothing to add to that, and so remained silent, waiting for him to come back out of his own deep thoughts.

"In any case," he said after a moment, shaking his head as if to clear it. "I think we should try the coronation. If it doesn't work then we can always keep researching, or perhaps travel to other cities and see if their libraries hold different information."

I grimaced. "I suppose there's no reason to say no."

He flashed me a grin. "That's got to be the least enthusiastic 'yes' I've ever heard from a woman, but in this case I'll take it."

I didn't share his smile. "I suppose at least someone will be happy. Idris will get that party he's been lobbying for."

Ambrose shrugged, still looking pleased and I couldn't bring myself to disappoint him. As I'd said, there was really no good reason to deny having a coronation. It wasn't much effort on my part, and if Ambrose was somehow right then it would be possibly the most important thing I'd ever done.

Still, for some reason I felt uneasy.

It was like a premonition, warning me of danger but not specifically what that danger was.

Days later, I would reflect that I should have listened to that gut feeling. Then, maybe everyone would still be alive.

12
LONNIE

THE GROUNDS OF THE OBSIDIAN PALACE, EVERLAST CITY

If I'd thought I'd have time to talk Ambrose out of the coronation, I was woefully and painfully wrong.

I assumed it would take weeks if not months to plan an event of that scale, but I'd wildly underestimated both Ambrose's determination for the coronation to succeed, and the staff's ability to make a party appear at barely a moment's notice.

Therefore it was only two days later when I walked down the castle steps toward the lit clearing on the edge of the woods with all the enthusiasm of a prisoner approaching the gallows. It felt similar to the time I'd had to walk down to nearly the exact same spot before the first hunt. Except this time, I didn't have Bael there to protect me.

Arriving with Bael was out of the question. Partly because no one had yet forgotten that he'd paraded me around like a pet during the hunting season, and partly because he had a well-earned reputation as being both terrifyingly dangerous, and something of a drunken slut who had fucked his way through every tavern in the capital.

I'd assumed, therefore, that they'd want me to walk in with Scion, who might have been feared by every man woman and child on the continent, but at least held on to some princely refinement in public.

Again, I was wrong.

Evidently, everything that had ever been said about Bael could also be said about Scion ten times over, with the added issue that he'd killed literally thousands at the behest of Queen Celia.

I'd suggested, entirely seriously, that we should be honest and the three of us should enter together. Unfortunately, I'd been shut down once more. Apparently I didn't want to give myself the reputation of being dangerous, murderous and unstable–no matter how accurate that perception might be.

In the end, we'd all agreed that it would be best for me to be seen arriving at the party alone. We might have been doing this for the sake of the curse, but there was some political benefit as well which could easily be ruined by a single wrong step.

I wasn't sure when I started understanding or caring about political nuance, but for once, I wasn't complaining.

As I no longer had a dedicated maid, and I couldn't bring myself to choose one from the mishmash of rebels and former palace staff who'd lived through the attack on the castle, I dressed myself in a plum purple gown that was both easy enough to put on without help and elegant enough for the occasion. The soft fabric draped effortlessly over my hips, and the intricate design of the bodice hugged my figure in all the right places. Its flowing skirt cascaded down to the ground, rustling with each step I took.

As I walked down the winding path towards the clearing, the distant sound of laughter and music grew louder. The forest around me was alive with fireflies and will-o-wisps, their glowing bodies creating a soft, ethereal light. Dozens of colorful tents dotted the area, each one adorned with intricate patterns and glowing from within.. The sound of fiddle music filled my ears, accompanied by the occasional burst of laughter and chatter from the partygoers.

Suddenly, I was hit with the strongest sense of Deja-vu.

I held my breath for a moment, fearful that the music would cause me to sway on my feet or forget where I was going, yet nothing happened.

I supposed that was yet another thing to have been changed by my magic. I was no longer susceptible to fairy music—or perhaps, I was finally hearing it as it was meant to be enjoyed.

I made my way into the clearing, nodding and greeting anyone who caught my eye. The party was a sea of dazzling faeries, their ethereal beauty enhanced by the flickering lights and lively music. I wondered briefly who they all were. The castle had been mostly empty for weeks–but then, I supposed that the nobles of the high Fae didn't live within the castle. These were the same city-dwelling nobles who I'd once been terrified to draw the attention of.

Now, as I strolled through the crowd, many of them bowed or curtsied at my passing. I scanned every face, looking for anyone I remembered, but I didn't see anyone who had ever been rude to me in the past, or went out of their way to terrorize me. It was for the best, I supposed. I was supposed to be cultivating an image of stability, not picking fights with the courtiers.

I kept walking through the crowd, searching for Bael or Scion, or even Ambrose. In the center of the clearing, I passed by a large raised platform, and looked up at it, startled. The obsidian throne stood upon it, looking dark and menacing in the flickering light from all the wisps and candles.

I'd only seen the throne outside the castle once before, and on that occasion it had been Penvalle who sat atop it. A tiny shiver crawled down my spine, like insects, and I quickly turned my back on the throne.

As I turned, I finally caught sight of a familiar golden tent. My smile widened into a grin, and I made a beeline toward the entrance.

Suddenly an idea occurred to me, and I reached out a hand to stop a passing servant. "Excuse me."

The girl jumped in surprise. She turned around, her blonde hair falling out of its bun, and her eyes widened with nervousness when she saw me. I wanted to tell her that she needn't bother with formality, but decided it wasn't worth the time it would take to convince her. I'd be gone soon enough, anyway.

I pointed at the jug in her arms. "Is that wine?"

"Yes, my lady."

"May I have it?"

She looked slightly confused, but thrust it at me anyway. "Of course, my lady."

I thanked her and marched toward the golden tent, my jug held out in front of me.

As I stepped inside the tent, the familiar sight of silk cushions and blankets covering the ground greeted me, along with trays upon trays heaped with an array of delectable foods. The air was filled with the rich aromas of spices and roasted meats, making my stomach grumble in anticipation. The flickering light from low hanging paper lanterns cast the entire space in a glow.

The only differences from the last time I'd carried wine into this tent were the people inside. Instead of the beautiful courtiers and half-naked dancers that had once lounged upon the cushions, there was only Scion, and a handful of nameless Seelie nobles.

As I approached, Scion looked up from his conversation. He's been chatting idly with a male I thought I might have seen around the castle once or twice, but stopped mid-word the moment he saw me.

I made a small bow, fixing him with a teasing smile. "Good evening, my lord."

Just as I'd hoped he would, he jumped to his feet to meet me.

With a wicked smirk, I deliberately stumbled over my own feet and dropped the jug.

It spilled across the ground, splashing Scion's expensive shoes. For a long moment he simply stared at me, seeming frozen to the spot. As he continued to stare, my confidence weakened and for a brief moment I feared I'd made a mistake.

Then, he blinked, and his eyes darkened with desire and hunger. I barely had time to register the change before his hand shot out and grabbed my upper arm in a vice-like grip and tugged me with him into the darkness.

* * *

A moment of dark disorientation later, we stepped out of the shadows onto a vaguely familiar stone balcony.

It was an open air terrace meant for gazing out over the grounds, and was probably no wider across than the average bathing room. The dark stone wall of the castle rose behind us, providing some protection from the wind. Even so. The air was slightly crisp because we were so high off the ground. Over the wind and the sounds of crickets chirping in the distance I could still hear the music and laughter from the party below.

I peered over the stone railing, and my head swum for a moment. The tiny people on the ground looked like nothing more than insects, the colorful tents like postage stamps standing out against the dark lawn.

I turned back around and leaned against the railing, smirking at Scion. "This is nice, but I must admit I'm confused. Is this really the moment to admire the view."

He took a step closer, looming over me. His lip curled in the ghost of a sneer. When he spoke however, his voice was soft. Coaxing. "What were you hoping to accomplish with that little stunt, rebel? Do you simply enjoy provoking me?"

"Always," I breathed.

He growled low in his throat, and his hand shot out to grip my hair tightly forcing my face up so I couldn't look away from his captivating eyes. He must have seen something in my expression that he didn't like—or maybe liked too much—because his fingers tightened, all but yanking my hair out by the root.

"Did you want all those people to see me punish you? Maybe you want me to make you get on your knees to lick my boots in front of all those people?"

I shrugged, feigning disinterest. "You couldn't force me to do anything I don't want to do, even if you tried," I hissed.

"True." His eyes lit up and his mouth curved into a satisfied smile. "But I think you'd want me to. I could have fucked your mouth right there and you would have loved it."

I let out an involuntary whimper and Scion grinned like a wolf flashing its jaws to its prey.

"Why didn't you?" I gasped.

"I didn't want an audience for this."

Unbidden, my mind conjured up the memory of the time he'd watched me across the lawn while some Fae woman knelt between his legs openly sucking his cock. The thought of it sent a tiny spark of anger through me. "Really? As I recall, you don't mind an audience, my lord."

His eyes flashed, and I was sure he knew exactly where my memory had gone. "Were you jealous, rebel?"

"Of you?" I scoffed. "Hardly. I didn't think she was that pretty, personally."

He laughed darkly before reaching down and gripping my chin forcing my face up to meet his gaze. "With you, there will never be an audience, because you're mine and I'd kill anyone who so much as looked at you."

He yanked me forward, using the hand in my hair to push me down to my knees on the cold stone floor of the balcony. Something low in my stomach clenched in anticipation.

I knew we were playing a game—that he wouldn't really hurt me—but some dark part of me hoped he might try. After all some pain could be fun, even life-affirming, and Scion knew more about how to cause pain than any other being on this continent.

I rose up on my knees, the cool leather of his belt brushing against my fingers as I inched forward. My hands trembled slightly as I reached for his waistband, feeling the warmth radiating from his body. With careful precision, I undid his belt and unbuttoned his pants, my heart racing with anticipation. As I snaked my hand inside, I could feel his thick cock pulsating with desire. Scion let out a low growl and his grip on my hair tightened when I ran the nail of my thumb over the sensitive head.

"Stop playing," he growled.

A smile curved my lips as I freed his cock from his pants, finding him already hard and ready for me. I leaned forward to replace my fingers with my mouth. I ran my tongue up his length, savoring the taste of him and relishing in the way he responded to my touch. Taking him fully into my mouth, I swirled my tongue around him, feeling him grow even harder with each passing moment.

I leaned back on my heels and took him out of my mouth just far enough to speak. I looked up at him through my lashes. "Is this supposed to be you punishing me?"

He looked down at me through a mixture of lust and defiance.

I drew in a sharp intake of breath as something soft and light brushed over my core, sending a spark of pleasure through me.

"What was-" I looked down and broke off, realizing that there were dark shadows swirling along the ground and all around where I knelt.

I gasped again, and it turned into a moan when again a feather light touch danced over my most sensitive skin. It felt like warm breath, but somehow more solid. As if he'd taken a paintbrush and lightly stroked my clit.

The shadows moved higher, covering my entire body and brushing against my neck, down my chest and over my tight nipples. My pulse quickened, my entire body coming alive as goosebumps erupted over my entire body and I felt myself growing wet between my thighs.

Then without warning, a tiny spark of pain lashed me, adding a small jolt of electricity to the stroking shadows.

I went back to teasing his cock, determined to give back just as much pleasurable torment as I was receiving.

Scion pushed my hair back from my face with his real hands, while his shadowy fingers danced over my skin, stroking and pinching every inch of my body. Pleasure and sensation poured over me, until I wanted to climb out of my own skin just to escape the exquisite pleasure of it.

"Look at me," he commanded, his voice shaking with authority as well as the effort to control himself.

I looked up, meeting his gaze as I sucked him deeper into the back of my throat.

Scion swore, and titled his head back groaning with pleasure. Then, abruptly he pulled back "You've got to stop that, rebel, or I'll come and I'm not nearly ready to be done with you yet."

Yanking me to my feet, Scion backed me toward the railing of the balcony. I glanced back once, feeling just slightly nervous as he lifted me until my ass was positioned firmly on the railing.

"Lean back," he said roughly.

I gave him an odd look. There was nothing behind me except open air and a fall that would undoubtedly shatter every bone in my body.

Scion's gaze flicked behind me, and smirked. "Trust me."

To illustrate his point, I felt the air behind me thicken. The shadows wrapped around me, cradling my body and preventing me from falling.

He slowly pushed my skirt up my thighs, then reached underneath the fabric and dragged his fingers over my throbbing core. With a smirk, he brought his fingers to his mouth and sucked. "You taste so fucking perfect, rebel."

He bent down, his strong arms lifting my legs and draping them over his broad shoulders, and pressed his mouth to my core.

My back bowed against the wall of shadows, and my eyes fluttered closed. Dear Gods.

He licked me slowly, sending shivers of electricity through my body. The sensation was overwhelming, each stroke of his tongue igniting sparks of pleasure within me. I could feel the heat building inside me and I moaned and writhed against the wall of shadows, my fingers tangling in Scion's hair as he continued to pleasure me with his mouth. The sensations were overwhelming, each stroke of his tongue igniting sparks of pleasure within me.

My back arched off the railing as I felt myself getting closer to the edge. Scion's hands gripped my hips, keeping me steady as he continued to devour me with his mouth.

"Let go, rebel," he growled against my skin, sending shivers down my spine.

And with one final flick of his tongue, I did just that. My body exploded in a wave of pleasure, my release crashing over me like a tidal wave. I cried out his name as I rode the waves, and Scion held me tight as I slowly came back down from my high.

He stood straight again, looking down at me with a predatory hunger in his silver eyes.

Without asking or waiting for me to recover, he reached out and tore the top of my dress down exposing my breast. His touch was electrifying as he trailed kisses down my neck and chest. He took my nipple into his mouth, his tongue rolling over it just as he'd done moments before. Every inch of my body felt alive under his touch, begging for more.

I wrapped my legs around him and pressed closer, grinding against him.

With a fierce growl, he released his grip on me and pulled me forcefully down from the railing. My feet stumbled against the ground as he spun me around, positioning me so that I was leaning over the edge of the railing, peering down at the dizzying drop below. The wind whipped through my hair and torn dress, grazing over my exposed skin and hardening my nipples.

Knowing exactly what he wanted, I pressed my ass against him. He pushed up my skirt and without any warning slammed every inch of his cock inside me.

I moaned as he filled me. My body instinctively arched towards him as he thrust in, filling me completely and causing my breath to catch in my throat. The sensation was overwhelming and I couldn't help but moan as he continued to drive himself into me with powerful, rhythmic movements.

Scion's thrusts were relentless, each one sending me closer to the edge of ecstasy. I gripped onto the railing for support as he pounded into me from behind, his movements becoming more urgent and animalistic.

I could feel my entire body humming with pleasure, my senses heightened by the rush of adrenaline and danger. With each thrust, I felt myself getting closer to a peak that I didn't want to come down from.

My stomach muscles tightened, but just as I was on the brink of release, Scion abruptly pulled out and turned me around. He lifted me up and carried me over to the adjacent castle wall, pressing my back against it and positioning my legs so that they were wrapped around his waist.

He kissed me fiercely, his hands roaming over my body as he held me against him. My heart thundered in my ears and the rough stone wall scraped against my back, but I hardly noticed.

Pulling back from the kiss, Scion looked me in the eye before deliberately bending to drag his tongue over the scar on my neck where he'd claimed me long before either of us really knew what that meant.

"Do you regret this?" he asked suddenly.

I looked at him sharply. "What? Why would you ask that?"

"You didn't have much of a choice. If you'd been able to choose, would you have let me claim you?'

I glared at him, almost angrily. In answer, I leaned forward and sank my teeth into his skin with all the force I could muster. A metallic tang filled my mouth as blood gushed between my teeth, carrying with it his raw power and unbridled desire. I could feel his body tense, before he entered me again, this time with a slow and steady pace that had me gasping for breath.

I could feel the heat building inside me once again, and this time I knew there was no holding back. I dug my fingers into his skin as he thrust into me deeper and harder, our moans loud enough that I was sure the entire court could hear us far down below.

With one final thrust from Scion, I cried out his name as waves of pleasure crashed over me. He followed soon after, burying his face in my neck as he rode out his own release.

"I love you," I said, feeling as if perhaps he needed to hear it.

"I used to feel as if I was sleepwalking through life. I didn't even fucking realize how numb I was until you woke me up." He shook his head, and looked up to meet my gaze, trapping me with his intense silver stare. "I don't know if I'll ever be able to be entirely happy in the way that others are. Maybe I'm still half asleep. But if so, I'm the luckiest bastard alive because that means I get to dream of you."

13
LONNIE

THE GROUNDS OF THE OBSIDIAN PALACE, EVERLAST CITY

Sometime later, Scion and I strolled between the colorful silk tents and reemerged in the midst of the revelry.

I looked around for any familiar faces, and didn't watch where I was going until I nearly collided with a line of twirling dancers, causing them to fall out of step with one another.

Scion reached out and lassoed me around the waist with one hand, pulling me backward just in time to avoid a collision. Pressing his chin into my shoulder and murmuring in my ear. "It's amazing how you can still be so damn clumsy. No wonder you never realized you were more than human."

I shivered, my toes curling when his warm breath fanned my neck. "Good thing you're there to catch me, then."

He chuckled softly, and tugged me closer against his chest. "Always."

I blinked to clear my mind before everything turned hazy once more, and tugged gently at his arm until he let me go. "Careful." I smiled over my shoulder. "It wouldn't take a lot of convincing to make me go right back to that balcony."

His silver eyes flashed dark. "Don't say things you don't mean, Rebel."

Oh, but I did mean it.

I didn't want to be anywhere near this party, anyway. Most especially, I didn't want to be anywhere near the ceremony that was meant to follow, and Scion had presented me with a much more enjoyable alternative.

"We should at least find Bael first," I mused, glancing back at the throngs of lively courtiers.

Scion raised an interested eyebrow. "Getting greedy, are we?"

I smacked his arm lightly. "That's not what I meant. I'm just sure we've been missed by now. Poor Bael has probably had to look after the druid all this time."

Before this week, I didn't know a single thing about coronations within the Fae court, but now I was better informed than I'd ever wished to be. Due to the time constraints, and the fact that we were mostly doing this for show, we'd forgone most of the formalities. There was no lavish parade or day's worth of celebrations. I hadn't had to visit every city in the capital and ask for their blessing. We hadn't even bothered to write to Overcast and invite the rest of the Everlast family.

The one thing we hadn't been able to ignore, however, was the need for a Druid.

Druids were priests of the Source. Most were humans who had gained power and immortality centuries ago due to continued exposure to the Source, but some had begun their lives as Fae. During the fall of Nightshade, most of the druidic order had been wiped out, but there were still some who roamed from province to province proselytizing for the Gods.

Ironically given the origin of my magic, I had never had any desire or reason to worship the Source, and was therefore a bit apprehensive about the robed stranger who would be performing my farce of a coronation. When he'd arrived earlier, having been sent for only days before, he'd given me such a searching look that I felt as if I were being examined from the inside out.

"I really don't know what the point of this is," I grumbled to Scion as we pushed through the rest of the crowd toward the raised platform and the throne. "I think Ambrose is deluding himself. What does it matter if I take the crown off just so someone else can place it back on my head in front of a crowd of strangers?"

"A crowd of our subjects," Scion corrected. "But I see your point. I believe Ambrose is simply trying to leave no stone unturned, so to speak."

"That's oddly charitable of you," I smiled. "Are you coming around to getting along, then?"

Scion's eye twitched with evident annoyance. "Let's not go that far, Rebel. I'm not sure I will ever do more than tolerate him."

"I don't know," I commented blandly. "You're immortal. Forever is a long time to hold a grudge."

We reached the edge of the enormous dais and paused. Finally, I spotted Bael on the other side of the platform. He looked up when I waved to him and his yellow eyes lit up. He mouthed something, but I couldn't understand him over all the noise.

"What?" I yelled.

He mouthed whatever it was again, and pointed to the man next to him. Indeed, it was the same robed druid as I'd met this afternoon. I groaned. That likely meant they wanted us to start the ceremony soon.

"I have the worst feeling about this," I muttered to Scion.

He looked down at me, his face contorting with concern. "Why?"

"I have no idea," I admitted. "There was nothing specifically wrong with the idea when Ambrose asked me about it, but I just…I don't know."

"Ambrose wouldn't do anything to hurt you," Scion said gruffly.

I raised my eyebrows. "I never said he would, but I'm surprised you think so."

Scion shook his head as if to clear it. "I'm sure it will be fine, rebel. You're likely nervous, but events like this always pass quickly."

"I don't know why you don't have to be crowned with me," I grumbled.

"Because we were never publicly wed," he replied, in a tone that implied forced patience. "And because I'm not the one who's going to break our curse."

It was an effort to keep the dread off my face, but still, I didn't argue with him. There was no point. In a few minutes either the curse would break, or it wouldn't, and that would be the end of that.

With a feeling of extreme trepidation, I took a step closer to the raised platform. There was a set of short stairs leading up toward the throne, and I stepped up onto the lowest one.

At that moment, the crowd seemed to part, and I stopped to see what they were all looking at.

My feet froze in place, and my jaw dropped open when Ambrose strode purposefully from the depths of the golden tent, his dark gaze fixed intently on me. I blinked rapidly and my heart skipped a traitorous beat.

I'd always had trouble picturing Ambrose amongst the glittering seelie court. He was certainly handsome, and carried himself with a raw power and confidence that could only be attributed to royalty. Still, there was something a bit too wild and unrefined about him that didn't seem to belong here among all the golden silk.

Now, I saw clearly that I'd been wrong.

The male striding toward us didn't look like he'd ever seen a battlefield. His hair was loose and perfectly styled to hide his tattoos and pierced ears behind a curtain of gleaming silver. Like Scion, he wore silver rings on each of his long fingers, and his blue silk jacket was open at the collar, showing just a hint of his muscled chest.

I swallowed thickly, finding my throat had gone dry.

Clearing my throat, I smiled widely by way of greeting, thinking that whatever I said he wouldn't be able to hear me over the tittering crowd. To my surprise, Ambrose didn't acknowledge me. In fact, as he grew closer, I noticed something slightly manic in his expression.

He stopped in front of us, breathing heavily. "Where the fuck have you been?"

I startled, taken aback by the anger in his tone, so at odds with the refined picture of elegance that was his persona tonight.

"We stepped out," Scion snapped, moving to stand more firmly in front of me. "That alright with you?"

Ambrose growled in frustration, and it was only then that I saw how his eyes were slightly unfocused, as if he were pretending to look at me but really staring at some distant point over my shoulder. I glanced behind me, and found nothing worth looking at.

I suddenly remembered the comment that Bael had made to me in passing–that seers were often out of touch with reality, and seemed strange when in the midst of a vision.

I assessed him more carefully, just as a bead of sweat rolled down Ambrose's temple and disappeared into his silver bright hair. He looked almost feverish.

"Wait," I hissed, putting out a hand to hold Scion back. "What's wrong with him?"

Scion cocked his head, glaring at his brother. Then he stiffened, and I could practically feel the moment he saw what I did. "What did you see?" he demanded urgently, his entire demeanor changing on a dime.

Ambrose blinked rapidly, his eyes sliding in and out of focus. He reached out and gripped Scion's forearm so tightly that his knuckles turned white, and I knew if he'd grabbed me like that my arm would have snapped. "Take her to the healer," he said. "Go now."

Scion looked at me, and I could see the conflict swirling behind his eyes. Before any of us could say or do anything, however, my dread came to fruition.

I heard Bael's voice over the crowd, calling to me and I turned over my shoulder to see him beckoning to the other side of the dais. The druidic priest had already taken his position in front of the enormous carved obsidian throne and was watching me, silent and staring.

In the same sharp moment I realized that the music had quieted. The crowd around me had stopped their shouting and laughing, and now only whispers rippled through the mass of assembled high Fae.

"I have to go," I muttered to Scion and Ambrose. "We can sort this out after."

"Wait!" Scion called after me.

But then, some melodious bell rang out over the evening, seeming to signal to all that we were about to begin. The wisp lanterns on the edges of the clearings went out, leaving only the dais illuminated and then, to my horror, the entire crowd moved as one.

Every single member of the court fell to their knees in a deep low bow, leaving only me, Scion, Ambrose and the priest standing. I couldn't even see Bael, and wasn't sure if he'd decided to bow or not, but as my gaze flitted over in that direction I caught sight of another figure standing in the shadows of the Waywoods.

Idris had not bowed, and was instead leaning against a tree watching me.

A shiver traveled down my spine and I faltered wanting to get as far away from this place as I could.

Except, then the druid was holding out a hand to me and somehow I was taking it, allowing him to pull me up onto the stage.

Here, I felt almost dizzy staring out over the crowd of bowing fairies. I knew from past experience that I had to tell them to rise or they might stay like that forever, passing out or falling asleep where they knelt rather than disobeying the custom. Unfortunately, there didn't seem to be any moment in which to address them.

The druid began to speak, addressing the crowd. After a long moment in which my brain struggled to make sense of what he was saying, I realized that I didn't understand him. Not only in an intellectual sense, but I literally did not speak the language.

He was saying something undoubtedly important, but he was saying it in the old language of the Fae. The language that was spoken in Nevermore and by most nobles, but had never been taught to me growing up in the kitchens.

I felt sweat bead on my brow and a nervous heat crept over my skin. What if he asked me something important? What if I had to agree to some bargain or pact that I didn't understand?

The priest finished his speech, and turned toward a small table that stood beside the throne. On it, the glittering obsidian crown sat within a carved wooden box. I eyed it nervously, as the druid reached out and took the crown, raising it high for all to see.

Again, he spoke, and though I couldn't understand the words his tone was easy enough to understand. *"Look here upon the glory of the crown,"* I imagined he was saying. *"This crown has been worn by every ruler of Elsewhere since its inception, and now it belongs to your new queen."*

My hands began to tremble with a mixture of anxiety and anticipation.

What if Ambrose had been right? What if I really was worthy of that crown, and in a moment everything would change?

The druid lifted the crown higher until he was holding it at eye level. He turned to me, and met my gaze between the jagged black points.

He was not as old as I'd originally thought, I realized as I looked into his face. Middle aged, with a worn, weathered complexion and piercing blue eyes. He said something and leaned toward me, as if asking a question.

I shook my head, my eyes wide and frantic. "I don't understand."

The priest looked confused, but jerked his head toward the obsidian throne behind us.

Right. Of course.

My heart pounding far too loud and fast, I took a step toward the throne. When the priest didn't stop me I assumed I was doing something right. I could do this. Sit on the throne and put on the crown. How hard was that, after all I'd done to get here?

With shaky hands, I lowered myself onto the seat, feeling the weight of all eyes on me as I took my place in front of them. The air was tense with anticipation, and I could hear my own breaths echoing in the silence.

Abruptly, a deep, rumbling sound reverberated through the clearing. My head snapped around, my heart racing as I tried to make sense of the unexpected noise. Was it my imagination? A trick of my anxious mind? But then I felt the vibrations under my feet and knew it was real.

The ground beneath me erupted into violent tremors, sending a powerful jolt up my spine. The earth quaked with an intensity that seemed to swallow the surrounding landscape. The trees swayed and creaked as if in protest against the sudden movement. The air filled with a low, guttural rumble that seemed to come from the very depths of the earth.

Before I could even comprehend what was happening, a pungent smell of sulfur and ash overwhelmed my senses. The acrid scent burned my nostrils, parched my throat, and left a coating of sour char on my tongue.

Immediately, my entire body tensed up. Everyone knew the Source of that scent. That sound. A tremble of fear rocked me and I looked up at the sky, already knowing exactly what I'd find.

For a moment, I thought the moon had disappeared from the sky, but after a moment I realized it was merely blocked. Blocked by an enormous swarm of dark, twisting shadows. The creatures emerged from the darkness like vengeful spirits. In the dim light of the clearing, their twisted and monstrous faces could almost be made out, contorted with either fury or anguish. They were like living nightmares, taking form and descending upon us as if we were their prey.

Screams sounded through the crowd. First a few, then many, as the nobles abandoned their kneeling position struggling to their feet as the ground shook beneath them. Many disappeared on the spot, but those who either couldn't or wouldn't shadow walk stumbled and crashed into each other in the chaos of their retreat.

Without thinking, I leapt to my feet. Before I knew what I was doing, I'd conjured a ball of flame in my palm and threw it as hard as I could at the oncoming mass of creatures.

In a fleeting moment, the ferocious flames hurled towards the oncoming mass, soaring through the air and igniting their ominous figures. The burning heat engulfed them, sending them careening into the sky.

For that brief moment, I allowed myself to hope that I had succeeded. That perhaps it was as simple as stopping the afflicted in their tracks. My heart swelled with hope.

But as quickly as it had come, everything went awry.

The fire turned in the air, hurtling back toward us with all the force of a boomerang. It crashed through the silk tents and into the center of the panicking crowd. In a flash, the whole clearing went up in flames.

The screams of the terrified revelers grew louder, mingling with the roar of the flames and the haunting shrieks of the afflicted.

The dancing fire illuminated the clearing, and now I could clearly see Scion in the crowd, crafting shadows out of thin air and using them to try and suffocate the burning tents. Beside him, Ambrose had found a sword and was brandishing it at the oncoming afflicted.

I surged forward, intending to join them in trying to help.

A sudden touch on my back sent a jolt of fear through my body, causing me to spin around in a defensive stance. But instead of a vicious creature, I was met with the intense gaze of Bael. His yellow eyes seemed to glow with intensity as he pulled me to him, trying to shield me from the chaos.

"Come on," he growled. "Hold on to me, I'm taking you out of here."

"No," I hissed, twisting in his arms. "We need to help."

I didn't know what I was planning to do, only that I couldn't just flee and save myself when so many others were in danger.

I wrenched myself free from Bael's grip and sprinted down the short set of stone steps, dodging through the throngs of frantic people. Bael was hot on my heels, his large hand reaching out to grab me again. As I pushed through the crowd, I spotted Scion and Ambrose fighting their way towards us. We locked eyes for a brief moment before they joined us in the middle of the chaos, flames licking at our feet.

The thick, acrid smoke filled my nostrils and burned my lungs, causing me to cough and sputter. My mind went numb as I surveyed the destruction before me. Strangely, I wasn't afraid. Confused, yes. Angry, certainly. But not afraid. We wouldn't die here–not tonight, not ever. I only wished the same could be said for everyone.

And then, just as quickly as it had begun, everything stopped.

The deafening screams and cries suddenly fell silent, leaving only a thick, eerie stillness in the air. The fires died, like all the air had been sucked from the world. The malevolent mass of afflicted seemed to evaporate, vanishing into thin air. The only thing that remained was the destruction. The ground was littered with charred debris and broken bodies, some crying out for help while others lay motionless.

Behind me, Bael grabbed my hand, and held on to it, as if afraid I might disappear too.

"What happened?" I gasped, only loud enough for Bael to hear.

Beside me, Scion shook his head. He wasn't looking at me, and I followed his gaze just in time to see movement in the crowd on the edge of the dais. I went stiff.

The bedraggled Fae parted, to let Idris stride into the middle of the clearing. He moved with purpose, climbing up on the dais and turning slowly like he was expecting applause.

As if sensing my eyes, he looked across the clearing and smiled the same benign smile he'd worn nearly every time we'd spoken. Only this time it didn't reach his eyes. He looked me up and down, a hint of sickly sweet disgust in his expression, before he deliberately turned his back on me.

"Friends!" He cried, raising his arms out to the sides as if welcoming the crowd. "Please don't be afraid. Nothing can harm you while I am here."

A sick feeling of dread bubbled up in the pit of my stomach, and I gripped Bael's fingers even harder.

The monster had shown his teeth, and he was bearing down on us about to strike.

Slowly the crowd began to surge. Those who had not shadow walked back to the city, or fled into the woods began to emerge from makeshift hiding places, looking up at the dais with a kind of hypnotic wonderment.

Idris bent down, and reached for a crumpled pile of robes heaped in front of the throne. I gasped, when a split second later I saw it wasn't a pile of robes but the body of the druid. I hadn't even noticed him fall. Idris dragged the druid's hood back from his face so that all could clearly see the dead, staring eyes that looked up blindly.

Shaking his head as if in sorrow, Idris returned his attention to the gathering crowd. "This was a man of magic," he roared, pointing down at the druid. "A dedicated worshiper of the Source who was cut down needlessly right in front of your eyes. I wish, for your sake, that this was surprising, but all I have seen of this court is violence, war, and treachery."

He plucked the obsidian crown from the priest's limp hand, and held it aloft, still addressing the crowd. "For years you've been deceived. Tricked. Dare I say, lied to by those who were supposed to keep you safe. Your lives have been made infinitely worse because you are ruled by royals with Unseelie blood in their veins, the descendants of the cursed and the condemned."

Beside me, I felt Ambrose go stiff, and Scion audibly growled. Bael gripped my fingers so hard it hurt, but I didn't even try to pull away.

Somewhere in the back of my mind, I recognized that this was bad–so much worse than I ever would have guessed, even though all my suspicions of Idris. No one in the entire kingdom of Elsewhere knew that the Everlasts were descendants of Aisling and the first Unseelie king. No one, except those who knew of their curse.

The crowd began to murmur, vicious whispers penetrating the air. They seemed to push closer to us, and immediately Scion threw out a hand. Shadows spilled from his fingers, creating a barrier around us, protecting us from the crowd.

On the platform, Idris threw back his head and laughed. His unnerving musical laughter was high and cruel, grating on the ears.

"Look how they hold you at bay with their magic." he shouted, spinning around to point directly at us. "The Slúagh queen who infects this court with her inferior blood, calls the afflicted to her and burns your homes to the ground. The butcher turned king, who leveled countless villages and holds the threat of endless pain over the heads of every person in this city. The Unseelie mutt who has further infected the gleaming court with the evil power of Underneath, and this—" he turned finally to Ambrose, sneering "—traitor, who holds no loyalty to either his blood nor his chosen family, and only seeks to use you as a pawn in his quest for power. These are the monsters you've followed blindly, because you had no other choice. Let me offer you that choice."

"Once, I knew a country where high Fae were prosperous. Where we did not have to tolerate creatures who are inherently beneath us. Where magic flourished. I believe Elsewhere can be that country again, but not until we have purged the curse on this land. Follow me, and I'll show you what this court was always meant to be. I'll build you a kingdom free from monsters, in the name of my mother, Aisling the Uniter."

PART TWO
Hide and Seek

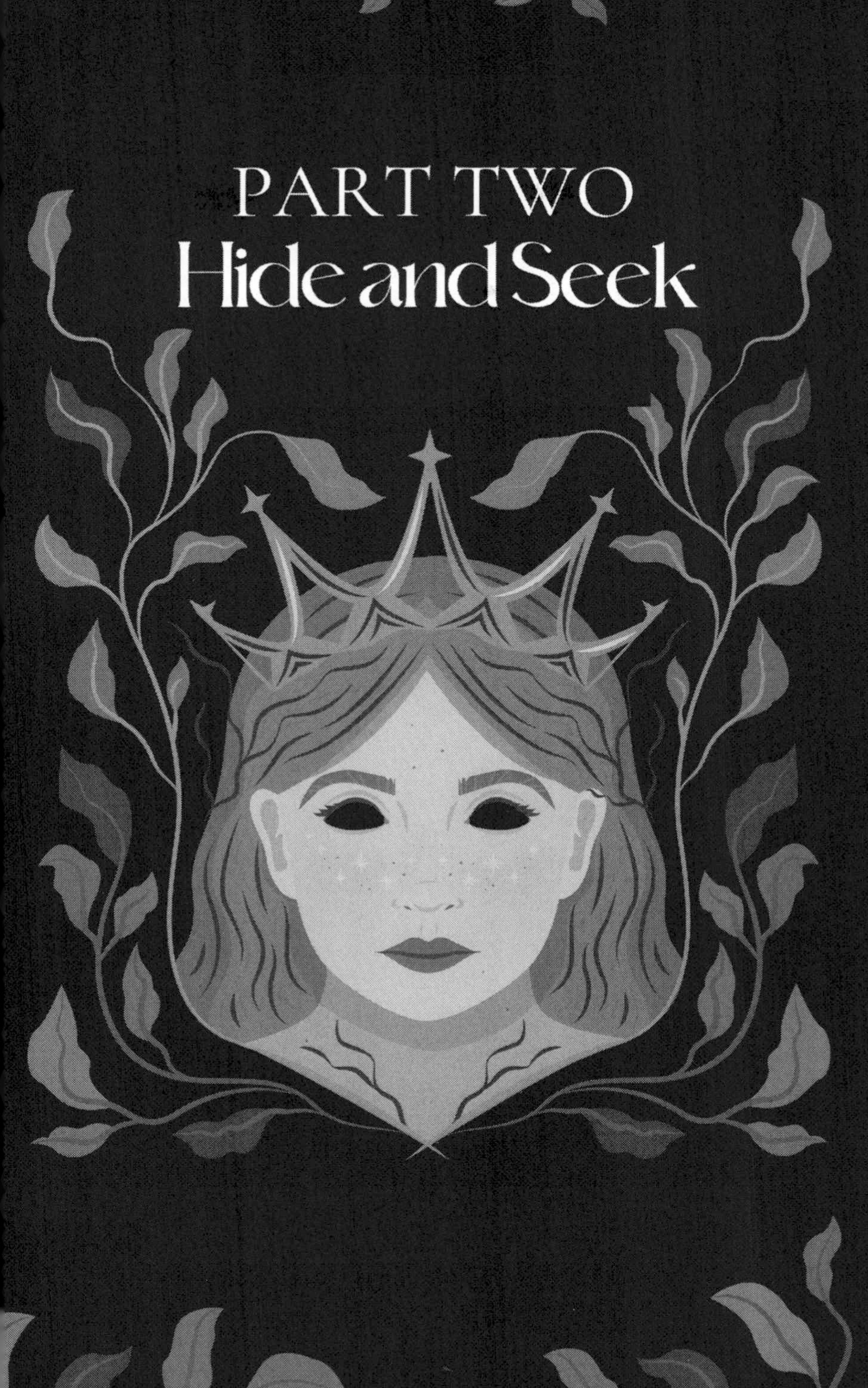

14
BAEL

THE GROUNDS OF THE OBSIDIAN PALACE, EVERLAST CITY

The monster in my head smelled blood.

The angry crowd pressed in around us, screaming curses and smashing their bodies against the semi-solid barrier that Scion had erected around us.

Over the heads of the mob, my gaze locked on Idris's manic smiling face. An involuntary growl escaped my lips, and I wrestled with myself, trying to hold the lion at bay.

I gripped Lonnie's hand so hard I was sure I was hurting her, but I couldn't force myself to let go. Instinct had taken over, and some irrational part of my mind screamed at me that if I let her go now we'd never see each other again.

"Bael!" Scion barked. "What are you waiting for? Fucking kill them."

I shook my head, struggling to focus on my cousin when the blood rushing in my ears had turned deafening. I knew what he wanted from me. I knew I should have acted immediately, but I was afraid that if I did, my body might give out.

I'd been spending increasingly more time sleeping or in my other form, trying to conserve what little energy I had, and using magic of this magnitude would undo any progress I'd made.

The answer was: I couldn't explain that. Possibly ever, but certainly not now.

Bracing myself, I gripped Lonnie's fingers tighter, and raised my free hand toward the crowd.

A different sort of tremor traveled through me, pulling power from the depths of my center. I gritted my teeth, and the closest row of angry courtiers fell. Those who had been pushing hardest against Scion's smoke screen, simply crumbled. They disintegrated on the spot, so far gone that even immortality couldn't protect them.

Lonnie gasped in horror, her hand flying to her mouth. "Stop!" she demanded.

I didn't stop.

As I knew and feared would happen, the moment I started I was unable to pull myself back from the edge of reason. Unable to fight the monster in the back of my mind who wanted to tear into the crowd, leaving no survivors behind.

"There are hundreds of them," Lonnie screamed. "You can't just—"

I growled, cutting her off. I didn't want to be told that I couldn't kill them all. I could—I wanted to, even. The mob continued to surge and I destroyed the next row of courtiers. The irony wasn't lost on me that this darkness, this love of violence, was exactly what I'd just been accused of.

"Stop!" Ambrose barked, echoing Lonnie but with a much more commanding tone." If you kill them all it only proves that fucking bastard correct."

I came back into myself long enough to glare at him.

Ambrose had no right to comment on the morality of killing hundreds of people. None of us did. That was the one thing that Idris had gotten right—we were all murderers, but I didn't truly care anymore. They were threatening Lonnie, and for her I'd flatten the entire city if I had to.

"We have to go, now," Ambrose ordered.

"I'm not going fucking anywhere," Scion spat. "I'm going to tear that fucker limb from limb with my bare hands."

I growled in agreement. There were clearly two opposing opinions within our small group, both grappling for dominance. Scion and I would gladly kill first, and ask questions never, whereas Lonnie had found an ally in Ambrose, both of them fighting for nuance.

"No. We have to find the healer," Ambrose yelled nonsensically.

"What fucking healer?" Scion roared over the noise of the swarming mob. "I'm not going to—"

He didn't get a chance to finish his sentence. In that second, Ambrose clearly decided he'd had enough.

He dropped his sword, evidently realizing he needed his hands free, and instead grabbed Lonnie's arm with one hand and Scion's shoulder with the other. As I was still clinging to Lonnie, I felt my stomach lurch forward, and then we were falling through compressed darkness.

In seconds, my knees crashed into hard stone. I tipped forward, entirely disoriented. My palms fell flat against the ground, and I panted, a wave of nausea washed over me and I choked, trying not to vomit.

It had been years since I'd been sick from shadow walking. The nausea and confusion lessened the more accustomed one was to traveling that way, and I'd been flitting in and out of the darkness longer than I could remember.

Squeezing my eyes shut for a moment to ward off the nausea, I sat up and looked around.

Where the fuck were we?

As I'd already known it would be, the clearing in the forest had disappeared. We'd left the mob and the remnants of the destroyed tents behind, and were now crouching in the middle of what looked to be a deserted road.

I looked around anxiously for Lonnie, and found her kneeling several feet to my left, her head in her hands. I couldn't tell if she was ill from the sudden travel, or holding back tears.

Likely both, I supposed.

Clearly thinking along the same lines as I was, Scion's angry shout echoed my thoughts. "What the fuck! Where did you take us?"

He'd gotten to his feet—evidently not as affected as I felt—and was marching toward Ambrose. Ambrose also stood, looking slightly pained. As I watched, he wiped a bead of sweat from his hairline with the back of his hand, before he schooled his expression to one of blank indifference.

"I would have thought you'd recognize shadow walking," he snapped at Scion.

"Don't give me that shit," Scion growled. "How did you do that? I've never heard of anyone bringing three others with them through the shadows at once."

"I'd rather not discuss it now," Ambrose said flatly. "We haven't traveled very far. We need to keep moving."

I got to my feet, my nausea finally subsiding enough to move. "You want us to run, you mean?" I barked angrily. "We don't run. Other people run from us."

"Which is exactly the problem," Ambrose said, his tone maddeningly calm and cryptic.

"So you're just expecting us to let that fucker go?" Scion yelled.

"For now, yes." Ambrose turned his back on us, walking a few paces down the road as if he could somehow trick us into following him. "Believe me, I know far better than you how this will all work out."

"Enlighten us, then" Scion yelled after him. "Your powers are working again? Fine. But we're not going to just follow blindly. You're not Celia, we don't take orders from you without even knowing why."

Lonnie got to her feet. "Perhaps we should wait to have this discussion until we're not in the middle of the damn road."

All three of us stopped and turned to look at her. Guilt washed over me. She was supposed to be our first priority always, and yet Ambrose's sheer presence had shoved such a deep wedge in the dynamic Scion and I had spent years cultivating that we were all but ignoring her.

"Are you alright, little monster?" I asked automatically, darting forward to steady her. I clasped her face in both palms and scanned my gaze over her, checking for injuries.

"Not particularly." She smiled weakly. "But I'm not hurt, if that's what you mean."

I nodded. Indeed, she looked shaken, but unhurt. Her face seemed pale, and her hair was a tangled nest, though that could hardly be considered unusual. I let her go, and she took a few steps in the same direction that Ambrose had gone.

Within seconds, she stopped and bent down. Her hands shaking, she tore several feet off the bottom of her long flowing skirt, tying the excess fabric around her waist like a belt.

"Where are you going?" Scion demanded, jogging after her. "We don't even know where the fuck we are."

"We're barely a mile from the castle," she said, the surety clear in her tone. "I used to walk this road nearly every day. Look:" She turned around and pointed over our heads.

Behind us, the tall dark spires of the obsidian castle rose against the dark sky, only illuminated by the reflection of the moon on the mirrored stone. From here, I couldn't hear any sounds of battle, or see any obvious signs of unrest. We were barely a mile away, and yet it felt almost as if we were in another world entirely.

"Come on," Lonnie said again. "We should keep moving. You're all loud enough to wake the dead, and the last thing we want is for anyone in this neighborhood to recognize us. Believe me, they won't be welcoming. We may as well have stuck with that mob in the clearing for all the difference it will make."

If anyone but her had suggested it, I was sure we'd all stand here arguing indefinitely. Instead, we followed her lead.

As we walked, I too recognized our surroundings. I'd never spent much time in Cheapside–the human village on the outskirts of the capital–but I'd been here enough that it was familiar.

"Why would you bring us here," Lonnie asked, turning her head to address Ambrose.

"I'm not entirely sure," he told her. "It was the first place that appeared in my mind, and past experience has taught me that the first place I can think of is usually where I'm supposed to be."

Scion coughed, muttering something under his breath. "Fucking condescending prick."

Ambrose ignored him, and we were silent for a beat, darting toward the center of the village. In a way, moving felt good. Like we had a purpose, even if we weren't going anywhere except away from whence we'd come.

Our feet echoed against the worn cobblestone streets as we made our way deeper into the heart of the city. The grand buildings that once lined the main roads were now replaced with smaller, shabbier homes crowded together. Each building's exterior was marked with years of wear and tear, giving them a weathered and neglected appearance. Some were even abandoned, their broken windows and doors hanging off their hinges.

"Before when you said we needed to find a healer, were you serious?" Lonnie asked Ambrose.

He cocked his head at her. "Very."

"Good. Then I know where to look."

I watched them in confusion, clearly having missed something. "What healer?" I hissed, leaning toward Scion. "What did he see?"

Scion just shook his head looking mutinous.

We carried on, deeper and deeper into the city. As we walked, my head began to pound in time with my footsteps. I squeezed my eyes shut, willing the pain to subside.

The first time one of these short stabbing headaches had hit me was in Inbetwixt, after I left the battle at the pier and found Lonnie and Scion still alive.

The pain had hit me out of nowhere, so intense it almost knocked me off my feet. It had been throbbing in my head the whole time we looked for the inn, during that ridiculous interaction with the bartender, and finally hit its peak later that night.

In the morning, however, I'd awoken to find Lonnie missing and I forgot all about the pain in my head.

That was, until it returned with a vengeance.

After the fight with my father, the headaches struck again, this time accompanied by extreme nausea and fatigue. Deep down, I knew something was wrong, but I refused to dwell on it. Instead, I gritted my teeth against the pain, and forced myself to focus on the road in front of me.

To my slight surprise and admiration, Lonnie really did seem to know her way around this city. She led us straight down winding street after winding street, managing to stay in the shadows. We hardly passed anyone as we walked, and the few we did pass were either drunks, swaying on tavern steps, or else averted their eyes the moment they saw us, minding their own business with an almost fanatical precision.

Finally, Lonnie stopped in front of a shabby stone cottage.

"There's only one healer in this city worth a damn," she muttered. "It's been almost two years since I've seen her, but I'd be surprised if she doesn't still live here. Ciara has been here longer than I've been alive."

Ambrose nodded sagely. "Let's go inside."

"Don't you want to tell us what we're doing here?" Scion snapped, clearly unable to hold in his frustration any longer.

"I will once we get inside," Ambrose promised. "Assuming this is the right place. I'll have to see it to know for sure."

I raised an eyebrow, and felt my respect for Ambrose rise ever so slightly. Grandmother Celia had never been willing to explain her visions, no matter how many times we asked. If Ambrose was willing to share even a hint of what he was planning, that was a vast improvement.

"Stand back," Lonnie whispered. "Let me knock."

I heard her breath catch as she stepped up the worn wooden door and knocked three times. The voices inside stopped, and then the sound of footsteps clattered across the floor and the door flew open and a pinched-face human woman stuck her head outside. "We're closed!"

The beam of light from the door crossed the dark street, illuminating Lonnie's red hair like a flaming halo. I watched her back stiffen as she looked up at the woman in the doorway. "Oh, shit," she muttered, seemingly without meaning to.

The woman's face contorted with disgust as she looked down at Lonnie on the doorstep. "You!"

"Yes," Lonnie said resignedly. "Hello. I'd say it was nice to see you again, but I'd really rather not lie."

I almost laughed. I knew Lonnie was serious—she didn't want to lie and scald her throat—but as one might expect the strange woman took her words as an insult.

Her look of contempt morphed into one of anger. "What are you doing here? Coming to spread your curse even wider? Drawing the attention of the Fae to good, hard-working people unlike yourself."

"I don't have time for this." Lonnie snapped. "Is Ciara here?"

"No!" the woman spat, trying to close the door in Lonnie's face.

"She's lying," Ambrose said passively.

The woman looked over Lonnie's head, seeming to notice for the first time that she wasn't alone. I watched the realization and then terror dawn in her eyes as she looked from Ambrose to

Scion to me in turn. She went as white as a sheet, and promptly fled back into the house, leaving the door hanging wide open. The sound of another door opening and slamming shut followed, as if the woman had fled out a back door.

"I wish I could say that was surprising," Lonnie sighed. "But that woman has always hated me."

"Why?" I asked, genuinely curious.

"Because she draws too much damn attention," Another strange voice replied.

My eyes snapped back to the door. For a moment, I thought there was no one there, but then I saw the shadow. The tiniest woman I'd ever seen stood in the doorway. She was so short, she was nearly completely obscured by Lonnie standing in front of her. Still, her size didn't stop her from glaring at us with wintery disapproval.

"Hello, Ciara," Lonnie said, sounding like she was trying to hide a smile. "It's good to see you again."

The woman gave Lonnie a long searching look, then sighed, turning back around and heading into the depths of her house. "You're later than I expected," she called. "I assume you've come for the book?"

15

LONNIE

CHEAPSIDE, EVERLAST CITY

"What book?" I demanded.

Ciara scowled at me and slammed a steaming kettle down on the table, making the liquid inside slosh over onto the worn wood. "We'll get to that, but first drink this."

I returned her scowl, leaning forward to assess the tea pooling on the table in front of me. "What is it?"

"Don't worry about that. You all look like you're going to drop dead at any moment, and this will help."

The three Everlasts and I were gathered around the ancient round table that stood at the center of Ciara's cottage. The room was dimly lit, with only flickering candles and a single small window allowing for a sliver of moonlight to cross the floor. Every inch of the tight space was utilized, with shelves of herbs and bottles stacked floor to ceiling.

Ciara herself was bustling around the tiny room, muttering to herself under her breath. As the local cunning woman, she was as close to a healer as existed in Cheapside, and the first person

I'd thought of when Ambrose brought us to the very road I'd once walked nearly every day, traveling back and forth between the castle and the human settlement. In fact, it was Ciara who I'd originally gone to see on the very morning I found myself in the woods where I met Bael and Scion for the first time.

Ciara was human–at least as far as I knew–but possessed a strong knowledge of magic. For years, she'd always known exactly when I was coming to see her, and unlike everyone else in the village, she never struggled to tell my sister and I apart. Still, just because I knew the healer in my former life and I'd come here for help didn't mean I was going to drop my guard so quickly.

I glanced across the table, searching out Ambrose's gaze as I reached for the dripping kettle. His eyes were closed, but as if he felt my questioning stare he opened one eye and nodded once. "It's just nettle root, love."

Ciara humphed loudly, placing her hands on her bony hips. "You don't trust me not to poison you?"

I smiled at her, showing a flash of teeth. "It's not personal. I hardly trust anyone anymore."

She humphed again, but looked slightly mollified. "I suppose that's not the worst way to stay alive. I have no reason to hurt you, though. I didn't help your mother escape all those years ago just to ruin everything now."

"That's true," Ambrose added.

Ciara turned and refocused her death stare on him instead. "I don't care for seers," she grumbled. "You're always blurting out things that no one needs or wants to know."

Ambrose raised a skeptical eyebrow at the old woman. "Do you have much to hide?"

"Of course. Don't go sharing all my secrets now, or I'll make you sit in the alley out back."

I cracked a small smile. Part of me wanted to see tiny old Ciara try to force the huge, muscular rebel leader to wait outside like a servant, but perhaps this wasn't the time.

Finally convinced it wasn't poisoned, I poured the steaming tea into four mugs and slid them across the table toward the men before turning back to Ciara. "Now what's this about a book?"

"Impatient, aren't you?"

I pressed my lips into a flat line, staring her down with every ounce of disdain I'd ever learned by watching the Fae court. It wasn't difficult. If Ciara realized what we'd been through tonight, surely she wouldn't have been so willing to make me wait.

"Fine," Ciara griped, eying my stoney expression. "Drink your tea while I go find it. I've had the damn thing so long I don't know where I put it."

"Is this really safe?" I asked Ambrose the moment that Ciara was out of the room.

He nodded. "She's a bit brusque, but the tea really is just nettle root. She's trying to help."

I waved him off. "That's not what I meant."

I'd meant, was it safe for us to be here at all? And more importantly, what were we meant to do here? Of course I'd been the one to suggest we go to Ciara, but now that we were here I wasn't sure I'd made the right decision.

Once again, I found myself turning to Ambrose. He was the one who had clearly realized something was about to happen before I even set foot on the stage. And he was the one who had insisted we needed to find a healer. He'd also just promised to explain himself when we got inside. It was time to make good on that vow.

"Did you see what was about to happen before I went up on that stage?" I asked.

Ambrose grimaced. "To an extent. Visions are always malleable. There were dozens of ways it could have happened."

"But did you know this before you suggested the coronation?"

"No," he said sharply. "I really thought a coronation might work. I suppose now we'll never know."

I grimaced. At least we'd been able to hold on to the crown. I was quite sure that Idris had intended to take it from us during the ceremony, and perhaps it was only the unexpected death of the priest that had prevented him from doing so. That felt like little consolation now, though. What use was the crown when the court had forsaken us.

As if reading my mind, Bael leaned forward putting his elbows on the table. "Why did the court turn on us so quickly? Not that I'd expect their loyalty, but neither have I ever known them to risk their necks. They certainly took to Idris quickly."

"It was like Penvalle," Scion growled under his breath.

I startled, looking over at him, my mouth parting.

Bael had once explained to me that the Everlast family had spent generations refining their powers and marrying to produce the most powerful possible offspring. As they didn't typically claim their mates due to the curse, they instead focused on building their power-base generation to generation.

There were three primary abilities that manifested in their bloodline. There were illusionists, like Scion. Seers, like Ambrose. And third, there was persuasion.

The former king, Penvalle, had used his persuasive magic to hypnotize the servants into enacting all his perverse fantasies. Bael's sister Aine had the gift as well, but rarely used it for fear of being turned into a frontline soldier as Scion had been.

"Is it possible that Idris could have that ability?" I asked the room at large.

It was Ambrose who answered. "It's not only possible, love, I'd put money on it. After all, he's our ancestor."

Scion sat up straighter, turning to look at Ambrose. "You believe he's really Aisling's son, then?"

Ambrose nodded. "Don't you?"

"I should have tried harder to talk to him," I complained. "We guessed this *days* ago but he kept talking in circles. I knew something was off. Why didn't I try harder?"

"I understand," Ambrose muttered, with a commiserating glance in my direction. "I want to know why I didn't see this coming,"

"Perhaps that's part of his ability," Bael mused. "Didn't you say that you only trusted Idris because you spoke to him when he first boarded the ship? Well fuck, what if that was because he wanted to persuade you to ignore any visions you might have about him."

Ambrose's face contorted into a grimace, and he remained silent. His eyes were unfocused, but there was a haunted look in them. It was as if he was physically present, but his mind was somewhere else.

"Perhaps he has persuasion abilities," I interjected. "But that can't be his only power. He called back the afflicted and put out all the flames."

"I still think we should have killed him right then and there," Scion growled.

"But could you?" Ambrose asked.

"Yes!" Scion and Bael said at the same time, both glaring angrily.

Before either Ambrose or I could reply to that, the sound of footsteps and creaking wooden stairs interrupted our conversation and Ciara bustled back into the room.

She paused in the doorway, an enormous leather bound book held in both hands. "Well don't stop talking on my account." She glanced around at the table where we'd all fallen silent. "This house has thin walls. You're not hiding anything."

I narrowed my eyes at her. "Good to know."

She slammed the large book down on the table in front of me, narrowly avoiding the puddle of tea that still pooled on the surface. Up close, I realized the book wasn't all that much larger than a normal tome. It was simply that Ciara was so small, it looked enormous by comparison.

Ambrose's hand shot out and he grabbed the book, his eyes flashing with interest. "Where did you get this?"

"Years ago, a servant from the castle left this item behind. It was on the same day that Rhiannon was taken away and her children were brought back to the palace. As such, I was skeptical of anything related to the royal family--" she glanced around the table, seeming to remember whom she was talking to "--no offense meant, I assure you."

"Oh, of course not," Scion muttered sardonically. "Why would we take offense?"

Ambrose ignored him and leaned forward toward Ciara, evidently fascinated. "Did the servant say anything about the book?"

"As it happens, she did. I wouldn't have taken it otherwise. She said to hold on to it and give it to the queen if she ever came looking. Of course, at the time I thought she meant Queen Celia. I wondered why the servant wouldn't give it to the queen directly, since she was coming from the palace, but she wouldn't tell me."

"And you kept it all this time?" I asked, suspicion heavy in my voice.

"Well, why not?" Ciara asked maddeningly. "It doesn't seem to be worth enough to sell, and what else could I do with it?"

"Did you read it?"

"I can't. It's all written in the old tongue."

Ambrose looked far happier than I'd possibly ever seen him. "Well, of course it is."

"Is this one of your grandmother's journals then?"

He nodded. "I should have guessed she'd do something like this. It's elegant, really."

I waited, expecting him to continue but he didn't. Instead, he pulled the book toward him and started flipping through the pages.

"Well, don't leave us in suspense," Scion barked. "What's so fucking elegant?"

Ambrose didn't look up from the book as he answered. "Clearly Grandmother left this here knowing we'd be here to find it, which means she was having visions beyond her own death. I didn't think it was possible, but it's the only explanation. We've been through every other journal in her office and the one we needed was being kept by the only person in this city you would go to for help? It's beyond coincidence."

I stifled a yawn. "I hope you're right."

I knew I should be more excited about the book. It was impressive if Celia had managed to leave it here for us years before she died. And more importantly. I was sure that Ambrose was right and the journal would hold some information about the curse or Aisling's heir–possibly both.

There was absolutely no reason why I shouldn't be leaping at the chance to pour over the book, yet for some reason I couldn't find the energy. Since the moment we'd arrived–the moment we escaped the mob–I'd felt like I was walking in a fog. Like I was so tired, that everything happening was barely penetrating my mind.

"Have more tea," Ciara barked, eying me warily. "You still look like death."

I stifled another yawn and reached for the half empty kettle. That small movement alone made the muscles in my arms scream, and I gritted my teeth. "Perhaps we should go find an inn or something and discuss this more in the morning. I don't know why, but I can barely seem to focus. I can't recall feeling this drained since the first hunt. I can barely lift my arms."

"I'm sorry," Scion said dully.

I glanced over at him, and found that he looked nearly as exhausted as I felt. He leaned back in his chair, arms crossed and head tipped back. His eyes were closed and if I hadn't just heard him speak I would have thought he was sleeping.

"Why are you sorry?" I asked.

Scion cracked one silver eye open. "It's my fault you're so tired."

I looked around the table blankly, feeling like I was missing something. "I don't understand."

Without warning, Ciara stepped up behind me and cracked a wooden spoon across the back of my skull. "Wake up, girl. You're smarter than this."

I lurched forward, yelping in surprise and pain. In the same instant, all three of the Everlasts had leapt up from their chairs, and were glaring at Ciara with murder in their eyes.

"Wait!" I put both hands up, trying to halt the impending violence even as my eyes watered. "I'm fine. Don't hurt her."

"Of course you're fine," Ciara griped, not seeming the least bit concerned over the three enormous Fae males, poised to rip her head from her body.

"Don't touch her again," Bael snapped, sitting back down with a threatening glare.

"Yes, yes," Ciara said with a roll of her eyes. "I understand. Any harm comes to your precious queen and I'll die a painful death."

I turned my entire body around in my chair to look at Ciara, rubbing the back of my head. "Yes, you will, but they won't have to do anything. Do that again and I'll kill you myself."

The old woman just shrugged. "Don't be so dramatic. Sometimes children forget to use their brains and they need the smarts beat back into them."

I scowled harder. I was starting to wonder if we'd made a mistake in coming here.

I glanced across the table at Ambrose again to find him already looking at me, his black eyes full of meaning. I bit back a sigh.

Evidently we had a larger reason for being here and my skull would simply have to pay the price.

"Would you care to explain what you're talking about?" I ground out. "What's so obvious that I need to have the knowledge *beat back into me.*"

"That one is your mate, is he not?" Ciara jerked her head at Scion.

My eyes widened slightly. "What makes you think that?"

She rolled her eyes. "I'm old but I'm not blind."

My eyes darted around the table, wondering what Ciara would say if I told her that Scion wasn't my only mate. Then again, maybe she wouldn't care. She didn't sound unsure, or even bothered by my having a mate–let alone that he was the queen's former executioner.

"He is," I finally admitted.

Ciara looked down her long nose at me. "Then you don't need to wonder why you're so depleted. He clearly used enough magic to halt an entire army's worth of people. In short, he overextended, so now your power is working twice as hard to keep you both alive."

I narrowed my eyes. Ciara had always known things without anyone having bothered to tell her, so I wasn't exactly surprised that she seemed to already know what had happened before anyone had the chance to explain it to her. Still, my knowledge of magic was much stronger now than it once was and I could no longer pretend to believe Ciara's foresight was simply intuition.

"You certainly seem to know a lot about this," I muttered, unable to keep the note of accusation from my voice.

Ciara chuckled. "Don't look so suspicious. Seer magic is the most common ability to manifest in humans with some distant

Fae blood in their ancestry." She jerked her head toward Ambrose. "Ask him if you don't believe me."

I grimaced. I didn't need to ask, I already knew she was right. My sister had been one of those part Fae seers. Yet, my understanding was that there was a vast difference between the occasional prophetic dream and the sort of magic Ambrose had.

"You seem unusually well informed is all," I said carefully. I didn't want to offend the woman, not if we needed to be here.

Fortunately, Ciara didn't seem to take offense. "Years ago when your mother was escaping the palace she needed somewhere to hide. I helped her find a house in Cheapside, but in exchange I wanted to know why she was running. She told me about your magic and tried to get me to give you a potion to suppress it. I told her such a thing didn't exist."

"Yes it–"

Ambrose cleared his throat, cutting me off before I could mention the potion he'd invented to do exactly what Ciara was describing. When diluted with other herbs, Gancanagh's dust could be used to suppress magic, yet for some reason he clearly didn't want me to talk about it.

"Right." I cleared my throat uncomfortably. "So you're yet another person who's known my secrets for years and never felt the need to tell me."

She looked entirely unabashed. "It would have done you no good to know sooner, but now you'd better learn fast or you'll do something stupid and end up drained–like today."

"I hate to agree but she's right, little monster," Bael said, still eyeing Ciara and her wooden spoon with obvious contempt. "Don't you remember what happened when I nearly drained you to get us out of Inbetwixt?"

I frowned and took a sip of my tea to give myself a moment to think.

In truth, I didn't remember the incident Bael was referring to because I'd been unconscious. Still, I understood what he was getting at. After the second hunt, our party had been attacked by the afflicted. Bael used a great deal of magic to hold them off, and then nearly drained himself to shadow walk both of us the long way back to the capital. Magical drain—or using too much power at one time—was the most common cause of death for Fae. I hadn't understood it at the time, but if Bael and I hadn't been mates and regularly sharing blood, we both would have died.

"This doesn't feel like a very good system," I said peevishly. "If every time one of you over extends yourself we could all die, then what's the point?"

"It's not supposed to be like this," Ambrose said gently, leaning forward across the table toward me. "True mates always have comparable powers, or the stronger partner would drain the weaker one by mistake. Because of your connection to the Source, you have so much power that you'd be in danger of draining even the strongest Fae in Elsewhere."

"That's the first smart thing any one of you has said," Ciara snapped. "Someone with power like yours would always have to have more than one mate, but I take it you haven't sealed all your bonds."

My eyes darted furtively around the table, and I shook my head. "No. Not yet."

"Well, if all your bonds were sealed correctly, sharing magic would be a benefit rather than a potential danger, but until you seal them you'll always be in danger of overextending."

I sighed loudly, and slumped my head forward against the table. "That's just perfect."

Bael reached over and ran his long fingers up and down my back. "It'll be fine, little monster."

I wanted to argue with him—no it actually would not be fine. That was the entire point, wasn't it? If we completed the bonds, they would all die, but unless we completed them we might die anyway. "I just don't know why nothing can ever be easy."

Scion laughed hollowly. "I stopped asking myself that a long time ago, rebel. I'm starting to think no one alive is ever truly happy."

Ciara bustled around the table and began throwing more handfuls of mysterious herbs into a second pot of tea. "So." she craned her head over her shoulder. "Explain to me why you haven't completed your bonds."

I glanced sideways at Ambrose, a question in my gaze. He shook his head once, which I took to mean that we were not about to start sharing the details of the Everlast family's curse.

"Er…it's complicated," I said awkwardly.

"Most things are, but as I see it, you don't have much choice. You'll have to seal things with these two eventually, better do it soon." She used her wooden spoon to point between me, Bael and Ambrose, a stern look on her face.

I cleared my throat, feeling heat rise to my cheeks. "Er, no. Not both of them, just him." I pointed to Bael.

Ciara frowned, looking confused, then shrugged. "Whomever it is. Don't waste any more time. A war is obviously brewing and you'll need all your magic to take back the kingdom. Unless, I suppose you want to give up the crown all together."

"No!" Ambrose and Bael said loudly, at the same time as Scion said, "There's an idea…"

I glanced at Scion, surprised. "I thought you of all people would want to fight for the crown. What happened to all that stuff you told me in Inbetwixt about being raised to rule?"

He sat up, looking slightly embarrassed. "Things are different now."

I opened my mouth to ask what Scion meant by that, but Ambrose spoke over me. "Giving up is not an option."

"Are you certain?" I asked, glancing around the table. "Maybe Scion is right."

"No," Ambrose said through gritted teeth. "He's not."

"I never wanted any part of this anyway," I said, following my own train of thought. "No one has ever pretended that I would make a great queen."

"Not yet, perhaps," Ambrose argued, "but you don't understand—"

I wasn't listening to him. "Maybe we're fighting a losing battle. Idris is technically the heir to Aisling. If things had turned out differently, he would have been the king anyway centuries ago."

"Exactly," Scion said, seeming to gain more energy with every word. "Maybe he's the worthy one, did you ever think of that? We're not even supposed to be a part of this."

Ambrose gritted his teeth, anger flashing behind his dark eyes. "Of course I fucking thought of that, but I'm telling you it's not the solution. We are not giving up."

"We don't have to do anything," Scion shot back. "There hasn't been a 'we' in decades. You can do whatever you like, but we don't need to be a part of it."

"You know why that's no longer an option," Ambrose growled.

"What would happen if we did stop fighting?" I asked, following my own train of thought.

Ambrose looked slightly haunted for a moment, then he shook his head. "It doesn't matter because it will never happen. I've given up everything for this."

"Well I haven't," Scion snapped, giving his brother a dark look. "You might have nothing left to lose, but I do."

"Yeah, you do because you've already completed your mate bond," Bael said, speaking for the first time in a while. "But what happens when you wake up one day and realize you're happy?"

I glanced at Scion, and held my breath, desperately wanting to hear his answer. Unfortunately, I never got the chance.

Ambrose stood abruptly, his chair clattering backwards against the stone floor. He slammed both hands down on the table, and I jumped startled by his sudden movement.

"Stop this," he growled. "We are not running away. I spent thirty fucking years making sure we'd all get here so there might be a better future for Elsewhere, and I'm not going to let anyone get in the way." He glared at me. "Not even you."

16
AMBROSE
CHEAPSIDE, EVERLAST CITY

"Where the fuck are you going?" Scion yelled as I grabbed the book off the table and stalked toward the door.

I ignored him, answering by yanking the door open and marching out into the street, slamming it forcefully behind me. The sound of wood against stone echoed through the quiet of the night, leaving a still silence behind.

The silence was…unsettling.

Aside from me, there didn't seem to be a single living soul on this street. Even the echoes of battle from the far-off castle couldn't reach this spot, leaving my heavy breathing as the only sign of life.

I ran a hand through my hair angrily.

I couldn't pinpoint the cause of this sudden surge of anger, but I was well aware of the growing pressure that had been building in my mind for days. Not being able to access my visions left me constantly frustrated, as if I had been disconnected from the most vital part of myself. Then, whenever a shred of the future did break through to my unusually inactive mind, it would be vague and confused. As if viewed through a veil.

Worse even than my lack of magic was the constant bickering with Scion, the never ending barrage of reminders that he had every reason to hate me. I was sure that soon he'd be pushed too far and demand that I leave them be.

But I couldn't do that. I'd never be able to do that, because of *her*.

Lonnie was the greatest Source of my ongoing frustration. My constant torment, and of course, she had no idea why I wavered between avoiding her at all cost and being unable to stay away.

With an aggrieved sigh, I slumped to the ground, taking a seat on the small stone step outside the back door. I put Grandmother Celia's book down on the step beside me, and then stared straight ahead, my vision swimming slightly.

The alley that stretched before me was littered with trash and debris, and the smell of rot lingered in the air. The cobblestones were cracked and stained with dirt and grime, and several houses had boarded-up windows. It was clear that this neighborhood had seen better days.

I closed my eyes and tuned it all out. I simply needed to meditate, I told myself. I needed time alone to recenter, and I'd be fine. I had to be fine.

I cleared my mind of all thoughts except the desire to see something–anything. It didn't need to be a world ending revelation, fuck, I'd settle for some idea of what tomorrow's weather might be.

After several long minutes of wrestling with myself, I finally latched onto a vision of the very alley where I now sat.

In my mind's eye, the little healer, Ciara, stepped outside her house and walked down the street, a basket in hand. She turned left at the end of the road, and the image dissipated.

I sighed with relief. It wasn't an important vision, or even a detailed one, but at least I'd been able to see anything at all.

Focusing harder on the details of the simple vision, I strained my mind for other possibilities. This was a simplistic, but useful exercise—one that my grandmother had taught me in childhood. Every single vision, no matter how mundane, could happen. Most small changes to the future had no effect, however some larger interventions would cause long term ripples that changed the future of thousands.

Once again, I saw Ciara walking down the street, but this time she turned right instead of left. I tried again, and Ciara walked down the street, turned right, then bumped into another woman. The two women exchanged tense pleasantries.

I ran through fifty odd scenarios of Ciara leaving her house, each one more unlikely than the last. In some iterations, I tried interfering. For example, if I went back inside and slit the woman's throat, she would never walk down the street at all.

Once I'd exhausted every possible version of the future, I sighed in relief. I didn't care about this street, or the healer or where she might be going, but at least my magic hadn't completely abandoned me.

My eyes flew open again, looking at the real street in front of me rather than the one in my mind. I felt markedly calmer than I had only moments ago. Remembering the book, I snatched it off the step and let it fall open on my lap. I supposed I could read it out here as well as anywhere else. At least out here, Scion wasn't glaring at me, and I didn't have to resist the urge to watch Lonnie too often, lest she become suspicious.

I bent closer to the book, squinting at the first page in the low light coming from under the door.

Without warning, Bael threw the door open behind me, bursting out of the house and nearly tripping over me as he bolted out into the ally. Startled, I watched, as Bael jerked to a halt and doubled over, vomiting across the stained cobblestones of the ally. I raised an eyebrow. I hadn't seen that coming.

I got heavily to my feet and walked over to my cousin. "You alright?"

Bael retched again, then glared up at me with contempt, wiping his mouth with the back of his hand. "What the fuck does it look like to you?"

I crossed my arms, leaning back on my heels. Nearly a year ago we'd stood together in the ally only a few streets over, just before I'd allowed myself to be captured. At the time, I'd thought my cousin was too young and inexperienced to be taken seriously, but he didn't seem that way now.

"It looks like you're ill. Are you allergic to nettle root or something?"

"What?" Bael said caustically, clearly not remembering the ingredients of the tea Ciara had served.

I shook my head. "Nevermind. What's wrong with you?"

Bael straightened, seeming temporarily finished vomiting. "Shouldn't you tell me that?"

I felt a muscle twitch in my jaw with annoyance. "I go back to meditating about it long enough to find out for myself, or you could save us some time and just tell me."

Bael matched my scowl. "I've got a migraine, that's all. It's making me nauseous."

I furrowed my brow. That was obviously bullshit, and at the same time must be at least partly true. He hadn't lied–indeed, I didn't think he'd stay conscious through the pain of a lie if his head was already hurting this badly. Yet, Fae didn't get sick often, and we certainly didn't get unexplained headaches.

"How long has this been going on?" I asked.

Bael's eyes darted to the side, looking uncomfortable. "Not long."

I raised an eyebrow. "Be specific."

Bael glowered at me. "I don't have to tell you anything. Leave me alone before I make you."

I snorted a derisive laugh. "You could try, but in this state I'd knock you unconscious before you ever lifted a hand."

"Give me a hundred years and I'd win every time," he grumbled.

I had no idea what the fuck that meant, and decided I didn't care to ask. Not when there were much more interesting questions at hand. "As you said, I'll work it out anyway. You may as well tell me everything."

Bael's scowl deepened. "I don't know what's wrong, alright? You have a better chance of figuring it out than I do, so when you do, let me know."

He shouldered past me, and plastered on a grin before striding back into the house.

I frowned. That was…odd, to say the least.

The only upside was now I had something to focus on. An actual challenge to exercise my powers without being hindered by the blind-spot that was Lonnie or Idris's interference.

By the end of the week I'd figure out what was wrong with him. I only hoped that would be soon enough to fix it.

* * *

The house was silent when I finally went back inside.

I'd lost track of time, caught in something of a meditative trance, reading Grandmother's notes and then seeking out possible solutions in the near distant future.

It had taken several hours, but finally I felt like myself again. I'd seen enough of the future to make a plan, and now needed to share that plan with the others.

I made my way up the small rickety stairs in search of Lonnie and the others. There were only two rooms at the top of the landing, so even if I hadn't known where to look it wouldn't have been difficult to find where they were sleeping.

I opened the door to a sort of store room. Like downstairs, there were drying herbs hanging from the low rafters, filling the entire room with a spicy floral scent.

There were no beds, but in the back corner of the room I found the others. They'd laid out their cloaks and what looked like a single borrowed blanket on the wooden floor.

Scion lay motionless, arms limply at his sides. His breathing was steady and deep, signaling that he was sound asleep. I couldn't help but smile; as a soldier, Scion had the ability to sleep in any place or situation. He probably found more comfort on the hard ground than on a soft bed.

Conversely, Bael was not asleep, and his yellow catlike eyes followed me as I approached. He looked wary, and we made eye contact for a brief moment. I tried to communicate without words that I had no intention of sharing his secret—yet.

Between them, Lonnie had her feet entangled with Bael's legs, and was using Scion's arm as a pillow. I thought she was asleep too, until her eyes flashed in the darkness. She sat up and looked at me. "Are you alright?"

I smiled to myself. She was always worrying about if we were alright, when really she was the only one who mattered.

"Fine, love." I said, quietly enough that I hoped not to wake Scion. "Better than fine, actually. I finally know what we need to do."

"Go back to the castle and murder Idris?" Bael asked, sounding somewhat hopeful.

"Eventually," I replied.

Both Bael and Lonnie looked taken aback, as if they'd expected me to say we should leave him in peace. If so, they'd gravely misunderstood my motivations. I would never advocate for either giving up or showing too much mercy to those who did not deserve it, but neither did I want to be rash. If we stormed back to the castle now, we might win, but the odds were slim.

Of the four of us, all but me had offensive magical talents. Except that no one was in top fighting condition.

Lonnie was still mastering her abilities. She'd come extremely far in a short period of time, but not far enough for a real fight. Bael was clearly in worse condition than he'd been letting on. I'd wondered earlier why he'd killed the mob of mindless courtiers in waves, rather than all at once. Now, I suspected it was because his energy was flagging. Scion seemed to think he was the one who had been siphoning Lonnie's energy, but now I wasn't so sure.

That left only Scion to face Idris alone, and I wasn't sure enough that he'd win to risk it. We didn't know the full extent of Idris's power, and thanks to whatever he'd said to me upon our meeting, I still didn't know.

"Well?" Lonnie blurted out.

I blinked rapidly, suddenly realizing I'd been silent for far too long, lost in my own contemplation. I shook my head vigorously. "Fuck, sorry."

"Another vision?" Lonnie asked hopefully.

Again, I shook my head. "Not this time. I just have a lot to think about." I took a breath. "I think we should travel to Inbetwixt in the morning."

"Why? Bael asked, his yellow eyes narrowing. In the dim light, his irises glowed, like that of an animal.

"Because I don't want to focus on Idris. Instead, we need to concentrate on breaking the curse."

Bael made a slightly angry noise in the back of his throat and Lonnie audibly sighed, her shoulders slumping. "Isn't that what we've been doing all this time?"

"Yes, but listen to me. You heard what Ciara said downstairs about draining, and she wasn't wrong. As long as your circle of bonds remains broken you'll never have enough magic to pull from to take on Idris, or to maintain power over the kingdom afterwards. His coup was public, and it will take years and many battles to regain the reputation we once had."

"It could also take years to find out how to break the curse," Bael growled.

"It could, but I doubt it." I held out the book to them. "Grandmother left us all her notes, and I've spent the last several hours deciphering them."

"I can't read this," Lonnie bemoaned, pushing the book back toward me.

"Here, then look at this."

I flipped to a page with a drawing and slid it back toward her. She and Bael leaned over the book as one, assessing. Lonnie opened her mouth, undoubtedly to ask questions, but I cut her off, already prepared to explain.

"This is that same crown we kept seeing pictured in the other books. Celia was clearly ruminating on it for years. Perhaps for decades, but here she's drawn it differently. See, instead of the three pointed crown with a jewel on each, she's made it a five pointed crown. Like the obsidian crown."

"You said the obsidian crown never had jewels." She eyed me suspiciously. "There were historical records and whatever else to prove it."

I smiled. This was the part of my theory I found the most interesting–the bit that confirmed for me that I was on the right path, finally, after so long of wandering aimlessly.

"I believe that it didn't have those jewels anymore by the time the Unseelie king stole the crown from Aisling and took her away from Aftermath. I already recognized one of the jewels as the diamond of Nevermore. I believe the others belong to Inbetwixt and Overcast."

I widened my eyes, expecting them to catch on and join in my glee at having finally worked something out.

"Did she dismantle the crown herself?" Scion asked.

I looked over at him, startled. I hadn't realized he'd woken up. "I believe so. It seems too much of a coincidence that Aisling had three mates, one from each province, and here we have dozens of drawings of the crown jewel of each realm set into the obsidian crown. But if she took her crown apart, spreading the pieces between her bonded, that would make sense."

"So we just need the stones?" Lonnie clarified. "That's it?"

"And a way to put it back together," I conceded. "But if we can do both…" I let my sentence trail off, leaving them to make the rest of the connections on their own.

"This is amazing," Lonnie beamed. She made a small lurching motion, as if about to hug me, then stopped herself. I bit back disappointment. It was such a small thing, but I felt like a starving man grasping for scraps. Anything she offered was better than nothing.

"I agree this is the best information we're going to get," Scion said. "We should leave for Inbetwixt tomorrow."

I looked sideways at him. "Are you agreeing with me?"

He scowled. "I'm agreeing with the best possible option."

I raised my eyebrows. Whatever he cared to tell himself.

"Why should we go to Inbetwixt first?" Bael asked, also looking much happier than he had when I entered.

"Because I'm almost certain that your friends in the thieves guild have the stone. Or, at the very least, they'll be able to help get it. There's a passage about it in the book. The stone used to be kept at the Lord and Lady's manor, but several years ago it was taken."

"Oh, good." Lonnie sighed in relief. "I wouldn't want to go back and see the Lord and Lady of Inbetwixt, anyway."

"But if we know Cross has the stone, why should we go there first?" Scion asked. "If we know they have the stone and have been presumably keeping it safe for a while, shouldn't we go look for one of the others first?"

I shook my head. "No, it must be Inbetwixt first. We'll need the thieves' help to reach the stone, but I'm not sure how much longer they'll be in the city."

Lonnie raised an eyebrow. "What do you mean?"

"Cross has spies in every city. Soon he'll know what's happened here, and I think he'll decide to take his group into hiding."

"When?" Scion asked.

"I'm not sure. It might be tomorrow, it might be in a few days. There are a lot of moving parts and I can't see all of them at once."

"Well that's fucking unhelpful," Scion snapped.

I glared at him. "I've just spent hours learning at least this much, you could be grateful to have at least some direction."

Lonnie pleaded with her eyes for us not to argue. "Thank you for trying."

I sucked in a calming breath. "I learned one thing for sure. Did you all know that Aine is still living with the thieves guild?"

They glanced at each other, exchanging looks of surprise.

"She is?" Bael sounded incredulous. "Why?"

I shrugged. "I don't know, but since she's there that opens up many other paths for the thieves as a whole."

"You can ask her tomorrow," Lonnie told Bael. Her expression had lightened, like the mere idea of having a plan had lifted some of the weight from her shoulders.

I found myself leaning toward her, then having to stop myself. Fuck, this was growing harder and harder to ignore. I'd thought it was bad enough on the boat, but somehow my feelings for her had gotten even stronger over the last months.

She couldn't know it, of course, but this conversation was the beginning of the end of my keeping the truth of our mating from her. She'd need her bonded circle closed to access her full power, and sooner or later I'd have to tell her.

17
LONNIE
CHEAPSIDE, EVERLAST CITY

I awoke the following morning to the feeling of cold fingers pressing into my cheek.

As if my body already knew what was happening before my mind had a chance to catch up, my eyes flew open. I sat bolt upright, already fully awake. "What—"

The same cold fingers clamped hard over my mouth, and my eyes widened to find Ciara peering back at me in the darkness. She pressed a long bony finger to her own lips, and jerked her head toward the door, indicating she wanted me to follow her.

If I could have, I would have let out a resigned sigh. Instead, I nodded, and waited for her to slowly pull her hand away from my mouth. She tiptoed toward the door to the hall, and stopped waiting for me to follow.

Once again, I'd slept plastered between Bael and Scion, and both were still sleeping soundly—clearly exhausted from the night before. Ambrose hadn't stayed in our makeshift bed with us last night, instead opting to sleep on the floor near the door. I looked down at him as I passed, and caught him looking up at me with one dark eye. Apparently Ciera hadn't fully succeeded in her attempts not to wake everyone.

I had the strangest urge to assure him that I'd be safe with Ciara. But then, that seemed overly familiar. He might be a friend of sorts—at least an ally—but I needed to stop treating him like one of my mates simply because he was always present. It wasn't fair to anyone—myself included.

Instead I gave Ambrose a brief nod of acknowledgement as I followed Ciara out the door into the hallway. The tiny woman scowled at me as I closed the door behind me. "Not so loud."

I rolled my eyes. "What's so important that you had to yank me out of bed?"

"I wanted to talk to you without all of them hovering around."

"Why, because they're Fae?" I said a bit defensively.

She looked at me oddly. "No, because they're men. By the Source girl, one would think you were dropped on your head as a child."

I pressed my lips together into a thin line. In fact, I had been dropped as a child—into a fucking volcano—but that probably wasn't what Ciara meant.

Ciara led me down the thin rickety staircase, and into her kitchen. I noticed that while it was still dark out, she already had a roaring fire going and a pot of yet more tea boiling away on the stove.

"Sit," she said briskly, pointing to the round wooden table. "I'm sure we only have a few minutes before you're missed."

"You should know that Ambrose is awake," I told her. "I'm sure he can hear us perfectly even from upstairs."

Ciara cocked her head at me, then glanced at the stairs. "Which one is Ambrose?"

I tried not to roll my eyes. I was quite sure that Ciara could tell all the Everlasts apart perfectly well, and her feigned confusion was more about putting distance between herself and the Fae royalty than anything else. Nevertheless, I humored her. "The seer. With the white hair."

Ciara humphed. "Awe well, it can't be helped."

"What's this about?" I asked her, finally sitting down at the table.

"I've made you a tea."

"More tea?" I gave her a dubious look. "I feel fine now. I wasn't injured, just tired, and a few hours of sleep has taken care of that."

"A few hours of sleep and my tea," she said stubbornly. "But this isn't like that. I've been steeping stoneseed root all morning for you."

"Oh," I said abruptly, glancing at the stove. "That's not—"

I broke off. I'd meant to say that wasn't necessary, but stopped short of scalding my throat.

The stoneseed plant was well known to prevent pregnancy, and I'd drunk it religiously since my adolescence. Now though, I realized with horror that I hadn't even thought of it in quite some time. My eyes widened, and panic consumed me as my hand flew unconsciously to my stomach.

"Don't look so petrified." Ciara rolled her beady eyes. "I daresay you're fine…for now."

"How can you be sure?" I asked hastily, not even bothering to deny the possibility.

Ciara looked me up and down and shrugged. "Just a hunch. You don't have the aura of a woman with child, but unless you want to make things even more complicated for yourself I suggest you make a habit of drinking your tea."

"Of course." I looked down to hide the flush heating my cheeks. "Thank you."

Ciara tisked disapprovingly, and turned to take the kettle off the stove. She immediately poured a large mug, and set it in front of me. "Let that sit for a few minutes before you drink it."

"Will it work better if it steeps?"

"No," she snapped, exasperated. "It's hot. You'll burn your tongue."

"Oh, right. Of course." I flushed again, and let my long curtain of hair fall in front of my face.

Ciara didn't bother me as I waited in embarrassed silence for the tea to cool. I couldn't believe this was the first I'd thought about mundane things like preventing pregnancy in weeks. Now, unbidden, the image of myself holding some nameless daughter popped into my mind. She looked like a version of Scion's nine-year-old half-sister Elfwyn, and I couldn't decide if the image interested or horrified me.

Hastily, I reached for the mug on the table and drank the entire thing in one gulp. Ciara was right—the last thing I needed right now was to complicate things further.

* * *

Several hours later, we thanked Ciara for her help and went out behind her house to shadow walk to Inbetwixt. Ciara didn't want to be seen by her neighbors assisting Fae of any sort, so it was just the four of us standing together in the dingy alley between houses.

The morning had brought a light rain, and the sky was completely gray. In the distance, the sky was lighter, and I hoped that meant the weather would be better when we reached Inbetwixt.

"How shall we go about this?" I asked, glancing around the group at large.

"What do you mean, little monster?" Bael placed a hand on the small of my back and grinned down at me. He looked healthier and more awake than he had in days, and I was relieved to see that his usual smile was firmly back in place.

"I mean, where are we meant to arrive in Inbetwixt?"

"I assumed we'd walk directly into the den," Scion replied. "Under normal circumstances I'd consider that rude, but I think Cross will forgive us given the circumstances."

"Do you know how to reach the thieves den?" I asked Ambrose.

He shook his head. "I'm sure I could work it out eventually, but if you are aiming for efficiency…"

Scion rolled his eyes and made a disgruntled sound in the back of his throat. "I suppose I can guide you."

"Excellent," I said loudly, before Ambrose could say anything that might make Scion change his mind. "See you all in a moment, then."

Without waiting for any of them to speak, I took a small step forward, falling into darkness.

It was only very recently that I'd been able to shadow walk at all, but as with all my other abilities I'd been practicing. Scion had once described it to me as if you folded a map, and walked in between the creases. I still wasn't entirely sure what he meant by that, but more often than not I found I was able to move from place to place without difficulty.

Indeed, when I opened my eyes again I immediately knew I was in the right place. The headquarters of the thieves guild was located in the very heart of Inbetwixt. The majority of the enormous compound was underground, with only a townhouse and a neighboring tavern representing the front-facing exterior. Unless you were invited inside, you would never know that some forty thieves lived and worked underground, moving all over the city by way of an enormous tunnel system.

I arrived in the middle of the den. It was a long room with a bar on one end and a large training ring on the other. Whenever I'd been here before, Cross and his crew used this room as both workplace and recreation. I'd never seen it entirely empty before.

I turned in a small circle, blinking to clear my eyes. Within seconds, Bael appeared beside me, followed closely by Scion and Ambrose.

"Cross?" Scion called, his tone wary.

His voice echoed all around the empty room, and no one replied.

"Where is everyone?" I asked nervously.

Silence answered me, as we all looked anxiously around. The entire guild was gone, and that either meant they'd fled…or someone had come here and taken them.

18
LONNIE
THE CUTTHROAT DISTRICT, INBETWIXT

"You said Cross would be here," Scion spat, crossing his arms over his chest.

Ambrose spun toward him, anger flashing in his dark gaze. "I also told you he was going to move his people out of the city in a matter of days. It happened sooner than I anticipated."

I tuned out their bickering and instead turned in a slow circle, scanning the large room for signs of where Cross might have gone. Everything looked the same as usual, though perhaps a bit cleaner than was typical. I noticed that the large wrack of weapons that usually stood by the training ring was empty. I swallowed a lump in my throat, hoping they hadn't needed those weapons for anything more than practice.

"Well, now what?" I asked the room at large.

The silence that answered me was deafening. No one seemed to know what to do, including Ambrose, who'd I'd expected to invent another plan on the spot.

With little else to do, we moved to sit at the deserted bar where Cross, Scion and I had once sat planning how to capture

Ambrose. A mostly silent hour later, we'd still not come up with a new plan.

I massaged my temples, feeling discouraged. I'd assumed that the jewel of Inbetwixt would be the simplest to retrieve—given that Cross possessed or at least had knowledge of every treasure in the city. Without his guidance, however, the city seemed enormous, and the task in front of us even more so.

"We could visit the Lord and Lady of Inbetwixt," I suggested half-heartedly.

"No point, love. They don't have the jewel anymore."

"Maybe they know who took it?" But even as I heard my own words, I realized how stupid a suggestion that was. There was only one thieves' guild in the city. If the jewel was stolen, either Cross had it somewhere or he'd sold it. Without him here to ask, there was very little we could do.

Scion glared at Ambrose, his lip curling in disdain. "That's it? You're out of ideas so easily?"

Ambrose set his jaw, looking like he was doing his best not to hit Scion.

I pinched the bridge of my nose and closed my eyes in frustration. I didn't know why I even cared. It wasn't my concern if they liked each other, or could even stand to be in the same room. Still, they'd been inexplicably getting along so much better for the past few days that I thought we might be on the verge of a real truce. Apparently the chaos of last night had put an end to that as quickly as it had begun.

"Does Cross have a vault?" I blurted out, more to interrupt the tension than anything else. "Perhaps if he stashed the jewel somewhere nearby we wouldn't need his help to find it."

"That's a good idea, rebel." Scion swung around on his stool to face me. His expression was perhaps slightly guilty, as if he realized that all the fighting was starting to get to me. "The only problem is I have no idea where it would be. There are thousands of miles of tunnels down here, and half the doors are hidden in the rock."

"I remember," I grumbled. "When we went through the sewers the last time we were here, I never would have been able to find the door without someone pointing it out."

Well, there went that suggestion just as quickly as it had come. I slumped back in my chair, drumming my fingers on the table.

Realizing he hadn't spoken in a while, I looked over at Bael. "What do you think?"

Instead of taking one of the bar stools, or even sitting at any of the small circular tables that took up a large portion of the room, Bael had decided to sit on the floor. He was leaning against the same wall where Scion had once nailed an incubus who had tried to attack me. Fortunately, the body had long since been removed, but I thought I could still see a hint of a blood stain.

At my question, Bael opened his yellow eyes and peered at me, half-lidded. "Were you talking to me, little monster?"

I frowned. He looked worse than I'd felt last night. Like he hadn't slept in days.

Evidently Scion agreed, because he walked around the side of the bar to get a better look at Bael. "What the fuck is wrong with you?"

"Nothing," Bael began. "...that you need to worry about right now."

I frowned. Clumsy technical truths were never a good sign. If he wasn't feeling well enough to think of a decent misdirection, something was undoubtedly wrong.

Before I could press him further, a heavy door at the end of the room flew open with a resounding bang, startling everyone in the room. In one swift and urgent motion, I was shoved behind the bar by Scion and Ambrose who stood protectively in front of me. Bael, who had seemed to be dozing off, was now wide awake and on his feet in an instant.

Part of me wanted to roll my eyes. I wasn't helpless anymore, yet they were all still treating me as if I was made of glass. Even Ambrose, who had no real reason to care what happened to me aside from the curse, didn't seem to be able to resist the need to shield me.

Maybe that was just Fae males in general. Aggressive, over-protective, and too controlling for their own good.

Suppressing the urge to complain, I leaned in close to Bael's broad back and peered around him. My eyes fell upon a mysterious figure who had just entered through the doorway. The person was cloaked in a dark garment, concealing their identity. But as they pushed back their hood, revealing a familiar face with a mischievous grin, my heart leapt with relief.

"Siobhan!" I exclaimed, my voice filled with relief. "Thank the fucking Source."

Siobhan was the closest thing I had to a friend among the thieves guild, and had helped us on several occasions in the past. She was Cross's favorite daughter, and often acted as his right hand on missions for the guild. The last time I had laid eyes on her, she was in the midst of a battle with Ambrose's rebels. I couldn't help but wonder how she would react to seeing him again in this setting.

At my shout, Siobhan's face changed from an expression of suspicion to a relieved grin. "I should have known it was you all, again." she called, striding toward us. "What are you doing here?"

I darted out from behind the protective wall of princes, and hastened to meet her in the center of the room. "We could ask you the same. We thought you'd all left."

"We have," she replied. "But you don't think father would leave this place unguarded, do you? We're taking it in shifts to keep an eye on the base."

"Where is everyone?" I asked.

She shook her head. "Sorry, can't tell you that. Father specifically ordered me not to tell anyone."

"Oh, he did?" Scion drawled, his voice growing louder as he came to stand behind my shoulder. "That fucker. We're supposed to be friends, but he can't even tell me when he's leaving the city unattended."

Siobhan looked up at Scion and smirked. "Sorry, my lord. You can complain to him yourself the next time you see him."

My brow furrowed in annoyance but it had absolutely nothing to do with Cross or the missing thieves. Absurdly, hearing anyone else—particularly someone as pretty as Siobhan—use the phrase "my lord" had set my pulse racing. *That was absolutely insane,* I told myself firmly. I shook my head quickly. I needed to get a grip.

I looked up at Scion and found him smirking down at me, looking a bit too satisfied for my liking. Clearly he knew—or had guessed—what I was thinking. My cheeks burned.

"So, what are you doing here?" Siobhan asked, clearly unaware of the silent conversation going on between Scion and I.

"Looking for you all," I replied. "We need your help finding something."

Siobhan's grin widened. "Of course you do. Well, I'll help if I can, but I can't leave the den until Arson arrives and that won't be for another two days."

"Hopefully you won't have to," I told her. "Come sit, we'll explain everything."

Siobhan nodded, stepping around me to approach the bar when she stopped short. Her large dark eyes widened as she looked at Ambrose, then she spun back around to look at me. "What the fuck is he doing here?"

I tried to smile, but I was sure it came off more like a grimace. "Another long story."

To my relief, Siobhan merely laughed. "I can't wait to tell father."

* * *

It took the better part of an hour to explain nearly everything that had happened since we'd last left Inbetwixt. Fortunately, Siobhan located some food and drinks from a nearby store room, so we were able to eat while we talked.

"I was born there, you know," she said conversationally, when I explained how we'd escaped the Underneath.

I swallowed the sip I'd just taken from my wine and shook my head. "No, I didn't know."

"You didn't?" Scion looked sideways at me, a hint of his old judgment in his gaze. "How could you miss it?"

I scowled at him. "I don't know. Why would I ask?"

"Most wouldn't have to ask because I'm Unseelie," Siobhan said.

"I wondered if you couldn't tell, since you didn't react when we first met."

"When we first met I couldn't tell the difference between seelie and Unseelie. I still can't, actually. You all seemed equally terrifying to me."

She grinned. "I knew there was a reason I liked you."

"So why did you leave Underneath?" I asked, suddenly realizing I had no idea how old Siobhan was. She called Cross "father" which had given me the impression she was younger than him, but perhaps not. Among the immortals, age didn't matter much beyond maturity.

"My parents left when Gancanagh came to power," she explained. "Then they were captured and killed by the Lord of Inbetwixt. I was captured as well, but the guild broke me out of prison in exchange for joining up. I've been with Cross ever since."

I frowned. "That sounds like they pressured you. Pulling you out of prison and then demanding service."

"Oh, they absolutely did." She laughed again. "But I wasn't bothered. We find a lot of members in the prisons actually. It's where thieves end up, obviously, unless they have the backing of the guild."

Hmmm. I took another sip of my wine, mulling that over. For some reason, my mind conjured up the image of the young guild recruits I'd seen Cross training the first time we'd visited the den. There were children there barely older than fourteen. Did they also find themselves having to choose between a lifetime behind bars or a lifetime of service to the guild?

"Why did they hate Gancanagh?" Bael piped up, jogging me from my thoughts.

Bael's tone was all innocence. He'd moved off the floor and seemed marginally better now that he was nursing a glass of whisky in one hand and an enormous tanker of water in the other. His expression was benign, as if his question didn't matter much. Yet I knew he cared about the answer very much–perhaps more than he should.

"Does it matter?" Siobhan asked. "From what I've heard he's not the king anymore."

Bael looked startled. "You heard that already?"

Siobhan looked at Bael shrewdly, and I immediately got the impression that he wasn't fooling anyone. She knew exactly who his father was. I supposed, if you'd ever seen King Gancanagh, it would be hard not to notice that Bael was his blonde double.

"Two months is a long time in the court of Underneath. From what whispers have reached me the entire court is in chaos. Without clear leadership, things have gone bad faster than you could even imagine."

Bael fell silent, looking troubled.

Sensing a change of subject was in order, I drew her attention back to me. "We heard Aine is still living with the guild."

Siobhan wrinkled her nose, looking annoyed. "Yes."

"You don't like her?" I guessed.

"I...she's what she is."

Abruptly, Scion laughed. "She's a bitch," he said in a tone that implied both admiration and affection for his cousin.

"Your words, not mine," Siobhan replied. Though, her expression said clearly that she agreed. "Father is quite taken with the princess."

Scion's grin immediately died, and his eyebrows shot up in mingled surprise and disgust. "Cross…and Aine?"

Siobhan laughed this time. "No, not like that. They're not together. Father merely thinks she's talented."

"Well that tracks," Bael interjected. "If she's finally using her magic regularly, her persuasion ability would be invaluable in the guild."

"It is." Siobhan looked sulky again. "The princess has quickly become part of the inner circle."

I raised my eyebrows. I had no particular strong feelings toward Aine. She was direct and often rude, and had never been overly kind to me. On several occasions, she'd clearly implied that she didn't think I was good enough for her brother or her cousin. However, she'd also wanted to accompany me to Aftermath and had fought the rebels on my behalf.

From Siobhan's tone, however, I didn't think Aine's character was in question one way or the other. I gathered that her resentment was really jealousy over whatever favor Aine had earned from Cross in these last few months.

"Oh," Siobhan said suddenly. "I forgot to mention. Your friend Iola is still living with us as well."

"Really?" I breathed. "Thank the Source. Is she doing alright?"

"Oh yes," Siobhan waved her hand in the air as if shooing invisible flies. "She's not much of a thief, but she gets along well with everyone. I think father may start using her in one of the shops we own as a cover."

I sighed in relief. "I'm glad. If you have a clothing shop, perhaps she could work there. She's a very talented seamstress. Who knows, perhaps you could turn a legitimate profit for once."

Siobhan grinned. "I'll pass that along."

I swirled the last sip of wine in my glass, trying to think what to say next. It was nice to catch up with Siobhan and to hear news of our missing friends, but still we couldn't pretend this was merely a social visit. We needed to find the jewel, and the sooner we did so and got out of the city the better off we would be.

Perhaps a direct approach was best.

"So what about the vault?" I asked. "Do you think we might find the jewel in there?"

Siobhan pursed her lips. We'd told her that we were looking for a lost Everlast family heirloom, carefully hiding the true nature of the jewel without directly lying. That much she seemed to believe, but she hadn't looked happy about helping us look for it. Now, she looked even less pleased.

"I understand what you're asking," she began, "and that this jewel belonged to you all to begin with. But I can't let you into the vault without father's permission."

"Tell us where he is then," Scion demanded. "I'll get his damn permission by tonight."

Siobhan shook her head. "I can't."

I put a hand on Scion's shoulder, sensing he was about to say something rash, possibly offending Siobhan enough that she wouldn't help us at all. He looked down at my fingers then up into my eyes, his expression unreadable.

"Where's the wine cellar?" Ambrose said loudly

I jumped, and spun around to look at him. He was sitting cross legged on the floor, his back straight and his eyes half closed. He'd been almost completely silent since Siobhan had arrived, and now when I looked at him I once again saw that disconnected distant look on his face. Excitement bubbled up in my stomach. "Did you see where the vault is?"

He tilted his head toward Siobhan. "She visits there many times in the future."

Siobhan scowled. "By the fucking Source. I'd heard the Dullahan was a seer, but that's eerie."

I grinned. "So I take it he's right?"

She nodded, looking none too happy about it. "I should tell you though, I wouldn't go looking for the vault. It's warded against thieves."

"That's fucking ironic," Scion grumbled.

Siobhan ignored him, speaking only to me. "The traps are good, so even if you did manage to find your jewel you might not get out. And before you ask me to help you break in, I don't know how to disarm them and I don't use combat magic. So, even if I wanted to help you, which I'm not sure I do, I can't."

I sighed, feeling discouraged again. There was a long silence in which I could practically hear Scion's brain working, and Bael gnashing his teeth.

Siobhan sighed. "I suppose I don't have to be a seer to know you're going to try anyway so I'll show you as far as the door, but that's it. Then I'm done."

My excitement returned at once and I grinned, jumping up from my stool. "Thank you. You don't understand what you're doing for us."

"Don't thank me," Siobhan grumbled. "I'm probably walking you straight to your deaths."

"Is it that bad?" I asked.

"Oh absolutely, but even assuming you make it out I would keep one eye open. You might be friends but if Cross thinks you've stolen from him he'll slit your throats while you're sleeping."

To my surprise, Scion laughed. "I genuinely hope he tries. I could use the exercise."

19

LONNIE

THE CUTTHROAT DISTRICT, INBETWIXT

Siobhan led us to the very same wine cellar where months ago Bael and I had joined the thieves before we all descended into the sewers. At first I thought we might be going that way again, and I braced myself remembering the horrible smell, and the way my boots squelched on the floor, stepping in Aisling only knew what.

Thankfully, we did not end up in the sewers.

Instead, Siobhan opened another hidden stone door in the wall and motioned for us to enter. The door creaked open, revealing a dark room.

"This is where I leave you," Siobhan said. "The entrance to the vault is over there. I recommend you step carefully once you're inside. You don't want to set off any traps."

"Thank you," I said automatically, peering into the dark within. Then, my mind catching up with me, I spun back around. "Wait! What are the traps?"

She didn't answer me, and when I looked back behind us she'd already disappeared. Moving as swiftly and quietly as a shadow.

I wondered if that was part of her Unseelie magic or if Cross had trained her to move without detection. Possibly both. With any luck, we wouldn't have to move through the vault in such a manner, because we might be many things but quiet was not one of them.

Sure enough, our boots slapped against the stone floor, echoing loudly off the ceiling as we entered.

"Damn," I hissed as we walked. "She might not have known how to disarm the traps, but she could have at least warned us what we're dealing with."

Ambrose stopped in front of me and I came to a halt behind him, blinking until my eyes adjusted to the dim light. After a moment, I realized the room was larger than I'd originally thought. Much, *much* larger.

We were standing within an enormous stone cavern. It was nearly half the size of the main room of the thieves' den. Stone pillars hung from the ceiling and the floor, and water dripped softly off naturally occurring stalagmites and stalactites.

"I expected another room like the den," I said to no one in particular.

"As did I," Scion agreed."This cave must have already been here before the city was constructed. Leave it to Cross to choose the most dangerous place possible to hide his treasure."

"Why is it so dangerous?" I asked. "Aside from the traps that is."

"Because of how old the cave itself is," Bael replied from where he walked behind me. "The old ones live in places like this."

I shivered and it had nothing to do with the chill damp air.

I'd met an old one once—an enormous murderous snake that was likely older than Elsewhere itself. It spoke in riddles and devoured Fae and humans alike, leaving their bodies mangled and floating in the quarry of Inbetwixt. I had no desire to encounter anything of that nature ever again.

As if my thoughts had made me paranoid, at that moment I could have sworn I saw something move in my peripheral vision. I quickly spun around, anxious to see who or what was there. Instead, all I saw was a skeleton propped up against the wall. Torn and moth-eaten rags hung off the bones, and beside the wretched person was a small pile of gold. Like whomever this had once been had died with their stolen treasure in their hand.

“I guess Siobhan was right,” I said with forced cheerfulness. “Some people don’t make it out.”

The men turned around to follow my gaze. Scion grimaced at the skeleton. “Cross is fucked in the head. He could have simply placed that there as a deterrent.”

"Well, if so, it’s a good one.” I shuddered.

Bael glanced back the way we’d come. “We need to make sure we can get back out once we’ve gotten the jewel. If the doors shut on their own, or…” he trailed off, looking meaningfully at the skeleton.

“Someone should wait here, to open the doors if something happens,” Ambrose agreed.

“Fine,” Scion said briskly. “You do that.”

“I didn’t mean me,” Ambrose snapped, widening his eyes meaningfully in my direction.

“He’s right, little monster. You should stay,” Bael said quickly. “If it’s really as dangerous as Siobhan claimed, I don’t want you anywhere near that vault.”

"Too late for that," I said acidly. "Anyway, how do you know I don't have to get the jewel myself? Like the hunts. Maybe it's part of being worthy."

"You don't believe that," Scion drawled, eyeing me with a raised eyebrow.

I pressed my lips together. He was right, I didn't believe I had to personally collect the jewel. Still, I'd be damned before I let them leave me behind.

"If that door does shut on its own, how am I supposed to help?" I argued. "I can't wrench a metal door off the hinges like any of you could. You'd end up just as trapped as if all four of us went, only you'd know I was on the other side of the door unable to help you. I know you all think I'm useless at fighting, but–"

"No one thinks you're useless," Bael said almost harshly. "We think you're too important to risk."

My chest swelled with warmth at those words, but I still wasn't going to give up. "You all keep trying to protect me from every tiny thing, but that can't last. Either I'm worthy of the crown or I'm helpless and need you all to save me. It can't be both."

Everyone fell silent looking both angry and also resigned. Like I'd made a good point, but not one they liked.

Scion turned to Ambrose. "She's right. It needs to be you. If the door closes, you'd be able to get it open, but more importantly, you're the most likely to realize if something is wrong."

"But I can't–" He broke off, giving Scion a meaningful glance.

"I said the most likely, not that I'm expecting total omniscience," Scion muttered, clearly agitated.

"Fine," Ambrose burst out angrily, turning on his heel and heading back toward the door. "Don't die."

"Don't worry, I won't," Scion replied dryly. "If I died while you got to wait safely outside, my spirit would be forced to return so I could kill you myself."

Bael laughed, but I didn't find anything particularly funny at the moment.

I waited a beat, warring with myself over…something. I wasn't entirely sure what was wrong with me. I felt itchy, like if I didn't at least say something–do something—I was going to crawl out of my skin.

Almost as if he read my mind. Or–I was embarrassed to hope it–he was thinking the same as I was, Ambrose glanced back over his shoulder at me. Our gazes connected, and a small shock, like static, surged through my veins.

Almost like he'd felt it too, Ambrose shivered, then smiled. "Stay safe, love. I couldn't bear it if anything were to happen to you."

I bit my bottom lip and swallowed thickly, recognizing his words immediately. It was the same thing he'd said right before leaving me in Underneath. Right after he'd kissed me…

A wild, untamed part of me wanted to do it again. I had the most bizarre desire to dart after Ambrose and press my lips to his, just in case we really did die and never see him again.

But I didn't.

Silently, I promised myself that if we came back–when we came back–I'd act on my impulse.

At least then the kiss wouldn't be a goodbye, but possibly a hello.

Bael, Scion and I continued on into the depths of the cavern, our boots echoing on the damp stone ground. The only other sound was our breathing and the occasional drip of water echoing in the darkness.

As we cautiously made our way towards the back of the cavern, a glimmer caught my eye. My heart raced with anticipation as the looming shape of an enormous door came into view. Its ancient stone surface was etched with intricate patterns and symbols I couldn't read or begin to understand.

I stepped forward, then glanced at Bael and Scion for confirmation before I reached for the door handle. My hands trembled as I yanked at it, fully expecting to find it locked.

Instead, the door swung open easily and I stumbled back, surprised by the momentum.

"It's unlocked," I blurted out, as if they couldn't easily see that for themselves.

Scion grimaced. "That's not a good thing, rebel. It probably means there's something worse on the other side."

I frowned, knowing he must be right. "I suppose we'll have to find out, won't we."

"I'll go first," Scion announced. "Bael, in back, and you stay between us, rebel."

Without a word, I switched places and followed him through the entrance and into a narrow stone passage. I'd convinced them to let me come along, I didn't need to push my luck by insisting on walking at the front.

The passage was pitch dark, the air thick with dust and mildew. I could barely see two steps in front of me, and on instinct, I conjured up a small flame in my hand to guide us

Bael looked at me appreciatively. "You're getting good at that, little monster."

I laughed nervously. "Don't congratulate me yet, I could easily still light us all on fire."

No one laughed, likely remembering the burning tents of the previous night. That had only been a mere day ago, but somehow it already felt like an eternity.

"I wonder what Idris is doing in the capital," I said, nearly as much to break up the silence of the passage as because I wanted to discuss my theory.

"Probably beginning plans for his segregated human towns," Scion replied offhand.

I gasped, only just now realizing he was probably right. Idris had been more than clear about his intentions for a "better" Elsewhere. He wanted high Fae to rule in isolation, with all other creatures separated off by walls and borders.

"You know what just occurred to me?"

"What's that, rebel?"

"Aisling was the one who created Underneath, right? Before she united the country, Unseelie were free to roam wherever they wanted."

"That's right, little monster. I suppose she passed on her segregationist ideas to her son."

"It's different," Scion growled. "Underneath was created to keep monsters from attacking the cities. Sending the humans away wouldn't protect them, or anyone else."

I had a retort ready on the tip of my tongue, but never got a chance to use it.

Suddenly, my foot landed on a thin wire that had been strategically placed across the floor. With a loud click, the corridor erupted into chaos as multiple bows were triggered, arrows whizzing past us with deadly accuracy.

"Get down!" Bael barked in my ear.

He didn't have to say it, I was already diving for the floor, covering my head with my arms. I'd recently had the experience of being pierced with a crossbow, and of all the horrible injuries I'd sustained I thought that might have been the most painful.

When the sound of the arrows flying overhead finally subsided, I lay panting on the rough stone floor. In front of me, Scion peeled himself off the wall, and walked across the passage to pick up one of the arrows, inspecting it. "Source forged," he said bitterly, throwing it back down onto the floor. "Don't step on any more of those lines, the arrows could actually do some damage."

"Thank you for that insight, my lord. I was really going out of my way to step on them intentionally, but now I'll do my best to avoid the deadly traps."

Bael laughed as Scion scowled, the tips of his ears turning slightly pink. "Just be careful," he muttered.

I shot him a grin. "Always."

I didn't step on any more traps, and finally I spotted a door ahead, signaling the end of the passage.

"I'll go first," Scion growled again, almost unnecessarily as he was already standing closest to the door. "Wait here to see if anything happens before you follow."

I nodded. I was tempted to point out that Cross had undoubtedly made this vault intending that any intruders would be Fae. All the traps were sure to be full of Source forged weapons, and

Scion wasn't much more likely to survive being hit by a dozen of them than I was.

I kept my mouth shut, though, as he stepped through the door. Pointing out the obvious wouldn't make our situation any easier, or less dangerous.

Scion stood perfectly still, just within the next room. Nothing seemed to be happening, but still I held my breath, letting it out only after several long moments. Taking another few steps into the next room, Scion beckoned for Bael and I to follow.

The room was far smaller than the cave-like entrance, and my flames illuminated every corner equally.

The walls were made of stone like the passage, but carved with dozens of looping decorations–like the symbols marking the door we'd first passed through to reach this point.

In the center of the room stood four imposing statues, each at least ten feet tall. The figures were carved out of solid rock, their fixed expressions all equally stern and unyielding. Each statue held a key in its outstretched stone hand, all of different metals. There was one silver, one gold, one bronze, and one that I thought might be carved from solid obsidian.

"What the fuck are those for?" Bael wondered aloud.

I furrowed my brow. "I assume one of them is the key to the vault. Or to the next room, at the very least."

"Which one?" Bael asked, not seeming to expect an actual answer.

I frowned. Which one indeed.

It seemed apparent that we couldn't simply grab every key and try them one after another. If Siobhan was right about the traps, then taking the wrong key was sure to have dire consequences.

I took a small step forward, and scanned my gaze over each statue in turn. Immediately, I saw they were not as identical as I'd initially thought. Two had more feminine looking features, while the other two seemed to be male. Three of the four had rounded human ears, while only the woman on the center left had the long pointed ears of the high Fae. Their carved stone clothing also differed slightly from one another. Each wore a long robe, but with different patterns decorating the hems. The closest statue carried a sword, while the one on the opposite end held a goblet of wine.

I bit my lip, thinking. If we were supposed to choose the right statue, there had to be some clue here somewhere. Cross had been the one to build this vault after all, and I trusted him to air on the side of the dramatic.

Turning in a small circle, I raised my flames higher to illuminate the room. My heart skipped an excited beat. Sure enough, the looping pattern on the wall was not a decoration, as I'd initially thought. It was words, carved directly into the stone. I leaned closer to read.

Silver but not silver.
Worth twice its weight in gold.
Forged of blood and ash.
What once was poison, now lies cold.

My pulse quickening with excitement, pointed at the words. "Look!"

Scion and Bael both turned as one, tensing as if they expected to be attacked. When they saw where I was pointing however, they relaxed.

"Silver but not silver?" Scion repeated, a mocking derision in his voice. "What the fuck is that supposed to mean?"

"Well, that's kind of the point of a riddle," Bael replied dryly. "What *does* it mean?"

Scion rolled his eyes. "I'm going to kill Cross the next time I see him. This is too much. Both of you, stand back."

"Why?" I said too quickly.

"Because I want to know what happens if we pick the wrong key. We could stand here trying to solve some damn riddle, or we could just try each key until one works."

"But if you take the wrong one it will surely set off a trap."

"I know," Scion replied. "But what kind of trap? The only way to know for sure how dangerous this is, is to test it."

Hesitantly, I stepped back toward the wall. Without commenting, Bael came to stand in front of me, blocking my view of the statues.

"You could at least let me watch," I grumbled, trying to edge out from behind him. "For all you know the floor will cave in if we pick the wrong key, and then it won't matter if you were in front of me."

"You're right, little monster." Bael grinned and grabbed my hand tightly in his fingers. "There. Now if it does fall in, I can shadow walk us both out of here."

"You're insane," I mumbled, but didn't pull my hand away.

Bael's eyes flashed, and I was sure he was thinking about all the ways he could show me even more insanity.

Once we were out of the way, Scion strode confidently toward the platform with all the statues. He reached out and snatched the obsidian key from the hand of the statue on the far right.

Immediately, another barrage of arrows flew through the air.

I let out an involuntary scream, my eyes going wide as Scion flattened himself on the ground, only narrowly avoiding the arrows.

"Alright." He got to his feet again. "That's good news."

"What, that you didn't get shot by arrows?"

"No. It's good that there's nothing more here than arrows. Stand back again."

One by one, Scion grabbed each key from the stone statue. He'd take the key, then hit the ground, covering his head until the arrows passed. He repeated this four times until the ground was littered with arrows, and Scion held all the keys in his fist.

"Brilliant," Bael said loudly. "That saves us some time."

Looking pleased with himself, Scion sauntered over to the door each of the four keys clutched tightly in his fist. We darted after him, and waited with bated breath as he tried the first key. Then the second. For each other I held my breath, practically shaking with anticipation.

But then—

"What the fuck," Scion barked, as I'd known he would the moment the fourth key failed to turn in the lock.

"I suppose Cross wasn't willing to risk anyone cheating." I threw him a sympathetic glance. "We'll have to solve the riddle."

"But how?" Scion demanded. "I've already tried them all."

"The keys must be a trick," I replied, already striding back to the wall. "They're there so that you focus on them and don't think too much about the riddle as a whole."

I stared up at the scrawled words on the wall, considering. I'd never had to solve a riddle like this before. Indeed, when would I have had the opportunity? But I did spend many years specializing in deception and misdirection. It was a few words, how hard could that be to uncover.

Minutes ticked by and a bead of sweat appeared on my brow. Some part of me felt sure that we could not stay here forever. That something would go wrong if we took too long to answer.

I read the riddle again, aloud, pronouncing each word slowly. "Silver but not silver. Worth twice its weight in gold. Forged of blood and ash. What once was poison, now lies cold."

"One of the keys is silver," Bael said, a note of uncertainty in his usually confident voice.

I pointed at the wall. "But it's not silver."

"What does that mean?" Bael asked.

"I have no idea."

I pressed my palms into my closed eyes, a familiar feeling of inferiority creeping over me. It was how I'd felt when I first realized how little I understood of Fae culture, despite having lived alongside it all my life. It was how I felt when the old tongue was spoken, and I couldn't understand. It was how, even now, I wondered if everyone around me was mocking me for my lack of education. My lack of experience. My unworthiness to be here.

Sometimes I wished to return to the valley outside Aftermath and imagine that none of this had ever happened.

Of course, that was ridiculous on a number of levels. Not least of which was that the city of Nightshade—now called Aftermath—hadn't been a city at all since the day I was born.

I took my hands away from my face, my eyes widening. My heart skipped a beat of excitement.

"Nightshade is a poison," I mused under my breath.

"What was that, little monster?'

I shook my head, still thinking, and read the riddle again. Silver but not silver…what once was poison now lies cold.

A smile spread across my face. "Wait, I think I've got it."

I dashed across the room and snatched one of the fallen arrows off the ground.

"Are you going to pick the lock?" Scion asked, obvious skepticism in his tone.

"Look—" I held up the arrow. "The arrow tip is silver, but not made from actual silver. It's made from steel, which is made from iron and carbon."

"Blood and Ash." Bael's eyes flashed with excitement.

"Exactly. And it's forged in the poison named city—"

"—which now lies cold," Bael finished for me, grinning widely. "Brilliant, little monster."

I grinned, feeling actually useful for once.

Scion stepped out of the way so I could approach the door. There was no slot for the arrow or anything so convenient as that. Instead, I held my breath in anticipation and scraped the arrow head over the metal keyhole.

At once, the door opened, a loud creak of hinges alerting us that no one had been here in quite some time.

I peered inside and gasped.

20
LONNIE
THE CUTTHROAT DISTRICT, INBETWIXT

A sharp gasp escaped my lips as the massive door swung open.

I'd been prepared for another hallway, or perhaps another room of traps, but we were not so unlucky.

A vast vault stretched out, overflowing with glittering treasure of all shapes and sizes. The gleaming gold and sparkling jewels seemed to radiate their own ethereal light, casting a spell over the room. I couldn't believe my eyes - it was like stumbling upon a secret pirate's hoard or a dragon's lair. My heart raced with excitement, pounding too hard against my ribs.

"Dammit, Cross," Scion breathed, looking around in wonderment. "How much do you think is in here?"

Bael laughed. "Does it matter?"

Scion shrugged. "I simply never thought about how much the thieves bring in. What is he planning to do with all this?"

"Build tunnels, apparently," Bael said blandly. "I don't suppose it was cheap to dig out a facility entirely under an existing city."

"Do you think there's more in here than in our vaults?" Scion asked, looking more curious than envious.

"No," Bael scoffed. "Close, though. We should be careful to watch him if he ever comes to dinner at the palace. Or I'm sure we'll find our vaults a lot lighter."

Both chuckled, then stopped abruptly. As if they'd remembered at the same moment that we didn't currently have a palace. Or any vaults, for that matter.

"Right," I said briskly. "How are we going to search this place?"

"I don't suppose you have some sense of these things?" Bael asked me, looking hopeful.

"Do I have a sense of where treasure I've never seen before is kept? No. If I did, I'm sure I'd be a rich woman."

Bael shrugged, looking slightly disappointed. "I suppose we'll just have to look, then."

We spread out and began to search. According to Celia's book the jewel of Inbetwixt was a large, oval ruby, about as wide as both my thumbs held together. Unfortunately—or fortunately, if you were Cross—there were dozens of loose jewels in the vault, all of which we had to carefully inspect before tossing aside.

For over an hour we searched in silence, only occasionally broken by a yell, and then a groan of disappointment every time one of us thought we'd found something.

I began making piles on piles of coins, trying to keep track of what I'd already seen and what I hadn't. There was more money in the small piles on the floor than I'd ever seen in my life until recently. Any one of these jewels could feed all of Cheapside for a year. Maybe two years if no one lived lavishly.

A tiny voice in the back of my mind whispered that I should take some. That we needed the money, now that we'd been expelled from the castle and anyway, Cross had stolen all this to begin with. He couldn't exactly complain about the taste of his own medicine.

I glanced over at Bael and Scion, both of whom were also making piles of jewels worth easily ten thousand silver pieces. Each.

They might be far more educated than I was in almost everything–they had tutors and had time to read thousands of books and learned to speak multiple languages. But this was not the first time I'd noticed that the Everlast family didn't grasp the value of money.

Of course, they knew how much it was worth, but they didn't really value it. None had ever had to earn anything, and as a rule they didn't carry money on their person. What if we had to trade for something in the next city? What if we had to stay at an inn and had no coins to pay for it?

Before I could further talk myself out of it, I grabbed a large handful of gold and shoved it hastily down the front of my dress.

"Hey!" Bael yelled.

I jumped a foot in the air and spun around, thinking he was about to scold me. Except, he wasn't even looking in my direction.

"What?" Scion asked, sounding grumpy.

"I think I found it." Bael held up a huge oval ruby to the light of my conjured fire, and inspected it. "We should have brought the book with us to compare the jewel to the drawing, but I'm almost positive this is the right one."

"Perfect," I let out a long breath of relief and jumped to my feet.

"Let's go, then. I don't want to stay here one moment longer than we have to."

"Let me go first, little monster," Bael said quickly, holding out an arm to halt me before the door.

"We've already been through here," I reminded him.

"I know, but still. I'd rather be overcautious than lose you."

He stepped through the door alone, grinning over his shoulder as he strode toward the statues. "I suppose you were ri—"

Bael's words broke off as a sharp, guttural noise of pain escaped his lips.

I screamed, downing out the sound of wheezing arrows as they flew everywhere, striking Bael repeatedly in the chest. My horror rose as I watched blood pool on the front of his already crimson jacket. The metallic scent filled my nostrils and the sight of it dripping onto the floor made me feel dizzy and sick. My screams became louder, echoing through the room and redoubling back on themselves.

Time seemed to slow down as I stood frozen, unable to tear my eyes away as he fell to his knees, slumping forward like a broken doll. The same frantic numb thought pounded over and over through my mind: *He was going to die here.*

We were all going to die here. Because I'd drain all my blood if it meant I could save him, and once I did, we'd all die anyway.

* * *

"Put him on the ground!" Ambrose yelled, darting toward us as we rushed out of the caves.

He reached for Bael's arm, helping Scion to lower him to the floor, then bent over Bael's body staring intently at each wound in rapid succession.

For once, Scion said nothing to Ambrose. He said nothing in general, stepping back to allow Ambrose more room to help. Scion's normally handsome face had turned the color of sour milk, and his scar stood out all the more prominently because of it.

Not that I could see much anyway, as blinding tears streamed down my face.

I'd screamed myself hoarse in the vault, and now my throat was in shreds though I hardly noticed or cared. I felt a bit light-headed, and blood streamed down my arms where I'd taken one of the arrows and slashed at my wrists, forcing my blood into Bael's open mouth. I was quite sure the blood was the only reason he was still breathing at all, though for how much longer, I couldn't tell.

I collapsed to my knees on the stone floor, and crawled over to Bael's, his once powerful form now limp and lifeless. My heart felt like it was being torn apart as I cradled his cold fingers in mine.

Ambrose knelt on Bael's other side, now running his fingers rapidly over the wounds. There were eight broken arrows sticking straight out of Bael's chest, as well as one in his shoulder. We hadn't dared to pull them out in the vault, knowing he'd bleed out instantly so Scion had snapped the lengths off to make it easier to carry him.

"We have to pull them out." My voice shook. "He can't heal while they're still in there."

"I fucking know!" Ambrose barked, more aggressively than I'd ever heard him speak to me. Seeming to realize what he'd said, he looked up at me and lowered his voice. "I know. I'm sorry. I just can't see how to get them all out before he loses too much blood."

I didn't say anything, merely lifted my still bleeding wrist back to Bael's mouth.

"No!" Ambrose yelled, knocking my arm out of the way.

"What are you doing?" I demanded angrily. "He needs blood."

"I know, but you can't be the one to give it to him."

"I already did!" I argued. "It's too late to worry about what happens now, if he doesn't have more he'll die."

"So will you," Ambrose snapped. "Even if we ignore the very real likelihood that you'll trigger the curse, you're still half human. You can't lose that much blood either."

"I don't care!" I yelled, about ready to shove him out of the way.

Ambrose ignored me, and shoved me back hard enough that I toppled into Scion's legs. I jumped back up, practically spitting venom, only to see Ambrose bite down hard on his own wrist and press it to Bael's still open mouth. I gaped, both surprised and relieved.

Suddenly, Scion had moved out from behind me, so quickly I didn't even see him until he was kneeling on the ground as well and slicing into his own arm.

"Will that work?" I demanded.

"Yes," Scion said shortly.

"But—" I began, unsure what I was even asking. I widened my eyes at Scion, exploring for him to explain.

I thought only mates shared blood. Perhaps Scion could help. Since they were both mated to me, they were loosely connected by more than family. Ambrose, however, seemed out of nowhere.

I didn't have the time to argue about it.

Suddenly, Bael coughed and sat up, his eyes opening. I let out a wail of surprise and misery, and forgot everything I'd been thinking about moments before. Any anger drained out of me, leaving only fear and the tiniest hint of hope behind.

"Don't sit up," Scion muttered, pushing Bael back to the floor. "We still have to pull these things out."

Bael allowed himself to be pushed back to the floor. A sheen of sweat had appeared on his brow, and I knelt behind his head and pushed golden curls off his face while Ambrose went about figuring out how to remove the arrows.

Bael's lips moved, and I leaned down desperately. "What did you say?"

"I said, don't cry little monster," he rasped.

"You're an idiot," I told him, still crying. "Completely insane. Why would you do that?"

He didn't respond to my question, instead holding back a shout of pain as Scion tugged the first arrow from his chest.

It didn't matter though. I didn't need to hear his answer to know he'd done it for me, and would do it again in a heartbeat even if it killed him.

21
BAEL
THE CUTTHROAT DISTRICT, INBETWIXT

"How do you feel?" Ambrose asked.

I grimaced and sat up, wiping sweat from my face with the back of my uninjured hand. "Like I'm dying."

"You are."

I felt my heartbeat speed up, almost in something like anticipation. Anxiety perhaps, that I was about to hear exactly what I'd been dreading for months.

The pain from the arrows was gone. Once the Source-forged steel that was poisonous to Fae was removed from my skin the wounds were able to close over quickly. Still, I felt weak and nauseous, and my head was pounding with yet another migraine.

After the arrows were removed and I'd consumed more blood than I'd ever even considered possible, we'd left the wine seller and returned to the heart of the thieves' den. I was now lying on my back in one of the slightly uncomfortable beds in the dormitory style barracks where the thieves usually slept when coming back from jobs.

Lonnie had laid in bed beside me for several hours, until finally Scion convinced her to wash the blood and grimy cave water from her skin. They'd left barely ten minutes ago, and I already missed both their presence.

"Did you hear me?" Ambrose asked roughly.

I looked up at Ambrose, who was leaning against the wall beside the door watching me. I didn't hate him nearly as much as Scion did, but I also wasn't at all comforted by my cousin looming over me. I wished he'd leave and let me sleep, but evidently he had something to say.

"Yeah, I fucking heard you," I grumbled. "Did your healing not work?"

He shook his head, his expression flat and slightly distant. Despite everything else, I found myself slightly annoyed by his attitude. My cousin had the worst fucking bedside manner of anyone I'd ever met–which was saying a lot, as I'd grown up with Scion.

Then again, he'd saved my life, so I probably shouldn't be so ungrateful.

I glanced down at my own chest, as if the arrow wounds might burst open and start bleeding once more. Before I could ask, Ambrose beat me to it.

"That's not what I meant," he said flatly. "Your wounds are fine, though I feel the need to point out it was stupid of you to allow yourself to get hit in the first place."

"I didn't allow myself to do anything,' I snapped. "You weren't there."

He raised an eyebrow, giving me a maddeningly superior look. "You're very decisive, you know."

I glared at him. "What?"

"You make clear decisions. Like, you never even considered letting Lonnie walk out of the vault first. That makes my job easier, because you don't create ripples of alternative futures the way most do."

"Alright…why do I feel like that's not a compliment."

"It's neither a compliment nor an insult." He shrugged. "It just means that unlike Lonnie or Scion, I can actually tell you with almost perfect certainty what your future holds."

"Enlighten me then," I grumbled.

"Your reactions are getting slower, as evidenced by the fact that you couldn't avoid these arrows. You're not eating anything. You're fatigued and struggling to use basic magic."

"What makes you–" I started hotly.

"Why didn't you dissolve the arrows in thin air?" he asked. "Six months ago, this would not have happened. In six more months you'll be dead. Likely a lot sooner."

I heard him, but rather than taking it in, suddenly I was pissed.

Ambrose seemed not only to be as quick tempered and moody as his brother, but he also gave off the impression that he didn't care about anything except the greater good. For all Scion's faults, he cared. He cared too much about everyone and everything until he nearly drove himself insane. I wasn't sure what Ambrose cared about, but I doubted very much that it was us.

"You're a prick, you know that?" I barked at him. "Fuck man, work on your delivery. Do you always talk to people like they're stupid while telling them they're going to die?"

Ambrose raised an eyebrow. "Would you rather I ignore this as you've clearly been doing?"

"Maybe," I snapped. "It's none of your concern."

He pushed off the wall and came to strand directly in front of my bed. "Actually, it is because if you die, then we all die."

I gritted my teeth and sighed, suddenly feeling exhausted. "So it's the curse?"

He nodded. "When did this start?"

"Right before Lonnie left us in that inn a few weeks ago."

He nodded, as if he'd already known that—or at least guessed. "What happened to trigger it?"

"I don't know," I said angrily. A slight burn scalded my throat and I coughed, before correcting: "I don't know for certain."

"What do you suspect, then?"

"I was…happy," I said, pained. "I didn't think it would happen. I haven't completed the mate bond because I know that would be too much."

He cocked his head to the side curiously. "Evidently that's not the only danger."

"I've done nearly everything right," I burst out bitterly. "Scion sealed his fucking mate bond and didn't even know it. How is this different?"

"Scion is constantly haunted by the years he spent in Aftermath. He loves Lonnie, but views the actual mating as more of a duty to her and the country than a gift he never expected to get to have. I don't know if he'll ever be truly happy, but if so, I doubt it would be caused by the bonding alone."

"That makes no sense," I snapped. "We were always told we couldn't mate or it would kill all of us."

"We were always told we couldn't mate because it might make us happy," Ambrose corrected. "It seems to me that the completion of the bond isn't the barrier to your true happiness. You love Lonnie, and Scion is your only friend—practically a brother. You're happy when all three of you are safe."

I sighed, feeling defeated. "So I'm killing us."

"Yes," he replied. "I think so. I'd always imagined it would be more immediate, rather than a gradual thing, but I don't think there's any doubt as to why you've been so ill. You saw them when you were hurt. Once you die, they'll both follow soon after."

"And you." I looked up at him sharply. "This will affect you too."

"Yes," Ambrose sighed, "but fortunately I'm not all that worried about it."

I laughed hollowly. "Why? You don't seem suicidal to me."

He scowled. "I'm not worried because you're going to leave."

"Oh, is that right?" I said sardonically.

He didn't rise to the bait. "Yes. You started getting sick when you believed all three of you would travel together to Aftermath, but it stopped when Lonnie left you. In short, being unhappy without her kept you alive. You'll leave again to keep her safe."

I scowled. I would do anything to keep Lonnie safe, but what he was suggesting felt impossible. Like I might shatter if I left just as quickly as if I stayed.

"How long?" I asked.

He shrugged. "I can't say. Once you leave, it will become even more difficult for me to predict the immediate future. I can't see Lonnie or myself, and Scion is unpredictable. I don't think it will be long, though. A few months at most."

"It won't be long until what?" I said shrewdly.

"Until all this comes to an end," he replied cryptically. "One way or another."

I dragged frustrated hands through my hair. "What are you expecting me to do? Just go wait in Overcast? Have tea with my mother and brother while I wait for you all to possibly die?"

"No," Ambrose said. "You know that would be pointless."

"This all feels fucking pointless."

He stood up, his face finally twisting into an expression of annoyance. "Sometimes I forget how young you are."

"Don't fucking do that. I'm not a child."

"No, but you have no concept of patience. You think waiting a year or five is a long time. Try spending eighty years making plans. Thirty years living in fucking Aftermath. Ten years to see your mate. Then perhaps you wouldn't complain about waiting a few months to get everything you could possibly ever want. I'd tell you to stop feeling sorry for yourself, but if that keeps you alive longer than perhaps it's worth it. Regardless, I'm not going to sit here and listen to you complain."

He turned and marched toward the door.

"Wait!" I barked after him. "Then tell me what to do."

"I can't," he said, his voice growing quieter as he walked away. "If I tell you what to do it will change things. All I can say is that if I just became the ruler of an entire kingdom, I might deign to spend some time there. It could be useful down the line."

AN HOUR LATER, I DRAGGED MYSELF UPSTAIRS TO THE MAIN HOUSE.

Cross's townhouse sat above the entrance to the barracks as both a front for the guild and an actual home for Cross and any of his guests.

I pushed open the door of the bedroom I'd once shared with Lonnie, and found Scion sitting on the bed. His legs were straight and he was leaning against the headboard, reading the leatherbound book that we'd gotten from the healer in Cheapside. Next to him, Lonnie was lying on her side wrapped only in a towel, her wet hair fanning out around her. She was using his thigh as a pillow and breathing heavily, clearly fast asleep.

Scion looked up when I entered, his eyes widening. "What are you doing walking around?"

"I'm fine," I waved him off. My eyes darted toward Lonnie. "What's going on?"

"She took a bath, came out here, and immediately passed out. Exhausted from the last few days, I suppose." He narrowed his gaze, still watching me carefully. "Are you certain you're alright? You don't look fine."

"Yeah, well, that has nothing to do with the arrows."

I quickly reiterated everything Ambrose had said, and Scion listened in tense silence while Lonnie slept, blissfully unaware.

"So you're leaving," Scion said flatly. It was more of a statement than a question.

I nodded.

Ambrose had been right. I'd won the throne of Underneath—my father's throne—then promptly left. The Unseelie kingdom was likely in disarray, and it was up to me to go control things. I couldn't help but remember how right it had felt to be there—how natural. Like home.

Scion started to rise, jostling Lonnie. I put out a hand. "No, don't wake her.'

"She'll be livid if you don't say goodbye."

I winced. "I know, but if I do I'm not sure I'll be able to leave."

He didn't look happy about that, but didn't comment on it. I supposed he knew what I was thinking, given that he'd done the same thing when we were planning to leave for Aftermath.

I moved back toward the door. "Tell her I love her."

"She knows that."

"Fine, then tell her I'm sorry, and I'm only doing this to keep her safe."

Scion raised an eyebrow. "She won't like that either."

I grinned. No, Lonnie probably wouldn't like to hear that but it didn't make it any less true. She was my entire damn world, and I'd do anything to protect her. Even if it meant I never saw her again.

22
LONNIE
THE CUTTHROAT DISTRICT, INBETWIXT

I woke up alone.

It took a long moment for me to realize where I was. Or, somewhat more importantly, why I wore nothing but a damp towel. Then, it all came rushing back to me–the vault, Bael's injuries, the blood and terror. It all felt a bit like a dream. Like one of those overly vivid nightmares that I used to have often, but which lately had not plagued me.

I knew it hadn't been, though. It wasn't a dream, and yet I glanced down at my wrists for confirmation.

I blinked in surprise when I beheld the smooth, unmarked skin.

I hadn't taken any blood from anyone else to heal myself, and usually I healed at the same rate as any other human. How odd.

On a hunch, I got up from the bed and walked directly over to the bathing room. I dropped my towel to the floor and stood naked in front of the long mirror, inspecting myself.

My skin looked entirely too smooth. Undamaged and unsecured by the many years of injuries I'd sustained as a servant and even afterward. I reached up and pressed my fingers into the point on my shoulder where a crossbow bolt had pierced me, and found no mark of it. I turned around, looking over my shoulder at my back. Once, there had been a jagged mark there from where the obsidian crown had cut into my spine. Now, of course, there was nothing. The only scar that remained was the imprint of Scion's teeth on my throat, which stood out pink and raw, as if it had only just healed recently.

I supposed with all the magic I was using, my body was responding.

Distantly, I recalled Lady Thalia saying something about this. She'd commented that it was lucky that my scars were fading so completely, but I hadn't thought about it much. Or indeed, bothered to check very carefully.

Suddenly, a wild thought struck me and I pushed my hair back from my face to inspect my ears.

I let out a sigh of relief when I found them unchanged. One, still round and human and the other jagged at the edge. Once, the large scar on my ear had been my greatest Source of insecurity, but now I hardly ever thought about it. The scar itself had disappeared like all the others. Though, I supposed, magic couldn't replace the missing flesh that had been torn off the top.

I glanced up at myself again, almost surprised to find that I was smiling.

This likely also meant that Bael would have no scars from the incident yesterday. In time, it would be as if it had never happened.

Cheered by that thought, I splashed some water on my face and went in search of something to wear.

For the last day or so, I'd had nothing to wear but the gown I'd had on when we escaped from the mob at the would-be coronation. I'd torn the skirt off to make it easier to move, but now I couldn't bear the thought of putting it back on. Not only was it filthy and bloodstained, it was damn uncomfortable.

After discovering that there was nothing in the bedroom, not even a robe, I wrapped myself in my towel once more. I opened the door slowly and poked my head out into the familiar hallway, listening.

There wasn't a single sound.

Of course, I hadn't really expected that there would be. We were the only people here, and I'd already gathered that Scion must have returned to the den to check on Bael. Still, I practically ran down the hall, nervous that someone might come upon me lurking the hallways in a towel.

I stopped in front of the first door on the right and poked my head inside. It was a store room, very like the one where Bael and I used to practice shadow walking. Not bothering to linger, I shut the door and moved on down the hall. I was sure there would be a dresser with clothes in it somewhere. This was Cross's primary residence, was it not? He must have other rooms for his guests, or perhaps a closet where Siobhan might keep extra garments.

Finally, my search paid off. I threw open the last door along the hall and found myself standing in a lavish bedchamber. It was much larger than the room I typically slept in, and to my relief there were two long dressers pushed against the wall facing the bed. I tiptoed quickly across the floor and threw open the top drawer. Immediately, I recognized the deep purple and red fabrics folded on top.

"Perfect," I muttered aloud, though no one was there to hear me.

Back when we'd first visited Inbetwixt, Scion had bought me enough clothing to outfit me for possibly the rest of my life. I'd hardly gotten to wear any of it, though, before we'd had to leave everything at the thieves' den and return to the castle.

I'd hoped that somewhere Cross had kept it all, and it seemed my hope was not misplaced.

I reached into the drawer pulling out a large stack of garments all in warm red and purple hues. Before I could go through everything carefully, a sudden rap on the window made me jump and look up.

My gaze scanned the room nervously as the tapping sounded again. I narrowed my eyes at the window, and crossed the room to fling open the heavy red drapes.

Sun steamed through the enormous window, illuminating the entire room. Outside, the city was awake and I could see people passing by below, some stopping to talk while others hurried by carrying shopping bags. Directly in front of me, Quill was flapping his enormous wings, hovering outside the window and tapping on the glass.

My eyes widening in surprise, I reached up and unlatched the window, throwing it open so that Quill could flutter inside.

"What are you doing here?" I hissed.

The bird swooped once around my head and landed on the bed. He narrowed his eyes at me, giving me a look that clearly seemed to say *"Where else would I be?"*

"I just assumed you were in the capital?" I told the bird.

"Assumed wrong, then, didn't you? Foolish child."

Indeed, Quill had not come with us to Cheapside, nor to Inbetwixt. I knew the bird didn't like Inbetwixt because the underground thieves' den made him nervous. Therefore, I'd assumed Scion had ordered the bird to watch the capital and report back to him in that strange unclear way in which they communicated.

"Well what is it?" I asked, wrapping my towel more firmly around me.

Quill hopped toward me, and I gasped when I spotted the purple ribbon tied to his front leg. I bent to inspect it and found that it wasn't a ribbon at all, but a tiny strip of my ruined dress. The fabric was holding a tiny piece of parchment to the bird's leg.

My eyes wide, I gently untied the fabric, having absolutely no idea what to think. I took the little scroll of paper and spread it out on the floor in front of me.

Little Monster,

I don't trust Scion to actually tell you why I had to leave, and maybe I'm not the only one because this damned bird wouldn't leave me alone until I wrote you this note.

I love you too fucking much and it's killing me. I told you back in the castle that if somehow my presence was hurting you, I wouldn't hesitate to walk away. Now I have to go if there's ever going to be a real chance for us to be happy.

I'm sorry. I promise we'll see each other again. You know I'll always find you.

He hadn't signed it, but he didn't have to. I would have recognized Bael's tone anywhere, even in writing.

"Where is he?" I demanded of the bird. "Where did you get this?"

For once, the bird only stared back at me–just a bird and nothing more.

Frustrated, I flopped back down on my ass and moved to lean my back against the dresser, my head on my knees. I supposed I couldn't say I was surprised.

Sad? Yes.

Angry that he hadn't said goodbye? Yes.

Worried? Absolutely.

But I was not surprised.

Something had been evidently wrong with Bael for some time now. He clearly hadn't wanted to discuss it, and perhaps I didn't either. Discussing it would have forced us to confront what I'd already long suspected. I was killing him, slowly, a little more everyday.

I'd known that was the case way back in that inn before I'd ever met Ambrose, and then it had been me who had to leave.

But even knowing that, I'd allowed myself to be happy. For these last two months, it was the first time I could remember being truly happy. Maybe not every moment, and certainly not when my mother died, but overall…this was the first time in my life that I'd known exactly where I was supposed to be and what I was doing. I wasn't afraid of where my next meal would come from, or that I might be attacked at any second. I wasn't being tormented by cruel court politics, or running for my life every other day.

I suddenly had a castle to live in, tasks to keep me busy, and two mates who clearly loved me. Things had been boring in a way that I desperately craved. And I couldn't bring myself to ruin it. I couldn't leave again, and I could ask too many questions of Bael in case he left instead.

Now, I supposed, it didn't matter. It had happened anyway. Bael was gone, I was running for my life again, and nothing was safe or comfortable or boring.

I didn't realize I was crying until I felt the tears dripping down my chin and onto my neck, and by then it was too late. I couldn't force myself to stop.

"Lonnie?"

I heard my name called down the hall, and shut my eyes. I recognized Ambrose's voice immediately, and wished I hadn't.

"I'm fine," I called back, my voice trembling and obviously distressed. "I'll come out in a minute."

Of course, he didn't listen.

I'd left the door open, and within seconds Ambrose appeared on the threshold looking a bit frantic.

Like all of us, he was still wearing his outfit from the coronation, although he'd abandoned his blue silk jacket at some point and now wore only the matching silk trousers and a white shirt with the sleeves rolled up to expose his tattoos. His long silver hair was no longer loose and shiny, but pulled back in a haphazard braid.

For a moment, he didn't seem to see me sitting on the floor. He turned his head to the right, finally and spotted me on the floor. I watched his face change too quickly to understand every emotion there. Watched his eyes dart over me wrapped only in a towel and widen just a fraction before he frowned with concern. Darting over, he bent down and knelt in front of me. "What's wrong, love?"

My chest shook, making it impossible to get the words out and instead I nudged Bael's letter toward him with my foot. He glanced at it, his eyes moving quickly, reading it far faster than I had.

"I'm sorry," he said after a moment.

I sniffed, getting my breathing under control, and finally looked up at him. "Why are you sorry?"

"Because I told him to go." He furrowed his brow, looking almost angry with himself.

"You did?"

He nodded. "I wasn't kind about it, either. Bael probably despises me now, but it had to be like that. He needed to leave, or I'm sure he wouldn't have lived another week."

I blinked at him, imagining that conversation. Picturing him being the sort of asshole that everyone expected him to be, all in service of the greater good.

It was probably always like that for him. Always having to play a role. Never able to get close to people because he knew exactly how it would end. He must have lived a very lonely life.

Without thinking or planning to do it. Without considering his reaction, and certainly without remembering I wore nothing but a towel, I surged forward and wrapped my arms around his neck. Ambrose went completely stiff, as if I were hugging solid stone, but I didn't care.

"Thank you," I muttered into his shoulder. "Thank you for doing that for me."

He just sat there for a long second, neither pushing me away nor raising his arms to hug me back.

With my face pressed into his chest I could hear his heart beating, and noticed when it sped up though he didn't say or do anything to make that reaction make sense. I pulled back slightly and stared at him.

He was looking at me with a kind of intense fire in his coal-black eyes. A hunger that nearly took my breath away, as well as an uncertainty that held me at arms reach. Like he wasn't sure if he was allowed to touch me like this. Or maybe, more accurately, like he wasn't sure what might happen to us if he did.

Remembering my promise to myself down in the vaults, I pushed up onto my knees. Like this, both kneeling, we were closer in height than we would have been on foot. I didn't have to stretch to reach him, or tilt my head all the way back to meet his eyes.

I inched closer until our faces were so close we were breathing the same air.

Ambrose had to know what was going through my head. He could have leaned forward and closed the small distance between our lips, but he didn't. Instead, he studied my face the same way I was studying his, and seemed to hold his breath, waiting.

I closed the last of that distance and kissed him, softly at first. Tentatively.

Ambrose didn't move, just sitting there frozen. There was only the memory of our last kiss, and the frantic sound of his heart that made me think he might want this. Want me.

When he continued to just sit there, I began to pull back, but then his hand shot out to stop me. He cradled the back of my head, tugging me closer and balling his fist into my hair.

A shiver of pleasure ran through my body when he parted my lips with his tongue. I opened for him, gasping into his mouth.

His hand stayed in my hair while the other gripped my waist, tugging me closer until I could feel every muscle of his sculpted chest pressed against me.

I wriggled impossibly closer, digging my own fingers into his hair and pulling, holding him against me. I felt my towel slipping down until it pooled around my waist.

In response, Ambrose growled low in his throat, and bit down on my lip until I tasted blood. He fell backwards out of his kneeling position so he was sitting on the floor, and dragged me with him.

His hands moved to my waist, lifting me until my knees landed on either side of his, straddling his lap. I pressed down, feeling him hard beneath me. The contact pulled a gasp from me and a growl from deep in his throat. He gripped me harder, his fingers digging into the bare flesh of my sides so hard I was sure I'd have bruises in the shape of his fingers.

I felt wild and alive, like I was burning up from the inside out.

Suddenly with a panicked jolt, I jerked my head back and looked around the room.

Ambrose blinked at me, as if dazed. "What are you doing?"

"Checking that I haven't set the room on fire." I muttered distractedly. "It's happened before."

His eyes widened at me, and then he laughed. A real laugh, that lit up his entire face making him even more handsome than he already was.

I glanced back down at us, a slight heat rising to my cheeks. I hadn't planned to do this. Hadn't meant for the kiss to go so far, but still, I wasn't bothered. I wanted more, to go further and to find out what it would feel like to have all that intensity focused entirely on my body.

But maybe now wasn't the time.

I could only imagine what Scion would do if he came up here looking for us. For some reason, I didn't feel as if I were betraying anyone. Still, I needed to talk to him before I said or did anything else.

As if thinking the same thing, or perhaps guessing where my mind had gone, Ambrose lifted me gently off his lap and stood up. "Come on," he said, as casually as if nothing had happened. "Get dressed. There's food down in the den, and I'm sure you're hungry."

I was hungry, actually, and I nodded slowly as I too got to my feet.

Ambrose reached out and dragged the pad of his thumb across my bottom lip where he'd bitten me, wiping away the drop of blood pooling in the center. A jolt of heat traveled through me, throbbing low in my stomach. As if he knew what I was feeling, his eyes danced with laughter.

Still looking directly at me, Ambrose brought his thumb to his mouth and sucked. "You taste fucking delicious, love. I can hardly wait to taste the rest of you."

23
LONNIE
THE CUTTHROAT DISTRICT, INBETWIXT

Nearly an hour later, I strode back into the den.

The smell of roasting meat and vegetables greeted me, and my stomach growled loudly as I approached the bar area. I hadn't even realized how hungry I was, what with my adrenaline running so high for the last day or so, but now I realized that my stomach felt as if it might cannibalize itself.

I was surprised to find both Scion and Ambrose sitting together at the bar. Each had a plate of food in front of him, and there was a third plate to Scion's right, presumably for me. They weren't talking to each other, but neither were they fighting–a vast improvement overall.

As I approached both males turned to look at me. Ambrose didn't react, leaving no indication that anything had happened between us upstairs, but Scion got to his feet to greet me.

I kissed him softly before drawing back and glaring at him with a sort of mock anger. "You abandoned me this morning."

He looked affronted. "I did nothing of the sort. I went to find us something to eat."

"Oh?" I raised my eyebrows. "I had no idea you could cook."

"He can't," Ambrose said over his shoulder, a note of humor in his voice. "Ask him how long he spent staring at these vegetables, practically praying for them to roast themselves."

"I don't have to ask." I laughed. "I've seen it before."

"If you're referring to that inn on the coast, that's unfair," Scion interjected defensively.

I was indeed referring to the several days we'd spent, jumping from seaside village to seaside village, in the days after Ambrose's army had taken the capital. I'd quickly learned that not a single one of the Everlasts had ever prepared their own food. Even Scion, who had spent many years in the army living far less luxuriously than while in the palace, struggled to concoct anything edible.

I crossed the room and perched on the edge of the table nearest the bar. "How is it unfair?'

"We were injured."

I grinned at him. "Your pride was injured, perhaps. If Iola and I hadn't been there you all would have starved."

"Untrue." He looked down. "We literally couldn't starve if we tried."

I opened my mouth to needle him again, but stopped. His words had jogged something in the back of my mind, raising a question. "Do you think I could starve to death? Or would that not be possible."

Scion shrugged. "I don't know. Why?"

"I've just thought, maybe that's part of why I survived the dungeon for so long when no other human could. I was starving, but maybe that couldn't kill me."

Scion didn't answer. He scowled, looking angry. I knew he wasn't angry with me for bringing it up, rather with himself. I reached out almost unconsciously and ran my fingers through his black hair.

"You may be right," Ambrose said thoughtfully, as he strode out from behind the bar carrying a plate of roast sausages and diced vegetables. "I'd rather not test it, though."

I smiled at him, and reached immediately for the plate. "This smells wonderful. I assume you made it?

"Yes," he replied. "It took me several years in Aftermath, but I eventually grasped the concept. There wasn't much food in the storage cellar. I wonder if they cleared most everything out before leaving."

Scion looked grateful for the change of subject. "I still want to know where they went."

"As do I," Ambrose replied darkly. "I'm not used to being so ignorant of other's movements."

Scion looked for a moment as if he might reply, but swallowed it, seeming to decide it wasn't worth needling his brother. I relaxed, grateful that for once they were—if not getting along, at least ignoring each other. That was about as much as I could hope for at the moment.

After we'd all eaten, the three of us sat around the table, passing the jewel of Inbetwixt between us and inspecting it. I held the ruby up to the light and looked carefully into its crimson depths, thinking hard.

"It really does seem to be just a gem," I said, finally.

"I think it is," Ambrose replied, taking it from me as I passed it to him. "The power isn't in the gem itself, but in the curse that Aisling placed on it and all the other parts of the crown."

"That the Source placed, you mean," I corrected. "She didn't have that magic herself, she bargained for it."

Ambrose waved me off. "Whichever."

I pressed my lips flatly together. Maybe it didn't matter, as he seemed to believe, but I couldn't escape the nagging feeling that there was something important in how the curse had come to be. Regardless, it wasn't anything I hadn't thought about before, and we had more pressing things to focus on.

"I think we should leave to look for the next gem as soon as possible," I said.

"Agreed," Scion said. "There's no reason to wait around here, especially with Cross missing."

"Where to next though," Ambrose asked. "Overcast?"

"I assumed so." I looked at Scion. "The rest of your family is there, wouldn't they be able to help?"

"...Yes," Scion said, after a long pause. "They could if they wanted to."

"But?" I asked, resigned.

Scion glanced at Ambrose. "But, they may not be so willing to help."

"That's foolish," Ambrose snapped. "This affects them just as much as the rest of us."

"Sure," Scion said acidy. "But do you want to try and explain that to Raewyn?"

Ambrose let out a sudden bark of laughter that made me jump. "Once, I asked Raewyn for help interpreting a vision."

Scion blanched, looking at him with incredulity. "Why?"

Ambrose's grin widened. "I was barely more than five, I hadn't yet realized what she's like."

"What happened?" I asked, glancing between them.

"She lectured me on the meaning of moon cycles for over an hour, before forgetting what we were talking about at all and leaving to play croquet. Raewyn isn't malicious she's just–"

"Stupid?" Scion suggested.

"I wouldn't say that either," Ambrose said thoughtfully. "Self-absorbed feels more accurate. She cares only for herself and her own ambitions."

"In my opinion, we should go to Nevermore next," Ambrose said.

"Do you say that because you know something, or is it just a feeling?"

"Both," Ambrose said. "I think that while the family might be reluctant to help overtly, they will defend the castle if Idris decides to storm it."

"Is that likely?" I asked, aghast.

"It's not impossible," he answered vaguely. "As of this moment, I don't believe Idris knows where we are or what we're trying to do. He's arrogant enough to just assume we've given up and gone into hiding somewhere. He also believes he's done a much better job influencing us than he really has."

"What do you mean?"

"I believe you were right. He said something to me during our first meeting that made me ignore obvious signs. Now that I've realized that, however, his influence has weakened significantly."

"It was like that with Penvalle," Scion interjected. "As a child he could influence me to an extent, but once I grew older and realized what his power was, it didn't work anymore. The entire court was aware of his talent, and therefore mostly immune. That's why he focused on human servants. I think we should send a message to Gwydion in Overcast warning the family. If they know Idris has the power of persuasion, they won't fall victim to it if he contacts them."

"That's a good idea," I agreed.

"I'd send the message to someone other than Gwydion, though," Ambrose said.

"Why?"

"Because Gwydion is exactly like his mother, though he hides it somewhat better. If it doesn't affect him directly, he won't care enough to remember. Why don't you send it to our mother instead?"

Scion raised an eyebrow. "Mother doesn't talk. How is she supposed to warn anyone?"

"I think the threat of more persuasion magic might give her enough incentive to tell someone. Trust me on this. Send it to mother."

Scion watched Ambrose for a long moment, then shrugged. "Fine."

"So we'll go to Nevermore first, then?" I asked.

"I think so," Ambrose said. "The Nevermore diamond is likely to be the most difficult to get, despite the fact that I know exactly where it is."

Scion looked sideways at his brother. "When was the last time you traveled too Nevermore?"

"Oh..." Ambrose suddenly looked deeply uncomfortable, and dragged a nervous hand through his hair. "Nearly forty years ago now."

Scion smirked. "That should make this an exciting reunion."

I glanced between them. "What are you two talking about?"

"We have a history with the court there, that's all," Ambrose said vaguely.

"We don't," Scion corrected, looking happier than he had all morning. "You do."

"Shut the fuck up," Ambrose growled, though with little real anger behind his voice.

"Well, I'm not looking forward to going either," I said, sulkily.

"Why not, love?"

"They speak the old tongue there. I won't understand a single word spoken, you will have to translate for me."

Scion frowned, but reached out to squeeze my hand under the table. "That will be no problem, rebel. I wasn't planning to leave you alone anyway."

I nodded, though I hardly felt better. Scion might be planning to stay with me, but lately, nothing had gone according to plan.

* * *

The closest I'd ever been to the winter island of Nevermore was when we sailed along the coast on the way to Underneath. Therefore, I had to be guided through the shadows.

If I was honest, I didn't think I'd be able to shadow walk that far anyway. It was a long distance, even for Scion, so it was agreed that Ambrose would take me and Scion would travel on his own. Having already proved he could shadow walk with three additional people in tow, I was sure Ambrose would have no trouble.

We collected the few things we'd brought with us–namely the book, the jewel, and the pocket full of gold that I'd stolen from the vault. Scion found some of Cross's clothes, so he and Ambrose could finally change out of their torn and bloody former finery. Ambrose unearthed a sword from one of the many store rooms, and packed a few days' worth of food into a bag.

And we were off.

Scion left first, walking directly into thin air and disappearing leaving not a single shadow behind.

Ambrose grabbed my arm. "Are you ready?"

I nodded, and let him tug me forward into the darkness.

For a moment we spun. The dark air pressed in on me from all sides, and I felt like I was being stretched and squeezed at the same time. Then, seemingly far too quickly, I tumbled out into the weak sunshine.

The first thing I noticed was the cold.

The chill wind whipped at my face, causing goosebumps to form on my skin. I inhaled deeply, taking in the salty scent of the ocean mixed with the earthy smell of pine trees, and opened my eyes.

I was kneeling on the ground on some kind of desolate beach, surrounded by jagged rockets, broken shells, and clumps of black seaweed. To my right, the dark ocean stretched out endlessly, disappearing on the bright horizon. To my left, there was a hill of dunes and scraggly bare trees, and behind that a wall of tall pine trees so dark I couldn't make out a thing between the branches.

I located Ambrose. He hadn't stumbled, and stood to my right facing the ocean, holding his hair back from his face with both hands as the wind whipped at it.

I stood as well, and turned around, staring back down the beach behind me. The sand seemed to go on forever, and there wasn't a single building or being in sight.

"Where are we?" I asked.

And where was Scion?

Ambrose turned around to face me, a half-guilty, half-annoyed look crossing his face. His brows furrowed and for a moment he didn't answer me. He brought his hand up to his face, shielding his eyes from the sun reflecting off the water.

He dropped his hands back to his sides. "Well, this *is* Nevermore."

An uneasy feeling settled in the pit of my stomach. "Right…"

"…Unfortunately I have no idea where on the island we are. It's been a long time since I traveled here. I might have miscalculated."

I bit back a sigh. I really couldn't complain—shadow walking wasn't an exact art, and many factors affected where one could travel. For example, you could only move between places you had traveled to before, and had to have some general understanding of the distance between two points. Those with more magical ability could travel longer distances, while the average Fae could only shadow walk a few miles at a time.

"It can't be that far to the city," I said, trying to remain hopeful.

Ambrose's eyebrows pulled even lower over his dark eyes. "Actually, it can. Nevermore is huge. Much larger than it looks on most maps, and a lot of it is mountains which are nearly impassable, even for me. Still, I'm less concerned about the distance as the time. It gets dark extremely early here and we don't want to be wandering around overnight."

"Why not?"

"Mostly because I'm not sure how much cold you can withstand before your human half succumbs to hypothermia, but there are also a great deal of monstrous creatures roaming the island. Species that don't live on the mainland."

"Like what?" I asked

As if on cue, a piercing cry filled the air. It sounded like a mix between an eagle and a banshee, and made the hair on the back of my neck stand up. I spun around, looking up at the sky and my heart leapt into my throat.

A massive bird soared directly above me, its wingspan stretching out almost as wide as the street itself.

No, wait.

The creature swooped lower and I saw clearly that it wasn't a bird at all. It was a monstrous looking woman with great bat-like wings protruding from her back. Feathers covered her neck and climbed down her arms, which ended in sharp talons.

Ambrose yelled beside me, and reached for my arm, yanking me nearly off my feet. His cry jerked me from my trance.

"What is that?" I demanded.

"That is one of those monsters I'd rather avoid," he ground out, dragging me forcibly down the beach. "We need to run!"

24
LONNIE
THE SOUTHERN COAST OF NEVERMORE

But I couldn't run.

My feet had stopped working, all my attention completely fixated on the monstrous woman. I gaped up at her, completely frozen to the spot.

Ambrose stopped trying to drag me behind him, and instead picked me up, throwing me over his shoulder like a sack of flour.

For once, I didn't protest.

Not because I was thrilled by being dragged around and carried, but because I couldn't seem to think of anything at all. That screeching wail of the creature was starting to sound enticing. Like music, heady and hypnotic. Begging me to come closer. To come swimming…

We ascended the hill of dry dunes, and darted into the trees. Immediately, the temperature dropped, and it seemed like the sun had been shut out. The needles of the pines were so thick, it could have been night and I would never have realized.

Ambrose dropped me back on my feet. He gripped my shoulders, and bent close to my face, forcing me to look at him. "Listen to me. Don't move. Just stay right there and don't move a fucking inch."

I only stared back at him, my brain feeling a bit fuzzy.

"What the fuck am I doing?" he cursed under his breath. "...completely pointless."

Then another wail pierced through the forest. Instinctively, I stepped forward and Ambrose shoved me back, hard.

A split second later, the colossal bird-like creature swooped low over our heads, diving between the trees.

Its powerful wings beating against the air as it aimed straight for me. Its beady eyes locked onto mine, its sharp talons extended and glinting in the sunlight. I could feel the rush of wind as it swooped closer and closer, until its claws grazed my shoulder, leaving behind deep gashes that seared with pain.

With a swift and practiced movement, Ambrose drew his sword from its sheath and swung it with all his might. The blade sliced through the creature's neck, severing its head in one clean motion. Blood spurted out of the wound, splattering onto the ground and staining Ambrose's clothes. He stood there, panting and covered in gore, his eyes tracing over me.

"Are you hurt?" he demanded, urgently.

I was, my shoulder was throbbing and I could feel blood running down my arm and chest. Though, that didn't bother me nearly as much as it should. The pain seemed to have jogged something in my mind, and I reached up tugging at my ears. "What the fuck was that?"

Ambrose looked relieved. "A siren," he said on an exhale. "Come on, we need to keep moving. Sirens live in flocks, and seeing one means there are three dozen more nearby. Keep running, I don't want to have to fight off all of them."

This time, I got up and sprinted alongside him into the dark woods.

"I thought sirens were supposed to be beautiful." I panted.

Ambrose chuckled hollowly. "They are, unless you threaten them. We must have landed near a nest."

It was all too familiar to run through the forest like this, with no light and no idea where we were going, sure the entire time that some great beast would descend on us and attack.

My heart raced as I pushed through the dense foliage, my feet pounding against the forest floor stumbling over rocks and slippery fallen needles. At least I wasn't alone. I could hear Ambrose's heavy breathing behind me the entire time, and knowing he'd kill anything that came at me kept me from constantly looking over my shoulder.

Finally, the deafening sirens faded into the distance.

Still, Ambrose didn't tell me to stop. I kept running, until the trees ahead seemed to thin. We burst out of the trees and onto a deserted dirt road, leading to the Source only knew where.

"That's far enough," Ambrose panted.

At his words, my legs buckled under me. All my exhaustion hit me at once and the adrenaline fled. The pain in my shoulder seemed to triple and I collapsed onto the cold ground, gasping for breath.

"Let me see your arm," Ambrose commanded, already reaching for my torn jacket.

I let him pull at the fabric and inspect the gashes on my shoulder. I was too tired to protest even if I'd wanted to.

"Why didn't the sirens affect you?" I asked through gritted teeth. "I kept thinking I needed to follow them."

"I've spent years training my mind's defenses," he said shortly, drawing back from me. "These wounds are shallow, and their claws aren't venomous or anything. You'll be fine…"

There was something in his tone that made me look up at him. "What is it?"

He ran a hand over the back of his neck. "I could heal it for you, but I don't have to. It's up to you."

My eyes widened with understanding. He was asking if I wanted blood.

Suddenly, I wasn't sure. I'd never been offered the choice before. My injuries had always been far too severe to even talk about alternate methods of healing. "I thought it was frowned upon to share blood with anyone other than your mate."

"I don't really care what's frowned upon."

True, I remembered. He'd even given blood to Bael only yesterday–something I still meant to ask him about. I supposed this would be the best moment if I was going to get answers about that.

"Fine," I said rashly. "I mean, yes. Please heal me."

Looking slightly surprised, Ambrose nevertheless dropped his bag and his sword on the ground and unbuckled the empty sword-sheath from around his waist–presumably so he could sit down without it getting in the way. Then, he sat down on the ground beside me and held out his hand in front of my face.

I stared at his hand blankly for a full ten seconds, nearly going cross-eyed, before I realized what was happening. He wasn't going to bite his own arm and just hold it to my mouth. No, he was expecting me to actually bite him.

This had never happened before.

A heat crept up the back of my neck, equally uncomfortable as it was intriguing.

I'd bitten Scion before, but that was different. And, in fairness, we'd always had sex either during or directly after. A casual bite felt wrong. Dirty somehow, and also deeply impersonal.

I'd gotten used to treating this sort of blood sharing as separate from anything intimate. It was like being fed medicine by a healer, except now that veil had been violently yanked away.

I might as well have crawled into his lap and bitten his throat for all the difference it made.

"Well?" Ambrose asked, looking slightly confused. "Are you waiting for something?"

Yes! I screamed in my head. I was waiting for one of us to do something rational and decide this was a terrible idea.

Instead, though, I took his hand in mine and pulled his arm closer to my mouth.

Immediately I realized how ridiculous this position was. I couldn't easily bite his wrist at this angle, and especially not if he wasn't going to make it any easier for me by shifting closer or turning his arm.

"Nevermind," I blurted out, dropping his hand. "I don't need it fixed that badly. I'll be fine."

"Suit yourself," he pushed back up off the ground, and walked over to retrieve his bag. I thought he sounded slightly relieved.

Nonplussed, I made to get up as well, pushing myself up on my palm before I'd thought through the consequences. I let out an involuntary sound of pain, somewhere between a scream and a groan, as agony shot up my arm and into my shoulder.

Instantly, Ambrose was back on the ground in front of me. This time he was far closer, leaning over me, as if checking for new injuries.

Without my meaning to, my eyes darted to his tattooed throat. In my mind's eye, I could see myself sinking my teeth into the point just above his collarbone where his neck met his shoulder. I could practically taste it, that rush of power and magic and desire all at once.

My heart beat once, twice, a third time in my ears and neither of us moved. His dark gaze bore into me, like he was daring me to act on every insane impulse that I hardly even recognized as my own. These ideas that felt both instinctual and like someone else's thoughts projected into my mind.

Distantly, I became aware that this had nothing to do with my shoulder anymore.

The sound of clopping hooves against the road and the distant jingling of bells pulled me back to myself. I looked up, past Ambrose's shoulder, and could make out a dark shape in the middle of the road coming toward us faster than any horse I'd ever seen.

Ambrose looked over his shoulder and swore loudly. "Fuck me."

"What is it?" I asked, nonplussed.

"I'm hoping it's just a servant," he said darkly.

"A servant to whom?"

Instead of answering, he got up and reached down, pulling me to my feet by my uninjured arm. I squinted into the growing darkness, and could finally make out a carriage being pulled toward us by two enormous white reindeer. I blinked in surprise, but there wasn't time to ask any questions.

The carriage drew steadily nearer to us, then stopped directly in the center of the road in front of us. The driver shouted something to the deer–a command which had to mean "Stop" or "Wait" just by the context, but which I couldn't actually understand.

Then, a figure in a heavy maroon coat that reached all the way to the ground climbed down out of the carriage. They walked toward us, and pushed back a wide, white fur trimmed hood.

My first thought was that I didn't recognize this woman at all.

My second thought was that she was far too lovely to be staring at Ambrose like she knew him…*well.*

She was clearly Fae, and had long chestnut brown hair and enormous honey brown eyes. Her face was slightly round, and her cheeks were bright pink from the cold. She walked up to us, looked at me for half a second, then smiled at Ambrose.

He swore again.

25
AMBROSE
THE SOUTHERN COAST OF NEVERMORE

"Fuck!" I swore loudly.

Cassinda laughed, and the sound made me stiffen. It was like glass shattering or a distant scream and knowing instinctively that something was about to go very wrong very quickly.

"Aren't you happy to see me?" Cassinda asked, in a tone that implied she knew the answer already.

"Not really." There was no point in lying. We both knew this was not about to be anything close to a happy reunion.

Oddly, Cassinda laughed again. "I would have thought you'd at least be grateful to get a ride back into the city. We've been out looking for you for over an hour."

My face twisted in confusion. "You have? Why?"

"Your brother arrived earlier. He's very handsome, and so polite too."

I laughed. Scion was anything but polite, but he'd undoubtedly realized it would be foolish to offend the ruling family of Nevermore so soon. Especially when we were so likely to offend them later, anyway.

"Scion would destroy you," I snapped at her. "Anyway, he's mated. Leave him alone."

She raised an eyebrow. "Yes, so he told me. It was the strangest story. Apparently, you were all supposed to arrive together but somehow you ended up way out here with your brother's mate. I'd say I was surprised, but I know you too well."

"You don't know anything about me," I ground out.

She smiled, and it didn't reach her eyes.

"Excuse me," Lonnie snapped angrily. "What the fuck is going on?"

I looked down at her, and only just then realized we'd been speaking the old tongue the entire time Cassinda had been standing here. *Shit.*

"I'm sorry, love," I said in the dialect of the mainland. "I forgot."

"Clearly," she replied dryly, still looking annoyed. "What's going on? Who is she?"

I bit back a groan. I didn't want Lonnie anywhere near Cassinda for numerous reasons, but I couldn't think of any way around it.

"This is the Lord of Nevermore's oldest daughter," I told Lonnie, trying to sound as impersonal as possible. "Scion reached the keep and sent everyone out looking for us. She's offering to take us back to the city."

Lonnie's eyes narrowed. "What were you two talking about?"

I ran both my hands through my hair, biting back the urge to let out another string of profanities.

Cassinda seemed to take my pause as her opening. "Hello," she said to Lonnie, in heavily accented common tongue. "Welcome! Is cold, yes? You come to castle now?"

I shot Cassinda a venomous glare, and continued to stare her down as I bent to speak to Lonnie. "Don't fall for this shit. She speaks the common language just fine."

Cassinda glared back at me for half a second, before she grinned. "He's right," she said to Lonnie. Her accent was still heavy, but the words were sharper and more confident. "I learned it many years ago when I believed I'd be going to live on the mainland."

"Why were you moving to the mainland?" Lonnie asked as she climbed into the back of the open carriage.

"Well, when I was going to be the queen, of course," she replied, her tone sickly sweet. "Didn't you know? He ran away to Aftermath to become some sort of radical only two months before our wedding."

Lonnie stopped, and looked over her shoulder at me. Her expression was a mixture of shock and anger. "You were going to marry this woman?"

I closed my eyes, and drew in a deep breath through my nose. This could not be fucking happening. "Unfortunately," I growled out, finally.

Cassinda scoffed as she climbed into the front of the carriage and took up the reins. "Come!" she said to Lonnie brightly. "I'll tell you about it on the way back to the keep."

"I can't wait," Lonnie replied bitterly.

* * *

I gnashed my teeth as we trundled up the dark road toward the keep.

The sun had set, and the temperature was steadily dropping by the second. Beside me, Lonnie was shivering so hard her teeth clacked together, but I didn't dare reach out for her. At the moment, I thought she might hit me if I tried.

On the bench seat in front of us, Cassinda kept up a steady stream of chatter. She mostly spoke in old tongue, seeming to realize it annoyed Lonnie, but every so often she would throw in a phrase in the common language just to needle her further.

I kept having to resist the urge to strangle her.

I was well aware that part of my rage at Cassinda had nothing to do with her and everything to do with what she'd interrupted.

In fairness, my mood had been erratic today, anyway. I'd barely been in control of myself since nearly the moment I woke up in the barracks.

I'd known the moment Bael left for Underneath because his future changed, becoming far more clear. I was grateful for even that much foresight. Bael's current trajectory implied this all might be over in a matter of weeks rather than months.

I had a strange sense of anticipation. I'd been working toward this moment for decades, and while it could easily end in my death I was still anxious to get to the end.

When Scion had come down to the den in search of breakfast, I promptly went upstairs to the townhouse. I was sick of arguing with him. It was difficult to maintain the animosity when I didn't hate him nearly as much as he hated me. I didn't hate him at all, actually.

After the conversation we'd had about Lonnie, I thought things might improve. And they had, for a short period of time, but now the tension was thick in the air once more. I knew he resented me for not being more helpful, directing our every move as Grandmother once did. I resented myself just as much, and if it wasn't for the fact that Lonnie was the one getting in my way I'd be resentful of her too.

I wandered the halls of the townhouse aimlessly, unsure where I was going. Then, I heard Lonnie's voice and the sound of crying.

I raced upstairs, my pulse racing. My immediate wild thought was that she was hurt, before I remembered that Bael had left overnight. Perhaps she'd just realized what happened. If so, I was just as much to blame for her misery as Bael was.

I found her on the floor of a guest room wearing nothing but a damp towel. My mind froze. I knew I was a prick for staring at her, wanting her, when she was so clearly upset but I couldn't make myself look away. I wanted Lonnie more than I'd ever wanted anything. The tantalizing fact that I could have her if I were only willing to tell her we were mates constantly beat at the back of my mind.

Maybe I was a masochist.

I could tell her. Even Scion–one of my greatest obstacles–wanted me to tell her. But I couldn't bring myself to do it. Telling her felt wrong. Like trapping her into something before she'd had the time to consider it.

Lonnie was shockingly oblivious to her own feelings, even now that she had more time and space to consider them. She'd fallen in love with Bael long before she knew anything about mating or magic, and still had to be convinced their bond was real. It was even worse with Scion, as both of them lacked self-awareness. They'd gone as far as sealing their bond several times over before either acknowledged its existence.

In other words, she'd been able to form real connections slowly because she had no understanding of what a mating bond was supposed to feel like.

Now that she did, I could tell her and she would undoubtedly believe me. But I would never know if she really wanted this, or simply believed it was inevitable. Worse still, there was the looming possibility that I wouldn't live past the battle I knew was coming, and how cruel would it be to leave her as a mate rather than as an estranged in-law? Even as I came upon her in her towel, I resolved not to tell her.

But then she kissed me and every promise I'd made to myself imploded. It was like she was breathing life back into me. Like my heart beat for the first time in a hundred years, and it only beat for her.

I'd never wanted to stop, but I made myself leave anyway. She was confused and overwhelmed and not looking for a mate, even if her long dormant instincts were pushing her to let me claim her.

That should have been the end of it, but of course it wasn't. The Gods clearly had an agenda today, and that plan involved fucking with me to within an inch of my sanity.

I'd shadow walked miles off course because I was distracted by Lonnie's very presence next to me. Then, she was attacked by the sirens and I had to withstand every instinct I had not to overreact to her injuries.

Then, she'd looked at me like she wanted me for more than the healing I'd offered her. She looked at me the way I looked at her whenever she wasn't paying attention. Like it physically hurt her to look, and she made herself withstand it because it was more painful to look away.

I waited, knowing that if she didn't take my blood soon, I was going to make her do it. I was ready to tear into my own flesh for her, and then I'd fuck her, claim her, make her mine right there on the fucking ground.

But then my worst fucking nightmare appeared in the form of Cassinda, and if I didn't already hate her as much as it was possible to hate anyone, I would have just because of her interruption.

I didn't know what my former betrothed was playing at. She hated me quite as much as I hated her, but for some reason she had fixated on torturing Lonnie from the very second she set eyes on her. It made no sense.

Pulling me from my thoughts, Cassinda herself glanced over her shoulder at me. "So, are you going to marry her?" she asked in the olde tongue.

I drew back, rattled by her change in tone. Did she know Lonnie was mine? Did it matter if she did? "Why would you ask that?" I hedged. "She's my brother's mate."

Cassinda raised her eyebrows so high they nearly disappeared into her hairline. "Right, but I *know* you. Are you going to marry her?"

I closed my mouth with a snap.

I'd entirely forgotten about how much Cassinda really did know. She'd spent a lot of time at the obsidian palace over the years, as we'd been betrothed nearly from birth until the day I left for Aftermath. Even if she hadn't been the daughter of the Lord of Nevermore, she would have had to be both blind and stupid not to notice something was wrong with our family. Unfortunately, she was neither.

The Everlast family had a long sorted history of rejecting our mates for fear of becoming too happy and triggering the curse that kept us all in a constant state of misery. But that didn't mean no one ever found their true mate. In fact, most of us did.

The common wisdom within the family had always been that we couldn't seal a bond, but that said nothing of keeping mates close. More often than not, a true mate was married off to a sibling or cousin, so they could be kept close.

Ironically, now that I'd seen this scenario play out between Lonnie, Bael and Scion I realized that we'd been going about things entirely wrong for years. It was a miracle that none of our ancestors had killed us all generations ago.

"Are you listening to me?" Cassinda asked.

"No."

She reeled back, looking offended. "You ass–"

"I meant, no. I'm not going to marry her. Not like you mean."

She narrowed her eyes at me, but said nothing, merely turning back around and focusing on the road ahead of us. I already knew that wasn't the end of this. I only wished I knew what Cassinda was trying to do.

* * *

It had started to snow by the time we arrived in the heart of Nevermore.

I'd given up and offered Lonnie my arm. Apparently, she was cold enough that she didn't care that she was angry with me. She'd pulled her legs up to her chest and curled her entire body into my side, and didn't sit up to look around as we pulled onto the main road.

The street was lined with round red-roofed houses, all with smoke rising from their chimneys and candles flickering in the windows. Here and there along the street, an evergreen shrub stood out from the snow, but otherwise everything was completely frozen over. Far up ahead on a snowy hill stood the keep–Nevermore's equivalent of a castle.

Unlike the other provinces, the island operated almost entirely independently of us, and governed themselves. They still technically answered to the crown, and the lord of Nevermore was not a king in his own right, but informally it was easiest to view them as a separate kingdom altogether.

As the reindeer pulled us up the hill and stopped in front of the huge stone keep, the wooden double doors flew open and Scion rushed out, trailed by a gaggle of servants who seemed to have been trying to make him eat something.

In a flash, he'd grabbed Lonnie out of the carriage and begun stalking back inside without saying a single word to me.

"Interesting," Cassinda said, a smile in her voice.

I whirled on her. I didn't care to know what was "interesting," I wanted to strangle her instead. "You drove slow on purpose."

She shrugged. "The reindeer needed the exercise."

My fingers flexed. I couldn't actually kill her. Right now, we needed Nevermore as an ally, at least as long as it took to find the jewel. I *really* wanted to, though.

"You do understand that she's the queen?" I bit out. "If nothing else, you should worry about what happens if the capital withdraws support from the island because you tried to freeze her to death."

"From what I've gathered, the capital is in a bit of an upheaval right now," she replied, still smiling. "I think I'll take my chances."

With that, she turned and stalked inside after Scion. I waited a minute before I went inside as well so I wouldn't have to walk directly behind her.

* * *

The Lord of Nevermore looked down at me from a platform in the center of his great all.

A large but relatively short man, 'from a platform' was the only way Bran of Nevermore would ever be able to look down at me and he seemed to be taking advantage of it.

I'd always thought he looked a bit like a bear. He had long dark brown hair and a matching beard that covered most of his face. His eyes were small and dark, and I'd once seen him eat an entire turkey leg in two bites.

"It's good to see you, Prince Ambrose," he boomed, loud enough for the entire hall to hear.

I gritted my teeth again. It had been a long time since anyone had called me "Prince" and I didn't like the sound of it. I never really had, but that was a different story altogether.

"Bran," I replied, pointedly not using his title. "How have you been keeping?"

He made an exaggerated show of looking around the hall and gesturing, as if to say 'Look around at all my wealth. Of course I've been doing well."

I forced myself not to sneer at him.

In a technical sense, Bran was a relative. He was my grandfather's cousin, which made him close enough to our family that he bragged about it, but not so close that we shared more than a dash of blood. He wasn't affected by the curse and neither were his children, which had made Cassinda a good candidate for queen consort. The fact that I hated her had been immaterial to the situation.

"Has my brother already explained what we're doing here?" I asked.

"Only in the broadest sense," he replied jovially.

"We're here because–"

"Wait!" he cut me off. "We can't have this conversation now. Why don't you all join me for dinner and we can talk it over then."

In other words, he didn't think he had enough of an audience and in case I said something he didn't like, or tried to attack him, he wanted there to be witnesses. It was all very predictable. Or, it would have been if I'd been able to see anything at all.

"Fine," I replied flatly, then glanced at the darkening window. I didn't know what time it was, and the sun set so early here that it might be midafternoon just as easily as midnight.

"We eat at 10:00," Bran added, seeming to sense my question. "Would you like to rest before dinner?"

"Please!" I said, enthusiastic for the first time.

"Wonderful. Cassinda can show you upstairs."

No absolutely fucking not. I'd die before going anywhere alone with that harpy.

"There's no need to bother her," I said. "A servant can do it."

To my great relief, he didn't press the issue. "Whatever you like." He waved me off. "You'll see her at dinner, anyway."

I couldn't fucking wait.

26

LONNIE

THE KEEP, NEVERMORE

I pulled my head back from Scion's throat, licking his blood from my lips.

We were ensconced in some upstairs guest room of the enormous stone fortress belonging to the Lord of Nevermore. The ceilings were low, crossed with dark wooden beams, and the furniture was all sturdy and low to the ground, looking nothing like the tall spindly style more common in the capital. On the wall there was a stylized painting of a brown bear lumbering through a forest. And underneath that, an enormous fire burned in a stone grate. I could swear I'd never been more grateful for anything in my life.

When we'd arrived, I'd been so cold I felt as if my very blood was freezing in my veins. I likely could have conjured fire to warm myself, but admittedly it hadn't occurred to me at the time. In so many ways, I still thought and behaved like a human. And, in truth, I'd been distracted by Ambrose's…betrothed? Partner? I wasn't sure what she was, but everything about her had set me on edge.

Scion had been just as on edge when our carriage finally pulled up in front of the castle. He'd grabbed me and carried me straight upstairs, without bothering to ask for permission or directions from any of the nobles.

Now, he was half sitting, half lying on his back on the bed, propped up against a wall of embroidered pillows. His hands were flat against my hips, holding me in place as I straddled his lap and sucked from his throat.

"Better?" he asked me, looking up through slightly hooded eyes.

"Much." I rolled my shoulders to demonstrate the healing. Then I leaned forward to lie more completely over Scion's bare chest, turning my head to press my ear to his impossibly warm skin. I could hear his heart beating steadily beneath me.

"I'd like to fucking kill Ambrose," Scion growled. "How does he have you alone for an hour, and you get attacked by sirens and nearly freeze to death?"

"I'm not sure that was his fault," I replied with a yawn. "Anyway, I was on that ship with him for nearly two weeks and he didn't manage to get me killed."

"Barely," Scion grumbled. "Sea monsters, Gancanagh, not to mention that friend of his shooting you with a fucking crossbow."

"Hmmm," I murmured, knowing there was absolutely no point in arguing. "I wonder where Riven is now. I haven't seen him in ages."

"Probably running errands for *The Dullahan,*" Scion sneered.

"You're determined to hate him," I commented. "And I get it, but it's not helping us at all if you can't get past it. We've already lost Bael, and you and I can't find these jewels all on our own. At the very least we'll drain each other the first time one of us has to use more magic than the other can handle."

I knew all too well that I was giving myself too much credit. It was highly unlikely–impossible even–that I'd be able to use so much magic that it would hurt Scion. But the other way around was more than possible. He'd nearly done it several times already. In any case, he seemed to take my point in stride.

Wrapping his arms around my back, he pulled me even closer and put his chin on the top of my head. "

"I keep thinking that maybe it would have been better if Bael and I just sealed our bond from the beginning," I mused.

"I don't see how," he replied, clearly doing his very best not to sound condescending. "That would just kill us all faster."

"Probably," I agreed. "But it didn't matter in the end, did it? Bael still left to avoid being too happy. If we'd sealed the bond, then you and I wouldn't be in such constant danger of draining ourselves."

I hadn't had much time to consider this since discovering Bael had gone. What with arriving in Nevermore, getting attacked, and meeting that woman, there hadn't been much time for contemplation. Now though, I couldn't help but wonder if we'd made a mistake.

"How did you heal Bael?" I asked, suddenly remembering the question that had been dancing in the back of my mind since last night.

Scion stiffened, his arms tightening more around me. "From the arrows?"

"Yes."

"You were there, rebel. It was blood, just as it always is."

I sat up again, looking down at him and letting his hands fall back to my hips. "I thought only mates could heal each other that way."

He shrugged. "We're both mated to you."

"And Ambrose?"

Scion froze, the hands that had been steadily sliding up my back and sides to graze over my bare skin stopped their ascent. His eyes darted to the side, and I knew instantly he was trying to think of a way to lie without actually lying.

"Ambrose is part of the family," he said. "We have the same blood."

I raised an eyebrow. I'd been exactly right. That was a technical truth if ever I'd heard one, which begged the question: What was Scion hiding from me?

Probably nothing so bad as what I was hiding from him, a tiny traitorous voice in the back of my mind argued. I'd promised myself I would tell him about this morning, but that wasn't the only thing I needed to confess.

"I kissed him," I blurted out. "Ambrose, that is."

Scion raised an eyebrow, and his hands resumed their slow path up my sides. "When?"

I bit my lip, anxiety riding me.

As a whole, I knew that Fae were not monogamous. They didn't have the same cultural norms around fidelity that humans did, likely because they had far fewer children than mortals. Once mated, however, they stayed loyal to that one person–or several people–for as long as their immortal lives allowed.

Scion didn't seem upset, but that didn't mean anything. He

could be plotting murder right now and his smile would prevent me from knowing until it was far too late.

"This morning," I said finally, then paused. "...and in Underneath. And–"

Scion cut me off before I could finish. He dug his fingers more firmly into my hips, holding me in place. Sitting up a fraction more, he leaned in to kiss me, undoubtedly tasting his own blood on my lips.

Without hesitation, I parted my lips and brought my hands up to his hair, deepening the kiss. I trailed my fingers over the back of his head, scraping my nails against his throat. He shivered when I stroked over the point where I'd sunk my teeth into his pulse, and I felt him growing hard beneath me.

In one swift motion, Scion reversed our positions, flipping me so I landed on my back, him hovering over me. He grazed his teeth against my throat, nipping softly. I whimpered, heat already pooling in my core.

"Listen," he said, mouth still brushing against the exposed tops of my breasts. "I don't really care how many times you kiss my brother. Fuck him if you want, just as long as you understand you're still mine. I own you."

"So I can go fuck whomever I want as long as I come back afterward," I asked nearly laughing. It was such a ridiculous idea that I'd even want to. But more than that, it was so out of character for Scion to suggest that it was almost comical.

Apparently, my mate didn't find it nearly as funny as I did.

A furious snarl burst from him. "Who are you talking about? Tell me!"

My eyes widened, startled by his suddenly furious face. "You just said–"

"If anyone else gets fucking near you I'll kill them. Don't for a moment believe I'd think twice about it."

My mind swum with confusion. He was contradicting himself. How could he not care that I'd kissed Ambrose, but be murderous at the idea of any other male looking at me. It made no sense, yet he hadn't cringed or showed any sign of pain. As ludicrous as he sounded, he at least believed what he was saying.

"I wasn't thinking of anyone," I said quickly. "I just don't understand how you could be so blasé about this. If you kissed someone else, I'd–"

I broke off, unable to finish my sentence. An all-consuming possessiveness had swept through my body. It was a rage, heating me from the inside out and making every one of my muscles tense. It felt so unlike me, so uncontrollable, that part of me wanted to smash something while the rest of me seemed to be looking on from the sidelines, wondering what the fuck was happening.

Scion looked down at me and his face relaxed. Instantly, he seemed to know what was happening, and he bent his head to trail kisses up my neck. "Maybe now you know what it's like for us," he murmured against my skin. "I'd always heard mating bonds stole your rationality, but I couldn't have ever guessed how true that would be."

I blinked, focusing on his mouth on my throat as my breathing returned to normal. "If that's what you feel like, I'm sorry I did that to you," I almost laughed.

"Why are you sorry?"

"Because you're so…controlled all the time. Regimented."

He smirked. "Not all the time."

He sucked hard on the scar on my throat and my toes curled, pulling a whimper from me. Reaching down and unbuttoning my pants with one hand, Scion stilled, his fingers hovering just over my aching core.

"Tell me you know you're mine," he commanded

"I'm yours," I echoed.

I gasped, words failing me and all my attention pulled back to him as he plunged his fingers beneath the fabric to rake through my growing wetness. Looking satisfied, he shoved my trousers down enough to drive two fingers inside of me and stopped, holding me tightly. My back arched off the bed and he held me there, trapped by his pitilessly unmoving fingers.

"I own every part of you," he breathed in my ear. "Your heart is mine. Your cunt is mine. And that doesn't change just because I have to share them."

I gasped, my legs actually shaking from the intensity. I rocked my hips, silently begging him to move his fingers, fuck me, *anything* to break the anticipation building in my core.

"Please," I heard myself beg.

"Tell me!" he barked, voice becoming a near yell. "Who does this cunt belong to?"

"You, my lord," I gasped.

"Good answer." He smacked my bare cunt with an open palm, sending a surprising jolt of pain and pleasure through me.

Scion reached down and undid his belt, keeping his eyes on mine the entire time. He moved so painfully slow, I was sure he was trying to torture me.

He flicked open the button of his trousers, but made no move to continue removing them.

"Get on with it," I growled.

He smirked. "I just like watching you squirm. You're so desperate for my cock you're shaking."

A small snarl bubbled up in my throat, and suddenly I wasn't content to lie here letting him tease me.

I rolled us again, pushing him back into the pillows so I could straddle his lap once more. He looked slightly surprised, but not at all unhappy when I dug my nails into his shoulders so hard small red beads of blood appeared beneath my fingers. I wasn't even sure he noticed.

Reaching behind me, I shoved at his open trousers and gripped his hard cock in one hand. "If I'm yours, shouldn't this belong to me?"

His eyes flashed pewter, and a hunger crossed his face. "Oh, it does rebel. Take it."

Rising up on my knees, I slowly sunk back down onto him, feeling his sharp intake of breath as he filled me. His body pulsed and throbbed inside of me as I began to move, my hips rolling in a slow and agonizing rhythm, just like the way he had teased and tortured me before.

Each movement caused a jolt of sensation to shoot through my body, igniting every nerve ending and sending shivers down my spine.

The smooth pad of his thumb brushed against my already sensitive clit, tracing gentle circles that matched the rhythm of my movements. Electric sparks of pleasure shot through my body, causing my stomach to tighten and my hips to move with even more urgency.

Mine! Mine! A voice in the back of my head chanted. *Mine!*

Every nerve ending was on fire as I raced towards an intense release, fueled by his skilled touch and our shared desire

No longer able to hold back, Scion lifted his hips, matching my every movement and sending me higher and higher.

My back arched as I rode him, and my breath became uneven.

The grip on my hip tightened, fingers digging in possessively. With each thrust of his hips, he pulled me down harder onto him, filling me deeper and more completely.

My knees began to shake, and I was sure I wouldn't be able to hold myself up much longer. All my muscles felt simultaneously too tight and like they were melting, becoming limp and useless.

"Look at me," Scion gasped.

I looked down, our gazes colliding. His silver eyes were all consuming, flashing with every emotion too fast to read.

Somehow, though, I understood.

"Fucking come for me," he demanded.

As if he could control my body with will alone, I shattered.

Waves of pleasure cascaded through me, causing my legs to tremble and my entire body to flush with heat. My senses were completely consumed by the powerful force of the orgasm, as if every nerve ending in my body had been set on fire.

I was burning, becoming one unending burst of flame, and my vision went white as I felt him follow me over the edge.

27
LONNIE
THE KEEP, NEVERMORE

What felt like an hour later, there was a soft knock at the door.

I sat up and looked confusedly at the door to our room. I could swear the knock hadn't come from that direction, yet I'd heard it, clear as day.

"Did you hear that?" I asked.

Scion looked over at me and shook his head.

His eyes were half closed, but he wasn't sleeping. His face looked less sharp, the firm ridge of his eyebrows smoothed out and his jaw considerably less tense than it usually was. Indeed, he looked as relaxed as I'd possibly ever seen him, even when he *was* sleeping. It seemed a shame to disturb him, but it seemed it couldn't be helped.

After a long moment, the knock came again. This time I was positive it was coming from the opposite side of the room. This time, Scion sat up as well, all the tension he carried with him like a noose around his neck returning to his face in an instant.

He stood up, and not bothering to get dressed, strode across the room toward a door I'd assumed was a closet. Without warning me, or giving me a chance to cover myself, he flung it open.

I yelped, and grappled for Scion's abandoned shirt, throwing it over myself like a tent. My head popped out of the neck just in time to see Ambrose in the doorway. He raised an eyebrow, then shouldered past Scion to enter the room.

"Bit cold for that," he said over his shoulder. "Don't you think?"

Scion scowled and reached for his trousers on the floor. "What do you want?"

Ambrose crossed his arms and faced Scion, turning his back to me. Perhaps he was trying to give me some privacy, but I didn't really care. We were far beyond that.

"We're expected downstairs for dinner."

Scion looked at the dark window with confusion. "Now?"

"Yes," Ambrose said bitterly. "I wish I could say they simply eat late here, but from what I recall that's inaccurate."

"You've spent a lot of time here?" I asked Ambrose, unable to keep the note of bitterness out of my voice.

He looked at me, and I could swear the corner of his mouth ticked up slightly. "Enough to guess that this dinner is in our honor."

"And what an honor it is." Sarcasm dripped from Scion's tone. He finished putting on his trousers and crossed to sit on the edge of the bed and pull on his boots.

"I think we should expect violence," Ambrose said.

Scion looked up at him. "You're serious? How foolish are they."

"I wouldn't underestimate them," Ambrose said warily. "Nevermore has a lot of magic compared with the mainland. They weren't as affected by the fall of Nightshade as we were."

"Why not?" I asked quickly.

He looked over at me quickly, and for a fraction of a second I caught his eyes darting over my bare legs, before snapping back up to my face. "They have a Source of their own here. Not nearly as powerful as *The Source,* but they draw a lot of power from the sea."

"What sort of magic does Cassinda have?" I blurted out. I internally cringed when I heard the clear note of jealousy in my voice, and prayed it wasn't noticeable to anyone else. That prayer went unanswered.

Ambrose smirked at me, a look of male satisfaction crossing his face. "You didn't like Cassinda?"

"How could I when I couldn't understand a word she was saying?" I hissed.

"I don't like her either," he said, almost like he was offering me consolation.

"But you were going to marry her?"

To my surprise, Scion cut in. "That means absolutely nothing, rebel. We don't marry for love."

"I know," I snapped, wishing I could control my voice better. "Bael told me you marry for power. So, what kind of magic does Cassinda have?"

"She's an illusionist," Ambrose said. "Grandmother would have preferred to find another seer, but there simply isn't one strong enough to make a good match. My mother is an illusionist, like Scion, so it seemed the most reasonable alternative."

I pursed my lips, thinking hard. They talked about their hypothetical future children like they were breeding particularly rare horses. It was so cold and disconnected it made my skin crawl.

And, as much as I hated myself for it, I couldn't help but wonder how I'd measure up. I didn't have the right powers to keep the dynasty growing. Worse, I was half human. What if my children were rejected and looked down on because they weren't illusionists or whatever else.

I shook my head and blinked to clear my mind. This was absurd. I'd never thought much about children before, except how *not* to have them. Clearly the stress and lack of sleep of the last several days was making me go a bit mad.

"Is Cassinda angry that you didn't marry her?" I asked, slightly distracted.

"Oh, absolutely," Ambrose said far too quickly.

My eyes narrowed. As before, when I'd considered Scion kissing another woman, I felt a stab of irrational rage so potent that I had to put a hand out on the bedpost to steady myself.

"Because she didn't get to be the queen," Scion blurted out, looking at me sideways with something like concern. "She wanted to be the queen, it wasn't about him specifically. Her father proposed she marry me instead about ten years ago, but obviously it didn't work out."

"Why not?" I replied through gritted teeth.

"For one thing, she's several hundred years older than I am. That doesn't always matter, but it's not ideal. Also, the situation with Thalia was more pressing. If Gwydion wasn't happy to take my place I would have had to marry her."

I had to drag my mind and swirling emotions back from the

edge of insanity to even begin to understand what he was referring to.

Thalia had explained to me once that she was sent to the capital to marry Scion because she'd found her true mate and the family was afraid she had enough Everlast blood to set off the curse. "I've always thought that was strange," I muttered, my voice returning to a normal register. "If Thalia had enough Everlast blood to potentially be dangerous, isn't she too related to you to marry?"

Scion scoffed. "That's nothing, rebel. For the entire year that Penvalle ruled there was a lot of talk about trying to force me to marry Aine."

"Aine?" I said, distracted. "But she's your cousin."

"Right, but that's irrelevant. She has the persuasion gift, which is more rare than illusion and objectively more powerful if it's used correctly. If a child could have both illusion and persuasion–"

"They'd be like Idris," I blurted out.

They both paused and looked at me, then each other.

"Did he use an illusion?" Scion asked no one in particular. "I didn't notice."

"He must have!" My voice grew louder with excitement. "What other power could banish the afflicted so quickly? What if he simply hid them, or–oh!" I exclaimed, my eyes growing even wider as an even better idea occurred to me. "What if they were never there to begin with? I remember thinking it was strange. I didn't smell the smoke."

Again, they glanced at each other.

"I'd say you're right, rebel," Scion said slowly. "But that doesn't help us now."

"How?" I demanded. "If we know what powers he has we'll know how to stop him."

"He means it doesn't change what we have to do," Ambrose added. "We still need to find the jewels and put the crown back together and have all your bonds sealed. Without that, it won't matter how we attack Idris. You'll be drained, and then there would be no point continuing anyway."

I narrowed my gaze at him. It sounded like he was saying that if I died, he'd see no point in continuing. But that was insane. Even if I died, the kingdom would still matter. Right?

Ambrose glanced at the window and then back at me. "It's getting late and there are no fucking clocks in this place. I don't know what time it is, but we likely have to get down to dinner. I've yet to think of a better way to get the jewel than simply asking Bran for it, and dinner is the only time to do it."

"Agreed," Scion replied. "Could we simply order him to give it to us?"

"Perhaps." Ambrose glanced at me. "But that would likely make him angry, and I'd rather avoid that if we can. All they need is the smallest push and they'll succeed from us tonight."

Scion nodded again, seeming to understand more than I did.

For something to do, I rose and crossed the room to the small bag of clothing and food we'd brought with us. I wished I'd packed a gown, but all I had was my magenta corseted coat from Inbetwixt and a pair of black trousers. Oh, and the crown, I supposed. "If I'm going I need to get dressed."

Scion looked perplexed. "Why wouldn't you be going, rebel?"

"I don't understand the language, and if you two have to keep translating for me it will look strange, don't you think?"

"I don't care what it looks like," Ambrose said hotly. "Still, I think you're right. This dinner will be difficult for you. Just keep in mind that they all understand the common tongue perfectly, no matter what they try to make you believe. If they use it, they want to make sure you understand."

I sighed. "This will hardly be the first uncomfortable meal I've sat through. I'm sure Cassinda has nothing on Raewyn."

28
SCION
THE KEEP, NEVERMORE

The Lord of Nevermore was a prick.

The hall was lively with activity when the three of us arrived in the dining hall. There was a raucous band in the far corner and several tables had been moved to create a space for dancing. They'd hung decorations as if it were a festival and now multicolored flags hung from every wall. Several tapestries depicting enormous brown bears were placed above the doors.

If I didn't know better—and perhaps even then—I'd say Bran had dragged every noble on the damn island out of bed, just for the pleasure of seeing us. That boded ill for our chances of success, and even worse for our chances of getting out of here without a fight.

The moment we entered the room, Lord Bran made an exaggerated show of greeting us.

"Prince Ambrose!" he boomed, his voice carrying to all corners of the room. "And Prince Scion. Welcome. Thank you for taking the time to share our table."

He openly ignored Lonnie, as if she weren't standing right there. I wasn't sure she realized that, because he spoke the olde tongue and all she would have understood were our names, but it didn't matter. I was livid on her behalf.

The snub was especially bold because Lonnie had worn the crown down to dinner—something I knew she despised, but which made the right statement. Anyone who wasn't sure of her identity before would now certainly know. And, more importantly, they wouldn't be able to feign ignorance.

Despite all that had happened—the coups, the rebellions, the destruction of the castle—Lonnie had still taken the crown from Penvalle by force. By the laws of Elsewhere, she was still the queen and the lord of Nevermore owed her his respect.

It was ironic, really. I'd spent months denying Lonnie's claim to the throne and wishing I could rewrite the laws to have her banished. Now, I was rabid to defend her claim, and would gladly step aside if I ever found myself between her and the crown.

We'd been directed to sit at one of the several long wooden tables lining the long room, which was both dining hall and throne room. At least they didn't dare to seat Lonnie at another table, and put her on the end next to me on one side and the wall on the other. It was only slightly rude, and suited me fine because it would be easier to protect her.

I didn't even care that they'd put Ambrose to the right of Lord Bran, treating him as the highest ranked of the three of us, whereas in reality he had no status at all. At one point, that would have made me angry enough to attack Bran right here at the table. Now, my only concern was how the three of us would be separated should something go wrong.

"What are they saying?" Lonnie whispered, leaning over to me.

My eyes darted around the table. I didn't know the nobles sitting directly in front of us, but from the way their ears had pricked up I guessed they spoke the common tongue.

Ah. Now I understood.

Bran was hoping that Lonnie spoke carelessly to me, not realizing that anyone could understand her. He'd probably placed his best common speakers all around us to pick up anything she let slide.

Under the table, I gripped her knee in a relatively obvious show of affection. Then, I leaned over and nipped at her ear, as if careless and drunk on lust. "Let's not talk now, rebel," I murmured. "I don't want the entire table to hear what I'm going to do to you later."

Lonnie looked at me sideways, her eyes narrowing. I prayed she understood what I was getting at. Don't say anything, we're not alone here.

She nodded, seeming to understand, and took a sip of her wine. I relaxed. I wasn't sure what Bran was playing at, or why he cared what Lonnie had to say but I wasn't taking any chances. The worst possible explanation was that Idris had somehow already reached Nevermore, and brought the lord over to his side. The kindest possibility was that Bran was nosey, and looking to exploit gossip for political clout. I wasn't willing to risk either option.

I wasn't afraid of Bran or his family, but the situation with Nevermore was complicated in a way I would never be able to satisfactorily explain to Lonnie in the little time that we had.

The island had been flirting with succession for generations, and it wasn't difficult to see why. Their culture was different from ours, as was their language. They were geographically separated from the continent, and they'd been governing themselves for centuries.

The problem was that we couldn't allow them to become independent.

Not only would the financial blow from their lost taxes take years to recover from, but their location made it critical that they hold our border. On the opposite side of the island from our continent, another powerful Fae kingdom, Ellender, occupied its own continent. We maintained a friendly relationship with Ellender, and their four high courts, but word had reached us that they were experiencing their own internal power struggles. We had no desire to get involved.

Nevermore's mere presence as a buffer made it unlikely that we would have to intervene.

Clearly, Ambrose understood the complicated situation on this island just as well as I did, because he was being very diplomatic while talking to Bran. I strained my ears to hear them over the chatter of the hall.

"We'd be happy to compensate you for the jewel," he was saying, his entire body turned toward Bran. "Or perhaps replace it with another treasure."

Out of the corner of my eye, I saw a flash of red and turned to look.

"Oh, fuck," I muttered under my breath.

"What?" Lonnie asked, turning around in her chair to see what I was looking at. I felt her stiffen and knew she'd seen exactly "what" I was looking at.

Cassinda was back, this time wearing a crimson gown with a plunging neckline and a jewel encrusted bodice. It was both too formal and too modern for Nevermore, making it clear she was aiming to make a statement.

She glided over and took the empty seat beside Ambrose at the head of the table. Seemingly without realizing she was doing it, Lonnie dug her nails into my arm. Her fingers were too hot—too hot—like burning coals.

"Easy, rebel," I said under my breath. The danger of anyone overhearing was far overshadowed by the danger of her lighting the hall on fire. "She could be naked and he wouldn't give a fuck."

She shook her head, and looked up at me, guilt and confusion in her eyes.

A spark of anger shot through me, but it had nothing to do with Lonnie being jealous over Ambrose.

This was getting fucking ridiculous. He knew they were mates—I knew they were mates—yet she had no idea. She couldn't understand what was happening, and was tormenting herself thinking she'd betrayed Bael and I. I couldn't keep watching this. If he didn't tell her tonight, I would.

"What are we discussing so seriously?" Cassinda asked loudly in the old tongue. "I thought this was meant to be a party."

Bran stood up from his seat, addressing the entire room. "My daughter makes a good point. I apologize for my inattention, but you see, Prince Ambrose has just asked me for a most enticing favor."

The table broke out in whispers. Cassinda—the fucking idiot—actually had the nerve to look hopefully at Ambrose. It was like she believed he'd returned to ask to marry her all over again.

An uneasy feeling washed over me.

Despite all we'd said upstairs, I thought my brother was wrong about his former betrothed. He clearly hated her, but the feeling didn't seem to be mutual.

"The prince has requested that I lend him the jewel of Nevermore," Bran announced.

The murmuring increased tenfold.

"Why?" someone shouted from the opposite side of the table.

Ambrose looked annoyed, but plastered on a smile before answering the question. "I don't require it for anything onerous, I assure you. I will only need the jewel for a few weeks, before I promise it will be returned to its rightful place."

The jewel would be returned to its rightful place in the crown before long. If Bran's court believed Ambrose meant to return it here, then that was really their blunder for not listening more carefully.

I was almost impressed.

Ambrose was good at this if he wanted to be, though all the tattoos and ridiculous earrings did make it hard to think he was merely a prince. He hadn't had those when he left the capital.

"We couldn't possibly part with the diamond," Cassinda said loudly. "Especially after we were so recently snubbed by the capital."

I raised an eyebrow. "What are you referring to?"

She looked down the table at me and smiled widely. When she spoke, it was in common tongue. "Only a few months ago our people were raving with excitement over the upcoming hunts, but then you canceled them so abruptly. We never got a chance to see our new queen defend the crown on our soil. The people were robbed of their chance to see her at all. One might even say that as she didn't complete the hunts, she is not the true queen, and we owe her no loyalty."

"Are you saying that?" Ambrose asked, his tone dangerous.

"I'm simply pointing out that one could make that argument, and how unfairly we've been treated by the continent. It makes one ask if we should reconsider if we are valued as a province, or if we may be better off on our own."

I closed my eyes. That bitch.

She knew we couldn't allow their independence, and now she was going to make some absurd demand in exchange for staying.

Beside me, Lonnie was grinding her teeth loud enough that I could hear every movement, but she wisely said nothing.

"That gives me an idea," Bran boomed, also in common tongue. "If you want the diamond, perhaps you should hunt for it? All those of us here today would happily stand witness. Some might even like to participate."

"No!" I blurted out before I'd had a chance to think about it.

Lonnie looked up at me. "If it's the only way, I could do it," she muttered. "I'm not nearly as breakable anymore."

"No," Ambrose echoed me. "We won't be playing any absurd games. We've done you the courtesy of asking for the jewel rather than ordering you return it. Don't take advantage of our generosity."

Bran's eyes flashed with anger. "You take advantage of our generosity every year in taxes. All we ask is to be afforded the same privileges as the other provinces. We expect to see the queen hunt."

They expected to see her blood soaking into the snow.

I vibrated with anger. It would be all too easy to just kill them all now. The consequences didn't matter. We'd have the diamond and Lonnie would be alive. Everything else could be fixed later.

I rose from my seat, lifting a hand in the air.

"Wait!" Lonnie yelled. She grabbed my arm and shoved it back down. "I'll do it. I accept."

Cassinda grinned wickedly. "Excellent. We'll see you out in front of the castle in an hour, then."

"E-excuse me?" Lonnie stammered. "An hour?"

"Of course," Cassinda said, her voice sickly sweet. "In Nevermore, the hunts begin at midnight. And conveniently, we are only one hour away."

* * *

"What the fuck were you thinking?"

The shout echoed all around the room, but for once, it wasn't me who was yelling.

We'd stood and left our seats, and were now standing back in our upstairs guest room. The moment I shut the door, Ambrose rounded on Lonnie, screaming at her loud enough that the entire castle could likely hear.

"I was thinking about saving the lives of three dozen people," she screamed back just as angrily. "You two were going to kill them. I could tell."

I glanced at my brother, who returned my look with a guilty one of his own. Clearly, I hadn't been the only one intending to end our dinner with a funeral.

"I told you," Ambrose barked, his gaze snapping back to Lonnie. "If they were speaking the common language they wanted you to understand. They were setting you up. Why the fuck do you think there were so many people here tonight, or how they're managing to set up a hunt in under an hour. They planned this."

"That makes no sense." Lonnie said hotly. She crossed her arms over her chest and scowled, not seeming the slightest bit cowed by Ambrose screaming at her. "They didn't know what you were going to ask. They couldn't have planned for this ahead of time."

I closed my eyes, pinching the bridge of my nose. I felt suddenly exhausted. "They didn't know about the jewel, no," I said, my eyes still closed. "But they were clearly going to ask you to complete the hunt anyway. They would have come up with some other reason to trap you into it. We just made it easier for them."

Lonnie faltered, looking slightly nervous for the first time. "Why, though?"

By the fucking Source. We'd fucked up.

I let out a long frustrated breath and fell backwards against the bed, putting my head in my hands. "We should have told you about the issues in Nevermore," I said angrily. "It seemed too complicated to bother explaining, but you should have known. They've been trying to become an independent nation for centuries."

"And you can't let them?" she asked, tapping her foot absently against the wooden floor.

"No. It's complicated."

"Don't say that," she snapped. "Acting like things are too complicated for me to understand is exactly what you just said you shouldn't have done."

"Fine."

I quickly ran through the highlights of Nevermore's succession attempts, and Lonnie listened with rapt attention.

"Alright," she said when I was finished. "Well there's one good thing about all that. They definitely won't follow Idris. We don't have to worry about him influencing them or coming here because they already reject the authority of the continent. It would be too hard to persuade them. I don't think he'll bother."

Ambrose smiled weakly. "That's a good point, love," he said in a tone that implied he regretted yelling at her. I could fucking relate.

"That doesn't help us now, though," I growled. "And the hour is almost up."

"I was serious downstairs. I can do this." Lonnie reached up and began braiding her long hair as she talked. "I've been training every day for months, and I've already survived two of these things even before I knew how to use magic."

I cocked my head at her, thinking. "You really only have to cross the boundary and you'll get the head start as usual. Once the wave of hunters are let in we can join you and help."

"Okay," she breathed, looking nervous but determined. She smiled a little sadly. "It's just like when we first met. Except Bael's not here to keep you from killing me."

"I'll keep everyone from fucking touching you, rebel." I growled. "You're going to be fine."

She nodded, and turned as if to open the door.

"Wait," Ambrose said, looking a bit pained. "One more thing, love. You should keep an eye on Cassinda."

My gaze flashed to his. He must have noticed her behavior at dinner just as I had.

"I'd planned to," Lonnie said darkly. "But any particular reason?"

"She thought she was going to be the queen," I answered, when Ambrose failed to speak. "She was two months from ruling, and it all got taken from her. She'll try to kill you for that crown."

I half expected Lonnie to panic, or start asking a thousand questions. But, as usual, my rebel surprised me.

"I hope she tries," She hissed, a slightly manic glint in her gaze. "I really need to burn something."

29
LONNIE
THE KEEP, NEVERMORE

Despite my bravado, I trembled as we made our way outside.

The bitingly frigid air was even colder than I remembered, and my trembling increased when we stepped out into the gathering snow.

There was already a large crowd waiting for us. None of them seemed to be cold, but then, all wore heavy furs, knit caps, and sheepskin boots. I supposed the only upside of my thinner clothing was that I might move faster and more easily through the hunting grounds. If I could move at all that was, and hadn't frozen to death before we even began.

One of the fur jacketed figures stepped forward and I realized before she even removed her hood that it was Cassinda. I glared at her with venom in my eyes. Once I might have given up on the spot. Said, "fuck it!" and let her be the queen. Now, I put my shoulders back and braced myself as she approached.

"Aren't you cold?" she asked me in her sickly sweet tone of mock concern.

I bared my teeth at her. She didn't scare me.

She was no worse than Aine or Raewyn had been when I arrived at my first hunt.

She was no worse than the other servants who had sneered at and excluded me my entire life.

She was no worse than Scion had been upon our first meeting, taunting and threatening me at every turn. Ambrose, who'd burnt down the castle and had me shot, Or Bael, who had left me with nothing more than a note.

And she was certainly no worse than my own mother, who'd never wanted me at all.

"Where are the boundaries?" I asked sharply.

Cassinda looked annoyed that I didn't seem willing to rise to her bait, but turned and pointed off into the distance. "The hunt begins here in front of the keep. You may run wherever you like, except into the center of the village or back into the keep. You may not shadow walk."

"What happens if I do?" I hissed.

"The hunt will become forfeit and you will leave here without the jewel." She smiled slightly, surely hoping I would break the rules and end up with nothing.

"You will have a ten minute head start, at which time anyone who wishes to may hunt you. If they kill you, they get the crown as well as the jewel."

"That's bullshit," Scion barked. "This isn't an official hunting night. If you kill her, the crown goes to me as her mate. No one is winning the right to be the queen."

Cassinda's expression soured. "You robbed us of the chance to fight for the crown on our own hunting night. Now you are trying to skirt the rules?"

"No, I'm telling you what the law states," Scion said dangerously.

"A law which will no longer apply to us if we choose to become our own nation."

"It's fine," I said quickly. "I agree. If you kill me, you get the crown."

Scion made a noise of protest and Ambrose pulled me back to look me in the eye. "This isn't wise," he muttered, ignoring the fact that Cassinda could certainly still hear us.

"It doesn't matter," I said firmly. "Idris is in the capital right now thinking he's doing the same thing. Someone is always trying to take the damn crown."

"Right, but this would be a legal capture," Scion muttered. "It's not a coup. It's essentially the same as what you did."

"Then I won't lose," I said flatly, turning back to Cassinda who was smiling.

"You've got more nerve than I expected," she said.

"Maybe," I agreed. "Maybe it's that I'm stubborn. Or maybe it's that I fully intend to kill you before you ever lay a hand on me."

"We'll see about that." Her face turning pink from anger, she turned and pointed at the skyline once again. "Do you see that mountain in the distance? If you wish to win by crossing the boundary, it is near the top. Otherwise, you will have to survive until sunrise."

"That's fucking insane," Scion interrupted again. "That mountain is three times further than the standard boundary, and climbing to the top is nearly impossible."

"Ah," Cassinda said grinning. "But In Nevermore we begin the hunt at midnight, not sunset, due to the fact that our sun sets so early and unpredictably. That makes the hunt only seven hours at most, and we have to have a way to compensate for that lack of difficulty."

"Is that true?" I asked.

Scion looked unsure but Ambrose nodded.

Shit. My strategy in the hunts had always been to run for the boundary. If I had to fight all night long that changed things significantly.

I glanced at Scion. "It's alright. I've never had you to help me before, and we both know you could take down this entire crowd at once if you wanted."

Scion nodded once, then set his jaw, still glaring at Cassinda.

I half expected Cassinda to try and tell me I wasn't allowed to have help, but she said nothing about it.

"Wait!" I asked her quickly. "What about the jewel?"

"What about it?" she snapped.

"Aren't you going to give it to me? To defend?" It was hard to keep the distain out of my voice.

Cassinda smiled, and reached up to undo the top button of her heavy coat. From beneath the fabric she pulled a diamond the size of a walnut hanging from a gold chain. "I'll take care of it for now."

I pressed my lips together, nodding. I didn't trust that woman, and didn't think it boded well for us that she had the jewel. Still, there was very little to do but wait and see.

* * *

As with my previous hunts, there was a certain amount of nervous standing around that happened before the event could actually begin. I wished desperately that I knew the time, to know how much longer we had to wait, but no one seemed willing to share it with me.

Finally, when I thought I might freeze to the ground where I stood, a low horn blew in the distance. I looked up, expecting to see the haunting figure of the hunter who wore the same deer skull mask that Ambrose had appropriated for his role as the Dullahan. Instead, all I saw was a fire burning far in the distance.

It was a beacon, as if someone had lit a fire on the very top of the mountain to guide me to the boundary. Unfortunately I had absolutely no intention of aiming for that boundary tonight.

"They'll blow the horn again, and then you run, rebel," Scion said. "When you hear the horn a third time you'll know we're right behind you."

I nodded, feeling truly nervous now.

Scion bent to kiss me, but I pushed him back. "Don't. There's no goodbye kisses. I'll see you in ten minutes." I glanced at Ambrose. "Both of you."

Ambrose opened his mouth to say something—I had no idea what. But then the horn blew a second time, and I turned and sprinted toward the road.

I'd run for a few short minutes when I had to stop and catch my breath. Despite my movement, the cold was unbearable. My muscles felt sore and stiff, and I couldn't feel my fingers or my face.

I didn't even want to know what not being able to feel my hands might do to my magic, and prayed I wouldn't have to find out.

Glancing behind me at the castle, I began to run again. It was only once I saw lights again, that I realized I was heading into the village we'd passed on our way in. Quickly, I veered to the right into a patch of dense trees.

The rules had been simple—no shadow walking, don't enter the village or the keep, stay alive until morning. Still, I had absolutely no qualms about breaking them if it meant I got out of this alive. I wouldn't shadow walk yet, but if things became truly dire the game was not nearly so important as my life.

Distantly, I realized this must be how the hunts felt for every other past ruler. They weren't afraid of dying so much as they were concerned about their image, their petty grievances, and holding on to power. How strange to realize I had similar concerns, and while I was far from comfortable sprinting alone through the cold, dark woods I wasn't frightened.

At least, not yet.

* * *

Several long minutes later I heard the third horn.

It was distant, making me wonder if I'd run further than I'd realized, but it was clearly audible over the howling wind and rustling trees.

I stopped in my tracks, panting from the long run. I felt somehow even colder now after all the running, my own sweat having turned to ice crystals against my skin.

The trees here were just as dense as the ones that Ambrose and I had run through near the rocky coast, but with the added difficulty that the ground between them was covered in snow and ice.

For the first time, I wondered how Scion and Ambrose would

find me before anyone else did. We hadn't discussed a plan or anywhere to meet. Now, that seemed like a grave oversight.

I turned to look back at the castle looming in the distance, its tall spires reaching towards the darkening sky. My eyes strained to make out any signs of movement and I thought I saw figures darting down the hill and disappearing into the shadows. They were all headed toward me.

Suddenly, a deafening chorus of screams pierced the air. At first, I thought it was the sound of the afflicted returning to haunt me

The hair on the back of my neck stood up as their cries echoed through the trees, seeming to double on itself, echoing back at me louder and louder.

This had to be Scion's illusion of pain.

The sound was familiar, the same one I would have heard if I had been in the dining room. It was the one Scion had talked about hearing on the battlefield for many years. And, I realized with a sickening lurch, it was the same sound the afflicted mimicked every time they appeared.

Apparently I need not have worried about saving the lives of the winter court. They were all going to die anyway, trapped in an endless cycle of pain.

I supposed I no longer needed to wonder where Scion was, nor about all the Fae chasing me. Still, I would need to find a hiding place, just in case anyone avoided the massacre.

I covered my ears as I ran, making myself keep going. Making myself put as much distance between me and the castle as possible before I stopped to hide.

Without warning, a deafening roar ripped through the air. I whipped my head around, eyes wide. My gaze fell upon one of the towering pine trees just in time to witness its trunk splitting in half and toppling towards me like an enormous falling sword.

Panic surged through my veins as an ear-shattering cacophony of cracking and splintering filled the air. The tall trees surrounding me started to split and sway, their trunks bowing towards me with alarming speed. Each crashing tree sounded like a thunderous drumbeat, closing in on me from all sides. I stumbled backwards, frantically trying to evade the crashing limbs and dove out of the way, covering my head.

It seemed like the forest itself was turning against me.

With a quick glance, I caught sight of a large boulder jutting out from the snowy ground. Without hesitation, I began to crawl towards it on my stomach, feeling the icy flakes seeping through my clothing and chilling my skin still further.

I reached the boulder and crouched behind it, cowering. I shook with cold, and for the briefest second I felt like the girl I'd been before. Hiding under a bush during the first hunt, praying that no one would find me. Praying that I wouldn't die here.

And then it stopped.

"If a tree falls in the forest and squashes a human, does she make a sound?" A female voice called out from somewhere behind me.

Shock and anger suddenly rushed through my veins. I stood up and spun around.

Cassinda was striding out of the forest where I'd just been and—I blinked. The trees behind her were fine. Not a single one broken or fallen. She grinned. "I thought you might recognize a good illusion, what with what your mate is doing back at the castle. But I took a gamble, and it turns out it was a good bet."

I bared my teeth at her. "Why aren't you writhing on the ground with all the rest of your court?"

She rolled her eyes at me, looking bored. "I'm an illusionist, so believe me, I've heard all about the new crown prince. *The queen's executioner*." Her tone was jeering. "I wasn't about to wait to find out how many bodies he can collect at once. I got well out of the way before the horn even sounded."

"So you cheated," I snapped.

She shrugged, causing the enormous diamond around her neck to sway with the movement. "Once you're dead there won't be anyone who can say if I did or didn't. Anyway, I doubt that will be what people remember from tonight. I'm fairly sure what your mate is doing is considered a war crime."

I was sure she was right, but she didn't sound all that broken up about it. These were her people, and she didn't care that they were all being tortured as long as she got to win the hunt she'd orchestrated just for this purpose.

She was the worst kind of ruler. The same kind as Idris, and to a lesser extent, that horrible lord and lady I'd met in Inbetwixt. None of them cared about their people at all. Which begged the question, why did we keep them? Long ago, Aisling had united the realms under one crown, but now we'd gone back to separate territories in all but name only. That couldn't possibly be the way things should be.

But I couldn't think about that right now.

Cassinda walked toward me, stalking me, and instinctively I backed up. I extended my trembling hands and Cassinda stopped in her tracks when fire burst from my freezing fingers.

It wasn't the best fire I'd ever made, and sputtered every time my teeth chattered. But evidently, Cassinda didn't realize that.

"You're an illusionist?" she accused.

I shook my head and tossed a flaming ball at the ground. A circle melted into the snow, revealing grass beneath. "Come touch it if you want. It's not an illusion."

She didn't move, seeming to take my word for it. I'd momentarily forgotten that she expected me never to lie.

For the first time, her eyes darted to the sides and she looked nervous.

"Afraid I'll burn down your forest and you with it?" I taunted her.

"The forest has nothing to do with us," she snapped. "It's innocent, and the home to many creatures."

I widened my eyes at her. She couldn't possibly be serious. She didn't care that the people were dying in agony up at the castle, but she was worried about a few trees?

Partly out of spite, and partly to see how serious she was, I held a handful of fire up to one of the nearby pines. Its bark began to smoke and with a cry of anger, she rushed toward me.

I pivoted on my back foot as if we were sword fighting, and held the fire up to her. It caught the tip of her long chestnut braid and the smell of burning hair engulfed the clearing.

"Wait!" she demanded. "I'll make you a bargain."

I scoffed. "I was taught never to bargain with the Fae."

"Then I'll offer you a challenge. Fight me without magic."

Her eyes widened, both earnest and determined and…something else. I couldn't explain why, but her eyes reminded me suddenly of Bael. His eyes were yellow and catlike, while hers were brown and so large they took up far more than their fair share of her face. Yet, there was…something. I couldn't put my finger on it.

I raised my eyebrows. "You cannot be serious."

"I'll even let you keep your weapons, while I—" she held up her hands to show me "—have none. I can tell you've been trained, it wouldn't be an unfair fight."

I stared at her. This was a terrible idea, and I was sure she was up to something. She'd already cheated once, and if I let her do it again then more the fool was I.

But even with magic, there was the very real possibility that she was stronger than me. I hadn't expected her to be so talented at illusion.

"You would be using no weapons?" I clarified, wanting to hear her speak the words again.

"No weapons, only my natural form," she promised.

A cold gust of wind blew through the clearing, bringing with it a flurry of snow. The icy drops hit my face and bare hands, and an enormous shiver passed through me. As it had been blown out like a candle, the flame in my hand flickered and died. I tried to flex my fingers and found them stiff and throbbing with cold.

Fuck.

I still hated this idea, but now it seemed I had no choice. If I was lucky, she was trained similarly to Scion. He was deadly with magic, but even he would admit he had never properly learned to use a sword. Maybe Cassinda would be like that. Too dependent on magic to realize how poor she was at fighting.

"Fine," I replied quickly. "No magic."

She smiled widely at me like she'd already won the crown. "It's a bargain."

I reached again for my knife and held it out in front of me. Only then, I looked directly into Cassinda's face. Her smile seemed to be growing wider. Her mouth stretched her teeth multiplying and her face elongated faster and faster.

I stumbled back, my heart pounding out of control. Oh shit.

Right in front of me Cassinda disappeared and in her place stood an enormous, shaggy, brown bear.

30
LONNIE
THE FOREST, NEVERMORE

I shadow walked.

I didn't care at all that it was breaking the rules, or about the bargain I'd just made. I was staring into the angry eyes of a two-thousand pound monster, and I wasn't going to just stand there and let her eat me.

She charged forward toward me, but I was already falling backwards into the shadows. The last thing I saw of her was her huge jaws opening wide, before I spun through darkness and reemerged on the road where Ambrose and I had first seen Cassinda.

I fell to the ground, panting.

What the fuck was that?

I wracked my brain, trying to remember if anyone had mentioned that Cassinda could turn into a giant fucking bear. I was sure they hadn't, and that seemed like the kind of thing I might remember. So what was going on? Was it simply part of her illusion ability?

Somehow, I didn't think it was.

Cassinda had said something about her "true form" and foolishly I hadn't thought to read into it.

This, too, explained why she made me think of Bael. She had an animal lurking behind her eyes, clawing at her to be let out.

I shivered, and this time it was only half due to the cold.

Getting to my feet again, I looked around. Behind me was more dark forest, and beyond that was the beach where the sirens were undoubtedly waiting to lure me into the ocean. To either side the road stretched out of sight, but right in front of me was a smooth hill, covered in snow.

I bolted toward it.

The snow was deep, and for once I was glad of it. My boots sank in up to the ankles, then as I walked further I sank to my knees, then my thighs. My body began to shiver so violently, I could barely move my feet. Still, I kept going.

I reached the bottom of the hill, where it began to slope sharply upward, and stopped. In front of me was a wall of white.

I put my hands out and was unsurprised to find that I was unable to conjure any flames. Gritting my teeth, I rubbed my hands together vigorously, trying to get some blood flow back into the tips of my fingers.

It hurt, and I bit back a pathetic sob as I continued to shake out my frozen hands, jumping up and down for all the good it might do.

Finally, I felt my hands begin to thaw.

I conjured a small burst of dancing orange flames, and thrust my hands out in front of me toward the wall of snow.

At first, nothing happened. Then, a small hole began to melt in the side of the snowy hill. I wanted to jump up and down again, but restrained myself, continuing to make the hole wider and wider with my flames.

If I could melt a cave into the side of this hill, and by some miracle the snow was deep enough, I could stay hidden in my cave until sunrise. There was even some faint hope the cave would keep me sheltered from the elements enough that I wouldn't freeze to death while I waited.

It was a good plan.

Or, if not a good one, it wasn't the worst plan I'd ever thought of.

I worked quickly, melting the snow until a decently sized cave emerged, wider on the inside than it appeared from the entrance. I was almost shocked at how well it had worked. The melted snow began to freeze again nearly as soon as I moved to the next section, which made the walls sturdy with ice. I tried melting all the way down to the ground, but discovered that beneath the snow the ground was wet and muddy, as if it had once been a swamp. I replaced the snow and merely packed the floor down to make it flat.

Finally, I straightened, feeling relatively pleased with myself. I was still cold, but not nearly as cold as I had been outside. Better yet, at least forty minutes had passed and Cassinda hadn't found me. That meant I had only six hours left until sunrise, and things were looking up.

* * *

I awoke to the sound of cracking ice.

I hadn't even realized I'd fallen asleep. I certainly hadn't meant to, and my brain felt sluggish. As if my blood was moving through my body at a trickle rather than a stream.

I shook my throbbing head and slowly blinked my eyes, trying to regain focus in the dim cave.

Suddenly, a loud thumping noise snapped me back to reality, and I remembered what great noise had awoken me in the first place. My hands trembled and my breath caught in my throat. With my heart pounding in my chest, I slowly turned my body towards the gaping mouth of the cave.

As I'd half known, half feared it would be, the enormous brown bear was blocking the mouth of my cave. It peered in at me, its jaws dripping and its beady eyes flashing with rage. The entrance was too small for it to walk through, but not for long. The beast was relentlessly thrashing and clawing at the ice, determined to break through and get inside.

Shock and fear immediately woke me fully, my adrenaline rising and bringing my temperature with it.

I got clumsily to my feet and reached for the knife in my boot with one hand and my flames with the other. The flames flickered in and out, my cold trembling hands refusing to hold them steady. Even if I'd wanted to, I suddenly couldn't even remember how to shadow walk.

The bear smashed its shoulders against the walls of my cave, and finally broke through. My flickering flame reflected in its black eyes, and went out.

I wasn't sure if I screamed out loud or in my mind as the hulking bear charged. It thundered toward me, its heavy paws smashing through the snow and ice as it closed in. Its breath billowed out in ragged puffs, and its fur stood on end as it prepared to attack. I shrunk back against the wall as the beast let out a fierce roar, lunging toward me.

Its enormous paw swiped out, raking my stomach. The force of the blow nearly knocked me off my feet and for the briefest moment, I couldn't feel the pain.

Then, I screamed. And screamed. And *screamed.*

The blood didn't spray, but rather gurgled out of me. Slowly at first, then faster, it poured out of my stomach and onto my hands. It dripped onto the ground making bright crimson patterns in the snow.

I choked, and was distantly surprised when the blood leaked from my mouth too, dribbling down my chin.

My vision swam and I struggled to keep my eyes open as the bear walked toward me, looming. I could feel the heat from its massive body radiating against my skin.

At least I wouldn't be cold anymore.

I clutched at my stomach, feeling blood pouring out of me so fast it soaked the ground around me and froze into huge scarlet sheets of ice. I was distantly aware of the frantic pound of footsteps, but I couldn't force myself to look up.

My legs buckled under me and I slid down the wall clutching my stomach. There were voices in the back of my mind, confused and talking over each other.

It didn't matter anymore. I was already dead…maybe?

I smiled slightly, delirium setting in. I'd nearly died so many times before, but this time felt different. I couldn't feel the pain anymore. I couldn't feel the cold.

I blinked…maybe?

A glint of light flashed past as a sword swung through the air and the bear's head rolled toward me. I stared down at it and blinked again.

A woman's head stared back at me…maybe?

My consciousness wavered. I let my head fall back against the wall, my eyes rolling into my head.

Realization settled in, overtaking madness. I knew I was dying. Knew I was more than half dead already.

I tried to conjure a happy memory. The faces of those that I loved. Anything to die with to make it feel as if it had all been worth something.

But I could find nothing. I could remember nothing.

All there was was fire and rage. Never ending rage at being unfinished. At being incomplete.

And then, somehow, I was climbing up a mountain.

As if in a dream, I climbed higher, but my feet wouldn't move. I went faster, but gained no ground. Still, I kept climbing and the wind whipped around me, bringing whispers on the breeze.

"Never make a bargain with a fairy," it seemed to say.

The earth was burning, the air thick with smoke, but still I climbed higher, my hands and feet slipping against the rocks.

"I'll kill anyone who hurts you, little monster."

I slipped further back, sliding down the rocks and I cried out but my voice was lost in the whispering wind.

"I love you enough for both of us."

Finally, I reached the top; clawing, scraping, begging.

"The new heir will be created, forged of Source fire."

I looked down over raging fire, opened my mouth, and screamed and screamed and *screamed.*

I kept screaming, but only then did I realize that I had no words, nor a voice with which to speak them. I was laughing and crying, but I had no eyes, no mouth, I had no body that was not consumed by flames.

And then, I was the flames; burning, blazing, Wilde.

I was fire.

I was creation and destruction; power and magic.

I was life and death.

I was the great equalizer.

I was *the Source.*

PART THREE
Truth or Dare

31
BAEL
UNDERNEATH

A breathtakingly beautiful woman knelt in front of me.

She'd approached slowly, her hips swaying and her dark curls bouncing around her shoulders, before lowering herself to the floor in front of my throne and bowing her head in reverence. "My lord," she murmured, her voice like honey.

Rising from my seat, I descended the stairs toward her with slow, deliberate steps, letting my gaze trail over her lovely features. I stopped in front of her, close enough to touch. "You may rise."

With a delicate gracefulness, she rose to her feet and took a step closer…

I swung my arm back with all my strength and smashed my fist into the side of her head.

Several courtiers gasped at the sound of the woman's skull cracking, and scrambled out of the way as she went flying backwards across the room. She landed in a heap on the stone floor, leaving the room in silence.

I squinted over at her. Hmm. That must have been thirty feet—possibly a new personal record. I should write that down.

"My lord!" A feeble voice stammered from somewhere to my right.

I held up a hand to halt him, my gaze still fixed on the woman. She looked dead, or at the very least knocked out, but I knew better.

The first time I'd had to fight one of these things I'd hesitated because it was female. Or at least, it looked female. The bruxa walked around looking like young, high Fae women, but once angered they shifted back into their true form.

And that true form was *disgusting.*

Sure enough, across the room the thing that had once resembled a young Fae woman leapt to its enormous webbed feet.

It towered nearly fifteen feet tall. Its body was gray and boney, and I could see its internal organs moving around beneath its paper-thin skin. It looked down at me with huge, milky-white eyes and snarled showing a mouth of brown fangs.

I snapped my own fangs together menacingly. *Come on, let's get this over with,*

Rising to the challenge, the thing charged running directly at me with enough force to bowl over a team of oxen. I waited until it was close, then I launched myself into the air and landed gracefully on four powerful paws. As I'd anticipated, the bruxa skidded to a halt, its weird milky white eyes going wide.

Not giving the beast a chance to recover, I lunged forward, raking at its hollow chest with my claws.

Within seconds the entire thing was over and I stalked back across the hall to lie on the carpet in front of my throne. That one was really too easy.

There seemed to be some sort of rumor going around Underneath that I'd make an easy kill. People were saying that I wasn't really Gancanagh's son. That I hadn't killed him, and that I was a weak seelie prince, sent here by the capital to turn Underneath into another high Fae city.

Now, challenger after challenger was showing up at the court to try and take the crown.

On my first morning here I'd had to fight seven duels, one after another, until finally one of my father's former servants told everyone to go home and come back tomorrow. Every day since had been exactly the same.

Eighteen hours a day, I sat in the throne room and waited for monster after monster to try and kill me. I would kill them instead, sometimes two or three per hour, and then I'd get to sleep for a few hours before we did it all again.

I loved it.

If not for the fact that I couldn't see Lonnie, I would have never wanted to leave.

I let my eyes roll back into my head, searching. Every time I thought of Lonnie—which was more often than was probably healthy—I always felt the urge to search for her. When they'd all been in Inbetwixt it was easy enough to watch her, but now they'd moved, and I wasn't sure which city they'd decided to search next.

I let my eye search several streets in Overcast before blinking and returning to the task in front of me.

On the other side of the room, the waiting challengers were recovering from their shock over the bruxa. I could hear the murmuring as they egged each other on, choosing someone to face me next.

I was eying a sturdy looking troll with a large spiked club, thinking he might be a fun challenge, when the voice of my advisor rang out again.

"My lord!" This time, unwilling to be ignored, Draven darted out from behind the throne and stood directly in front of me.

Draven was a short, thin man who didn't look like he would be much in a fight. He reminded me a bit too much of Mordant, making me predisposed to hate him. Still, he still might prove useful. There were so many things about Underneath that I didn't know.

"I believe we should conclude for the day, your majesty," Draven said imploringly.

"Why?" I growled, before remembering he wouldn't understand me. I abruptly shifted back. "Why?"

He looked nervous, and averted his gaze from my lack of clothing before continuing. "I have a list you might like to go through."

"A list?" I didn't think I'd ever sounded so disgusted in my life.

"Yes. Of potential challengers. I'll gladly explain further once…" he trailed off, jerking his head meaningfully at the group milling around the edges of the hall.

"Once there's no audience?" I guessed.

"Precisely."

I rolled my eyes. "Fine. Send them away until tomorrow. I'm going to take a bath, I'm covered in guts."

He looked revolted, but bowed. "Yes lord."

* * *

Though I'd only suggested the idea to avoid Draven, I still returned to my chambers and took an extraordinarily long bath. Partly because I hadn't had the chance to bathe in far too long, and partly because I'd finally located Lonnie and wanted to watch her.

I soaked in the hot water as I watched her arriving in Nevermore. She climbed into some sleigh with Ambrose and I practically vibrated with anger at how cold and miserable she looked. Why wasn't Ambrose doing anything to help her? Who the fuck was that woman driving them?

My bath water churned, and I struggled to get my leaking magic back under control.

Then, thankfully, Scion appeared and took her back into the castle. At least someone gave a fuck if she froze to death.

I watched Lonnie for nearly an hour longer than I should have. First to make sure she was alright and that her injuries were healed. Then, because things turned more interesting.

Whatever conversation Lonnie and Scion were having had quickly gone from serious to heated. I raised my eyebrows, my pulse beginning to race as I watched Scion slap her bare cunt with the palm of his hand.

Was it fucked up to watch them? Absolutely. But I was so far beyond caring. Anyway, I reasoned with myself, it wasn't as if I hadn't seen it before.

I gripped my cock beneath the water, squeezing tightly as I watched her climb on top of him and begin to move. She rolled her hips, tits bouncing, her mouth parting in ecstasy. I wished I could be there. I wanted to suck on her pretty nipples and play with her clit while she got herself off on Scion's cock.

I lingered long enough to watch Lonnie come, then yanked myself back to the present. Unsure if I felt more or less relaxed than before, I got out of the bath and went to track down my advisor.

* * *

The halls of the palace of Underneath were just as long and winding as those in the obsidian palace. I wasn't yet familiar enough with the castle to quickly shadow walk from room to room, so I had to walk at a normal pace. It was a slow process, and it took me at least ten minutes to get anywhere.

Lost in thought, I wandered down the dimly lit hallway, unaware of my surroundings. Suddenly, a loud caw and the sound of flapping wings jolted me out of my reverie. I stumbled backwards as a large raven landed on my shoulder, its beady eyes staring directly into mine.

"Agh!" I yelled, flailing my arms to shake it off. "What the fuck! Get off me!"

Quill squawked in outrage, but his talons just dug deeper into my flesh, gripping my shoulder as if his life depended on it.

Which, it motherfucking did, because I was finally going to make good on my longstanding promise to kill the evil thing.

I'd never liked Scion's horrible bird even when I was a child. I was a cat, and therefore the bird and I were natural enemies. But that wasn't the problem. I was positive that it wasn't merely a bird as Scion claimed. It had some sort of malevolent presence. A dark soul trapped inside it that brought destruction wherever it went.

I grabbed for the birds neck, trying to choke it until it let go of me, but it pecked violently at my hand.

"Agh!" I yelled again, drawing my hand back quickly to escape the razor sharp beak.

I spun down the hallway, slamming into walls attempting to shake the thing loose—or better yet smash its head against the stone.

When that failed, I tried magic, but I couldn't get the aim right. I destroyed several paintings, a vase, and an entire damn wall before giving up.

Eventually I collapsed on the floor, entirely spent. The bird sat on my shoulder, cooing softly.

"What are you?" I panted, not sure if I was asking the bird personally or the gods themselves. "Do you realize I've killed several dozen monsters in just the last day alone? Trolls, goblins, brexa are no problem, but then there's you."

The bird chattered, and I could fucking swear it was laughing at me.

"What do you want from me?" I demanded. "I wrote your letter. What else is there?"

The bird cocked its head at me, its huge fathomless eyes peering into mine. I could swear it was saying. "Take me with you, you stupid prick."

I threw my hands up in indignation. "Fine. Fine! You can come to the meeting. It's not as if I can be rid of you anyway. Demonic fucking bird…"

I was still muttering when I stepped into Draven's office, Quill still on my shoulder.

The advisor glanced at the bird, then looked away, evidently deciding not to ask. I had kept him waiting a long time, and I supposed he was hoping to get this over quickly.

"Well, what is it?" I asked flatly.

Draven's eyebrows angled in annoyance. "I thought you'd like to know that you've rallied the support of two thirds of the country in only a matter of days. It's impressive, certainly. Some credit must be given to your father, of course. Gancanagh was an unusually stable ruler, and the continuity of father to son makes many feel confident in your leadership. The majority of the support, however, is coming from news of your many duels, so that credit is yours alone."

I raised an eyebrow. He was being far too complimentary, and many years' experience had taught me that when advisors were too kind it meant bad news was coming swiftly.

"Who's the other third who doesn't support me?" I asked.

"Ah." Draven laid out a list on the nearby desk and gestured for me to look.

I read through it quickly. None of the names were the slightest bit familiar. "These are all challengers?"

"Not exactly," Draven said. "These are influential citizens who do not wish to challenge for the crown, and are instead voicing their lack of support publicly. They think you are too seelie to lead the Unseelie."

"Why?" I snapped.

He gestured at me vaguely.

"Your…appearance doesn't help. We are a kingdom of monsters in search of other monsters to lead us."

I grimaced. If only he knew how well that described me. But apparently that didn't matter because I looked like high Fae. Ironically, in the other court, I was too Unseelie. There didn't seem to be any way to win such an argument.

"I can't say I knew my father well." *Or at all.* "But it would be hard to deny we looked similar."

"True," Draven agreed. "But Gancanagh spent the majority of his time in his beast form."

I grunted in some vague agreement. I could do that. The only problem was I couldn't speak in that form as my father had been able to. But perhaps with practice?

"If you want my advice…" Draven hedged.

"That's why you're here, isn't it?"

"Yes. Well, I suggest that you choose a name from this list and make an example of them. Call them here to fight, or go to them. It makes no difference. All that matters is that the duel is seen."

I raised my eyebrow. That wasn't a bad idea. I leaned over the list again. "Who?"

He pointed at a name at the very bottom of the list. "I would suggest you start here."

I frowned. I had no way of knowing if that was a good suggestion or not.

On a whim I would undoubtably regret later, I turned to the bird on my shoulder. "What do you think?"

Quill tittered, and it sounded like. *"I thought you'd never ask. You must be less stupid than you look."*

The bird hopped off my shoulder at last. I quickly reached up to massage the tender flesh as I watched the bird reading the list—No, it was *looking* at the list; birds couldn't read.

As if it could hear my thoughts, Quill looked up at me before pecking his beak into the center of one of the names.

I picked up the list, peering at a tiny hole in the center of the name "Apophis." *No last name.*

"Right," I said briskly. "I'll go meet with that one, then. Where do I find him—or is it a she?"

Draven's eyes widened and he trembled slightly. "Lord, I'm not sure—"

"*Where do I find them*?" I asked again, every word over-pronounced.

"In the mountains, lord. Apophis is a dragon."

32
LONNIE
THE CAVE, NEVERMORE

I awoke wrapped in warmth and confusion.

My awareness returned before I opened my eyes, and for a long minute I lay there marveling at the feel of my own body. I could feel my heart steadily beating. Feel my arms and legs, my fingers and toes. I could feel the slight burn of thirst in my throat, and hear the rushing of wind in my ears.

I wasn't sure I'd ever been grateful for those things before, but suddenly they seemed marvelous.

I squirmed slightly, and realized I could feel other things, too. *So many other things.*

My eyes popped open, and several realizations hit me all at once.

Firstly, I had no memory of how or why, but I was lying on top of Ambrose. The warmth of his skin seeped into mine, as his bare chest rose and fell with each steady, sleeping breath. I was draped completely over him, my bare breasts pressed against his sculpted chest, my legs tangled with his, and…other areas…fit together entirely too well not to notice.

Secondly, and to that point: we were completely nude.

I was distantly aware that I should have been bothered by this, but instead I could only fixate on where we were and how exactly we'd gotten there.

I raised my head slightly, and it all came flooding back to me in a rush.

We were still in the snow cave.

That explained the position I'd woken up in. It seemed as if Ambrose had removed his cloak and laid it out on the floor, separating us from the icy ground below. Then, he shed his clothes, and mine, and used every scrap of fabric to cover us. I couldn't complain. Without his burning skin, several degrees warmer than mine on average, I would have surely succumbed to the cold.

I glanced behind me, more memories coming back in a steady stream.

Outside the door, I could see that the sky was still dark, and to our left… I turned to look, already knowing and fearing what I would find. Cassinda's dead body, reverted to her human shape, lay on the snow in a puddle of frozen blood. Her head was lying several feet from her body and staring up at me with wide eyes, already turning the milky-white of death.

I recoiled. *By the Source…*

Instinctively, I flexed my stomach muscles. I was half expecting to find my insides shredded, but the pain was gone.

What had happened here?

My movement roused Ambrose and he murmured in his sleep, shifting.

Slowly, he opened his eyes, blinking several times. He looked up at me, and his eyes shot open fully. "You're alive!"

I frowned at him. Was it that bad? Why couldn't I recall all the details of what had happened?

Ambrose didn't seem to notice or care that I hadn't responded. His eyes, often distant, were suddenly blazing fire.

He sat up, inadvertently taking me with him as I tumbled sideways into his lap. Without preamble, he gripped my face tightly in both hands, and slammed his lips down on mine.

I gasped in shock and his tongue thrust between my parted lips. I moaned into his mouth, angling my head so he could kiss me deeper, more completely. His hand found my hair, while the other tugged me closer, holding me trapped against his chest.

Every press of his mouth and swipe of his tongue sent liquid heat racing through me, igniting every nerve in my body and leaving me breathless and wanting more.

My mind finally catching up with me, I crawled into his lap, letting all the clothing that had been piled on top of us fall away.

Abruptly, he pulled back, gasping. "I'm sorry."

My brow furrowed in confusion, my breath still coming out ragged. "Why?"

"I didn't mean to do it like that. Like this…" he looked down at all the clothing falling uselessly on the ground all around us. "You were far too cold."

"I know," I whispered, chasing his mouth. "I'm fine."

I want this. I want you. You're mine.

He shook his head again, seeming determined to act as if I hadn't been lying on top of him. As if he hadn't just kissed me like the world was about to end.

"Let me see your stomach," he demanded, reaching for me.

A spark of irritation shot through me, but I obliged, guiding his fingers to trail over the smooth skin of my abdomen. "I'm fine." I told him. "You're doing, I assume?"

I didn't really remember much of anything after the bear swiped at me. I must have been losing my mind from blood loss and cold, and anything and everything felt like a dream rather than something that had happened to me only hours ago.

I might have been surprised to find myself healed, except that I was alive. He must have given me his blood, or I surely would have never woken up.

"You healed me." I said, more of a statement than a question.

He shook his head. "I tried, but—" he broke off, looking at a complete loss.

"But what?"

His expression was chaos. Confusion, guilt, anger, relief. There was so much there I couldn't pick out any one emotion individually.

"I thought you died," he said finally.

My eyes widened. "What happened?"

"I'd been searching for you," he said, distractedly. "I couldn't find you anywhere. Scion was stuck up at the castle holding all the other hunters back, so I was alone."

"Is he alright?" I demanded.

"I assume so. It hasn't been that long. The hunt is still going on."

I bit my lip. If I'd been injured as badly as I remembered then I was sure Scion and Bael would have felt it. They were probably going out of their minds now, wherever they were.

"I found your footsteps in the woods," Ambrose continued. "But then you disappeared. I assumed you shadow walked."

"I did. Your fiancé was trying to kill me."

"She's not my fucking fiancé," he growled, gaze suddenly snapping back to mine. "If I could kill her again for hurting you I would do it a thousand times over."

I shivered, liking the angry growl in his voice, but now that he'd begun I wanted to hear the rest. I wanted to understand. "Then what happened?"

"I kept looking for you on foot. Then, I *saw* you. In a vision, which has hardly ever happened. I sprinted all the way here but I was too late. I killed the bear, but you were barely conscious. I could hear your heart failing, so I cut open my arm and gave you as much blood as I could force you to swallow."

He held up his left arm and showed me a deep gash from wrist to elbow. It was still oozing slightly, not healing like it should have.

"Why would you use a Source forged blade?" I demanded.

"I wasn't thinking," he said angrily. It was as if he was relaying the story to himself as much as to me, words pouring out of him faster than he could process them. He looked at me, black eyes flashing midnight. "You were fucking dying in front of me. I would've torn my own heart out and given it to you. It's already yours, anyway."

I gasped.

What did he say?

He was staring at me with so much intense emotion raw on his face that it stole my breath. I could hear my own heart beating so loud that it seemed to echo between us. My entire body was humming, my skin buzzing, heat building all over my body.

Then, the realization hit me all at once.

It wasn't sudden or shocking, but rather sensible. Like a piece of a puzzle finally snapping into place, giving me the answers I'd been craving for my entire life.

He was mine.

My stalking shadow. My lover. My *mate.*

And with that realization came a sense of completeness that I'd never felt before, not even with Scion or Bael. It was the knowing that I was finished. I'd found all three, and now I was done searching.

I rose up on my knees so we were close to the same height, and moved so close that we were chest to chest once more.

His breathing was ragged, uncontrolled, and I could almost see the way he was holding himself back. Had been keeping himself on a leash for months, so that we could finally get to this moment.

"Do you know?" he asked, his tone almost desperate. "Please tell me you know, because I can't…I can't fucking do this anymore."

"Do what?" I asked, my lip curling slightly.

"I can't keep pretending that I don't know you're mine. Playing the villain, or the brother, or the friend. I can't keep pretending that I don't want you. I'm shit at it, anyway."

He was, I realized now. He'd dimmed himself for my benefit, waiting for me to have the realization on my own. But he hadn't shut down completely, and if I'd been less oblivious things could have been different.

I lifted my hands to his chest, just below his shoulders, and ran my palms slowly up I could wrap my arms around his neck. "Stop pretending, then."

He growled low in the back of his throat, and I felt him growing hard against my stomach, but still he gave me one last opportunity to flee. "Be careful, love. Think about what you're asking before it's too late."

I brought my face so close that our lips brushed as I spoke. "I'm asking you to fuck me. I'm asking you to mark me and claim me."

"Why?" he demanded. "Say it."

"Because I'm your mate."

33

AMBROSE

THE CAVE, NEVERMORE

"How?" I growled, my hand making the slow ascent up her back to grip her hair. I wrapped my fingers around her curls and pulled, tilting her head back far enough to give myself access to her neck.

"How?" Lonnie echoed, her voice high and breathy.

I trailed my tongue slowly over her skin, tasting her, drawing a path from her collar bone up to swirl my tongue around her ear before leaning in to whisper. "How were you going to let me fuck you?"

Her eyes widened, and she dragged her tongue slowly over her bottom lip. "You tell me."

"Were you going to let me take you?" I asked. "Could I use you however I wanted? Would you let me split your pretty legs open and own your perfect cunt however I liked?"

"Yes," she gasped.

Good.

I pushed her still further, reaching down to draw my fingers through her folds. She was wet and ready, practically melting on my fingers. I wanted to taste her, to suck her off my fingers then feast on her cunt until she was crying. First though, I was going to make her wait. I wanted her to beg me to let her come. Beg me to fuck her, and when I finally did I wanted it to imprint on her very being so she was irreversibly changed.

I pulled my fingers out of her cunt and offered them to her lips. "Suck," I commanded. She seemed surprised, but eagerly complied. It reminded me of how willing she had been back in Underneath, the one time I let myself give in to my desires for her. But now, as I watched her obediently suck on my fingers with hooded eyes, I couldn't help the stirring in my pants. She was such a contradiction - stubborn and defiant during the day, but perfectly submissive in bed.

"That's enough," I said, pulling my hand away from her mouth. Pinching her nipples hard enough to make her yelp, I sat back down on the cloak spread out on the floor. Despite the cold, I spread my legs wide and pulled her onto my lap. She straddled me and began grinding down on my already painful cock.

Placing one hand on her back and using the other to push away strands of hair from her face, I warned her to be careful. But she couldn't resist rolling her hips again, making me hiss in desire. It would have been easier to tease her if we were both dressed, but as it was, she was only one movement away from impaling herself on me.

"I'll fuck you when I'm ready," I told her. "Be patient." She pouted and rolled her hips again, almost letting the head of my cock slide inside her.

But before that could happen, I grabbed fistfuls of her ass and redirected her movements, leaning forward to take her nipples into my mouth instead. She moaned and arched into me as I trailed kisses up her neck and found her lips with mine.

Unable to resist any longer, I kissed her slowly, savoring every moment of finally having this woman in my arms after years of wanting her. Lost in our passion, I didn't stop her when she shifted forward and the head of my cock slid into her wetness. She was so ready for me, making it almost too easy.

"Well," she breathed, no longer moving her hips. "Are you going to fuck me now?"

I stayed still, barely inside her, fighting the urge to thrust forward and finish this. I wanted to take my time with her, make this moment last after waiting for so long.

"Not yet, love," I said, lifting her off of me and laying her on her back. With her legs spread open on either side of my knees, I could tell she knew exactly where this was going and couldn't wait any longer.

Leaning down, I pushed her legs wider and fastened my mouth over her cunt. She closed her eyes as if in pain, but let out a soft breath as I slowly licked up and down, driving her wild with desire. Moving to her clit, I sucked lightly and teased until she couldn't control her moans and whimpers anymore.

She rested her feet on my shoulders as I continued to pleasure her, lost in the taste and feel of her after years of only imagining what it would be like.

She made a sound between pleasure and frustration, and tried to lift her hips. I placed a hand flat on her stomach, exactly where she had been injured only hours before, and shoved her back down.

I sat up so I could watch her face, replacing my lips with my fingers. I rolled her clit between my thumb and forefinger, then shoved another finger inside of her. Then two.

"Oh, Gods," she moaned. "Please."

"What do you want, love?"

I expected her to say she wanted to come or for me to fuck her. But instead she said "Everything."

My eyes widened.

I didn't know why I liked that answer or even what she meant, but I decided to give it to her anyway.

Still alternating between thrusting my fingers inside of her and rubbing little circles on her clit, I bent my head to press a kiss to the inside of her inner thigh.

She didn't even seem to notice at first, but when I dragged my teeth over that spot, she paid attention.

“What were you doing?” she moaned, her breathing uneven again. I could tell she was close.

“What would you have done if I marked you there?” I licked the skin of her thigh again to illustrate my point.

She didn't say anything, just kept writhing against my hand.

I pulled my fingers back until she looked at me, clearly rebellious.

“What would you have said if I marked you there?” I asked again.

“That you might as well have written your name on my cunt.”

I smirked. She shouldn't have given me any ideas.

Leisurely, I went back to stroking her, wanting her wound up and ready again before deciding where to brand her.

“I want you on your hands and knees,” I told her.

She looked at me as if contemplating an argument, but wisely stayed silent. Scrambling up, she knelt on all fours in front of me.

Kneeling behind her, I pressed my face against her cunt from behind, lapping at her already sensitive core.

She yelped and tried to stand up. With one hand, I pushed her back down. "What did I just tell you, love?"

"But—" she didn't even seem to know what to complain about.

I laughed and dragged my tongue from her clit all the way up to her ass.

"Are you going to let me fuck you here?" I asked her, pressing the tip of my finger against that most sensitive area.

I could tell by her silence that her eyes had widened.

I smacked her ass, just to get her attention back on me. I kept lapping at her and finally she answered with a low moan of pleasure. "I don't know."

"You should probably get used to it," I told her semi-seriously.

"Why?"

"You have three mates, love."

She didn't seem to know what to say to that, so I took pity on her. Gripping her hips, I pulled her back towards my face, devouring her until her legs were trembling and she was moaning my name over and over again like a chant.

Finally, I could feel the fluttering of her muscles and hear the change in her voice. I pushed her leg out to the side so I could sink my teeth into her inner thigh.

She screamed from the combined force of her orgasm and the pain of the bite. Her scream was so loud that I was sure they could hear her all the way back at the castle, but I couldn't care less. All I could think about was her blood pouring over my tongue and the permanent mark on her thigh that proved she was mine.

Lonnie collapsed forward onto the ground, panting. I waited a full ten seconds before drawing her back to me and gently turning her to lie on her back.

She blinked up at me, dazed.

"You don't think we're done, do you love?"

She laughed softly. "I need to catch my breath."

I grinned, satisfied by how wrung out she looked. "Fine, I'll start slow."

She had whimpered as I grabbed her knees and dragged her towards me, lifting her hips to line them up with my own.

In one long stroke I slid into her, then paused, closing my eyes. She had been so fucking wet and still trembling from her orgasm, it had been like torture to have to go slow.

But I had promised her I would.

I slid back out and in again, moving so slowly that I was certain that after a moment she would be begging me to go faster. To fuck her hard and real, in the way that claimed her just as much as that bite ever could.

Sure enough, after a minute, Lonnie sat up and scrambled back into my lap, straddling me as before. She didn't ask before she seated herself on my cock, and gripped my hair drawing my face back up to hers for another kiss.

I let her take control then, riding me, rubbing herself and drawing a second shuddering orgasm from her lips.

She moved faster and faster, riding out her pleasure, and finally I gripped her hair and shoved her head down against my throat.

I didn't need to tell her what I wanted, or when. She already understood. It was instinctive.

So as my stomach muscles finally contracted, and I let out a shout, spilling inside her, she sunk her teeth into my throat.

The effect was immediate.

I had heard it wasn't always like that, but perhaps since I had known she was my mate for so long, been watching her, waiting for her for so many years the bond instantly snapped into place.

I sucked in a breath and closed my eyes, wondering for half a second if this was the moment it all ended. The moment we found out I was wrong about the bonding in the most brutal possible way, and I simply dropped dead on the spot, still buried inside her.

But it wasn't. I took another breath and everything was fine—better than fine. For once, everything was good.

I thought that might have been the happiest I had been in a long time. Possibly ever.

Which begged the question, what was still missing?

34
BAEL
UNDERNEATH

A dragon. A fucking *dragon.*

I'd never seen one before, and I practically vibrated with excitement as I shadow walked up to the mountains. A *dragon.*

And best of all, I might get to fight it.

When Draven had said the name on his list of dissenters was a dragon, I almost didn't believe him. For one thing, no one was quite sure if they existed anymore. They lived so far into the mountains that many Fae believed them extinct. For another, why was this particular dragon against my leadership? When had he said that, and to whom?

I couldn't wait to find out.

I shadow walked on to the path near the tallest mountain. Draven, who was not completely useless as it turned out, had pointed to the mountain and then shown me a painting of the path. It was a quick way to avoid having to walk up the entire peak, and for that I was grateful.

I'd intended to go alone, but of course, I couldn't.

"I don't know why you can't at least fly," I grumbled to the raven on my shoulder. "Come if you want, but do you have to sit there all the time?"

Quill tittered. *'My, aren't you weaker than you look.'*

"And aren't you heavier than *you* look?"

I rolled my eyes. I thought I might be going a bit mad talking to the bird all the time. But, I supposed, there wasn't really anyone else to talk to here.

I certainly wouldn't say the bird was growing on me. More like, he simply wouldn't leave. I wondered if Scion had put him up to this, sending him to watch me and report back. If so, I had no idea why. He seemed busy at the moment, and I hadn't seen Quill visit him to make any reports.

I walked down the mountain path and reached the mouth of the cave. It was surprisingly apparent from the road, and looked unguarded. I frowned. It didn't seem to be a secret where the dragon lived, but I supposed visitors weren't often welcome.

Well, with any luck he'd be expecting me. I'd sent Quill with a message that I planned to visit yesterday. I'd heard nothing back, but I didn't expect to. Either the dragon would be waiting to attack me the moment I walked in, or perhaps he had some demands we could negotiate. Either way was fine with me.

I stepped inside the cave, my footsteps echoing off the damp walls, and looked around.

It was an enormous cavern, very like the one beneath Cross's den. I couldn't help but remember the burn of arrows through my flesh as I walked on, the musty scent of earth and ancient stone filling my nostrils.

Arrows were unlikely, I reasoned with myself. A dragon wouldn't need traps. If anything, I should be more nervous about being swallowed whole while my back was turned.

Quill still riding on my shoulder, I made my way deeper into the darkness. After a few moments, the passageway opened up into another vast cavern, illuminated by shafts of sunlight peeking through cracks in the ceiling.

My eyes scanned the rocky expanse, searching for any sign of the dragon. Yet, all I found were empty alcoves and abandoned bones of what looked like past meals.

A shiver ran down my spine, half anxiety half excitement.

"Any ideas which way to go?" I asked Quill.

As he often did, the bird did seem to have an opinion. He leapt into the air and flew off, venturing deeper into the cave. Sighing, I jogged after him, squinting to see where he'd gone.

He just had to be a black bird flying into darkness, didn't he? Why couldn't Scion have had a parrot? I supposed it might ruin his tortured image.

I grinned, stifling a laugh.

I continued jogging, my feet crunching on bones and gravel. As I rounded a bend, I stopped short, staring wide eyed up at the room before me. "Shit."

I was standing in an enormous treasure room, ten times the size of Cross's vault, but just as packed with treasure. There were gold coins, lost crowns, jeweled necklaces and loose stones *everywhere.*

As I approached the mound of treasure, my eyes scanned over the glinting objects. I reached down and plucked a tarnished coin from the ground and held it up to the light. This wasn't currency I recognized. It must have been old. Older than Elsewhere itself, maybe.

I needed to get out of here. The dragon clearly wasn't in this room, but if it caught me here my visit would likely become far more difficult.

I turned around, looking for Quill, when something flashed out of the corner of my eye. I turned, expecting movement, but instead found myself staring at a large wooden chest tucked away in the corner. There wasn't anything remarkable about it. It was plain compared with the rest of the room. In fact, the only interesting thing I could see was that etched onto the lid was a familiar crest. The Everlast family emblem blazed on the top.

I marched over to it, curiosity piqued, and threw open the lid. "Fuck."

I stared down at a glittering sapphire, twinkling up at me from an otherwise empty chest. It looked far too familiar.

I ran my fingers through my hair. Perhaps I should have expected something like this. After all, Ambrose had sent me to Underneath, and the bird was a bit too helpful

I grabbed the sapphire and examined it. It was the exact size and shape of the jewel of Inbetwixt, like they were meant to mirror each other. I hadn't pursued the book as carefully as Ambrose, but I was sure the overcast jewel was a sapphire.

Taking a deep breath, I stuck the gem in my pocket.

Immediately, and as I'd half expected, a deafening boom erupted behind me . It was followed by another and another, like the pounding of giant footsteps.

The ground trembled beneath my feet as a monstrous roar echoed through the air, causing my hair to stand on end. And then, with one final resounding thud, the dragon emerged from its hiding place, its massive form casting a shadow over everything around it. Its scales glistened even without much light to reflect off them.

“Thief!” It rumbled.

I closed my eyes. “Shit.”

35
LONNIE
THE ROAD TO OVERCAST

With the diamond in hand, we fled Nevermore.

The moment dawn broke and the horn sounded for the final time, Ambrose and I were already prepared to leave. We'd met Scion on the road, where he was already searching for us, and the three of us shadow walked off the island without returning to the keep.

After all, we'd gotten what we came for–albeit in a more violent and traumatic fashion than any of us would have liked. Cassinda was in possession of the jewel when she died, and we were able to collect it from her severed neck with very little fanfare.

In fact, there was no celebration at all.

We might have collected the second jewel, but it had cost all of us far too much.

Even the brand new bond between Ambrose and I was not enough to cheer me. I could feel it pulsing in my chest, somehow identical to the bond I shared with Scion and yet…not.

Now was not the time to consider it, however. Not when my

brain was sluggish and every movement and thought felt like a chore.

It did not help that we hadn't slept. Hadn't eaten anything, and hadn't had a chance to bathe and wash the blood from our hands—both literally and metaphorically. We'd had to abandon our food and extra clothing in the keep, and worst of all, we lost Queen Celia's book.

"Don't worry, love," Ambrose said, with a forced confidence I was sure he didn't feel. "I've practically memorized that book. We'll be fine without it."

I didn't look at him when he said this. I didn't really want to know if he flinched at the pain of a lie.

To avoid being separated again, Ambrose guided both Scion and I through the shadows. Though he hadn't commented on it, it was obvious to me that Ambrose had some unusual measure of control over his shadow walking. Maybe that explained how he'd managed to be no where and somehow everywhere at once for the last ten years that Scion had searched for him. Maybe it didn't matter anymore as long as we were all on the same side.

Ambrose brought us to a small woodland inn along the north-bound road between Overcast and Inbetwixt. We ate and bathed and slept a few unbroken hours before we had to leave again, pushing on toward Overcast.

In order to give Ambrose a break, we had bought horses from the innkeeper and set off at a leisurely pace towards the north. Despite the fact that it would still take us a full day and night to reach Overcast, we were in no particular hurry. We hadn't yet determined where the final jewel was located, and even though no one said it aloud, I could tell that both Scion and Ambrose were reluctant to face their family.

"I've been thinking a lot about the other night," I said that afternoon as we rode.

As he rode ahead, Ambrose turned his head to look back at me with a smirk. "Is that so, love?"

I felt my cheeks heat. "I meant about Cassinda."

Both my mates growled in displeasure. Scion had felt the moment that I was clawed by the bear, but hadn't been able to reach me in time for it to matter. I could tell the incident haunted him, and I only hoped his scowl would lessen with time.

"What about her?" Ambrose barked.

"When she mauled me. You said you thought I died. I'm starting to think maybe I did—at least for a moment."

I'd posed the statement as casually as I could, but still, both males yanked back on their reins, and turned around in their saddles to face me.

"Do you remember it?" Ambrose said, his voice brittle like broken glass.

"No," I began, but then mid word I realized that wasn't true. "I mean, yes. I do. Sort of. I think I was in Aftermath."

"You mean you dreamed about Aftermath?" Scion clarified after a long moment.

"No. I mean I think I was in Aftermath."

I told them both what I could remember of my strange dream or vision or whatever it was. About climbing up the mountain, about screaming at the flames, and how for a moment I could swear I was those flames.

When I finished, Ambrose frowned, looking worried. "I'm not sure what that means, love. Even if I could see your future, I don't know if I would know how to interpret that."

Scion looked more angry than worried. "It sounds a bit like your soul tried to return to the Source and the Source spit you back out."

I laughed, but stopped abruptly when I saw that he was serious. "That's impossible."

"I also would have said it was impossible to drop a baby into the Source and have it come out whole. There's a lot of magic in the world that we don't understand, especially in Aftermath."

I fell silent again. For some reason, at that moment, I missed Bael.

Of course, I missed Bael all the time. It was like a low hum in the back of my brain reminding me that I was still missing something vital. Like a severed limb.

But now I missed him for his perspective and his humor. I was sure he'd have taken me seriously about Aftermath, even if it sounded absurd.

Sometimes I needed Ambrose's pragmatism, or Scion's strength. At the moment, I needed Bael's flexibility.

As we rode further north, the dense canopy of trees began to thin, revealing a landscape of twisted and gnarled trunks, like a tangled web of knotted tree roots. The air grew damp and musty, reminiscent of a swamp, as the sunlight filtered through the sparse branches above. The ground beneath us became soft and squishy, the sound of our horses' hooves sinking into the muddy terrain. It was as if we were entering another world entirely, one where nature ruled with untamed chaos.

"Are we growing close?" I asked.

"Somewhat," Scion said evasively.

"We're still a good day's ride away, love. We should stop and make a camp, unless we want to ride all night."

Without speaking, we all came to the mutual decision that riding all night was not something we wanted to do.

After hours of riding through the muddy wetland, our horses were exhausted and in need of water. We finally came across a small stream with a grassy bank. We quickly dismounted and tied our horses to a nearby tree, allowing them to quench their thirst. As they drank, we set up camp on the soft grass.

I took it upon myself to make a fire, and gathered some nearby wood before putting out my hands to conjure a flame.

To my utter shock, the flame in my hand was enormous, at least twice the size as before, and it was more blue than orange, as if burning hotter.

"Look at this!" I yelled, afraid the flame might go out at any moment.

Both Ambrose and Scion came running. Ambrose drawing his sword, and Scion glaring as if he was more than ready and willing to inflict some pain on my imaginary attackers.

"What happened?" Scion demanded.

"I'm fine." I rolled my eyes. "But look at the flames!"

They both turned to look, but it was Scion who spoke first. "Is your power increasing?"

I cast a sideways look at Ambrose. "Maybe. Have any of yours?"

Scion waved his hands around, as if shooing flies, then shrugged. "I can't tell."

"What were you trying to do?" I asked.

Rather than answering, he pointed toward the stream. At first, I thought the horses were gone. But then, if I squinted, I could still make out the outlines.

"That almost worked on me," I told him. "So maybe you are stronger."

He shook his head. "If I am, I doubt that's proof of it, rebel. I think it's simply that I'm not trying to hurt you. Only combative magic doesn't work on you."

"And you?" I asked, turning to Ambrose. He was the one I was the most curious about, given that our mating bond was newer. I wasn't sure how a seer might draw on other's powers the way Scion or I did, but perhaps there was some benefit to him as well.

Ambrose scowled, though not as if he were mad at me. More as if he were thinking very hard and struggling to find an answer.

"I need to meditate," he said finally, shaking his head. "I can't wait until Bael is back with us so I can see again."

"Any idea when that will be?" I asked hopefully.

He shook his head, no. "Sorry, love. Even if I knew I couldn't tell you. It might shift things."

I sighed, saying nothing as he wandered over to a nearby tree to meditate. I knew he was right, but I was starting to get seriously annoyed with whoever was pulling the strings of our future, and not understanding why only made things worse.

THAT NIGHT, I SLEPT ON THE GRASSY BANK BETWEEN MY MATES.

Or rather, I tried to sleep. For some reason, I couldn't. I envied Scion, who was sleeping soundly to my left, one hand on my hip and the other under his head like a pillow. I wondered if the army had trained him to sleep anywhere, because he always seemed to be more comfortable than the rest of us.

On my other side, Ambrose was also lying awake.

I rolled onto my side to look at him, finding him staring up at the sky with an intensity that implied he might read some secret message among the stars.

"What are you looking at?"I asked so quietly I was practically mouthing the words.

He shook his head. "Just working through some things. The future is complex, and I'm not used to being around other people so often."

I frowned slightly offended, and leaned back.

Likely seeing my movement, he turned on his side as well to look at me. "I didn't mean you…at least, not all the time." He grinned. "What I do takes a certain amount of alone time to think without distractions or making others feel like you're ignoring them."

Ah. That, I could understand.

"So you're 'alone' now, so to speak?" I asked.

His smile widened. "Something like that."

"oh, I suppose I'm disturbing you. Sorry."

I made to roll over again, facing Scion, but Ambrose grabbed me and pulled me back. I found myself tucked under his arm, pressed into his side. Our faces were suddenly very, very close.

"You're never disturbing me, love. I can't believe I'm lucky enough to have you at all."

Ambrose leaned over, capturing my mouth in a slow, languid kiss. Warmth filled me from within, curling my toes. Then, he angled his head, bringing his hand to my cheek, and the kiss turned hotter. More possessive. He sucked my bottom lip into his mouth and I whimpered, letting him steal the sound from my lips with his own.

My body was loose and coiling at the same time. I could feel my temperature rising, and my pulse beating insistently in my core.

A sound behind me made me go stiff. *Shit.*

I bit my lip. I wasn't good at this sort of thing. I had never been the most tactful person, and now I felt we were walking through a battlefield every time the three of us were alone together. It had been difficult enough before, but now that I'd chosen both of them how could I navigate the path between their feud?

Breaking away from Ambrose's kiss, I rolled back over, explanations already rising to the tip of my tongue. I was expecting to see Scion looking at me with fury in his hypnotic eyes. I expected him to storm away, or perhaps demand that I choose between them—something I didn't even want to try and think about.

What I did not expect was for him to be watching me, with something like interest playing across the lines of his too-handsome face.

"You're awake," I whispered, feebly.

Scion's lip curled and his eyes flashed with dangerous humor. "As are you, rebel."

I opened my mouth to say something else, but then I caught the heat in his gaze. He was watching me–more specifically watching my mouth–with that single minded focus that used to scare me, but now made heat pool in my core.

Speaking of which, I shivered as Ambrose moved closer to my back, pulling me against his chest and trailing his mouth up the column of my neck.

Scion and I looked at each other in the darkness, and his eyes flashed again. Like a challenge, beckoning me forward.

I shot a hand out and pulled Scion closer. He didn't seem to need much encouragement. He kissed me hard, parting my lips easily as I whimpered against his mouth.

Ambrose nudged the underside of my jaw with his nose, and I turned my face slightly, meeting his lips instead.

Fuck, I wanted to sleep every night like this–sandwiched between them and passing lazy kisses back and forth. But how far could I push this–push them–before their individual love for me was outweighed by their mutual hatred of each other?

Aiming to find out, I trailed my fingers down my own stomach to the hem of my blouse, and began to inch it slowly up my skin.

A distant shout of laughter stilled my hand. We all froze, as if turned to stone, and waited to see if the voice came closer.

It did.

The laughter grew louder as someone approached, followed by the voices of several men and the clopping of horses' hooves.

I pivoted, disentangling myself slightly and tried to sit up. As one, both Ambrose and Scion threw an arm over me, clamping me back down to the ground.

"Our horses are hidden," Ambrose breathed in my ear. "But we're not."

I gave him a sideways look, wondering why on earth it mattered.

But as the voices grew nearer, the question answered itself.

These were soldiers. They wore the same black obsidian armor Scion typically wore, and looked to be escorting several carriages. Almost like…

"A royal procession," Scion breathed as they trundled past.

My heart beat sped up. That couldn't be any of the Everlasts, which could only leave one person.

"Idris is traveling with a procession as if he's the rightful king?" I growled low in my throat, surprising myself with my own reaction. "Where do you think he's going?"

"Only one place he could be going," Ambrose said. "To Overcast. And the fact that he's forcing the party to ride through the night instead of making camp makes me think it's urgent."

"Serious, but not urgent," Scion corrected. "If it were a truly urgent matter he'd shadow walk. If he's bringing the carriages he'd still be trying to keep up appearances."

"For whom do you think?" I asked. "He usurped you all from the throne—at least, temporarily. Why would he care about the rest of the family?"

Scion chewed on his lip. "Technically, he usurped you, and us by extension. He may have no issues with the rest of the family, and is possibly looking for allies."

His words rang too true for words and I grimaced, watching the procession. There were so many carriages that it might take a full twenty minutes for them all to pass, and in the meantime we needed to keep our voices low and not be noticed.

That was apparently easier said than done.

"Halt!" A shout rang through the woods, and was echoed by all the other soldiers down the line. "Halt! Halt! Halt!"

The carriages rolled to a stop and I peered into the darkness, unable to tell what they were looking at.

"There's something over here, my lord," one of the guards shouted. "Something in the water."

"Shit," Scion swore under his breath. "We need to go, now."

"But what about the horses?"

"The horses are what they're looking at, rebel. They've likely spotted the movements in the water, but we need to go.

"Let me see!" A familiar voice cried, opening the door to his carriage with a flourish.

I stifled a gasp. Idris was dressed like a king, his clothing screaming both wealth and status. He walked with purpose toward the steam, took one look, and turned around to speak to the guards again. "Fan out. I want the entire wood searched in case they're still here somewhere. They've probably shadow walked far away by now, but we won't take chances."

"Uh, who are we looking for, my lord?"

"The descendants of that filth who killed my fathers and siblings and destroyed my mother, and their dirty half-human whore."

"Uh, who's that my lord?"

Idris snarled in evident frustration. "Find the Everlasts, and that girl they keep dragging around everywhere. Bring them all to me."

"Yes, lord."

I trembled with fear. We needed to stand up to walk into the shadows, but if we did, would we be seen immediately? What would we do if they charged straight at us?

Like he could read my mind, Ambrose reached over to me and grabbed my hand. "Don't move, love."

"What?" I hissed. "But they're searching for us."

He nodded. "Don't move. Just wait."

"Wait for what?" Scion hissed.

"Wait....now!"

Ambrose's face lit up with an excited grin, but the sound that followed froze me in fear. It was a roar like no other I had ever heard before - deep, guttural, and coming from a beast larger than any I had ever seen. As the ground beneath us trembled, I instinctively covered my head and bit down on my tongue until it bled, desperate to stifle the scream threatening to escape my lips.

A massive dragon, with scales as dark as coal and wings that spanned the width of a small town, soared overhead, casting a shadow over the forest below. Its powerful wings beat against the air, causing trees to sway and branches to snap like twigs. With a deafening boom, it landed on the forest floor, its talons digging deep into the ground. The roar that followed shook the entire forest, leaving a ringing in my ears.

My heart raced as I gazed up at the fearsome creature, my fear palpable in the trembling of my voice. "What the fuck is that?"

"That–" Ambrose said, jumping to his feet. "–Is our ride. Shall we?"

My head swirled with confusion and terror as I struggled to make sense of what he was saying.

But then, I raised my gaze up to the beast, and instead saw a figure perched on its back, frantically waving at me. A grin spread across my face, and I laughed, my fear falling away in one perfect instant.

Bael was back—and he'd brought reinforcements.

36
LONNIE
THE ROAD TO OVERCAST

We rode the dragon all the way to Aftermath.

I clung to Bael the entire time, both exhilarated and terrified at the same time. Thankfully, the dragon was so large that looking directly downward wasn't feasible. Unluckily, that didn't prevent me from knowing the ground was there, and how very far away it was.

In a comically short amount of time compared to traveling by horse, we could see the mountains of Aftermath in the distance. They stood out, painted orange and purple against the sea of brown and green.

"I've only just thought," Bael said over the wind. "Where are we supposed to land?"

"Anywhere flat?" Scion snapped.

"No, I mean where is it safe to go? Aftermath isn't exactly habitable."

I was startled, realizing he was right. Unless I intervened, we were going to end up landing right in the center of all the afflicted and Wild magic.

"I know where we can go!" I yelled as the dragon swooped lower. I pointed down, and behind me Ambrose reached out and gripped my thigh, squeezing in acknowledgement. "Good idea, love," he murmured in my ear.

I smiled. I could only hope it was a good idea; it certainly felt like the best one I had had in a while.

We landed in an enormous meadow of sunflowers, miraculously blooming despite the toxic scent in the air.

The very moment he helped me down from the dragon, Bael reached for me. He pulled me to him for a deep bruising kiss that left me gasping.

"Hello, again." he said. "I missed you."

I pressed my fingers against my throbbing lips "I missed you too. But wasn't that dangerous?"

"One kiss won't kill me." He threw me a wink. "Probably."

Before I could scold him for being so flippant about his own death, he'd darted away to say something to his dragon, leaving me to focus on where we'd landed.

We were standing on the edge of the field. To our right was the Waywoods, and to the left, the base of a gigantic purple mountain. Directly in the center of those was a tiny wooden house.

I was certainly shocked to find it standing, but even more shocked that it was unchanged. I walked up to the house and pushed the door open, only for another wave of shock to wash over me. Everything was exactly as it had been when we left, down to Rosey's books on the shelves and the paint scribbles I had etched on the wall.

"How is this possible?" I breathed, looking around at the room in wonderment. "It's all exactly the same as it always was."

I looked up at the three hulking figures in the doorway. Ambrose looked around the house and frowned. "That is odd. I don't suppose there's anything unusual about this meadow?"

"I don't think so," I replied. "Aside from being so close to the Source."

"It's odd that only this land seems to be thriving while everything around it is swamp or barren wasteland."

I nodded, but was admittedly distracted by the sight of them in my little house. They didn't fit. The house was small enough as is and built for a single woman and her two small children. This kitchen wasn't meant to accommodate three enormous Fae warriors. I thought about the beds and blanched. I had no idea what we were going to do.

"Come in," I said quickly. "And shut the door."

I led them into the adjoining living room. It wasn't much larger than the kitchen, but it didn't have a loft above it, so the ceilings were higher. At least they weren't in danger of hitting their heads.

Bael flopped into an old moth-eaten armchair by the fire, and Ambrose leaned against the adjacent wall. Looking slightly lost for a moment, Scion finally elected to sit on the floor, leaving me unsure who to sit with.

Not that I'd expect them to be jealous, but there was definitely a certain amount of negotiating we'd have to work out. Maybe we should construct a calendar. My face split into a grin and I chuckled to myself.

"What is it, little monster?"

"I was merely thinking we might need some sort of formal schedule."

Bael laughed, but to my surprise, Scion actually seemed to be thinking it over. "I doubt it, rebel," he said finally. "Things will work themselves out."

Making my decision for me, Bael gripped my hips and pulled me back onto his lap. I immediately sunk into him, enjoying his warmth just as much as his familiar scent.

Without even realizing I'd done it, I shoved my nose into Bael's neck, breathing against the skin of his collarbone.

"Don't," Bael said, a little more sharply than I was used to. Then, as if he'd heard himself, his eyes softened. "Sorry, little monster. I couldn't hold myself back from kissing you, but we shouldn't push it further. I don't want to ruin everything right before we might finally break this damn thing for good."

I was a little disappointed, but he was right. Anyway, he'd reminded me how many questions I had about tonight.

"So now can you explain the dragon?" I asked Bael. "And you," I rounded on Ambrose. "When did you know he was going to turn up?"

"I just met the dragon the other day in Underneath," Bael said conversationally. "Bit of a funny story, really. He caught me stealing from him."

There was a collective gasp around the room, and Scion blurted out: "You fucking idiot!"

"Listen," said Bael defensively. "I wouldn't have been there if your foul bird didn't send me."

Scion's face twitched, the corners of his mouth fighting to turn upward. Like he really wanted to smile, but was insistent on looking disapproving anyway. Eventually, the smile won out and he grinned. "Quill's with you?"

Bael nodded. "He'll be along shortly, I'm sure. The dragon flies faster."

"But why were you stealing from a dragon?" I demanded. Everyone knew that was a death sentence. Even me, and I was hardly an expert on magical culture.

"I went to talk to him," Bael replied easily. "I was waiting in his cage for him to show up to chat, when I spotted this." He pulled a large blue gem from his pocket.

"Is that the jewel of Overcast?" Scion asked, reaching out to grab it.

"I expect so," Bael said, waving us off. "So, I couldn't leave it there. Not when I knew that's what you were all out looking for."

"Right…" I hedged. "But how did you get out?"

"The dragon–his name is Apophis by the way–showed up and saw me take the jewel. I offered to fight him for it."

"You fucking idiot," Scion said again, shaking his head.

"No." Bael's eyes widened. "That was what saved me actually. He thought it was very noble. Nevermind the fact that I just really wanted to fight a dragon."

I twisted on his lap to look him in the eye. "So he let you go?"

"Yes." Bael grinned. "And we ended up making a deal. I get to keep the jewel and the throne, but he's going to be my new advisor and keep an eye on things when I can't be there. It's perfect really, given that I'm fairly sure my other advisor was trying to get me killed. He had this long list of monsters that I needed to "talk" to. I looked at the list more carefully after I saw the dragon. Most of those creatures can't even talk."

We all gaped at him for a long silent moment.

"So, that's it then?" I asked finally. "That's the final jewel."

Looking very surprised himself, Ambrose nodded. "I suppose we should see if they fit into the crown."

"But wait!" I said, suddenly realizing. "Did we leave the crown in Nevermore with everything else?"

I was flabbergasted. I couldn't believe I hadn't realized that. We'd brought so few things with us on this journey, the crown should have been by far the most important.

To my surprise, Ambrose smiled. "Don't worry about the crown, love. As Bael just said, the raven will be along shortly."

"You gave it to Quill? When?"

"I did," Said Scion flatly. "In Inbetwixt. It seemed too important to lose."

I felt my smile growing wider. "But he's a bird? Where would he keep it?"

"I don't think that's a normal bird, little monster," Bael said with an affected shutter, making his eyes as wide as possible. "It *knows* things."

I rolled my eyes. They were all absolutely insane–all three of them.

"Fine, so we'll wait here for Quill," I said. "But what about Idris? I don't like that he traveled to Overcast and seems to know how to find us."

"He has no idea how to find us," Scion said.

"But in the forest he knew we were there immediately."

"That's because he saw the illusion," Ambrose explained. "He had the same power. I think he must recognize it. I think it's most interesting the way he spoke about you, love."

"Why?" I grumbled. "It's nothing I haven't heard before."

"Because I don't think he realizes who you are. Or rather, who your magic made you. He's focused on us, but doesn't seem to realize you're the greater threat."

I laughed. "No I'm not."

"Once we get all the bonds sealed, you will be," Scion said. "Removing Idris from the palace will be easy, but it only works if he's surprised by you. If he finds out about your magic, or the crown, we'll have entirely different problems to contend with."

I swallowed, nodding slowly. He was right. The fight with Idris suddenly seemed immaterial–an after thought to be defeated once the true enemy was conquered. That enemy had always been the curse.

"I'm sorry," Bael blurted out.

I turned to look at him again. "Why?"

His brow furrowed in anger. "I'm the only one who can't seal the bond with you."

"Your only difficulty is being less fucked in the head than the rest of us," Scion said. "I wouldn't say that's a bad thing."

Bael still looked angry. "If I could–"

"If you could fuck me on the floor this second and seal the bond, it still wouldn't fix things."

Bael raised an eyebrow. "It certainly wouldn't make them worse, though. Shall we try?"

I rolled my eyes. "I'm saying that we'd still need to break the curse eventually. What if we have children one day? Do you want them to be constantly miserable and unable to find their future mates? And what about the kingdom? It's not just you who is affected, it's everyone. Idris and his segregated towns are just the newest version of an old problem."

"Which is what?" Bael asked.

"That this kingdom is divided. It might be one continent, and one kingdom in theory, but it isn't. Just look at Nevermore."

"And Inbetwixt," Scion added. "Their lord and lady have been a pain in my ass for years. The guilds are really running that city, but without real power they have to operate underground which makes things more dangerous for everyone."

"And Overcast," Ambrose said. "They're nothing more than a vassal state where we send soldiers we don't want in positions of power. They're all living in near poverty because the marshes make it impossible for large trade routes or farming."

"And Underneath," Bael said. "It's surprisingly civilized and well managed down there, but their population is stagnant. There's almost no children because there's too many incompatible immortal species in one place, and they all keep killing each other out of boredom. The hedge is keeping thousands of different species from thriving."

"If we get the kingdom back, we'll tear down the hedge," I promised.

Bael smirked. "I already have a kingdom, little monster. I'm tearing the hedge down regardless. It will just be a matter of if our own soldiers are going to come fight me on it."

"They won't if I have anything to say about it," Scion growled.

"I think this is the point…" I said slowly.

They all looked at me, but fell silent simply waiting for me to explain.

"Aisling was the Uniter. She mated with the lord of every realm and made them all work as one connected kingdom, but then when the Unseelie king forced her to be with him things fractured. Elsewhere cannot be ruled by any one person. No one person is worthy. It has to be a bonded group, each with separate strengths, working together."

A ringing silence answered that pronouncement. No one seemed to know what to say. The words had felt heavy, but now that I shared them I seemed lighter.

Like somehow, somewhere, the gods were smiling.

I gave a little nervous laugh into the silence. "So are we going to try and reunite the crown tomorrow?"

When no one immediately answered I glanced toward the window. I couldn't precisely see the Source from here, but I could see the base of the mountain that cradled it. I wondered which path my mother took up the mountain. It seemed absurd to climb to the top with an infant, after just giving birth no less.

And the longer I looked at the mountains, the more uneasy I felt. The more I couldn't banish the memories of that…vision…I'd had when I may have died.

A large part of me hoped this would all be simple. That reuniting the jewels with the crown would be all it took to break the curse, and that Idris would be easily removed right along with it.

But I wasn't that naive. Not anymore. Even if I fixed the crown, surely there would be more. A test of worthiness, one might say.

"Actually, I thought you might try to reunite it tonight" Ambrose said, breaking through my thoughts.

"Tonight?" I squealed. "Why? How?"

"The crown is simply another Source forged weapon," he said. "Like a sword."

"Who forges weapons in the Source?"

"Source forged weapons all came from before the fall of Nightshade, love," Ambrose replied. "The forge might still exist on the mountain somewhere, but I couldn't tell you how to use it."

"Well then what are you suggesting?" Scion snapped.

Ambrose looked at me again. "Source fire, love."

My eyes widened, and I realized what he was expecting me to do–had probably always meant for me to do–and it made sense. It seemed right. Seemed poetic even that we'd all be here to witness it.

Three very different jewels, brought together to unite one crown, and the weapon who would forge them into something new.

37
LONNIE
AFTERMATH

That night, I used my fire to forge the jewels back into one crown.

For once, something felt easy. There were no hiccups, no accidental house fires, and no attacks from prowling monsters. I went to sleep hopeful, nearly excited for the following morning when we'd take the crown up the mountain to the Source.

In the morning, however, nothing felt quite so magical.

I stared out the tiny window in the kitchen. It was barely dawn, the sky a mix of peach and violent purple against a backdrop of gray.

I couldn't precisely see the Source from here, but I could see the base of the mountain that cradled it. I wondered which path my mother took up the mountain. It seemed absurd to climb to the top with an infant, after just giving birth no less.

Not only absurd, but impossible. It simply couldn't have happened the way she remembered it. She would have died.

Unless... a tiny voice in the back of my head whispered. *Unless there was some kind of Godly intervention.*

Was that crazy? Was it crazier than the idea of a sixteen year old new mother climbing an active volcano with her baby, and coming out unscathed?

Somehow, I didn't think it was. I was starting to convince myself that there must have been some magic at work that day.

That Aisling had chosen me herself.

I realized that subconsciously I'd been viewing Aisling as an evil figure. As the one who'd cursed the men I loved and made it impossible for any of us to be happy.

But that wasn't right at all.

Aisling had been a queen as well. She'd had three mates of her own. She had children, and subjects who she took care of. She'd brought down this curse on the Everlasts out of grief, and possibly, out of a desire to see her kingdom thrive again. And then when she saw the opportunity, she gave me the power to carry that plan out for her.

The only thing I couldn't understand was: why me?

It was the one thing I really wished I could understand as we prepared to go up the mountain. What made me the vessel for her plans? Why did the Source erupt on my birthday? What was I supposed to do when I reached the top of that looming jagged horizon?

BAEL'S DRAGON HAD WAITED FOR US IN THE MEADOW OVERNIGHT, and now we sat atop its back again, climbing higher and higher into the sky.

We didn't talk.

Surely no one wanted to voice our fears aloud—but I was sure that we were all thinking the same thing: We could, and very likely would, die today.

And the longer I looked at the mountains, the more uneasy I felt. The more I couldn't banish the memories of that…vision…I'd had when I may have died.

A large part of me hoped this would all be simple. That reuniting the jewels with the crown would be all it took to break the curse, and that Idris would be easily removed right along with it.

But I wasn't that naive. Not anymore. Even if I fixed the crown, surely there would be more.

A test of worthiness, one might say.

The dragon flew in great wide circles over the jagged peaks, and I forced myself to look down if only to see where we might land.

I took a moment to gather myself, using my hands to brush away the stray bits of ash and debris that had invaded my eyes. As I slowly opened them, I squinted down at the majestic mountains below.

In the distance, looming over the landscape like a titan, was an enormous volcano. Its fiery red and orange hues reflected off the surrounding terrain, creating an otherworldly glow. The ground rumbled beneath us, a constant reminder of its power and unpredictability.

It wasn't difficult to see why anyone would choose to worship the Source even now when it had done so much inadvertent harm to so many. Nor was it hard to understand why the gods might have forged such a place. It was lovely and terrifying at once. Glittering and deadly.

We swooped low over the smoking mountain and as the smoke wafted over us, I felt the prickle of magic that flicked against my senses.

"What if it warps us?" I asked.

"It only warps the powerless, love," Ambrose said from where he sat behind me. "You've seen how the Source works before. It's both a magnet and a power supply. It wants to find hosts, but if the body can't tolerate that much magic the person becomes afflicted."

I sincerely hoped that meant our dragon would be immune as well, and dug my nails into my palms as we swooped lower and lower.

"There's nowhere for him to land," Bael bemoaned.

He was right. The dragon couldn't very well perch over the volcano, and he was so large there weren't places he could land safely.

"Have him land on that ridge," Scion said, pointing toward a plateau some one-hundred yards down from the summit. "We can walk from there."

"Climb," I corrected him. "The rock is steep, If we fall…"

"I don't believe we will," Ambrose said confidently.

"Do you know that for certain?"

He kept his mouth shut, and I knew with a sinking feeling that meant he didn't want to lie.

THE DRAGON LANDED WITH A WHOOSH, AND WE ALL SLID OFF ITS back onto the rocky ground.

The air was impossibly thick, the heat so strong it felt like a physical presence. Like wading through smoke and water. If this was what it felt like here, I couldn't imagine what it would be like once we reached the top and were able to look down into the bubbling pools of molten magic.

Again, my dreams pricked at the back of my mind. Plaguing me.

I felt as if I'd been here before. Felt I'd done this before.

As with so many of my dreams which later came true, or had some strange message embedded into my subconscious, I felt sure the vision I'd had while dying meant something. I just didn't know what.

"Shall we go?" Bael asked nervously.

I looked around at him. His usually smiling face was grave. He looked like he might like to grab me and bolt all the way back to valley below.

I put a hand on his chest. "Just think," I said with a joking smile. "In a couple of hours we can complete our bond."

He looked at me very seriously. "If this is what we have to do to complete it, I don't need to. I love you enough as it is. I'll go back to Underneath, or—"

He broke off as I kissed him.

There was just something about Bael that made everything seem possible. Safer.

With him, I could join the Wilde hunts and survive because he'd kill anyone who hurt me. Of course I loved all my mates equally, but there would always be something about knowing Bael was the first to really see me. The first to think I might be worth something.

I pulled back from the kiss and he looked a bit dazed. Still, that panic in his eyes had lessened. He took a large step back. "It'll be easier to walk up this in my other form, and easier to drag you out of there if something goes wrong."

I nodded, watching as he shifted into the enormous lion. He was so big that he was still nearly as tall as I was while on four paws, and I petted his nose when he walked up to nuzzle against my shoulder.

In silence, we all began to trudge up the side of the mountain. At first I clutched the sharp obsidian crown in my hand, but as the terrain grew more challenging I gave up and tied it to my belt. I couldn't help but recall that tying the crown to my belt had done nothing to keep it from stabbing me in the back once before.

We climbed higher and the thick air grew even more suffocating and noxious. I choked on the sulfuric scent and the ash that swirled on the wind.

Still, I kept going.

The back of my mind kept whispering to me that I was mortal. That this couldn't be done. That I'd suffocate or burn to a crisp before we ever made it to the top.

Still, I kept going.

Flashes of my dreams—my visions, perhaps—mingled with what was real. With what the wind whispered to me.

"What did you say?" I asked, whipping around.

"Nothing, rebel." Scion looked at me with more concern that I was used to from him. Perhaps I looked mad. Deranged. I felt like I could come unhinged at any moment.

"I don't like it here," I said, though some veil of lucidity.

Scion laughed hollowly. "I don't think anyone does."

"Someone must. For years, the priests in Nightshade prayed at this spot."

"True," Ambrose agreed. "But notice how few stories there are of visiting the Source and being granted a favor. Aisling—and now your mother—are the only one's I've ever heard of."

I nodded, but said nothing. I was not able to find any words for how I felt to hear that.

How had mother done this? How was I doing it now? Was it really some godly intervention? Or simply that voice that pounded in the back of my mind at all times. *I will not die here. I will not die…*

The ground got steeper, the rocks sharper and more jagged as we climbed. Even my mates were struggling to find footholds that would not send them careening to the ground.

And then finally, as I was sure my lungs would burst and my skin would melt from my bones, the ground began to even out.

I stared out ahead of me in awe at the enormous fissure in the mountain and swayed before it, hypnotized by the swirling, churning lava hundreds of feet below.

"Wait!" Scion said, gabbing my arm and pulling me back. "You're too close to the edge."

I realized he was right and that I'd been teetering far too close to falling.

I looked at Scion and Ambrose. There was only the three of us to decide what to do next, as Bael couldn't talk in his lion form.

"Well?" I asked.

Ambrose looked some combination of angry and confused. I didn't have to guess what he was thinking. He'd been working for this for so long, and now he was blind. He didn't know what to do anymore than we did.

I tried to remember everything I'd ever heard about Aisling. Everything my mother had said about the Source.

And again, the whispers began in the back of my mind. I could not tell if they were real or visions, but I heard the voices as clear as if they were standing beside me.

"The queen poured her power into you, and the force of it caused the Source to erupt." My mother said.

Bael's voice from so long ago seemed to laugh. *"Aisling begged the gods to help her, and the Source erupted."*

"As long as the crown is not returned to the worthy wearer, the obsidian kingdom will know everlasting misery."

I felt Scion's hand on my shoulder, once again pulling me back. "What are you thinking, rebel?"

But I couldn't speak to him. Couldn't scream over the voices in my head which were growing louder and more insistent with every passing second. I could no longer recognize who was speaking, only hear the echos of their words.

"...she told me to bring her heir back to her."

"...I don't believe there is any one person who is worthy, so I set out to make one."

"...The new heir will be created, forged of Source fire."

And I was the Source, wasn't I?

I was creation and destruction; power and magic.

I was fire.

"...I'd tear out my heart and give it to you."

"...I love you enough for both of us."

"...I'll always find you, little monster."

And then, with sharp clarity, I understood.

I gripped the crown in my hand so hard that it bled as I darted forward.

"No!" Someone shouted behind me, grasping for me, but I pulled away.

For once I wasn't questioning anything. I had no confusion. No curiosity. I simply knew that like there was no one ruler, there was no one worthy person. The worthy had to be forged by sacrifice to the Source.

And I knew, as surly as I'd ever known anything, that I *would* die today.

I looked down over raging fire and didn't hesitate. I jumped, plunging downward. *Down and down and down.*

The voices above me rose in a cacophony. They screamed and screamed and *screamed.*

I screamed too, but not with terror or sadness. Not with pain, but like a battle cry. I screamed with anger. With relief.

And then, it was over.

And it was beginning.

I was life and death.

I was the great equalizer.

I was the flames; burning, blazing, Wilde.

38
SCION
THE SOURCE

I heard myself scream before I'd realized I'd opened my mouth.

My shout chased Lonnie out of sight, the sound echoing all around me, reflected back from the other screams of horror and pain.

Bael roared and leapt to the edge of the rocky fissure, staring down as if he planned to follow her.

My mind was blank.

Perhaps I'd follow her too?

And then all at once I felt a strange weightlessness wash over me. It was like darkness fell away and for the first time I could see colors clearly. I could laugh fully, and feel true pain. I felt as if I could taste vinegar and realize it had been wine all along.

I knew the curse had lifted, knew we were free at last…

But somehow, I'd never been more miserable. More caged. More alone.

"No…" I heard myself say. "No! She's coming back."

I was so sure that my throat didn't even twinge. Lonnie would be back. She was the fucking Source. She had the power of Aisling, and fire couldn't kill her.

"She'll be back," I said again, just to reiterate the point.

Ambrose turned to look at me. His face looked shattered. Dead. He'd turned as white as his hair, and while his eyes were focusing on me, they weren't really seeing me. "She won't," he said, tonelessly.

"Shut up!" I barked, moving toward the edge where Lonnie had jumped. I looked down and tried to make out anything other than churning molten lava and smoke. "She's coming back."

This time, my throat burned and I realized with a sickening jolt that I was becoming less sure by the second.

"No, she's not," Ambrose said again.

"After everything this is the end? I don't fucking accept that. Bring her back!" I shouted at the Source, my voice echoing across the mountains so loud I was sure even the fucking gods could hear me. "Bring her back you fucking evil—"

My voice cracked.

I swallowed the lump that was beginning to form in my throat. I couldn't remember the last time I'd cried. Perhaps never. But the fact that I could access that depth of emotion now, only because she was gone…

I didn't believe it.

This couldn't be happening. She wouldn't have done this. Wouldn't have left us all like this.

I looked at my brother, desperately. "What happened? What happens to her now?"

He shook his head, his eyes glazing over as if he were staring at something so far in the distance he couldn't make it out. "I don't—"

"Don't fucking tell me you don't know!" I raged. "You know everything! Tell me what happens to her!"

"Nothing!" He lunged forward at me, screaming in my face. "Nothing happens to her! Nothing happens to us! This is how it ends."

I shook my head, disbelieving. Uncomprehending. "That's not right. That can't be right."

"Yes, it can," he said, his voice dark and furious. "Lonnie is gone so she can't be blocking me, yet I see nothing after this. That means we die here. There is no future after this."

A new wave of darkness settled over me. All my newfound senses were dull. Muted. Taken over by this malignant presence hovering over me.

That presence was death, I thought vaguely. It had come to collect Lonnie and settled over all of us. Waiting. Biding it's time until we joined it willingly just to be near here again.

And I would, I realized. I'd follow her whether I jumped into that volcano or not, I was already dead.

I might be immortal, but I was not living. She was my entire life, and now I'd die with her.

I stood there for a long moment. It might have been an hour for all I knew. And then, vaguely, I noticed that Bael had said nothing since his initial roar of shock. Not a single word.

I looked over at him, not precisely curious. I wasn't sure if I could feel curious ever again, but just…searching.

Bael had reverted back to his human shape. His clothes had gone the way of his lion form and he was kneeling naked on the rocky ground, his eyes closed.

"What are you doing?" I asked him. He didn't move and I spoke louder, striding toward him. "What are you doing?"

Bael's voice was flat, almost tranquil and he didn't open his eyes as he answered. "Praying."

My face twisted in anger and I scoffed. "Are you fucking serious? You're praying?"

I felt a new wave of anger. It was offensive somehow, to be praying. To be speaking to imaginary figures and silent gods when this was happening, here and now, and there was nothing any of us could do! I couldn't understand how he could be so calm when I wanted to rage and scream more, vent my anger on whomever was nearest.

"Come sit," Bael said.

"Fuck you."

This time he opened his eyes and looked at me. "Don't you understand?"

"Understand what? Why you're acting like nothing has happened?"

His mask of tranquility slipped and he glared at me, the lion pacing behind his eyes. "Don't you understand what she was doing? What she wanted from us?"

I couldn't even speak. As far as I could tell Lonnie hadn't known what she was doing any more than I did now.

Or, perhaps she did. Perhaps she'd aimed to break the curse, but at the cost of her life what was the point?

"There have only ever been two eruptions of the source," Bael said, his tone maddeningly even. "Once, when Aisling, a person who was defined by her love and goodness lashed out in rage and prayed to punish her enemy. Second, when Lonnie's mother, who was hateful and angry every second of her life, had a moment of selflessness and prayed to save a life she didn't believe was worth anything."

"I don't have time for this shit," I demanded.

"Don't you get it?" His voice rose. "We're monsters. None of us has ever done anything good in our entire lives just because it was the right thing. We're selfish, always and we don't deserve to have the crown because of it. We're not *worthy*."

Ambrose made his way over, and stood behind me. "So what are you expecting us to do?"

I glanced at him over my shoulder. "You're not buying this shit, are you?"

"The future is…moving," he said vaguely. "What are you trying to do, Bael?"

"Do something selfless."

"She's your mate," I said. "Wanting her back isn't selfless. That's the definition of selfishness."

"I'm not asking for her back because she's my mate. I'm asking for her back because she's worthy. I'm asking the source to send her back for *them*." He pointed vaguely out at the land below the mountain range. "Because she made all of us better and without her to unite it, the kingdom will suffer."

Beside me, Ambrose fell to his knees like Bael was doing. He closed his eyes and began moving his lips very fast as if he were mouthing the words in his head.

I stood frozen, watching them.

Then, I knelt too, but I couldn't think. Couldn't get past the rage and disbelief. And even if I could, I didn't think I could be unselfish. Not when it came to Lonnie.

I'd wanted her since the moment I saw her. I wanted her entire life, in whatever form I could have it. I wanted her attention and admiration. I wanted her body, all her thoughts, and every single sideways glance across the room. I even wanted her hatred and her fear. I'd protect her. Keep her. Consume her…

Nothing about me was selfless, but especially not when it came to her.

I couldn't pretend to care about strangers because I didn't. If I was honest with myself, the people of Elsewhere meant nothing to me.

I'd fought for them because I was ordered to.

I'd ruled them because I was born to.

I'd interacted with them only so far as I had to.

I only cared about a few people in the goddamn world, and they were all on this fucking mountain. I even hated half of them.

I opened one eye and looked at my brother whom I'd vehemently hated my entire goddamn life, but who had saved my life when it counted. Who Loved Lonnie as much as I did. Who unlike me at least believed in something, and wanted the world to be better.

And on my other side, was my other brother. Not of blood perhaps, but of choice so many times over I'd lost count. Bael had never wanted to be a king, but now he was because Underneath needed him. He'd done what I couldn't and focused on the purpose rather than the power.

The only honest thing I could say was that I wanted Lonnie back *for them*. Not for everyone, but for my brothers as much as for myself.

An enormous tremor rocked the ground beneath me, and my eyes flew open. Before me, enormous plumes of smoke were rising out of the source. The ground trembled again as if it might crumble beneath us. I looked up, my eyes wide, and my mouth falling open.

The sky was black.

39
LONNIE
THE SOURCE

In my dream, I was in a throne room.

Sunlight leaked through the windows and streamed onto the glittering stone floor. Outside, a field of sunflowers danced in the breeze and behind that, a purple mountain rose in the distance so tall it ascended out of sight.

I turned slowly in a circle. The room was familiar, yet not. I'd seen it before, but when?

The sound of footsteps in the hall followed by laughter made me halt. Was I even supposed to be here? What would happen if–

A woman walked into the room, her long purple gown trailing on the floor. In her arms she was carrying a small black-haired child. Her face was obscured, her head turned back, talking to someone in the hallway behind her.

"Come along, darling," she was saying to the person trailing her. "Let's go to the window and watch."

A tiny girl, with curly red hair like the woman's ran after her on chubby toddler legs. The girl bared her teeth in something between a smile and a snarl, and let out a growl.

"Yes, you're very scary," the woman said, turning back around.

I stepped back, startled.

I realized at that moment that I'd expected the woman to be me, but it wasn't. She had red hair, but the similarities ended there. Her face was more striking, and she was undoubtedly pure Fae.

She walked across the room, passing right by me as if she didn't know I was there, and stopped beside the window looking out over the sunflower field. She frowned, and hugged her child closer.

I took a step toward them, wanting to see what they were looking at. But before I could reach them the dream changed.

I was in the same room again, but the woman and her children were gone. In their place were three tall Fae males, all dressed in some form of armor.

"We have to close the fucking border," a cruelly beautiful blonde was saying, pale blue eyes flashing with anger. "I don't care how many soldiers they send."

The man to his right–dark skinned and muscular–rolled his eyes. "Of course you don't care."

"What the fuck does that mean?" the blonde growled, dangerously.

The third man grinned, looking like he'd heard this argument a thousand times before. "Because you don't care about anything. Obviously."

"That's not fucking true and you know it."

"Fine," the grinning man amended. "You care about *one* thing. But Aisling won't like this, so if you don't care about what we think, go ask her."

The dream changed a third time, and now I was standing beside the red-haired woman on the top of a stone tower, watching soldiers march across the meadow.

"Princess?" a voice called from below.

Aisling turned as the blonde man emerged from the staircase behind her. His face was softer when he looked at her, but retained its cruel beauty. He stopped short, seeing the soldiers all across the field. "So, it's too late."

Aisling nodded. "I only hoped we'd have more time."

The dream changed for a fourth time and I was standing out in front of the castle where Aisling was arguing with a figure in a stag skull mask. She was flanked by the three men from the throne room. This time, all four of them were wearing crowns. One obsidian, one diamond, one sapphire, and one ruby.

A fifth time, and the cruel blonde man was picking up the dead body of the little red-headed girl and sobbing.

A sixth time, and the laughing man took a sword to the abdomen, pushing his friend out of the way.

A seventh, and the four of them were lying in bed making plans. They all knew they were going to die–to drain–but they thought maybe Aisling had the best chance to live. Maybe she could pull from all of them because she was their source…

Again and again and again, faster and faster there were more scenes. More moments. More misery.

I watched all their pain, until eventually I wasn't me anymore. I was merely a silent spirit lurking in a story that was not mine to tell, watching, waiting, listening.

I watched as one after another all the men died.

Their children died.

The land around them which had once been green and lush turned hot and desolate.

I watched as the red-haired queen, Aisling, became more desperate. More reckless. Without her family she had nothing. She was only rage and power.

And I watched as her will shattered, and she begged for the source to take away her misery and give it away. Spread it everywhere, to everyone, to Elsewhere.

I watched for so long that it became my story too. I was no longer standing beside Aisling, but I was her, watching through her eyes as she cursed her enemies, wishing for them to feel the pain she'd felt.

I wished for time to turn back to when the land was united, and my family was whole. So I lay down my bargain: Only when the land could be as it once was, would the misery end. Only when the crown went back to the worthy, could I finally rest.

For though I'd long since returned to the fire, I'd spread too much of myself to the land and given them my power bit by bit.

Every time my name was spoken, I was bound tighter to the land. Trapped here. Kept in the dark by the power of thousands of voices calling to me, invoking my true name and bidding me to care for them.

In all this time I'd become the gods to which I once prayed, but I was still angry. If I'd ever cared for the people I could not remember it. I'd been trapped without family, without love, for so long that I knew only vengeance. Only everlasting misery.

But in all that time I was trapped, I watched. And I waited. And I listened.

Then one day, I saw the solution. The power kept me tethered, so why not give it away?

I tried to send the magic outward, but it turned Wilde and corrupted everything it touched. I tried again to draw it inward, but that took it from the creatures who needed it to survive, and drove the land into greater chaos.

I was so tired, and I knew there was no hope.

I would not die here, but oh how I wished I could.

So I tried one last time.

I watched a new red-headed woman living in the valley where my castle once stood, her belly growing larger by the day.

I waited for her to come to me, high up on the mountain.

I listened to her invoke my name and make her demands.

And in granting her prayer I chose my vessel–my heir–and I gave my power away in the hope that it might come back to me when it was worthy.

40
LONNIE
THE SOURCE

The last time I died, I awoke to warmth and confusion. This time, I woke to smoke and ash.

As I slowly opened my eyes, I was met with the sight of the jagged edge of the cliff jutting out in front of me. The same cliff that I had impulsively leaped off just moments before.

Or, was it moment? Minutes? Hours?

I wasn't precisely sure, and I supposed it didn't matter. All that matters was getting back to my mates.

I got to my feet. My clothes were gone, as was the crown, and the hot rock below my feet burned slightly as I took a step away from the edge. The ground seemed to tremble, and the smoke had thickened, turning the sky black with soot.

I knew we needed to get off this mountain, but I couldn't force myself to move once I turned and saw the row of my mates all kneeling on the dusty ground with their heads bowed in prayer.

My chest swelled with an overwhelming sense of relief and triumph. We'd actually made it. Against all odds, we were all still here, alive and breathing. Nothing else mattered.

Without meaning to, an anguished sound of shock and relief escaped me. I wasn't sure if I wanted to cry or laugh, and somehow I was doing both, my entire body shaking and my chest heaving for breath

Clearly hearing my sobs, my mates stood as one, running toward me.

Bael was the first one to reach me, wrapping his arms around my figure and holding me tightly. He buried his face in my hair, and he too was laughing and crying at once, tears escaping him as he grinned through the wetness seeping into my hair.

Then, Ambrose was there and he was just watching me in wonderment. In awe. I reached for him around Bael's arm and gripped his hand tightly, assuring him I was there.

Finally Bael pulled back and simply looked at me. His arms stayed around my waist holding me loosely as I turned to look at Scion and waited.

"How?" Scion demanded, running his hands over my face again and again.

I shook my head. "Think she heard you. Or, I heard you. I'm not certain."

"And it just gave you back?" Scion demanded, shaking me slightly.

Scion seemed so shocked, so over-rot, so twisted into knots that it was coming out as anger whether he meant it to or not. I thought of the cruel blonde man crying over his little girl, and ached inside.

"I'm fine, my lord," I said. "See? I'm fine."

He stared at me for so long I began to wonder if he was going to speak at all. Tentatively, I smiled.

Then, whatever thought had been running through his mind seemed to break. He took an aggressive step toward me, grabbing my face between both hands, and crushed his mouth to mine.

I gasped, opening my mouth instantly to the kiss, letting him ravage my mouth with his tongue, searching, tasting.

Bael still held me against his chest, letting me use him for support as Scion kissed me. He moved the hand that was nearest to my belly, and began to trace small patterns on my bare skin. I shivered, pleasure creeping over me and moving up my spine.

I arched my back into him, moaning against Scion's mouth. I could feel both of them growing hard for me, and my lower belly tightened in response.

There would be time for explanations later, but not now. I wanted to feel something. Anything, if only to prove I was alive.

Another hand joined us, wrapping around my waist. I pulled back from Scion to see Ambrose beside me, waiting his turn.

Without hesitation, I twisted back and pulled his mouth to mine. He kissed me fiercely, easily parting my lips as I whimpered against his mouth.

"Don't hold back," I whispered against Ambrose's mouth. Though I directed it at him, the command applied to all of them. I wanted more from them, everything they had to offer.

"I won't, love," Ambrose promised. "But…"

I pulled back, narrowing my eyes at him. "But?"

"Perhaps we should get off this mountain. Otherwise 'dying to be inside you' will take on a whole new meaning."

LATER THAT NIGHT, I WALKED OUTSIDE ALONE.

We'd finally exhausted ourselves beyond the point of no return, and half-walked, half-crawled, into the house to sleep.

Unfortunately, though I was exhausted beyond all reason, sleep would not come.

I had too much to think about. Too much to do.

I stood on the front stoop of my old house and looked up at the sky. It was almost peculiarly clear. Seeming too innocent as compared with the black plumes that had just this morning covered the sky.

The source had not erupted as we expected. Its final act seemed to be returning me from within the fire, and now it had gone quiet. I suspected when we climbed the mountain to look the fires within would have gone cold.

Out of curiosity, I raised my hand and conjured a flame. To my relief, it danced there just as strong as it ever had before. Maybe it was a parting gift from Aisling. Or maybe it was simply that I didn't have to become the fire to wield it.

Still, this felt like an ending, of sorts.

I knew the curse had lifted when I returned both the crown and myself to the source, letting Aisling free at last. I did not think any of my mates had really had the time to consider all that the ending of the curse could mean. What it might mean for us, but also for the greater kingdom.

This also felt like an ending for me. It was a death and rebirth. A complete destruction of who I'd been in my mortal life, and a new beginning for who I might become instead.

Though I had no wish to test it—dying twice was enough—I was almost positive that plunging into the source had killed whatever was mortal inside me.

Though, I might live for five hundred years, but I would still always feel human. Now, that didn't seem like such a bad thing.

"What are you thinking about, love?"

I jumped and looked up at Ambrose. "What are you doing up?"

"Alone time," he told me.

I nodded. "Me too."

He sat down on the doorstep beside me, and I was glad of it. We could be alone together.

"Well?" He asked after a minute.

"What?"

"What are you thinking about all alone?"

"Honestly?"

"Always."

"I"m thinking that whatever we do next is important."

"How do you mean?"

I sighed, putting my face in one hand. "I want things to be different. I don't want to go start another war, or track down Idris. If he comes to us then I'll defend us. If he hurts anyone, I'll protect them. But I don't believe we need to be the aggressors anymore. If we're going to be a kingdom full of monsters, I want it to be because we knock down the border wall. Not because we kill everyone who opposes us."

"You're talking about mercy," He stated.

"Yes."

We were silent for a long time. Alone, but together.

Finally, I turned to him again. "You know what else I've been thinking? That Queen Lonnie is a stupid sounding name."

He let out a bark of laughter, then swallowed it, evidently not wanting to wake up Bael and Scion. "Why on earth are you thinking that?"

"Because I thought true names had no purpose once you had magic, but they do. Aisling proved they do. If enough people know your name they can call you for help. I like that idea. And Queen Elowyn sounds much better, don't you think?"

"I think you can be whatever queen you want, love. There's a long future ahead of us to figure it all out."

EPILOGUE
Rose and Peregrine

LONNIE

SIX YEARS LATER

"Would you like me to lie?"

Iola chuckled and gave me an apologetic glance, brushing a stray strand of hair away from her face. "No, I'm well aware of how awful it is already."

My nose scrunched up in disgust as I turned around, taking in the entire room. It truly was terrible, and I couldn't think of a single helpful thing to say that would not inadvertently scald my throat.

"It's…large." I landed on, grimacing slightly. "And I'm sure you'll make it lovely eventually."

She grinned. "Thank you. I think so too…eventually."

We stood in the drawing room of the abandoned home, once belonging to the Lord and Lady of Inbetwixt. Despite being the largest building in the city, the house had stood unoccupied for the past five years, ever since Cross ascended to his position as Lord. Obviously he had a house already, and hadn't wanted anything to do with the mansion.

The entire building was now shrouded in thick cobwebs, layers of dust coating every surface. The remaining furniture was dilapidated and covered in grime, and cracks snaked their way across the walls like crooked veins.

Despite all that, Iola was planning to turn the home into an orphanage for abandoned children of any species. So, despite its current rundown state, I couldn't help but see the potential for something wonderful.

"It's taken us years to build the mountain palace, but it was worth it in the end," I said bracingly. "This will be too. You'll see."

"Thank you again for funding it, my lady."

I waved her off. "It was no trouble, we have far too much money to keep to ourselves. And I keep telling you to call me Lonnie."

"Yes, my lady," Iola said quickly. "I mean, yes Lonnie…ma'am."

I sighed and rolled my eyes. She was a lost cause.

"Did you want to stay for tea?" Iola asked hopefully.

I bit back a groan. "I do. I really, really, do. But I can't. I'm only in the city for the day and I have so many meetings planned I've barely given myself time to breathe."

"You could have someone do that for you, my lady," Iola pointed out.

"Oh, I am." I laughed. "Ambrose is in Nevermore hearing petitions today, and Bael is in Underneath for the rest of the week. I'm starting to think I need three more mates just to keep the continent running smoothly."

She laughed and her cheeks reddened slightly. Iola had never quite wrapped her mind around how it could work that I was married to three males at once, but she was far too polite to ask about it.

"And Lord Scion?" Iola asked. "Where is he this week?"

"Ah." I smiled. "Waiting for me outside. Would you care to say hello?"

Iola shrunk back. "Oh, no my lady…that's alright."

I grinned. Despite living with the thieves guild for the last six years, Iola was still a bit frightened of Fae. I hoped that would improve for her with her work on this new project.

After all, Fae children raised by humans weren't always so bad.

I STEPPED OUT OF THE DREARY, GRAY WALLS OF THE ORPHANAGE AND into the blinding sunlight. The bustling street was filled with people talking, laughing, and the shouts of vendors hawking their wares. I shielded my eyes with my hand as I walked down the stone steps and scanned the crowd for my husband's familiar face.

Without any warning, a small boy with obsidian black hair appeared in front of me as if out of thin air. My heart skipped a beat and my eyes widened in alarm as he teetered on the top step, a look of surprise etched on his face. In a split second, I reached out to catch him but my fingers only brushed against the empty space where he had been.

What in the name of the Source?

I whipped around, searching for my son. "Peregrine?"

Just as suddenly, Peregrine appeared again, this time standing in the middle of the cobblestone street. "Mother, look!" he demanded, waving his small arms at me. "Looook!"

I hurried down the steps, reaching out to grab him once more, but he vanished once again.

"Don't look so nervous, Rebel."

I whirled back around and found Scion leaning against the garden wall outside the orphanage. I was 100% certain he hadn't been standing there a second before.

"Not you too," I hissed.

He looked unabashed. "Children learn by example."

"So you're just shadow walking all over the city, and what…?" I raised an incredulous eyebrow. "…making him chase you?"

"Yes!" His eyes gleamed with pride. "He's doing well, don't you think?"

I furrowed my brow. "How well he's doing is irrelevant. He's only five!"

Scion was undeterred. "That's a good thing, rebel. That means his power will be unusually strong."

I frowned, staring out onto the street where Peregrine was now fading in and out of sight as he bent to pet a scruffy-looking stray cat. The cat obviously had no idea what to make of it, and was watching the occasionally invisible child with extreme wariness.

"I just thought there would be more time," I explained. "How are we going to keep him from wandering off the continent every time we have to scold him?"

Scion kissed me on the top of the head. "It will be fine, rebel. He has four parents to go search for him, not to mention a large collection of aunts and uncles."

I supposed that was true, though I still found myself worrying as we watched Peregrine pick up the enormous gray cat, which was nearly as large as he was, and disappear with it.

"Wait!" I whirled on Scion. "Where's Rose?"

"Aine is watching her," he said, as if this were no cause for concern. "I let them go back to Cross's."

"Oh, lovely," I said sarcastically. "So I leave for an hour and come home to one child I can't see, and another one who will want to be an assassin when she grows up."

Scion looked for a moment like he was going to argue, but then changed his mind. He grimaced. "You're right," he finally said, reluctantly. "We should probably go check on them."

"Good. I have to go by the den anyway to speak to Cross."

Scion looked sideways at me. "Anything I should know about?"

I shrugged. "I'm not sure yet. We can ask him together."

WE ARRIVED AT THE THIEVES' DEN JUST IN TIME TO SEE AINE FLYING backwards across the room.

There was never a dull moment.

Aine somersaulted in the air and managed to land on her feet in a crouch just outside the training ring. Then she jumped, like a spitting cat, and rounded on her opponent.

I turned, watching with benign interest. Then, my eyes went wide again as a whiling streak of curly red hair shot past me.

"Rose!" I yelled, "Stop that."

I shouldn't have been at all surprised when my daughter didn't stop. She barreled toward her aunt, a tiny whirling ball of rage.

Where Peregrine looked like Scion in miniature, except for the single white streak that always peeked through his jet black hair, Rose was the complete opposite. Her long mane of red hair was always a mess, and if I made her sit too long while I attempted to tame it she would growl and flash her cat-like yellow eyes at me.

Now, Scion stepped forward and casually plucked Rose off the ground mid-stride. For a moment, her little legs kept moving, and then she stopped, glaring at Scion.

"What?" Rose said defensively, her angelic face and tiny sweet voice at complete odds with the clear threat of violence in her cat-like yellow eyes.

"You know what," Scion told her patiently. "It's unwise to challenge your aunt…at least, not where your mother can see you."

Rose grinned widely. "Can we fight later?"

Scion's eye twitched. He seemed to be struggling with himself, clearly torn between encouraging this behavior in our daughter, and a desire to see what she might be capable of.

"Perhaps," he said finally, putting her down. "Go play with your brother."

Rose scoffed and rolled her eyes. "He's boring. He never wants to play any of my games, and when he does he won't even try. It's no fun winning when he won't even try."

I pinched the bridge of my nose. "Why don't you go see his new cat."

She shrugged. "Alright."

She walked away and I stared after her. Sometimes I wasn't sure whether I should be proud or horrified at how much she reminded me of myself.

"Are we keeping the cat?" Scion muttered out of the corner of his mouth. "Quill won't like that."

"Quill is the least of my concerns at the moment."

Suddenly remembering Aine's presence behind us, I whirled around and glared at her. " What are you doing? You should know better than to fight a child."

"I should," she agreed, picking at the edge of her fingernail. "But that particular child is far too much like Bael."

"Meaning what?" Scion asked flatly.

"Meaning she'd pick a fight with a mirror if she could. I'm merely exercising her talents."

"You're merely trying to mold her into one of your 'family.'" I snapped, putting a lot of emphasis on the word.

Aine grinned wickedly. "Why can't it be both?"

Our meeting with Cross was long and uneventful. There were a lot of changes brewing in Inbetwixt that we had to remain aware of, but overall he seemed to be on top of things.

In fairness, there were a lot of changes brewing in every major city on the continent. It had taken several years of continuous work, but we'd finally stamped out the last of the coup attempts and anyone who might have supported them. We'd removed the governing lords and ladies of each province, and taken a more hands on approach to leadership.

Bael split his time between our castle and his seat in Underneath. When he wasn't there, his dragon, Apophis, kept an eye on things for him and sent back regular reports.

Ambrose managed Nevermore, which was still constantly threatening succession but with less and less seriousness with every passing year. Now, the threats were less legitimate plans for a war of independence and more hyperbolic threats. *"If I can't get my boat fixed before spring, I'm organizing a secession!"*

Technically, Scion was in charge of Overcast and the former capital, but in actuality he had very little to do. Thalia and Gwydion managed Overcast, and as we no longer resided in the obsidian palace, the capital had become far less of an issue. Scion effectively "retired" from being royalty the moment our children were born. He'd spent years believing he would never truly be happy, but all that changed the moment he learned he would be a father.

Now, it was Scion and I who shadow walked the children back to our new castle.

The castle stood in a field of sunflowers, inexplicably blooming despite the slight hint of smoke that still lingered in the air. To the right was the edge of the waywoods, and to the left rose an enormous purple mountain. In the garden we'd left my tiny wooden house for the children to play in.

We made our way up to the castle and immediately ran into Ambrose He greeted the children, then me, kissing me lightly on the lips.

"How was the island?" I asked.

"Cold," he replied. "But otherwise fine. How was Inbetwixt?"

"Fine," I replied, smiling slightly. There was once a time when I'd have balked at flitting in and out of various provinces as if it were no more complex than walking down to Cheapside. Now, a trip to Inbetwixt was no more remarkable than "fine."

Giving me another quick peck on the mouth, Ambrose turned his attention to Scion. "Come down to the training room. I have something to show you."

Scion's eyes lit up. "New swords?"

"Yes!" Ambrose looked equally excited. "The dwarves in Nevermore have started forging Iron differently. They're trying to replicate Source forged steel."

"Is that possible?" Scion asked, already moving toward the direction of the stairs.

Ambrose jogged beside him. "I'm not sure yet. Want to go find out? We'll see if I can put another scar on your face."

"Not the face please," I called after them, shaking my head. It was moments like these I missed when they hated each other.

"Morning little Monster."

I slowly opened my eyes to find Bael leaning over me, a smirk playing on his lips. I sat up. "Is it morning?"

Bael gestured at the still darkened window. "In a manner of speaking. It's past midnight, at least."

"What are you doing here?" I whispered. "I thought you were in Underneath for several more days."

"I missed you," he replied with a sly grin. "Apophis is taking care of things for me."

"And you?" I asked, tilting my head inquisitively.

"Well, right now I thought I would take care of you," he said, bending to tracing his lips along my collarbone.

Goosebumps erupted all over my chest and arms as he continued lower, pressing kisses on the tops of my breasts and lightly sucking on my nipple through my nightgown sending ripples of pleasure through my body.

"Wait," I gasped, glancing at Ambrose and Scion who were both asleep next to me.

"Do you want to wake them?" Bael asked, leaving the decision up to me.

"Not this time," I grinned. "Come with me."

Taking his hand, I dragged him across the room and led him out into the hall. As we walked, I glanced around nervously, making sure no one was watching us before darting down the familiar path.

"Who are you looking for?" Bael chuckled, following me closely. "It's your castle, no one cares what we do."

"Our castle," I corrected with a smile. "And I know, but let's not scandalize the servants any more than we already have. I can relate to their discomfort."

Bael laughed and shook his head as we reached the door at the end of the hallway. With one more quick glance around, I pulled it open and we stepped out into the tranquil courtyard garden. The scent of blooming flowers filled the air and fireflies and wisps danced about us in the moonlight."

Bael raised an eyebrow at me. "This is different. Not that I'm complaining."

I turned to face him, running my fingers up his toned abdomen through his shirt. "Hasn't it been too long since you pinned me against a tree?" I teased. "I seem to recall that being a favorite pastime of yours."

"And I remembered when you pretended to hate it."

"Well, remind me now why I changed my mind."

Obligingly, he picked me up, holding my ass firmly as I wrapped my legs around him. Finding the nearest tree, he moved me so my back was flat against the trunk and we were almost nose to nose.

He looked down at me with a clear hunger in his eyes, running his hands up my bare legs and over my stomach to cup my breasts. Squeezing lightly, he ran his thumbs over my nipples, scraping with his nails. A tingle traveled through my entire body and landed in my core. I arched my back, pressing my chest more firmly against him.

"I need you to take this off right fucking now," he said, plucking at my nightgown.

"You do it," I gasped.

"If I do it, little monster, there will be nothing but sheds."

I wholly believed him, so I tugged the gown over my head, leaving me completely bare.

With a growl, e moved his lips down my neck, across my collar bone again. His teeth scraped against the healed over scars that were my mating marks. First Scion's bite, then his own. I shivered, hoping he'd find Ambrose's bite next.

As if reading my mind, he moved his mouth lower.

I gasped and grabbed onto one of the branches above me as he sank to his knees, draping my legs over his shoulders.

He stared at my bare cunt for a moment, right in front of his face.

"You were so pretty, little monster. You should always sit like this."

"That might make dinner difficult," I joked. "Or hearing petitions. Should I sit on the throne with your face between my thighs?"

He looked up at me, eyes flashing dangerously. His mouth curled up in a smirk. "Absolutely. Your throne, then mine."

I nodded. That was a bargain I would easily agree to.

Bael's breath feathered over my sensitive core, then he pressed a firm kiss to my clit. I gasped. Then my gasp became a moan when he sucked harder on my clit, scraping his teeth, and at the same time thrust two fingers inside me.

I writhed against his mouth. My nails scraped against the branch above me, scrabbling for stability as Bael opened his mouth, dragging his tongue over and over my folds

"You're fucking delicious, little monster," he murmured

His fingers curled against my inner walls, and I screamed loud enough to wake the entire castle. My entire body shuddered and I closed my eyes, gasping for breath.

I slumped against the tree, my chest heaving for breath. Then I let my legs slide off his shoulders. My feet touched the ground again, and he crowded me against the tree, forcing me to tilt my head all the way back to look at him.

I was suddenly very aware that I was entirely naked, and he had taken off a single article of clothing. There was something sexy about that. Dark and forbidden, it made my pulse pound in my core once more.

Bael smirked at me, seeming to know exactly what I was thinking.

He reached down and undid his belt, but didn't remove his pants. His eyes darted to the side, and I followed his gaze. There was a low stone bench beneath the tree, intended for quiet commune with nature. We were about to desecrate that bench.

Next thing I knew, Bael sat down on the bench and tugged me into his lap. He pulled out only his cock, leaving the rest of his body completely covered.

I let out a breathy moan when I felt his tip nudging against my soaking wet entrance. I pushed my hips forward and rocked against him, sliding his cock back and forth over my entrance.

He growled, and gripped my hips tightly, pressing me down until I was seated fully on his lap. I was impossibly full. The pressure was intense, and oh so good. "Fuck."

He throbbed inside me. "Bounce on my cock, little monster."

I shifted my knees to the couch on either side of his hips, and wrapped my arms around his neck. Then, I rose slowly, sliding him out, and back in again. His grip tightened, and I knew I'd have bruises on my hips in the morning. I fucking loved it.

I moved faster as he reached for my breasts and sucked one nipple back into his mouth. Pleasure began to build inside me once more, and short gasps escaped me as I ground down on him, rocking my clit with every stroke.

"Fuck, little monster," he growled against my skin, so engrossed he said nothing else. "Just like that."

I moved even faster, and he helped, lifting my hips with both hands and slamming me back down again over and over. My clit throbbed, and my legs began to shake both with pleasure and exertion.

Sensing me slowing down, Bael lifted me off his cock and

returned to the tree. He slammed my back down against the trunk, and thrust into me once more.

I moaned, and raised my hands over my head as he circled both my wrists with one large hand. In this position, I was just along for the ride, loving the burn of pleasure and friction as he fucked me so hard my head bounced against the bark.

Warmth spread through me again, and I squeezed my eyes shut tight. Clearly sensing my coming release, Bael licked back up my throat once more. His mouth hovered over my fluttering pulse point. "I love you so fucking much."

Then sank his teeth into my skin.

Every muscle in my body seemed to tense. My toes curled, and I squeezed my legs around his back, holding Bael more tightly against me.

We both shouted at the same time, his yell muffled by my blood in his mouth. He shuddered, and grew harder inside me, before collapsing forward and pressing his face against my chest.

For a long moment I simply listened to our combined breathing, the pound of my own heartbeat and the sizzle of magic that seemed to hum everywhere all at once. Then, I pulled back to look at him.

"I think the throne room should be empty," I said on a breath.

His gaze met mine, and in an instant his surprised eyes heated once more. "Lead the way, my queen."

I took his hand, my pulse racing. I felt bewitched. Beguiled. Positively Wilde.

THE END

THE WORLD OF
Wilde Fae

BOOK ONE RECAP:

Lonnie Skyeborne is a human kitchen maid living in the capital of Everlast with her identical twin sister, Rosey. Unlike her sister, the Fae have always taken a particular interest in Lonnie, making her an outcast among the other servants. The twins are orphans, however, they still follow their mother's lessons: always lie, never make bargains, and never get noticed by the Fae.

In Elsewhere, the monarch proves their worthiness for the crown through a series of "Hunts." The monarch is "the hunted," and anyone who wishes to take the crown becomes a hunter. On hunting day, the monarch enters the arena. They must then either cross the finish line or survive until morning to keep their crown. If they die, the person who killed them becomes the new king or queen.

When the previous matriarch of the Fae royal family, the Everlasts, dies and her son Penvalle is crowned as king, the hunting season begins, however no Everlast has lost a hunt in over seven thousand years.

On hunting day, Lonnie meets two of the Fae princes, Scion and Bael. The princes realize that she is unaffected by their illusions, and Lonnie finds herself the unwilling recipient of their attention. Later, rebels attack the capital, and Rosey is revealed to be among them. Rosey is killed while trying to assassinate King Penvalle, and in a fit of rage, Lonnie kills the king before escaping into the woods. As it is a hunting day, she unwittingly becomes the mortal queen of the Fae.

Prince Scion throws Lonnie in the dungeon, believing she is also a rebel, and acts as king himself. He shows his cousins, Bael and Aine, a prophecy written by their grandmother before her death that says Scion will be the last Everlast king.

One year later, Prince Bael finds Lonnie in the dungeon and offers to help her win the next Wilde Hunt if she helps him obtain the crown (over Scion). Lonnie has no choice but to agree, and Bael heals her by giving her his blood. Bael wants to seal their bargain with a name oath, but Lonnie will not reveal her true name to him. They seal it, instead, with a kiss.

Lonnie narrowly survives her first hunting event with Bael's help and moves into the palace. Despite her title as queen, she is met with hostility from the Fae. Scion threatens her constantly, and the rest of the family refuses to acknowledge or help her.

Lonnie becomes obsessed with finding Ambrose Dullahan. She sneaks into the village to investigate what her sister was doing prior to her death and goes searching for her journals. Meanwhile, she begins having erotic dreams about Prince Bael and (occasionally) Prince Scion and grows closer to Bael while training for upcoming hunts.

Meanwhile, the rebel forces are growing stronger in the north, and Scion demands that Bael stay away from Lonnie. Bael disappears, and no one will tell Lonnie where he went.

At a ball, Lonnie dances with Prince Scion and feels a strong sexual tension between them despite the fact that he swears he intends to kill her. Lonnie's friend and servant, Iola, is mysteriously poisoned but saved by Bael's brother, Prince Gwydion, in exchange for learning Lonnie's real name.

One afternoon, Lonnie is attacked on the grounds and nearly killed by rebels. She consciously attempts to use the power she has alluded to several times, and nothing happens. Scion and Bael come to rescue her, and Scion is shocked at how worried he is for her safety. He kills all but one of the attackers and tells the survivor to spread the word across the kingdom that Lonnie belongs to the Everlasts. No one is allowed to hunt her.

Bael takes Lonnie back to the castle and once again feeds her his blood. He tells her a story about Aisling, the first queen of Elsewhere, and her three mates. The story ends with an explanation of a curse on the kingdom and the Everlast family:

"As long as the crown is not returned to a worthy wearer, the obsidian kingdom will know everlasting misery. If ever any member of the royal house should experience a moment of true happiness, all those who share Everlast blood will wither and die."

The night before the second hunt, rebels attack the castle and break into Lonnie's room. Meanwhile, Lonnie has snuck out to the village to look for Dullahan and her sister's missing journals. She runs across the royals and their court throwing an orgy in the woods. Bael sees Lonnie and tells her to leave, as she isn't safe, but ultimately gives up trying to stay away from her. Bael stops short of them having sex and tells her to leave. Prince Scion witnesses this encounter and is jealous.

Lonnie leaves, only to find her sister's journals in the palace garden. She returns to her room and finds that it has been ransacked in her absence, and there is a note from the rebel leader, Ambrose Dullahan, requesting that she meet him to speak during the second hunt.

Lonnie feels she cannot go to Bael (her closest ally) for help after their encounter at the party, so she returns to her old servants' quarters and sleeps there. Bael learns of the attack and is terrified that Lonnie has been hurt. He finds her and reveals that by feeding her his blood for the last few weeks, he has been sharing his powers with her, and that wouldn't be possible if she were entirely human. He also reveals that he believes they are fated mates, but they cannot be together because of the curse on the Everlast family. Finally, he demands to know the truth of who she is, insisting that he knows she's been lying to him as he can feel her powers through their bond.

In the Epilogue, Prince Scion ventures down to the dungeon, where he speaks to Lonnie's former cell neighbor. This is revealed to be Ambrose Dullahan, the leader of the rebels and Scion's estranged brother. Scion agrees to Let Ambrose go in exchange for his help interpreting Queen Celia's prophecy.

BOOK TWO RECAP:

In a flashback, we learn that Ambrose Dullahan believes he is working for the greater good of Elsewhere by rebelling against his family (The Everlasts). He is a powerful psychic and has spent 30+ years attempting to force events to occur, thus creating the future he thinks is best.

Knowing that he needs to speak to his brother, Scion, at some point in the future, Ambrose intentionally gets caught by the royal guards and thrown in the palace dungeon. Ambrose thinks about how he will be "blind" for the next several weeks until Scion comes to see him, as he cannot make predictions about himself, only those around him. Then, he realizes that Lonnie is in the cell next to him. He calls her his weakness, and the Source of everything.

In the present, it is hunting day in Inbetwixt. Lonnie is making her way up the quarry and attempting to win the second hunt. She is distracted from the hunt by thoughts of Bael's revelation that they might be mates, but she is unharmed because Prince Scion has threatened to kill anyone who touches her. She encounters a monstrous snake, and considers using magic to escape. Lonnie remembers how her mother told her never to use her magic or something horrible would happen, and thinks about how she doesn't know how to use it because she has never tried. Ultimately, she escapes after bargaining with the snake; telling it her true name, Elowyn, and swearing to return at a future date with a gift of royal blood.

Meanwhile, back in the capital, Scion believes that Ambrose Dullahan will use the second hunt as an opportunity to attack the castle, and demands that his family stay behind to fend off the rebel army. Scion is in a foul mood, due to the bargain he struck with his brother, Ambrose, early that morning. Ambrose told Scion he would marry Lonnie, and now he has been freed from the dungeon.

Bael agrees to stay behind initially, but is distracted and irritable. He tells Scion that he believes Lonnie is his mate, and Scion is horrified. Scion realizes that Ambrose's marriage prophecy now makes sense, as the Everlasts have a long history of marrying fated mates to close family members, since they cannot claim them due to their curse.

Bael learns that Lonnie has encountered the snake, and leaves immediately for Inbetwixt to help. He rushes to her aid, and they argue about their feelings for each other and have a sexual encounter.

Lonnie wins the hunt, and she and Bael return to the camp where the court has gathered to watch the hunters. Lonnie's servant, Enid, is in her tent and reveals that she brought all of Rosey's journals with them to the hunting grounds. Bael and Lonnie read part of Rosey's journal, which turns out to be mostly accounts of her dreams from the previous year. Bael theorizes that Rosey may have been a seer, like his grandmother and Ambrose, which could be why Ambrose was interested in her. Lonnie questions Bael about the powers of himself and the other Everlasts, but refuses to admit to her own possible magic. Bael's powers are explained–he has limited power over time, which manifests in the ability to destroy objects or enemies. He can also see echoes of times past, in the form of spirits.

The following day, the court procession rides back to the capital. Bael teases Lonnie, showing her he still has the ability to conjure fire. This is a power that he has only gained through their blood sharing, and is rightfully hers. She is terrified, due to her mother's warnings that her magic would cause something horrible to happen. Before she can voice this concern to Bael, they are attacked by a hoard of afflicted. Bael exhausts himself, using nearly all his magic to escape the afflicted and protect Lonnie. Because they are connected, he accidentally drains Lonnie's life-force as well to save them. Lonnie and Bael make it back to the obsidian castle, where Lonnie collapses into Scion.

Scion spends several days calling multiple healers to revive Lonnie, who has not woken up since the incident. Bael, meanwhile, is also unresponsive but stable. Scion realizes that Bael used too much magic to escape the afflicted, and has drained Lonnie. Knowing that it will temporarily bind her to him, Scion feeds Lonnie his blood and resolves never to tell her or Bael about it.

While passed out, Lonnie dreams about an unknown masked fairy. She wakes up to find Scion with her, and they fight. Scion reveals that Bael has been trapped in his cage since the incident with the afflicted, and will eventually recover on his own. Lonnie demands to see him and is denied.

Scion and the other Everlasts explain that they believe the afflicted were sent by Ambrose Dullahan to destroy the capital. Lonnie fears they are wrong, and that she is the cause of the afflicted, but doesn't tell anyone.

Scion wants to go search for Ambrose in Inbetwixt, and needs Lonnie to go with him. Lonnie will not agree, and demands to see Bael. Scion abducts her and forces her to accompany him against her will.

Lonnie is furious with Scion the moment they arrive in Inbetwixt and attempts to escape when he binds her to him with a shadow rope. They ultimately agree to stay in Inbetwixt for three days, and if they cannot find Ambrose Dullahan, then Scion must take Lonnie back to Bael in the capital.

Lonnie and Scion go to speak to the Lord of Inbetwixt to ask for the soldiers to help search for Ambrose. The Lord denies the request, due to thieves stealing ships from the harbor. Lonnie suggests that they address the problem with the thieves, so that the soldiers will be available, and everyone begrudgingly agrees.

It turns out that Scion knows the thieves, and he and Lonnie immediately set off for the guild headquarters. The guild leader, Cross, turns out to be a former member of Scion's army unit, and a close friend. Cross agrees to help them find Ambrose. Later that night, a shapeshifting incubus attempts to sexually assault Lonnie by pretending to be Scion (whom he assumed was her mate). Scion dismembers the incubus and nails him to the wall of the thieves den.

Over the next few days, Lonnie and Scion live with the thieves and plan a heist to locate Ambrose. Lonnie continues to dream about the mysterious masked fairy. While on a shopping trip to the local market, Lonnie and Scion discuss their different understandings of how to rule a country and the greater good. Having been raised to rule since birth, and then spending years in the military, Scion believes in using any means necessary to protect the largest number of people. He acknowledges that he is not sorry for imprisoning Lonnie, because if she were a threat to the kingdom it would have been worth it to him.

To locate Ambrose and his rebels, the thieves determine that they will need to break into the local brothel and steal the madam's client book. Lonnie and Scion agree to provide a distraction, although Scion is dubious about putting Lonnie in danger. In the brothel, they are mistakenly poisoned by "Gancanagh's dust," an illegal Fae drug which causes insatiable lust. They nearly have sex, but after biting Lonnie's neck Scion comes out of the trance and takes her back to the thieves den.

The following morning, Lonnie is horrified by what they did while under the influence of Gancanagh's dust, and the fact that the mark on her neck seems to be permanent. Scion tells Lonnie not to be embarrassed because he would still want her anytime, all she has to do is ask.

Lonnie and Scion speak to Cross, and learn that while they were under the influence of Gancanagh's dust, he and his thieves were able to steal the client book. They discover that the Lord of Inbetwixt's son is a rebel, and go to confront him. The son tells them that the rebellion has been shipping Gancanagh's dust in and out of Underneath, and tells them he hopes they burn up with their castle.

That night, the thieves have a party, and Lonnie and Scion dance. Back in their room, Lonnie tells Scion she wants him. They have a sexual encounter. Scion panics, thinking that he may have real feelings for Lonnie, and Lonnie realizes she can no longer lie.

Overnight, Lonnie dreams that the obsidian castle is burning and Bael is trapped. In the morning, Lonnie's ability to lie has returned, and she and Scion return home to the capital. There, they find the castle under attack by the rebels.

Scion is concerned with retrieving the obsidian crown because without it their curse cannot be broken. Lonnie wants to find Bael, who may be stuck in his cage inside the burning castle.

Scion admits he cares about Lonnie, and traps her in the stables to prevent her from getting hurt.

Lonnie manages to use magic to escape the stables, and appears in the castle. She helps her friend Iola escape, then goes looking for Bael. Lonnie finds Bael, and discovers that his "monster" form is an enormous beast-like lion. He saves her life, and they reunite.

Bael goes to help Scion and the rest of his family. Scion is able to use Lonnie's fire magic, and doesn't understand why. Bael tells him he believes that Scion is also one of Lonnie's mates, but Scion disagrees. He feels guilty for getting between Bael and Lonnie, and tries to apologize for his feelings.

Meanwhile, Lonnie runs into Ambrose Dullahan on the grounds. Ambrose has taken the crown, and wants Lonnie to leave with him. He promises her information if she will go with him, and implies her mother is still alive. Ambrose mentions to Lonnie that it is possible for two fated mates to be together, because Bael's parents were mates. His real father is an Unseelie named Gancanagh.

The castle collapses, and Lonnie assumes that both Bael and Scion have died. She lets out a burst of magic, and accidentally summons the afflicted to her. Bael, who was not harmed, is able to calm her down.

Lonnie, Bael, Scion and the rest of the Everlasts who survived the battle (Gwydion, Aine, Thalia and Elfwyn) all escape. They flee to a nearby coastal town, and commandeer an inn.

Bael and Lonnie finally have sex, but cannot complete their mating bond because of the Everlast curse. The following morning, Scion kisses Lonnie before telling her to stay away from him from now on.

Lonnie announces to the group that she will not be participating in the third hunt. She intends to travel to Aftermath and search for her mother so she can finally learn about her magic and who she is.

BOOK THREE RECAP:

A week after the events of book two, Lonnie and the Everlasts are in Inbetwixt. They are living in the thieves' den with Cross and his guild, and hiding from the rebel army. The rebels have taken over the capital and Ambrose Dullahan (formerly Prince Ambrose Everlast) is living in the obsidian castle. Everyone thinks Ambrose wants to kill Lonnie, but Lonnie is unsure since he didn't try to attack her during the battle.

Lonnie has been practicing her magic and has almost learned to shadow walk. She is intent on traveling to Aftermath to look for her mother, who may be still alive. Bael will be traveling with Lonnie while the rest of the Everlast family goes to Overcast to wait out the war. Scion is undecided on where to go.

The tension between Scion and Lonnie has hit a breaking point since their last visit to Inbetwixt and he is now avoiding her for fear of betraying Bael.

When Lonnie and Bael leave for Aftermath, Scion refuses to go with them. However, when Lonnie is attacked by rebels and shot with a crossbow Scion feels her pain and rushes to find her. He heals her with his blood and they have sex, but Scion does not feel a mating bond. He deduces that Lonnie is not his mate, but that he is still in love with her and must continue to avoid her.

Bael and Aine, as well as the thieves guild, fight off the rebels. Aine decides to stay with the guild, while Bael leaves to find Lonnie and Scion. He finds them, and the three decide to travel to Aftermath together. While staying at an inn, Bael gets angry with Scion for being oblivious about Lonnie. He insists they are both her mate. Scion has sex with her in front of Bael to "prove" they are not mates, but it turns out they actually are. Realizing she has now inadvertently sealed her mating bond with Scion, which could trigger their curse, Lonnie resolves to leave.

Lonnie tries to escape the princes and is captured by Ambrose Dullahan. Ambrose revels to the reader, but not to Lonnie, that he cannot see her in his visions but has spent many years trying to watch her. He met her once as a child and she gave him her true name, at which point he realized he had no power over her (meaning she has more magic than he does). He has been fascinated with her for over a decade.

Ambrose brings Lonnie to his ship and they set sail for Underneath. While on the ship, Ambrose forces Lonnie to spend time getting to know him, a question for a question. Lonnie learns about he sisters involvement in the rebellion as well as her mother's. She finally has time to truly grieve her family and spends many days depressed before Ambrose resolves to snap her out of it. He teaches her to fight and they begin getting along.

Meanwhile, Bael and Scion are searching for Lonnie. They seek out the serpent in the quarry to ask how to find her. The serpent reveals that due to Scion and Lonnies mating bond they are now married, making him the king of Elsewhere. It also tells them to travel to Underneath. They kill the snake and head to Underneath to find Lonnie, but are captured by the Unseelie king, Gancanagh, who happens to be Bael's real father.

Back on the ship, Ambrose has a vision of Bael and Scion being captured. He helps Lonnie go after them. They arrive in Underneath and pretend to be visiting the court on business. During dinner, Lonnie and Gancanagh's wife are attacked by an assassin. Lonnie kills the assassin but believes Gancanagh is trying to have her killed.

Ambrose and Lonnie have to share a room and they share a romantic encounter. Lonnie wakes up unsure how to feel about it. Ambrose leaves to go hunting with Ganacanagh and Lonnie tries to find Bael and Scion.

Gancanagh's wife, who keeps her face covered, helps Lonnie find the dungeon. Lonnie frees Bael and Scion, and the veiled queen attacks them. In the ensuing fight, the queen is revealed as Lonnie's mother in disguise.

A prisoner in the dungeon tells Lonnie he has been there for seven thousand years. He asks Lonnie to free him, which she does in exchange for his help saving her mother from the crumbling dungeon. Bael, Scion, Lonnie and the unknown prisoner carrying an unconscious Raewyn, run for Ambrose's ship.

Gancanagh sees them leaving and tries to stop them, but Bael kills him. This makes him the king of Underneath.

On the ship, Bael Scion and Lonnie solidify their relationship. Meanwhile, Lonnie is still thinking about Ambrose. She is unsure where things will go from here, but plans to finally lift the curse on the Everlasts once and for all.

The Everlast Family Tree

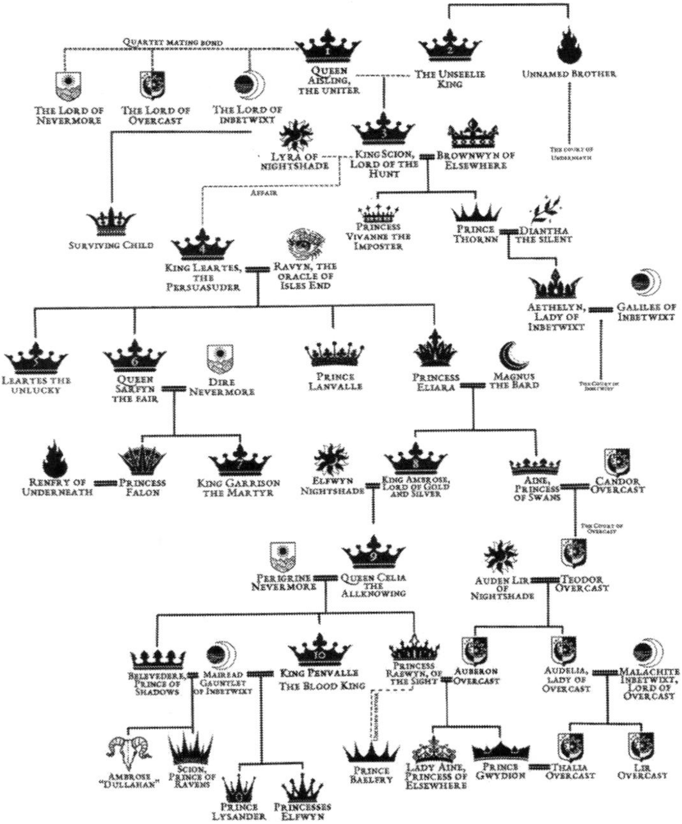

Quartet mating bond
The Lord of Nevermore
The Lord of Overcast
The Lord of Inbetwixt
Queen Aisling, the Uniter
The Unseelie King
Unnamed Brother
The Court of Underneath
Lyra of Nightshade
King Scion, Lord of the Hunt
Brownwyn of Elsewhere
Affair
Surviving Child
Princess Vivanne the Imposter
Prince Thornn
Diantha the Silent
King Leartes, the Persuasuder
Ravyn, the Oracle of Isles End
Aethelyn, Lady of Inbetwixt
Galilee of Inbetwixt
Leartes the Unlucky
Queen Sarfyn the Fair
Dire Nevermore
Prince Lanvalle
Princess Eliara
Magnus the Bard
Renfry of Underneath
Princess Falon
King Garrison the Martyr
Elfwyn Nightshade
King Ambrose, Lord of Gold and Silver
Aine, Princess of Swans
Candor Overcast
The Court of Overcast
Perigrine Nevermore
Queen Celia the Allknowing
Auden Lir of Nightshade
Teodor Overcast
Belevedere, Prince of Shadows
Mairead Gauntlet of Inbetwixt
King Penvalle The Blood King
Princess Raewyn, of the Sight
Auberon Overcast
Audelia, Lady of Overcast
Malachite Inbetwixt, Lord of Overcast
Ambrose "Dullahan"
Scion, Prince of Ravens
Prince Lysander
Princesses Elfwyn
Prince Baelfry
Lady Aine, Princess of Elsewhere
Prince Gwydion
Thalia Overcast
Lir Overcast

CALENDAR

- January — Danú (Da-new)
- February — Imbolc (Im-blk)
- March — Ostara (Ow-staa-ruh)
- April — Walpurgis (Wal-pur-gus)
- May — Beltane (Bel-tayn)
- June — Litha (Lee-tha)
- July —Annwn (A-noon)
- August — Lammas (la-muz)
- September — Mabon (Mah-bon)
- October — Samhain (Sow-wen)
- November — Bálor (Baw-lor)
- December — Yule (Yule)

PRONUNCIATION

- "Acacia" —Uh-kay-sha
- "Aine" — An-ya
- "Aisling" — Ash-lin
- "Apophis" — Uh-pow-fus
- "Ambrose" — Am-broz
- "Auberon" — O-ba-ron
- "Baelfry" or "Bael" — Bale-free or Bale
- "Beira" — Bay-ruh
- "Belvedere" — Bell-ve-dear
- "Caliban" — Cala-ban
- "Cassinda" — Cah-Sinda
- "Celia" — See-lee-uh
- "Ciara" — Keer-ah
- "Dullahan" — Doo-luh-han

- "Elfwyn" — Elf-win
- "Elowyn" — El-lo-win
- "Gancanagh" — Gan-can-ah
- "Gwydion" — Gwid-ee-in
- "Iola" — Eye-oh-luh
- "Kaius" — Kai-us
- "Lysander" — Lie-san-der
- "Mairead" — Muh-raid
- "Mordant" — Mor-dnt
- "Penvalle" — Pen-vail
- "Raewyn" — Ray-win
- "Rhiannon" — Ree-ann-in
- "Roisin" — Row-sheen
- "Scion" — Sigh-on
- "Siobhan" — Sh-von
- "Slúagh" — Slew-uh
- "Thalia" — Ta-lee-uh

GLOSSARY OF CHARACTERS

If you need an instant character index, here it is! This information is as of the end of *Lords of the Hunt,* so there are many spoilers in here for that book, but none for *Lady of the Nightmares*. I hope this is helpful!

PRIMARY CHARACTERS AS OF *LORDS OF THE HUNT*:

LONNIE SKYEBORNE:

At the start of *Lords of the Hunt,* Lonnie is a twenty-year-old kitchen maid, but by the end of book one, she is twenty-one and the first human queen of Elsewhere. She has no known powers and is not a particularly adept fighter, however, she is unusually good at surviving deadly circumstances and alludes several times to having powers that have not yet been revealed. Due to drinking Prince Bael's blood in *Lords of the Hunt,* she was temporarily able to use his powers.

Lonnie has curly red hair, brown eyes, and a scar on her ear where the tip appears to have been torn off. She is extremely mistrustful and fearful of Fae, who killed her mother and sister. Her mother taught her to avoid Fae at all costs, but the Fae have always been extremely interested in her. During *Lords of the Hunt,* this is not fully understood but seems to be attributed to giving off a magical scent or aura. Bael and Scion note that she "tastes like magic." She seems to have some immunity to the Everlast's powers but insists that the immunity doesn't extend to all Fae.

Lonnie may be the fated mate of Prince Bael, but that has yet to be confirmed. He believes that she is. Lonnie has also expressed sexual attraction to Prince Scion, although she does not like him.

By the end of *Lords of the Hunt,* Lonnie has been revealed as an unreliable narrator as she lies often to protect herself from the Fae. As Bael says, Lonnie lies so often that she herself isn't sure what the truth is anymore.

SCION, THE PRINCE OF RAVENS (SIGH-ON):

"The Prince of Ravens" is the kindest name given to Prince Scion, the heir apparent of the Everlast family. He is also sometimes called the Prince of Nightmares, the Queen's Executioner, or the God of Pain.

A former soldier in the queen's army, Scion spent his adolescence and adulthood fighting rebels in Aftermath. Scion's magical ability is illusion, which he primarily uses to inflict crippling pain on opponents in combat. He also creates shadowlike visual illusions. Like a bomb, the prince can clear entire battlefields on his own, so often his presence is enough of a threat to end a conflict. Scion hates the northern rebels due to his experiences fighting them and reacts harshly to any mention of them.

Scion is described as handsome and dangerous, with black hair and magnetic silver eyes. He is second in line to the throne after

Penvalle. His father was Celia's first son, Belvedere, who is dead. His mother is Mairead, who is now married to Penvalle. He often expresses that he dislikes everyone, including his family, but this is shown to be mostly untrue in practice. He views lifting the curse on his family as his responsibility and believes he is destined to be the last Everlast king. He has two half siblings through Mairead and Penvalle (Elfwyn, 9, and Lysander, 15) and one significantly older brother through Mairead and Belvedere (Ambrose).

PRINCE BAEL (PRONOUNCED "BALE" NOT "BAY-EL"):

Bael is the youngest of the adult children in the Everlast family. He is described as angelic-looking but slightly unnerving. He has blond hair, yellow catlike eyes, and unusually sharp teeth. During *Lords of the Hunt,* he tells Lonnie he was twelve during the fall of Nightshade, making him about thirty-three years old.

Bael is as powerful or possibly more powerful than Scion but is not in the running to be king because his powers are chaotic and potentially dangerous. While it is not clear by the end of book one exactly what the full extent of Bael's magical abilities are, he is seen to have some powers relating to conjuring smoke as well as making objects turn to ash. It is mentioned that he has "bad nights," and he has a cage in his bedroom.

Publicly, Bael's parents are Princess Raewyn and Lord Auberon, but it is an open secret that he has a different father than his two older siblings (Aine and Gwydion).

Bael wants Lonnie to win the Wilde Hunts and give him the crown but says that he does not personally want to be king. His best friend is Scion, and he believes Lonnie to be his mate.

LADY AINE (AN-YA):

Raewyn's daughter, Bael and Gwydion's sister. Aine is thin and willowy, very tan, with curly honey-colored hair. She is a cynic with unclear motives. She is good friends with Scion and her brother Bael. Her mother wants her to marry her cousin, Scion. She is a princess like her brothers but is never called Princess Aine. She mentions to Lonnie once that she hates her title. Her magical talent is unknown.

PRINCE AMBROSE EVERLAST/AMBROSE DULLAHAN:

"Dullahan" is a major player in the rebellion against the Everlast family and the person responsible for Rosey attempting to kill King Penvalle. It was revealed at the end of *Lords of the Hunt* that Dullahan is actually Ambrose Everlast, Scion's brother. His parents are Belvedere and Mairead, and he is a seer like his grandmother Queen Celia. Since the death of Queen Celia, Ambrose is now the strongest seer alive. Ambrose had a letter sent to Lonnie asking her to meet him during the second hunt and then was released from prison by his brother, Scion, later that same night. He is the visual opposite of his brother, possessing black eyes and silver hair.

CALIBAN:

Lonnie's former lover, Caliban, is a guard at the palace. While Caliban and Lonnie did not have any great affection for each other, he did help her stay alive in the dungeon. He is often used by Scion to do errands he does not want to take credit for (like bringing Lonnie food). The last time we saw Caliban, Scion had him stationed in the dungeon, guarding Ambrose.

PRINCESS ELFWYN (ELF-WIN):

Penvalle and Mairead's daughter. She's nine with black hair and silver eyes and has similar powers to her half brother Scion, whom she idolizes. Elfwyn tried to kill Lonnie in *Lords of the Hunt* because she thought Scion would be proud of her. She has no personal ill will toward Lonnie.

ENID:

Lonnie's former nemesis turned sometimes ally. Enid is a maid in the kitchens who is only out for herself and her own survival. She doesn't dislike Lonnie but wouldn't lay down her life for her either.

PRINCE GWYDION (GWID-EE-IN, RHYMES WITH GIDEON):

Bael's older brother, Gwydion, is a healer with an excellent court reputation. He is large and muscular, very tan, with curly dark blond hair. He is everyone's friend, and even the servants say he's not that bad. He is betrothed to Thalia. During *Lords of the Hunt,* Gwydion showed his cunning side by forcing Lonnie into an alliance in exchange for healing her friend Iola, who had been poisoned.

IOLA:

Lonnie's former maid and friend Iola was poisoned at a ball but is recovering due to Lonnie's bargain with Gwydion.

PRINCE LYSANDER (LY-SAN-DER):

Penvalle and Mairead's son. He's fifteen, and his powers have not yet emerged. Lysander hates Lonnie for killing his father.

MAIREAD GAUNTLET (MUH-RAID):

Scion, Lysander, and Elfwyn's mother, Penvalle's wife. She has the power of illusion but doesn't use it. She has not spoken much in years. She is originally from Inbetwixt (for more on this, see the glossary entry on Inbetwixt). Mairead has technically held the position of princess (through marriage) and queen consort, but she is not treated as such.

MORDANT:

The Everlasts' stuffy and prejudicial head of staff.

KING PENVALLE (PEN-VAIL):

Celia's only living son at the time of her death, Penvalle is murdered by Lonnie early on in *Lords of the Hunt*. Prior to his death, Penvalle was cruel and barely sane and considered to be dangerous even by other Fae. His magical ability was mind control.

He was married (not mated) to his brother's former wife, Mairead, and father to Lysander and Elfwyn. Prior to his death in *Lords of the Hunt*, it was mentioned that Penvalle and Scion looked very similar.

PRINCESS RAEWYN (RAY-WIN):

Queen Celia's daughter. Raewyn married the lesser lord Auberon Overcast and has three children: Gwydion, Aine, and Bael. Raewyn's greatest ambition is for one of her children to take the throne so she can rule by proxy. She is a seer like her mother but far less powerful. She is very accurate, but her visions are random and infrequent.

ROSEY SKYEBORNE:

Lonnie's mild-mannered identical twin sister. Although Lonnie and Rosey look the same, Rosey does not attract attention from the Fae in the same way as her sister. She is much less rebellious and cynical as a result. She writes daily in journals and seems to have no secrets until she suddenly is seen to be part of the rebellion against the Everlasts. In the month or so prior to her death, Rosey was very sick and drinking tea from a tree that only bloomed at night.

THALIA OVERCAST (TA-LEE-UH):

Gwydion's fiancée. She was originally brought to the royal court as a bride for Scion (they are both illusionists) but is now betrothed to Prince Gwydion. This situation has not been explained as of the end of book one. Thalia is described as pale and unusually beautiful, even for a fairy, but always looks like she was recently crying.

Thalia is technically a cousin of the Everlasts several times over. She is a first cousin of Gwydion (her mother is his father's sister). She is also a second cousin through Queen Celia, who was her great-aunt.

MENTIONED OFF PAGE OR DEAD AS OF *LORDS OF THE HUNT*:

QUEEN AISLING THE UNITER:

The long-dead historical queen of the Fae who first united all the provinces into the country of Elsewhere. She had three mates, but her story ended tragically when her family was murdered and she was violated by the Unseelie king. She cursed the king, leading to the curse on the Everlast family.

PRINCE BELVEDERE:

Scion's father, Mairead's former partner, Penvalle's brother. He was the heir to the throne before he was killed in the war with the rebels.

QUEEN CELIA THE GREAT:

The longest-reigning Everlast queen, who has just died as of the beginning of *Lords of the Hunt.* She was a very powerful seer who left letters for some members of her family with instructions after her death. Only Scion's letter has been revealed so far.

RHIANNON SKYEBORNE:

Lonnie and Rosey's mother. Seen only in flashbacks in *Lords of the Hunt,* Rhiannon was a changeling child stolen from the human realm and brought to Elsewhere to serve the Fae. She was stolen as a child (not an infant) and lived in the North of Elsewhere (Nightshade). Eventually, she became the mother to Lonnie and Rosey. She spent her entire life training her daughters to hate the Fae, likely due to her own upbringing and early memories of being stolen.

She was taken away by Fae soldiers for punishment due to some unknown transgression and never seen again. Prince Scion was part of the group that captured Rhiannon.

A/N: When Rhiannon is speaking a language that Scion does not understand in LOTH, it is English. Being a changeling, Rhiannon speaks English, while her daughters do not.

THE KING OF UNDERNEATH/UNSEELIE KING:

The monarch of the separate realm below the border.

THE KING CONSORT:

Queen Celia's late husband and father/grandfather to all the Everlasts, who died before the events of book one. Though it is not relevant to the events of *Lords of the Hunt,* his name was Peregrine, and he was from the province of Nevermore. For more on this, see the glossary entry on Nevermore.

GLOSSARY OF PLACES

ELSEWHERE:

The country where the story takes place. It is located "beyond the veil," somewhere in the North Atlantic Ocean.

EVERLAST CITY (INTERCHANGEABLY "THE CITY OF EVERLAST" OR "THE CAPITAL"):

Not to be confused with the Everlast family, this is the capital city of Elsewhere. It is named after the royal family. It is mostly populated by wealthy Fae (some noble, some not) and free humans. There is a large class divide between even the poorest Fae and the wealthiest human.

The capital city is extremely small compared to other cities in Elsewhere in terms of both size and population. In technical terms, it is more of a vassal township than a city, being only a tenth the size of Inbetwixt. It is bordered by the Waywoods on one side and farmland on the other.

The most important (and only) landmark is the obsidian palace. The palace is over seven thousand years old and built by the former Unseelie King of Underneath. The palace is the southernmost structure in Everlast, and there is nothing but untamed wilderness between the palace and the Hedge.

NEVERMORE:

The richest and most insular of the four provinces, Nevermore sits on an island slightly separated from the rest of Elsewhere. They speak in a different dialect than the mainland (Referred to by the characters as "the old tongue") and are governed by a council rather than a single governor. Nevermore might govern themselves if not for their friendly relations with the Everlast family and prosperous trade with Inbetwixt. Queen Celia's late husband, the king consort Peregrine Nevermore, was integral in making sure that Nevermore did not succeed from the rest of the kingdom. The royal-appointed governor now acts as an ambassador. Their climate is temperate to cold, and most of the island is covered in mountains. The Fae of Nevermore live peacefully alongside some species of non-combative Unseelie, such as dwarves and sirens. Since the fall of Nightshade, Nevermore now has the highest population of druids and witches (human magic users). Fae with particular magical talents in Nevermore tend to possess mental abilities like mind-control and clairvoyance.

INBETWIXT:

Inbetwixt is a trading port that grew into a city of travelers with a violent reputation for being unwelcome toward outsiders.

They have the largest and most diverse population of non-noble Fae, Unseelie, free humans, and hybrid monsters. Their climate is warm and often rainy. They are bordered on all sides by the Source Mountains, the Waywoods, the Wanderlust, and the

Undertow, making it easy for Inbetwixt to control access to the city. Every road in and out is guarded, and tolls are high.

The governing noble family of Inbetwixt has been loosely at odds with the Everlast family for the last century. Lady Mairead Everlast was born Mairead Gauntlet in Inbetwixt. She was not a noble but the daughter of a wealthy merchant who met Crown Prince Belvedere while he was traveling with the queen's army. Mairead was a talented illusionist and came with a large dowry, and therefore, her non-noble blood was completely ignored by Queen Celia and King Consort Peregrine, who favored Prince Belvedere above their other children. This incident enraged the Lord of Inbetwixt and his family, and they are still bitter about it.

OVERCAST:

Overcast is a small but relatively prosperous northern seaside province known primarily for its political neutrality and lack of army. Their governing noble family is heavily enmeshed with the Everlasts, as they are all not-so-distant cousins. Their governor is Thalia's mother (Lord Auberon's sister), but it will likely soon pass to Thalia's brother.

Overcast sits in the shadow of the Source Mountains, directly downwind of Aftermath. In the years since the disaster that destroyed Nevermore, they have had increasingly erratic weather and are now struggling to deal with the toxic clouds rolling in from their neighbors to the northwest. There are only two ways into Overcast: through the Wanderlust or across the Undertow. It is far easier to cross the Undertow, especially in the twenty years since the fall of Nightshade. Thalia marrying into the Everlast family is intended to ensure that Overcast is not overlooked and cut off from the rest of the country, as they need their own expanded water access unhindered by Inbetwixt. The population of Overcast is almost entirely Fae, and there are no free humans in their city.

AFTERMATH:

Previously called Nightshade, the mountain province of Aftermath sits at the northernmost part of Everlast. A third of the population died in the initial volcanic eruption, with another third dying in the following weeks from injury, starvation, and effects of the Wilde magic. Survivors quickly fled to the valleys on the opposite side of the mountain, closer to the Waywoods, and most eventually left entirely. Aftermath is considered mostly uninhabitable, with a climate similar to Underneath.

After the disaster, Queen Celia began sending prisoners and slaves to Aftermath to assist in rehabilitating the area. This punishment was viewed by many as cruel and unusual and led to the beginning of the organized rebellion.

NIGHTSHADE (ALSO SEE AFTERMATH):

Nightshade was the fourth province in Elsewhere until the disaster roughly two decades ago that destroyed the land and population. Their city was very large and beautiful, having been built by Queen Aisling as the original capital of Elsewhere, and they were an area of high magic concentration. Despite this, they did not pose much political threat to the Everlasts as most of the population were highly religious academics. The noble court of Nightshade trained spiritual leaders and magical practitioners and sent them out to proselytize to other courts about the way of the Source.

UNDERNEATH:

The home to all hostile Unseelie and monsters, The Underneath is part of the continent of Elsewhere but separated from the kingdom by the Hedge. It is ruled by the Unseelie King. The Hedge is patrolled on the Everlast side at all times to prevent any monsters or Unseelie from crossing over into the capital.

WANDERLUST:

A large marsh between Inbetwixt and Overcast, populated by thousands of Underfae. It is extremely easy to get lost in the marsh and wander forever in the fog or sink into the waters. Crossing it is difficult without an undersea guide.

THE UNDERTOW:

A small sea filled with pirates and traders.

THE WAYWOODS:

A seemingly endless forest that stretches through the middle of the country. No one person has ever explored every part of the Waywoods, and it is said that there are things in there that predate the Everlast family themselves.

FORT WARFARE:

An enchanted prison on an island in no-man's-land on the west side of the continent. It is used most often by the Everlast family, but they do not exclusively control it.

THE HEDGE:

The wall separating Underneath from the capital of Everlast.

MOONGLADE LAKE:

A lake in the capital that is rumored to be enchanted. Queen Celia walked into this lake when she decided to return to the Source.

THE SOURCE:

The volcano that is believed to be the Source of all magic. Gods are said to live in the mountains surrounding the Source.

GLOSSARY OF TERMS, ITEMS, AND CREATURES

FAE:

The dominant species, Fae have become the ruling class by numbers alone. They are also called Seelie, to differentiate them from the Unseelie, but this is typically not a necessary conversational distinction to make. All Fae possess some inherent magic and are immortal (though not impervious to death), but only some possess unusual magical abilities. Fewer and fewer Fae are born with special abilities with each generation.

HIGH FAE:

Fae of the noble class. Sometimes interchangeably used to mean Fae with magic, but typically referring to social standing.

"FAIRIES":

Catch-all term for anything non-human, including High Fae, monsters, hybrids, Underfae, etc.

UNSEELIE:

Sentient non-human, non-Fae creatures. The Unseelie are not always malevolent (though they often are). In Nevermore, some of the non-hostile Unseelie, like dwarves and sirens, live alongside the Fae. On the continent, almost all Unseelie are confined to Underneath, although there are some exceptions (like Beira, the palace cook). Some examples are succubi, spriggans, púca, incubi banshees, and shape shifters. The Unseelie are different than monsters, which are abundant everywhere, although some are just as dangerous.

UNDERFAE:

Magical creatures that cannot speak or be reasoned with but are sentient (like pets). Will-o-whisps and all the plant guardians fall into this category.

SLÚAGH:

A rude name for humans. This roughly means "the crowd" or "the army," but the intention is to mean "peasant" or "sword-fodder."

THE WILDE HUNTS:

The competition where the ruler proves their worthiness to keep their crown. There are five hunts, the first taking place on May 1 and the last one taking place on June 21. Every hunt is in a different province in this order: the capital, Inbetwixt, Nevermore, Overcast, Aftermath. Anyone who wishes to challenge the monarch for their crown must kill them on hunting night and take it. If the monarch dies, the hunts end until the following year.

MOONDUST TREES:

Trees that only sprout leaves at night. Their leaves are white and turn to dust in the morning.

THE COMMON TONGUE:

The language spoken most commonly on the continent. It is used by both Fae and humans.

THE OLD TONGUE:

The language spoken most commonly below the Hedge (Underneath) and in Nevermore. This is where the word "Slúagh" originates.

The Everlasts speak old tongue because their grandfather, Peregrine, was from Nevermore. Now, they complain that others don't speak it, when in reality, if they had not been forced to learn, it is likely they would not have bothered.

ABOUT THE AUTHOR

USA Today and International bestselling author Kate King loves sassy heroines, crazy magic, and alpha-hole heroes.

An avid reader and writer from a young age, she has been telling stories her whole life. Ever a fan of the dramatic, she lives in an 18th century church with her husband and two cats, and often writes in cemeteries.

ALSO BY KATE KING

WILDE FAE

Lords of the Hunt

Lady of the Nightmares

The Last Heir of Elsewhere

A Kingdom of Monsters

WILDE THIEVES

The House of Doublecross ~ 2025

ENCHANTED LEGACIES

A Thorn in Every Heart ~ 2025

THE GENTLEMEN

Red Handed

Thieves Honor

Damned Souls

THE BLISSFUL OMEGAVERSE

Pack Origin

Pack Bound

Pack Bliss

STANDALONES:

By Any Other Name: A Deliciously Dark Romeo and Juliet Retelling

Made in the USA
Middletown, DE
26 October 2024